A FAMILY OF STRANGERS

A FAMILY OF STRANGERS

SANCHONA

FIVE STAR

An imprint of Thomson Gale, a part of The Thomson Corporation

Detroit • New York • San Francisco • New Haven, Conn. • Waterville, Maine • London

THOMSON

GALE

LIBRARY OF CONGRESS CATALOGING-IN-PUBLICATION DATA

Sanchona.
   A family of strangers / by Sanchona. — 1st ed.
       p. cm.
   ISBN 1-59414-543-1 (alk. paper)
   1. Australia—History—1788–1851—Fiction. 2. Botany Bay (N.S.W.)—
Fiction. 3. Penal colonies—Fiction. 4. Women prisoners—Fiction. 5. Irish—
Australia—Fiction. 6. Mistresses—Fiction. I. Title.
   PR9619.4.S26F36 2006
   823'.92—dc22   2006024541

U.S. Hardcover:
ISBN 13: 978-1-59414-543-8
ISBN 10: 1-59414-543-1

First Edition. First Printing: December 2006.

Published in 2006 in conjunction with Tekno Books.

Printed in the United States of America on permanent paper
10 9 8 7 6 5 4 3 2 1

Dedicated to the memory of my parents,
"Wong" and Ah-Hock.
Wishing they were here.

ACKNOWLEDGMENTS

I'm obliged for the help I received from my fellow writers in the Internet Writers Workshop who played a significant role in getting this novel published. They are too many to list, so I shall just name a few: Robert Crouch, Carlton Hommell, Waid Woodruff, Larry Stanwood, Lee Hauser, Edita Petricke, Judson Jones, Sue Bolich, Mike Crowl and Sandra I. Smith. Thank you, all!

CHAPTER 1

The sun was high overhead, but that August day felt cold to Kate O'Neal. She closed her eyes, and tears rolled down her face. Ma would be ashamed of her if she were alive. Fifteen years old, and she was behaving like a babe, afraid of her own shadow. How did she let mere strangers and their fears get to her? What did they know of this Botany Bay, this faraway place? They'd never been there before.

She licked her lips and inhaled sharply. The stink of mud and rotting flesh that hung over Portsmouth Harbour gave her empty belly a stir. She clasped her hand over her mouth. *No! I will not puke.* She needed a distraction. With a force of will, she looked around her, at the men and women, those bound in irons and chains, who shared her sorry plight.

Her heart started pounding. One of the men was staring at her. She shrank from his view. Pressing her hands against her chest, she struggled for calm.

Eejit! The man had simply looked her way. Did she think every man who looked at her planned to attack her? Of course not. No more. She would be brave.

Her resolve changed nothing. Her heart continued to beat very fast.

"Silence!" The word thundered above the squall of seagulls, killing at once the murmur of conversation. It came from a man with a red kerchief covering his head, who had appeared from nowhere and now stood just some five paces from the crowd of prisoners. He had an arm wrapped around a musket that had a bayonet protruding from its end. "I'm Twiggs, and for now, you're all in me charge." He glared at them in turn, as if he'd like to swallow them up whole and be rid of his problem. Kate reminded herself to be careful, not to draw his special attention. She'd learned that any attention from a man could only bring her grief.

"And that be the *Merry Mersey*," Twiggs said with a sweep of his arm. " 'Tis me job to get you all aboard."

His tone alarmed Kate. She stared at the ship that looked too small for a long voyage, but come what may, she knew she'd be aboard that transport before the day grew much older.

She never had a say in anything, especially not since the day her mother died. Her father had sent her into service with the Rustands for the price of a handful of silver. The Rustands had her thrown into prison for daring to defend herself. And Newgate Prison had been her first bitter taste of her new future.

She recalled the stench of urine and unwashed bodies and remembered the curious gleam in the women's eyes as they stared at her when the guard first thrust her into the prison cell. Afraid these unfriendly women might tear into her, she'd been extra careful not to knock into any of them as she made her way to a less crowded corner. No one stopped her to ask questions; or remarked on the bruises on her shoulder and face. She almost wept as tension leached out of her.

Some time after supper, a supper she didn't have for lack of means to pay for it, a guard sought her out.

"Been told ye'll be leaving us tomorrow for Botany Bay," he said in a booming voice.

The women around her gasped.

The guard sniggered. "Ye've got yerself some powerful enemies. Why else would ye be going to that heathen place ahead of everyone else here?"

From the looks of pity directed at her, Kate reckoned Botany Bay had to be worse than Newgate Prison. Here the women fought each other for every inch of advantage; there was no room for charity. Meals had to be paid for. Since she possessed nothing but the clothes on her back, she'd probably starve to death. How could it get any worse? Would she have to pay for water in Botany Bay? For the air she breathed?

The guard stared at her for some moments more, then laughed and left. As the women settled down to sleep, Kate couldn't help overhearing snatches of their conversation. They were talking about her, and their tone suggested her future was dire indeed.

She was awake when the guard came to fetch her at dawn. He sounded kind, too. "Now, don't you worry none about Botany Bay, you hear?" Then he smirked. "The sea might get you first."

Kate dropped her face into her hands in despair. Her one act in mindless retaliation was costing her dearly. If only she'd . . . but there was no turning time back.

Now she watched Twiggs order one prisoner at a time to board the rowing boat, making them sit at the exact spot he'd selected, shouting at any who missed it by even an inch.

The boat was beginning to fill when a male prisoner baulked. "I ain't climbing into that. Can't you see that boat be sinking already? I ain't drownin' with them all."

Twiggs thrust the bayonet into the man's arm. "Move!" he shouted.

Kate quickly averted her gaze from the widening bloodstain on the man's sleeve, only to end up staring into Twiggs' face. The cold look in his eyes set her heartbeats galloping, and she feared he might lash out at her because she stood so handily close to him. But he only glared at her and the other prisoners, before he returned his gaze to the wounded man who was scrambling his way into the boat without another word. Twiggs gave a grunt of satisfaction, then waved another prisoner, a woman, into the boat, telling her firmly where she was to sit. Then it was Kate's turn.

The boat dipped and rocked under Kate's feet. She lost her balance and fell heavily onto her seat. A sharp pain from injuries barely two days old made her cry out before she could stop herself. She quickly sat down between the woman and the side of the boat, determined not to attract any more attention.

Her gaze fell on the seawater, an arm's length away. Her belly knotted. The sea was so close.

All too soon, the sailors pulled on their oars, and the boat surged forward. The movement almost threw her against the man behind her. She recovered her balance, then tried to catch a last look at the land she was leaving behind. Likely she'd see nothing but open sea till she reached Botany Bay. But she couldn't see much over the heads of the people behind her. With a sigh, she turned to face forward.

An icy spray attacked her. She wiped away the moisture from her face, gasped when she noted that an arm of the sea had reached out to engulf the boat. She shrank back with everyone else. The boat rocked dangerously, and frightened cries filled the air.

Holy Mary, Mother of God! She didn't know how to swim. Surely she would drown, but nothing dire happened. Then she spotted Twiggs in the bow. *Eejit,* she thought. Would he be in the boat too, if it was going to sink? She had to have faith. God would protect her.

Then a man shouted, "Look at that!"

Kate stared in horror at a rope ladder swaying against the side of the ship. The howl of protests around her became a roar.

"Silence," Twiggs cried, pointing his bayonet at the protestors.

"Unless you can sprout wings and fly, you'll all climb that ladder, by God!"

The male convicts climbed first, grumbling loudly. The female convicts followed. Kate, who climbed last, scaled the ladder carefully. She couldn't risk a slip. She gasped in relief when she reached the top of the ladder, even smiled at the sailor who helped her onto the deck, then directed her to join the rest of the women by the starboard rail. She crossed the deck with arms and legs trembling from the strain of the climb. Timidly, she joined the group of twenty-five women. A far greater number of men stood in small groups close by. She had never seen them before.

The crowd suddenly opened a path for a runty-looking fellow. He stopped in front of the women. His lips parted in a broad grin showing rotting teeth. "Ladies, listen up. I'm Roger Blackton, and by Captain Mowat's order, you're in me charge till we reach Port Jackson. Now, before we do anything else, you're gonna get a haircut. We must get rid of them vermins now, mustn't we?"

"Haircut? Bloody hell!" a woman cried.

"I ain't got no vermins. The bloody nerve, I say!" another shrieked.

Curses flew. The women argued. They cried. Many pleaded. Blackton appeared unmoved until someone bargained to keep her hair.

Seven women chose to take their chances with the sailor holding a pair of shears. Penniless, Kate had no choice but to submit to the haircut. In quick order, the sailor hacked off her long black hair, leaving behind a head of uneven stubble. She knew she must look as ghastly as those women who went before her, but she didn't weep like they did. Looking pretty meant nothing to her.

Then Blackton ordered the chains removed from the women's

wrists. A few called for him to remove their leg irons too. He ignored them.

Two sailors handed out woollen caps and sets of new garments to the women. Kate gaped when a cap went sailing past her and fell overboard.

"That's what I think of yer bribe!" someone yelled.

Kate hugged her new clothes and cap close as she watched two more caps follow the first into the sea. She couldn't afford to be so reckless. At least now she owned something more than what she had on her back.

At Blackton's next instruction, she froze.

Blackton shouted again, "Ladies! 'Tis time for your bath!"

"Bath? Did he say 'bath'?" a woman asked. Alarm rippled through the crowd of women.

"Nobody's giving me no bloody bath," a voice yelled. "Ye want a bath, ye take it yerself, ye bastid!"

"Silence!" Blackton bellowed, then retreated a few hurried steps when above a dozen women rushed up to him.

"I don't care about me hair, but I'll pay not to take the bath. I'm too young to die," one woman said.

Blackton held the women back with an outstretched arm. "Sorry, ladies. Can't be done. I got me orders."

Kate frowned. She'd taken regular baths all her life, and they hadn't killed her yet. Did these women know something she didn't? What did that matter? She should keep her mind on the sailors. The reason they were hanging around had become clear to her.

But wait. Maybe Blackton meant them to take their bath in their old clothes. Why else would he have his men hand out new garments?

Just then Blackton clapped his hands and settled the question. "Come on then, strip and take your bath, ladies, or me men will help you do it."

14

One of the sailors yelled, "Aye, Roger, give us the word!"

"You hear that, ladies?" Blackton asked.

"You black-hearted sod!" a woman cried and began stripping. The rest slowly followed. The sailors cheered.

Kate undressed quickly. She could deal with the pain that came with her injuries by ignoring it. The bleeding from her torn innards presented a problem, but there was no help for it. After making sure the rag between her legs stayed as secure as she could have it, she stripped, then sidled her way into the centre of the group. She crossed her arms, clutched her shoulders then hunched low, making herself as small as she could behind a wall of naked bodies.

The women kept shifting about, and Kate moved with them so their bulk would continue to shield her. She caught glimpses of two bold women posturing and waving at the sailors.

"Aye, me laddies, are you drooling now?" one called out.

"Here, wouldn't you like a taste of this?" hollered the other.

How shameless, Kate thought, just as cold water came splashing down on her. It seemed to come from every direction. Many women screamed and shrieked. They retreated, ran this way and that, trying to avoid a drenching. Kate stayed with them. Her ears burned from their loud curses. Her face flamed from the sailors' even louder cheers.

She thought the bath would never end, when Blackton shouted, "Enough!" Her first thought was to cover herself. Dressed, she looked around and sighed. The sailors had begun to move away.

Two guards guided the women down a hatch into a dark world, a corridor lit only by the flicker from the occasional oil lamp. Kate listened to the women's groans and curses as they bumped into piles of stores and chests stacked along the sides of the passageway. She soon spouted her own newly learned swearwords as she stubbed her toes and banged her knees. She tried to be careful, but that didn't stop the sharp edges of obstacles on her path ripping her skirts. The guards led them onward, seemingly oblivious to their charges' plight or the stench that filled the passageway.

They wended their way down another hatch and along another corridor. Kate found no relief from the stale smell surrounding her. Blinking her eyes did not help her see any better in the darkness. Would she ever catch sight of the wide-open sky again?

The women slowed to a stop. A door creaked open, then one of the guards said, "Step inside your quarters, ladies."

Pushed from behind, Kate quickly found herself inside the cabin. She immediately searched the walls for a window. Nothing. *Dear God.* How could twenty-six women survive the voyage in this small dark hole? Maybe that guard at Newgate Prison had good reasons to suppose she wouldn't last the voyage.

And she was here only because of that devil, Lord Oliver. Sure, she'd done a bad thing, but didn't Lord Oliver deserve it? She still ached and bled from his brutality. Where was justice? Would Lord Rustand consider punishing his son for beating and raping her? No. Only the maid who'd dared to fight back deserved punishment. And who but Lord Rustand would have her convicted of the theft of his wife's silk handkerchief and sent off to Botany Bay to serve her seven-year sentence at once? Did he plan to have her suffer untold hardship before dying on the voyage?

Kate clenched her hands into fists. Well, she wasn't going to die to oblige Lord Rustand.

The door slammed shut, then the crush of bodies eased a little as the women spread themselves out. They sat on the deck in groups, and conversation soon filled the cabin. Someone laughed. Another followed.

Kate blinked. What did these women have to laugh about in

these awful circumstances?

A while later, the door creaked open and crashed against the wall. Three sailors pushed their way inside. They dropped an assortment of goods on the deck and left.

"That's me bag!" a woman cried, rushing forward to claim it. "Never thought I'd see it again when they took it off me." In an instant, the others swarmed over the pile, screaming and jostling each other to get at the bundles.

Kate looked away, wishing she had something to claim. Then she saw the door opening again.

Roger Blackton stepped into the cabin. He clapped his hands and shouted, "Ladies, your attention, please."

Kate barely heard him over the din. Many of the women seemed unaware of his presence. Some were too busy quarrelling. Others were digging into the pile, or rummaging through their bundles, probably checking to see they'd not been robbed.

"Ladies!" Blackton roared. The noise abated.

"That's better." He smiled thinly. "You can look for your possessions later. Now, let's get you organised. See yon raised platforms? Them be your beds—four of you to one berth."

Kate stared at the bunks. Four women in a berth that wouldn't take three? Some of them would have to use the floor. Indeed, she preferred the floor to being squashed in the bunks.

An irate voice objected, "We ain't some bloody straw you can stuff into a pallet—"

Blackton held up a hand. "I'm sooo sorry, ladies. Captain Mowat didn't know he'd have such fine guests as yourselves. But we'll manage, won't we?"

No one answered. He raised his voice. "Won't we?"

A murmur of agreement from many of the women seemed to satisfy him. He smiled, then strode to the doorway. He poked his head outside and rapped out some orders. Five sailors trooped into the cabin. They dropped their load of packages, left, only to return with another. When the door finally closed behind them, Blackton started pulling one woman this way and pushing another that way. A large woman resisted.

"Move, I say." He gave her a shove. She yelped as she fell against another woman. He grabbed her and dragged her several paces away. "I'll have me four messes, and you, stay with this one."

The woman whined, "You could have said so. Don't have to push nobody around."

When he had the women divided into four groups, he handed out bowls and spoons, blankets and sleeping pallets, braziers and cooking pots. Next he shared out the food parcels.

"Are we to get more food every day then?" a woman asked.

He chortled. "Lady, this lot has to last you a week."

"A week!"

A shrill voice wailed, "We'll starve!"

"Ladies, ladies! Calm yourselves. Nobody's going to starve, I promise you. If you want more food, why, you only have to tell me. I'm an easy enough fella."

"Aye, and what's it gonna cost us?" an angry voice demanded.

He rubbed his hands. "Whatever I consider a fair price."

CHAPTER 2

The silence in the cabin held while Blackton closed the door behind him, then slammed the bolt home. For a long moment no one spoke a word, then a voice said, "Right, I'll be leader of this here mess."

Before anyone could protest, three other women snapped up leadership over the remaining messes. Kate's heart sank. She should have expected this. As leaders, these women could keep a larger portion of the food rations for themselves. How could she survive the long voyage without her fair share of the meagre supplies? She didn't have the means to buy more food from Blackton.

She had to speak out. She must, but a stout woman beat her to it. "Here, you can't just make yourselves leaders!"

"Are ye goin' to stop me then, Flo?" With one hard push, the first bully threw her to the floor. The three others moved in with a kick each.

Kate flinched at the sound of the thuds, ashamed she was thankful it was Flo and not herself taking the punishment.

The first bully bent over the cowering figure on the deck. "So, are ye goin' to stop me, Flo?"

Flo shook her head and moaned. "No!"

The bullies nudged each other and laughed. For a while, the rest of the women remained silent. No one seemed ready to gainsay the bullies. Then a whisper started, and conversation resumed.

A voice said, "It takes one bloody year to get to this Botany Bay, you know?"

Someone squeaked. "A bloody year? Surely not!"

"We can't live through a year of this," a shrill voice wailed.

A chill started in Kate's heart. She would now learn what lay ahead of her. It could only be more hardship and strife.

"Look at them measly food they give us," the shrill voice continued. "Mouldy bread and biscuits that could break your teeth. I'll wager there be weevils in them flour too. Damn Blackton for a miser. We'll starve, I tell you."

Murmurs of agreement followed, when a new voice cut in, "So pay for your food, Daisy. It'd be no different from jail. Them bloody sailors be men, and they can jolly well pay for their pleasure."

Kate couldn't repress a shudder. Did the world consist only of men who wanted to rut, and women willing to oblige them to survive? Well, not her. After Lord Oliver, she'd rather die before she spread her legs for a man.

"What else did your friend tell you about Botany Bay, Lizzy?" Daisy asked.

"Them natives there be strange buggers."

"Hey? How's that?"

"Me friend say they got black skin. Black as coal and shiny too."

Someone chuckled. "Pull me other leg. Why don't you?"

"I ain't making this up," Lizzy protested. "I swear!"

The chuckles grew. "Sure, Lizzy. They all got black hair, black eyes and maybe black teeth too!"

"Black all over? Just fancy that!" Daisy said.

"And they don't wear no clothes, neither," Lizzy continued. "I says to me friend, wouldn't they all freeze to death in winter then? But me friend say there be no winter in Botany Bay. 'Tis very hot out there, even in December! He reckons 'tis the hot sun that's cooked the natives' skin, turning it all black—"

"Rubbish. Them be cannibals! That's why," Flo said.

" 'Cannibals'? What's that?" Daisy asked.

"Those that be eating human flesh, you fool!"

Kate's mouth became very dry. People who ate people? Surely, Flo had to be lying. Try as she might, she could not recall the Bible mentioning cannibals. But wait. These women also believed taking a bath would lead to their deaths. Could she trust any of them?

"Blimey! Ain't they got nothing better to eat?"

"I knew it, I knew it!" Daisy wailed. "The government's sending us to feed them natives in Botany Bay!"

Lizzy gave her a push. "Who'd want you for a meal, you skinny bitch?"

Flo tossed her hair and scowled. "Well, do you want to hear the rest of me story or not?" When the noise subsided, she continued, "Me friend say, 'tis how you can tell if a man eat human flesh. His skin will turn black as coal—"

"I'd die before I eat human flesh. I'm a Christian woman, I am!" Daisy cried.

Kate pressed her hands over her ears, but she couldn't completely shut out their words. She shifted closer to another group and concentrated on their conversation instead. These women were sharing stories about their past, and Kate listened to their tales till her eyes grew tired.

She woke to hear several women complaining of hunger. The mess leaders took charge, passing out chunks of bread and keeping larger pieces for themselves. No one raised a word of protest.

The guard visited them twice a day: first to deliver two buckets of fresh water, then to clean their waste containers. Without the sun to guide her, Kate used the guard's visits to count the passing days. Five days later, two women complained they were dying, several others puked on the deck.

"Listen!" Lizzy said. "Can you hear them creaking? Bloody hell! We've sailed! Why didn't the guard warn us?"

No one bothered to answer her. Most of the women were unhappily spilling their latest meal onto the deck. The cabin reeked of vomit and the smell reminded Kate of her voyage from Loaghaire to Holyhead with Lady Rustand and her two small daughters. That was the day she left Irish soil for the first time, and now chances were she'd never see Ireland again, ever.

Lizzy pestered the guard when he came with the water. "You gotta help us clean away this awful stench of vomit, or we'll never get better."

"It'd just be a waste of time, lady. The cap'n's expecting some bad weather shortly."

"Bad weather!" Flo cried. "What bad weather?"

"You'll see."

All too soon, the ship heaved and rolled like an enraged beast. The flickering flame of one small lamp in the cabin didn't allow Kate to see clearly. She dodged the best she could the bowls and pots and other heavy objects as they flew around the cabin as if celebrating their newfound freedom. She also swerved away from contact with the other women's feet and elbows.

Kate realised she had to find a support to cling to quickly, before she grew too weak from battling the storm. She fought her way to the boxes that served as beds only to find the three bullies there before her. It took another half hour before the rest of the women joined them. Still, the ship continued to buck and plunge, apparently determined to shake everyone loose from their timber posts.

The torture seemed unending, and Kate wondered if the ship would split asunder and end their misery, when the storm seemed to weaken. But the reprieve proved all too short. The storm had merely paused to gather more strength. Kate's arms ached from clinging to the post. Her ankles hurt from the leg irons. Why had Blackton not removed them? Did he think the women would escape from a locked cabin in the middle of the sea? *Eejit!*

A drop of water fell on Kate, then another. Surprised, she looked up at the ceiling and choked on her despair. Seawater came dripping down from the deck above, the drops growing bigger all the time. Kate knew everything would be drenched before too long. Sure, their belongings would dry, eventually, but the food would be ruined.

The raindrops of seawater turned into a torrent. The oil lamp went out. Soon, water collected at Kate's feet. Each time the ship rolled, the water sloshed against the bulkhead, first on this side, then on the other, washing over the women, who whimpered and moaned. Some prayed for deliverance. Kate wondered at the few women who yelled out their prayers. What? Did they think God might not hear them over the cries of their fellow sufferers and the roar of the raging storm?

Exhaustion clouded Kate's mind. Her future looked bleak. Why, then, was she battling on? Maybe death . . . She thought to let go of the timber post, but her fingers refused to work. *No, no! I mustn't think like that. God would provide.* First she had to hang on for a count of a thousand, she told herself. She began counting, then started on a second thousand, and then a third . . .

She was still counting when Lizzy said in a raspy voice, "The storm's over. Can you all feel it?"

A general murmur greeted the news. Some of the women began to stir. Kate heard someone wading around in the ankle-deep water and wondered where she found the energy to move.

"Every damn thing's sodden!" Lizzy called out. "And the food's ruined."

"We'll starve." Daisy moaned.

Kate didn't know about the others, but it looked like she'd have to survive on water till Blackton delivered their rations in another four days.

"Maybe Mr. Blackton will replace them rations." Lizzy's voice sounded hopeful.

"Not that scoundrel!" Flo said. "I know his kind."

"But it ain't our fault!" Daisy said.

"You ask him then."

The deck had drained dry before the guard came with their drinking water. He located the cabin's oil lamp and lit it. Kate was glad to see again.

Lizzy tugged on his sleeve. "Our food's ruined. When will we get new supplies?"

"We're all busy, and I ain't got no orders about them food, but I'll get you something to clean up the mess here."

"Where's Mr. Blackton? Tell him, I'll pay for me food," Flo said.

"I'll pay too," a chorus of voices joined in.

He nodded and turned to leave.

Lizzy stopped him. "What about them sick women? They need a doctor to—"

He laughed. "Lady, don't be daft. The cap'n ain't interested in no sick convicts. The dead go over the side to feed them fishes."

"God save us!" Lizzy cried.

"Listen," Flo said. "We don't like them sick women here. How about moving them out?"

"Sure, when the cap'n or Mr. Blackton give the order." He brushed them aside to step out of the cabin, then slammed the door in their faces.

Flo stared at the closed door, as if frozen, then said something to the two women beside her. The three of them then dragged the five sick women to the farthest corner. Lizzy approached the sick women and when Kate saw she was trying to help them, she joined her. However, there was little they could do for the sick women, except keep them company. Death eventually claimed two of them.

Kate thought she ought to cover the dead women's faces but she was reluctant to sacrifice her only spare gown to do it. Then when she saw Lizzy stripping one of the women of her petticoat and used that to cover her face, Kate did the same for the other woman. The others only looked on and continued to keep their distance.

When the guard next called on them, Flo grabbed his arm. "You gotta take away them dead bodies."

He brushed off her hand.

"Where's Mr. Blackton?" Daisy asked. "It's been three days since the storm, and we're fair starved! Did you tell him we'd pay for the food?"

"Sure," he said and left.

"Ignore the bastard, Daisy. You'll get no help from him," Lizzy said.

When the third woman died, Flo threw a fit. "Listen. We gotta do something. Do you fancy waking up next to them rotting bodies?"

"What can we do?" Daisy asked.

Footsteps sounded outside their cabin. Flo cried out, " 'Oi there. Help us, please. We got three dead bodies in here." Even though a few other women joined in the cries, the footsteps soon faded into silence.

Later that day, Blackton surfaced with two sailors bearing packages, which could only be the week's rations. He had the dead women removed, then directed the rest to even up their numbers in their messes.

Kate waited for Flo to ask about replacements for the ruined rations.

"Mr. Blackton?" Daisy pointed to the packages. "Are those to replace what we lost in the storm?"

Blackton stopped twirling the cabin's padlock around his finger and frowned. "Replace? Why would I do something so foolish?"

"But it ain't our fault we lost our food in the storm!"

"How be it me fault then, eh?"

"Wait a minute. This lot don't look right to me, Mr. Blackton," Flo said. "Can a bundle of food be missing?"

Blackton shook his head. "I don't make no mistake about food rations, lady. The cap'n don't like such mistakes."

"We're fair starved," Flo cried, "and now you give us less food than before. Are you trying to kill us?"

"Less food?" Blackton frowned. "Now, you didn't think I'd be giving away food for twenty-six when there be only twenty-three of you left?"

"But—"

Blackton backhanded Flo in the mouth. She went sprawling onto the deck. Kate gasped and backed away from Blackton. So did the others. Flo sat up and spat out a tooth. She used her sleeve to wipe the blood running from her mouth. Blackton took two steps closer. Flo raised her arms over her head and cowered. But he walked past her, tossing his padlock from one hand to the other. "I ain't taking no lip from no female. The cap'n's given me a free hand to deal with you lot." He turned his gaze on Flo. "Do you have any more complaints?"

Kate hoped Flo would remain silent. Surely she didn't want to lose another tooth? No one said anything.

"Good." Blackton nodded. "Can I trust you to even up your numbers, or must I do it for you?"

"We'll do it ourselves," Lizzy said.

A week later he returned, smiling broadly. "Ladies, have I got news for you! There be some gentlemen aboard this here ship asking to have a lady companion. To be sure, 'tis a fair exchange. You provide him with a bit of comfort, and he'll be providing you protection, food and all. What do you say?"

"We'll not be locked up no more?" Flo asked. "How about these here leg irons?"

"I'll remove them shackles, of course. And you're free to move about the ship as you like after. What do you say, ladies? Deals don't come any sweeter."

Much to Kate's surprise, sixteen women took up his offer. He led them out of the cabin, and when he returned later, he smiled at the remaining women. " 'Tis not too late to change your minds, ladies."

Kate looked away. Nothing would persuade her to rut with a man, not even for the promise of as much food as she could eat for the rest of the voyage.

The two sick women said nothing; the remaining four only smiled.

Blackton shrugged and called out, "Jimbo!"

An old sailor stepped into the cabin. He removed the seven pairs of leg irons from the women and then left without uttering a word.

"Ladies, you're free to move about the ship. Make sure you don't get into no trouble, hear? Now, before I go, would any of you want to do some washing to earn a bob or two?"

Kate stepped forward.

"Anybody else?" He looked at the four healthy women.

They looked at each other and laughed. "Do we look like washerwomen?" one of them asked.

Blackton shrugged, then looked at Kate. "All right. Let's go."

The sun hurt her eyes when first she stepped out of the hatch. The discomfort was soon overtaken by the glorious pleasure of being in the warm embrace of bright sunshine and fresh sea air. Then one look at Blackton standing some ten feet away, beckoning to her, had her hurrying to join him. She listened closely when he gave her directions to the cabins of the six men who'd pay to have their laundry done, then waved her away.

Alone once more, she slowly approached the railing for a better look at the sea and sky in the distance. Resting her folded arms on the timber railing, she leaned forward and drew in deep breaths of cold air. Was she really standing on the top deck, free of her shackles, free to move anywhere she wished? She pinched herself to be sure she wasn't dreaming, then sighed. If only she didn't have to go below deck again.

Reluctantly, she tore herself away from the railing. 'Twas time she met the six men who would pay her to do their washing. She had to earn some money, money she might need to pay for food to see her through the voyage.

Each of the men appeared glad to see her. They handed her their dirty linen, and with her arms full, she headed back to her cabin with plans to do the washing the next morning.

She stopped at the doorway and stared at the blankets draped over four strong ropes strung across the cabin. Four makeshift rooms. How clever. It wouldn't have occurred to her to think of this. She was about to ask the four women where they got their blankets and ropes, when a group of sailors came to the cabin door, forcing Kate to move farther into the cabin. With welcoming smiles on their faces, the four women moved forward to greet the men.

Bits of their conversation drifted in whispers to Kate, just enough for her to make sense of them.

Holy Mother of God. How could they be so shameless? Discuss payment to rut with the men? Kate put a hand on her chest to calm her thudding heart while she watched four sailors follow the women behind the blanket partitions. Within minutes, a series of low grunts and gasps filled the cabin. Kate wanted to rush away and never return, but the group of sailors blocking the doorway gave her pause.

She retreated to her corner of the cabin, which was as far as she could get from the sailors, only not far enough. In despair, she curled up on her pallet and threw her blanket over herself. Her hands held over her ears didn't cut out the rhythmic sounds. All at once Lord Oliver loomed large in her head, growing ever larger. The whap, whap, whap she remembered of the leather strap he used to slap the palm of his other hand had her sweating. Kate knew what he would do next, and so she began pushing hard to get him out of her mind, but he wouldn't budge. The sound of her pounding heart swelled to fill the head.

She couldn't breathe. Pulling the blanket off her face, she took in huge gulps of air. The grunts and gasps now thundered in her ears. She forced herself up on shaky legs, then took a step forward, then another and another. Ignoring a spate of offers from the sailors at the doorway, she pushed past them and fled from the cabin.

The piles of stores along the corridor didn't slow her down. She bumped her way to the open deck. The cool wind soothed her fears. Sailors going about their duties calmed her nerves. She didn't want to return to the cabin below, but as the sun dipped into the sea, she knew she didn't have a choice.

She found the cabin clear of sailors.

One of the women greeted her warmly. "Here, come join us for supper. Never mind Mr. Blackton's rations. Look, we got food aplenty. I'm Josie. What's your name?"

"I'm Kate."

Josie waved at the woman who wore large, dangling earrings. "Clara, Kate's going to share our meal."

"Oh, I couldn't do that," Kate said, stealing a glance at the two sick women nibbling on some cheese. Apparently, they had no qualms accepting charity.

Clara drew her shoulders back and looked down her nose at

Kate. "Why? 'Cause we're soiled doves?"

"Oh, no. I couldn't take anybody's food for free."

Clara narrowed her eyes. "You want to pay us for it?"

Kate took a deep breath. She'd worked in the Rustands' kitchen for a year and she'd learned how to prepare tasty meals. "I don't have any money, but I could cook for you."

Josie grabbed Clara's arm and looked at Kate. "You want to cook for us?"

Kate nodded. "In exchange for your food."

"Why Kate, how sweet of you," Josie said. "We'd love for you to be our cook. Ain't that right, Clara? Now, come and eat with us."

Later, Kate looked at Clara. "What are 'soiled birds'?"

"No. That's 'soiled doves,' lass."

"C'mon Clara," Josie said. "We're more like petals of a flower. Sounds real pretty, don't it?"

Clara chuckled. "All right, 'petals' then."

Kate looked from Josie to Clara. "But what—"

Clara heaved a loud sigh. "Birds, flowers—they be names for whores, luv."

Josie laughed. "I'll be Pink Petal—how's that?" She turned to her other two friends. "Kitty, you be red, and Rose can be rose."

Clara rolled her eyes, and Kate smiled. How strange, she thought, that in their terrible circumstances, these women could laugh at themselves.

She remembered being told that whores were sinful people, that they were to be shunned by all decent folks. Now, she looked at the four women before her and decided that fallen women could be decent and kind too.

She took a deep breath. She'd made some friends, and she'd have enough to eat the rest of the voyage. Her future didn't look so bleak or the cabin so crowded anymore. Why, she might even find Botany Bay a better place than she'd been led to expect. Then she remembered. What if the natives were cannibals? Was she to escape being food for the fishes only to end up in the cooking pot to feed the natives in Botany Bay?

Chapter 3

The cool breeze caressed Kate's face as she leaned into the port railing and gazed into the distance. Her vision blurred. Tightening her grip on the handrail, she tilted her head back and took a deep shuddering breath while blinking away her tears.

How very odd. She was a convict trapped aboard the *Merry Mersey,* and yet she'd never felt so free in her life.

Six men aboard had hired her to be their washerwoman. The first time they'd paid her, she couldn't believe it was happening, not even when the coins rested in the palm of her hand. She'd searched out a quiet corner above deck and then stared at the coins and cried.

On her father's farm in Ireland, her time was never her own. There was always something that needed doing. If not looking after the children, cleaning or cooking, it was taking care of Ma, who was too weak to do many things for herself.

She never got to see any money either. Da paid, ever so reluctantly, for food they couldn't produce themselves, or for clothes and shoes for herself and her two older brothers when they outgrew the ones they wore.

Nor did she see any payment for the work she did for the Rustands. The cook, the housekeeper and later the governess kept an eagle eye on her, to see that every moment of her time was properly spent serving the Rustands. Exhaustion took care of her nights.

Now, though she was a convict, her time was her own, and

best of all, she was paid for her work. She closed her eyes and took another deep breath as she listened to the creak of spars and lines, the snap of canvas straining in the wind and the occasional shouts of sailors aloft while trimming the sails. She thought of the happy hours watching sea creatures that stayed close to the ship, some just showing their little sails, moving low in the water. Others looked unbelievably tame, leaping playfully alongside the ship.

Best of all she was thankful to have work that kept her away from her cabin for long periods of time. Sure, she'd taken the four prostitutes, the Petals, for her friends, but she couldn't bear the way they earned their living.

She was no longer troubled by the sailors. They usually ignored her, repelled, no doubt, by the stubble on her head. She would spend long hours above deck, oftentimes till after the sun sank into the sea.

That the ship carried more than convicts and crew surprised her. There were at least a dozen women she'd never seen before. She took those dressed in quality garments for paying passengers and those who were not, for wives of the ship's crew. Although the women, whether convict or free, crossed each other's path, none stopped to exchange a word of greeting.

After a while, Kate turned away from the railing, picked her way around a pile of stores and sat on a bale. To her right, two sailors strained to shift a huge sea chest.

"Damned woman," said the shorter man. "How often are we going to be running her errands eh, Joe? She wants this chest, then that chest—"

"As many times as she wants, so the cap'n says. He must like her."

"The cap'n? More like her husband's paying the cap'n to keep her happy. Here, let's tie this monster to this stack." They began loosening the ropes securing a pile of stores.

A tiny figure caught Kate's attention. The little boy couldn't have been more than six, but already moved around the deck with the boldness of a sailor. He ran for the port railing. Before Kate could blink, he'd straddled the railing twice his height. Leaning out, he peered into the water. Kate smiled, wondering what had him so entranced. He stretched out a little further. Kate held her breath, afraid a slip might see him fall overboard. When he straightened up, she sighed in relief. She followed his gaze to a woman dressed in drab garments who had her arms full of washing.

"Look, Ma!" the boy shouted, then leapt onto the deck. He gave his mother a wave before heading for the pile of stores. He scrambled to the top with ease, then spread his arms and grinned, revealing a gap between his front teeth. With a blood-curdling yell he leapt to the deck below. Laughing, he climbed the mound again.

A sudden gust of wind swept across the foredeck. The boy's mother clutched her washing and turned her back to the wind. The shawl across her shoulders broke free and danced across the deck. She gave chase.

Kate heard a loud whoop, then the little boy flashed past her, running after the shawl.

The wind caught the sails, and the ship rolled. The two sailors cursed as they fought to keep the sea chest and crates from sliding away. The ship rolled again, sending the crates towards the starboard railing.

Kate's belly clenched when the boy tripped over a coil of rope, then crashed onto the deck, screaming. She had jumped to her feet, when the ship rolled again. The two sailors shouted. The crates they chased had changed direction, rumbling after the boy.

Kate gasped. Those heavy objects would surely crush the little body. Mindlessly, she dove after the boy, grabbed his arm and yanked him towards her as the crates rumbled harmlessly past, just inches away. Suddenly her legs could no longer support her. She dropped to her knees while cradling the boy.

"There, there," she whispered. "You're all right. Don't cry. You're safe now."

Kate became aware of someone beside her. The boy's mother. With tears streaming down her face, she stretched out hands that trembled for the boy. "Robbie, oh Robbie."

Kate struggled to her feet with the little boy still clinging to her neck. Carefully, she passed him to the woman. "He's just frightened," Kate said. "I don't think he's hurt."

"Thank you. Thank you so much," the woman said. " 'Twas so stupid of me to be chasing after the shawl. The shawl, the bloody shawl isna worth risking Robbie's life. If I dinna give chase—"

"Don't blame yourself." Kate patted the distraught woman clumsily on her shoulder. "Your Robbie's safe now."

"I'm Fiona MacAlister. I dinna ken what I'd do if I lost me Robbie. Thank you, thank you so much. If you ever need me help, let me know. I'll be glad to be of service to you. Och, Robbie, you mustna be so careless, you hear? I wilna have it!"

The next day, Kate was mid-way through her washing when Fiona approached to exchange a few friendly words. Two days later, she stopped by with Robbie for a longer conversation. Kate was sorry to see them go below deck a while later, and she didn't see Fiona again till the next day. Soon they met almost every day, and Kate knew she'd made another friend, apart from the Petals.

One day, Fiona told her the ship would be stopping soon at Tenerife in the Canary Islands, maybe for a week or so to take on water and supplies and probably make some repairs, too.

The *Merry Mersey,* she said, would then use the trades, the northeasters, to head for Rio de Janeiro in South America.

They'd stay there maybe a month, then catch the southeasters to cross the Atlantic Ocean to Cape Town. After another month, they'd use the westerlies to get them the rest of the way to Port Jackson, New South Wales.

"You mean Botany Bay, New South Wales."

"Botany Bay's a nearby harbour, lass. We'll be stopping at Port Jackson."

"How long—"

"We'll get there in about eight months."

"Fiona, when do the convict men come above deck? I've never seen them."

"You canna be serious. Oh Kate. The cap'n, he'd never allow the convict men out of their cabin. He wants no trouble from them. They get food and water and won't be let out till we reach Port Jackson."

"Oh."

"Aye. They be treated worse than beasts in the hold. Me Jamie say they have these holes in the bulkhead for the guards to put the muskets through to shoot at them if they make trouble."

"To kill them?"

"Aye."

"How many have they killed—"

"None yet. Me Jamie say Cap'n Mowat be easier on the women 'cause he think them too weak to be dangerous."

Kate shuddered. "How do these men manage?"

"They dinna fare well at all. Saw some of them when they landed in Port Jackson—scrawny and ill—"

"You saw them at Port Jackson? You've been there before?"

"Aye. Twice—"

"Twice? Then you can tell me! I've been ever so worried! Is it true? Do the natives there have black skins? Do they eat human flesh?"

"Aye, they have black skin. But eat human flesh? I canna be sure, but I'll ask me Jamie for you." Fiona hesitated a moment, then laughed in a self-conscious manner. "I've been meaning to ask you, lass. You speak like a lady. You ain't a lady, are you?"

Kate laughed. "I'm just a farm girl who used to work for milord and milady Rustand, as their kitchen maid, then as companion for their little daughters. I'm no lady. Oh, no! I sat with the two girls when they had their school lessons, and the governess used me to get them to work harder."

"How?"

"Well, the girls laughed at me because I didn't know how to read or write, do arithmetic, paint or embroider. The governess taught me some of those things. So, if their little ladyships wanted to keep laughing at me, they had to stay ahead of me, see? They used to laugh at my Irish ways too, so I learned to speak like them, behave like them, so they couldn't make fun of me anymore. I must seem funny to you—part Irish farm girl, part English gentry-like."

"Oh, no. I'm puzzled, is all." Again Fiona hesitated, her brow drawn in a frown. "Kate? I've been meaning to speak to you. Do you ken New South Wales be naught but a Godforsaken land?"

Kate didn't like the sudden turn of conversation. "Why do you ask?"

"We been talking, me Jamie and—" Fiona took a deep breath and began again. "Me Jamie say you've not taken a man for your protector, Kate. Why not?"

Kate looked away for a moment. "Don't you fret, Fiona. I don't need a protector. My friends have more food than they can eat. I cook for them and get to share their meals. I live very well, I promise you, without a protector."

Fiona shook her head. "Och. I dinna like to be poking me nose into your business, really. But me Jamie say—" She drew a breath. "You ken that New South Wales be a penal settlement, Kate? All the convicts there have to work. Well, there be plenty of work for the men. They can be made to work at anything. There ain't much in the way of work for the women—"

"That can't be right! Women can do almost anything: the washing, the cooking, the cleaning. Even the farm work—"

"Nay, lass. The government men, they dinna think women can do the hard work, like clearing the land or building the roads and houses. Aye, you're right. Women can do everything you say and more, but there ain't enough of these jobs to be going around, not in the new colony, you ken?"

Kate frowned. "What do the women do?"

"Och. That's the rub, Kate. Men have their needs, but there be too many men in the colony and not enough women to go around. So the men apply to the government to get a convict woman for themselves. A settler man who dinna really care . . . well, he betters his fortune by putting his woman out to whore for him, you ken? Well, that's what me Jamie say—"

"To whore for him? No, no! You're trying to frighten me."

"Nay, I'm not, I promise you. There could be worse. Me Jamie say that most whores usually end up diseased and sick. Then no men would go near them. I'm very sorry, Kate. We dinna wish to see you in such straits."

Kate's belly turned over. "No." She flinched at the pity in Fiona's eyes. "No. I won't be a whore! Oh, what am I to do?"

"Seems to me like you'd be wise to get yourself a kindly protector on board ship. Me Jamie say the men who take on a convict woman on this here ship be officers or men plump in their pockets. Every man who want to keep a woman with him has to pay Cap'n Mowat a goodly sum. Then he has to pay for her keep. If you take up with a man on board, and if you pleases him well enough, 'tis likely he'd keep you when you land. Then you dinna have to worry about the future. A rich man will surely keep you to himself."

Kate turned away and buried her face in her hands. "Oh Fiona. I can't . . . I don't ever want to rut with a man!" She pulled herself together, then lifted her head and stared into the horizon. "What am I going to do?" Unmindful of the tears streaking down her face, she turned to Fiona. "When I worked for the Rustands . . . Well, their son and heir, Lord Oliver, he took a fancy to me."

"Oh," Fiona said.

"No, no. 'Tis not what you think. Where do you suppose I got these bruises? He came at me with a leather strap and just wouldn't stop. When I fought him, he punched me. The rutting was bad, but worse was when he forced me to . . ." Kate raised her hand to her mouth, sick with the memory. "I bit him," she said defiantly. "I'm not sorry I bit him. I wish I had hurt him more."

The sobs just broke out. Fiona slipped her arms around her and held her close. "I'm thinking maybe you hurt him and his family enough, Kate."

"I never want to rut with another man, Fiona. I'd rather die—"

Fiona tightened her hold. "Shush . . . Yon Lord Oliver's a terrible baistie and no mistake. I ain't saying there be no more men like him abroad in the world. Believe me, not all men be like that. Look at me Jamie, a giant to be sure, but he's such a lambkin, you wouldna believe. Who knows? Maybe, you'll meet a man like me Jamie one day. You'll ken how wonderful it can be between a man and a woman."

"No, Fiona, I just can't."

Fiona appeared to struggle with her words. Then her expression lightened. "Kate, you ken the whores? You've heard them with the men, surely? Do they seem to be in pain? Fearful? Think about it."

Kate thought of nothing else the rest of the day.

If Fiona was right, she couldn't hope to avoid spreading her legs for a man. And wasn't she lucky? She had the luxury of a choice: lie down for one man or do it for many.

Well, she couldn't afford to feel queasy over the foul act of rutting. She had to overcome her revulsion, but the mere thought of submitting to another like Lord Oliver sent shivers through her. One thing was clear: she needed to learn all she could about this darker side of life. It wouldn't be pleasant, but it was time she stayed in the cabin with the Petals to find out for herself exactly how a whore earned her living.

The Petals kept only one oil lamp burning and the blankets down when they conducted their business. From her corner in the cabin, Kate braced herself as she watched and listened to her friends satisfying the sailors. At first, she had to quell her urge to flee from the cabin. Then she became puzzled. Wouldn't the Petals scream if the sailors hurt them? But Kate only heard their soft whispers and moans, their urgent words of encouragement and occasionally, loud mystifying cries. After the men had gone, she saw all four of her friends laughing and joking with each other. What was the truth? Was Fiona right? Did she have nothing to fear from rutting?

Rose approached her, snapping a pair of shears she'd borrowed from a sailor. "Time for another haircut?"

"Maybe later."

Rose gave her a knowing smile. "Ah. Changed your mind and thinking of joining us, eh?"

"I wouldn't be any good at this, Rose."

"Why not? It ain't so hard," Josie said.

"I don't like a man's touch."

Rose and Josie looked at each other, then shrieked with laughter.

Clara wiped tears of laughter from her eyes. "You don't think we enjoy what we do, do you, Kate?"

"I don't know. You all seem happy enough with the men."

"Kate! Don't be silly! 'Tis all work, girl," Rose said with a broad grin. "Just work."

"But—"

"I know," Kitty said. "You've been listening to us, haven't you, duckie? Did you like our cries of pleasure, our sweet words of loving?"

The three others snickered. Kate hung her head.

"Kate, Kate!" Kitty said. " 'Tis just a bit of play-acting, you know? The men likes it. Gets their blood running hot and fast, and they gets to finish that much quicker. 'Tis just work, nothing more."

Kate heard a soft moaning. It grew louder. Surprised, because all the sailors had left, she looked behind her and stared at Josie. After a moment, she snapped her mouth close and glanced back at the others. They were doubled over, with their hands over their mouths, but that didn't smother their giggles.

Josie cried, "Yes, luv. That's it, luv. Ooh. Ooh." Cries of her pleasure filled the cabin.

The three other Petals fell on each other, laughing hysterically. Kate buried her burning face in her hands. The laughter around her swelled. In a moment, Kate found herself laughing too. *Bloody Josie!*

The Petals taught Kate the basics of their trade, revealing the many tricks they practised, and competed with one another to share their experiences.

"No. You're making that up, Josie," Clara said.

"No. 'Tis true. Swear to God."

"You never did that! Don't you lie now," Rose cried.

Josie cleared her throat. "All right, all right. But I heard of it from me friend, Chelsea."

"She lied!" Kitty said.

"How would you know, pray tell?" Josie said. "No! Never say you've tried it too? You didn't!"

"That's for you to find out." Kitty laughed and turned to Kate. "Close your mouth, luv. Now, what else can we learn you?"

CHAPTER 4

The *Merry Mersey* did a roll, and Jeremy Kendrick, who lay curled up like a ball, moaned piteously. Moments later, he scrambled out of his bunk and made a dash for his chamber pot. He retched and coughed till his face and throat burned, but his stomach refused to yield its sorry contents. Wiping his mouth on the laced cuff of his sleeve, he got to his feet. The ship rolled again, almost throwing him to the deck. He lurched into the bulkhead, cracking his skull. Too dazed and tired to curse his rotten fate, he silently slumped onto his bed. He drew a deep breath and instantly regretted it.

A *dead* rat? He shuddered. He'd suspected there might be one somewhere in his cabin, but preferred to believe it was his imagination. He could no longer deny the fact now. *Damn!* Couldn't the stupid creature pick some other place to die? Well, he was in no condition to locate and then get rid of the putrid carcass. He'd just have to ignore the stench.

A pox on you, Emeline!

His troubles had started with that henwit. If only he'd tossed away her note imploring him to call at her townhouse two weeks ago. . . . His belly churned again and he groaned in misery.

Recalling what happened that day gave him no joy. But he remembered clearly how she'd greeted him with smiles, then led him coyly and in unseemly haste to her bedchamber. He barely controlled his distaste and tried not to think of her body, scarred by childbearing and wrinkled with age. It pleased him better to dwell on the expensive trinkets and the small bag of gold coins she'd slip into his pocket before they said goodbye.

Like the times before, he smiled at her. Then whispering honeyed words into her ears, he slowly removed layer after layer of her clothes. He untied his cravat, and as he stripped down to his stockings, he caught a glimpse of her large bottom as she climbed into bed and under the bedcovers. A shudder of revulsion washed over him, but he pasted a smile on his face and joined her with feigned enthusiasm.

"Emeline, open this door at once!" The loud voice was accompanied by heavy thumping. "Do you hear me, Emeline?"

Emeline froze, her eyes rounded in horror.

Jeremy stared at her and shook with fury. He'd be doing the world a favour if he strangled the fool. What could she be thinking of, to send for him when her husband was still in town? How could she not fear discovery? She had more to lose than he—her marriage, her children and her reputation. *Damn.* He should have known the woman was not to be trusted.

Despite his trembling knees, he stumbled out of bed and grabbed his clothes. His hands turned clumsy as he hastily dressed. Try as he might, he could see no way out of his predicament.

"Jeremy, what are we to do?" Emeline begged. She scrambled out of bed and fluttered around him. "Oh, the scandal. I can't bear it. What if he kills me? Oh God! Jeremy, you've got to help me."

He wished the woman would just curl up and die. "Calm yourself, Emeline. His lordship may go away if you keep quiet."

The door shook. Emeline grabbed his arm, hampering his efforts to put on his boots. "He's not going away, Jeremy. Why is this happening to me? He wasn't supposed to come back for another two weeks. Are you leaving? Yes, yes. Go now. Before he finds you—"

She couldn't wish him gone more than he, but the only other exit lay in a row of windows three stories above ground.

"Emeline, if you don't open this door, I'll break it down!" the earl said.

Jeremy knew he had no option but to confront the henwit's husband. He turned to Emeline, deciding to put on a good face in an untenable situation. "Get dressed, my dear, and don't worry. Everything will be all right."

"How?"

"Trust me," he said, praying the earl would want to avoid a scandal. "Everything will be fine."

Indeed. All might still be well if the old fool would just forgive Emeline. After all, Emeline had been his countess for more than ten years, and she'd done her duty, provided him with his son and heir. Surely she deserved some consideration? If forgiveness wouldn't serve, he could banish her into the country for the rest of her life, but no, the lackwit meant to turn his wife's indiscretion into the season's scandal.

"Name your seconds," the elderly man said. "Bleinford and Wainbridge will act for me."

With a calmness he didn't feel, Jeremy assured the earl his seconds would call on Bleinford and Wainbridge and then took his leave.

A miserable jewel-encrusted snuffbox and a small diamond pin were all he had left to show for his liaison with that stupid tart. *Damn.* He should have stuck to his original scheme of fleecing young blades fresh from their schoolrooms. Wet behind their ears and eager to test their wits in games of chance, they'd provided him with rich pickings. He was a fool to believe he could make a better living pleasuring neglected wives on the sly.

Well, he had no intention of risking his skin for any woman, and certainly not for an old crow like Lady Emeline. Perhaps he could leave the country for a year or two? That should be enough time for the earl's wounded pride to heal and the ton to become engrossed in some other scandal so that his return to London might not even be commented upon.

Where should he go? The continent held no appeal for him; it never had. The people there did not speak the King's English, and he had no intention of learning French or German. Besides France was presently in political turmoil. It was his object to evade the possibility of injury in a duel. Why would he jeopardise his life and limbs in a French war that had nothing to do with him? Scotland? No, not that inhospitable land.

New South Wales! Yes, the new penal colony would suit him fine. Many adventurers had made their fortunes in foreign lands, like India and China, and he could do very well in this New South Wales and return to England a wealthy man.

Suddenly his future did not seem so dark. He acted quickly before rumours of the upcoming duel spread far and wide. He called at the New South Wales Corps headquarters at once and purchased a lieutenant's commission. The *Merry Mersey* had a last-minute cancellation, so he bought passage. Under cover of darkness, he boarded the transport and, out of fear of chancing upon an acquaintance, resisted the urge to step ashore again.

They would call him a coward. So what if they did? Only a fool would risk death to keep his reputation. Reputations could always be redeemed. Had it not been the case with Edward Rutherford and Anthony Wakefield? Their gold had dazzled many into having faulty memories. Well, time and gold could be his friends too.

His cabin on the *Merry Mersey* proved no bigger than a barmaid's room in a second-rate inn. He thought to confront the ship's captain. Was he not a lieutenant of His Majesty's Army? Did he not pay a king's ransom for the passage on this transport? He deserved a bigger cabin. Then reality took hold of him. He had to leave the country to avoid a duel. He had to take up his army commission or forfeit his money, which he could ill afford to do.

He looked around his cabin and shuddered in revulsion. How could he endure months living in such cramped quarters, in near darkness and breathing in stale air?

The fact of the matter was he didn't have a choice.

The moment the *Merry Mersey* set sail, his stomach heaved. Even if he was prepared to cut his losses, he was too late to do anything about it. There could be no turning back. He realised he had become hostage to the ship and the sea.

His ailing stomach gave him no peace. The mess in his cabin gave his stomach a bad turn. He needed help. He needed someone, anyone, to take care of his cabin and clean up after him.

When the deck stopped shifting, Jeremy decided he had to do something to improve his situation. Armed with two handker-chiefs, he stumbled his way to the open deck. A sailor pointed out Captain Mowat, who cut him off halfway through his explanation. "Roger will take care of you, Lieutenant Kendrick."

Jeremy stumbled back a step in astonishment as the captain brushed past him. Mowat had been polite enough when they first met, and he'd arranged to provide Jeremy his meals for the voyage. How dared the man show him such disrespect now? Had he forgotten he was dealing with an officer of His Majesty's Army? Goddamned scoundrel!

Jeremy was about to give the captain a piece of his mind, when the deck shifted, and Jeremy lost his balance.

A hand grabbed his arm and steadied him. "Lieutenant Ken-drick? I'm Roger Blackton. How may I serve you, sir?"

Jeremy took an instant dislike to Blackton. He forced himself to look away from the morsels of food clinging to man's beard and proceeded to explain his situation.

Blackton smiled. "You'll find the services of a convict woman most helpful, then."

"Excellent. Let me have one."

"As soon as I can arrange it, sir. By the bye, you know there'll be a fee for this service?"

"Yes, yes. I'll pay whatever is needed. Just get me the woman."

He waited for Blackton to show up with his convict woman. Time passed, but there was no sign of the captain's lackey.

Then the storm hit. It slammed Jeremy about like a ball, bouncing him on the deck and smashing him against the bulkheads. His chest hurt for a breath of air, his belly mutinied. In desperation, he clawed his way to his bed and clung to the timber post for support.

Thank God, his oil lamp continued to burn. To go through this misery and do it in the dark would be more than he could endure. Then droplets of rain fell on his head and arms. He thought he'd gone mad. How could there be rain in his cabin? He looked up at the deck above, saw the growing droplets and wondered if things could get any worse.

His cabin soon collected an inch of water that rose to two inches, then three. His cold and sodden body ached from its battering against the cabin walls and deck. For a moment he wondered if he should have stayed and faced the earl. So what if the earl killed him? At least death would have been quick, and he'd be spared this terrible torment.

When the storm finally passed, he stood in six inches of dirty water. He looked about, wondering how he could endure another such punishment. His glance fell upon his metal chest. Alarmed, he waded over and pried open its cover. "Thank God," he cried, peering inside. His clothes and papers had escaped the watery onslaught.

His misery increased by the day. He had to lie on his wooden bed without benefit of his mattress, which was drying very slowly. His efforts to get a new mattress brought him no joy.

For the first time since he boarded the ship, he was glad of the poor lighting. At least he didn't have to see the filth that had piled up in his cabin.

If only he had someone to look after him, to clean his cabin and his clothes. He longed to hear a human voice, to know he still lived. Where the hell was the convict woman Blackton had promised? If only he felt stronger, he would confront that damned scoundrel.

Blackton showed up the next day. "Sir, Cap'n Mowat's given his permission to release the convict women today. Do you want the services of one?"

"Yes. Yes!"

"If you recall, sir, there be certain conditions to go with the woman. There's the cap'n's fee and, for as long as she stays with you, the expense of her meals."

"Yes, fine! When can I have her?"

Blackton gave the waistband of his trousers a tug and smiled. "You'll have to pay me before I can let you have the woman, sir. Cap'n's orders."

Blackton accepted the coins and flashed Jeremy a wink and a smile. "I'll be letting you have Daisy. She's the best of the lot, sir."

An hour passed before he showed up with the promised woman. "Here's Daisy. I'm sure you'll be very happy with her, sir."

Jeremy stared at the creature Blackton pushed at him. *Daisy? A flower? She doesn't even look half human!*

Before Jeremy could say anything, Blackton had rushed off. Daisy asked a question. Jeremy never heard the words, only the shrill tone in her voice, and it chased goose bumps up his arms.

Best of the lot, the scoundrel said. No wonder he'd run off so quickly. Daisy was naught but a bag of bones draped in rags, with a rusty door hinge for a voice. The unconscionable rogue.

"Well, don't just stand there, gawking like an idiot! Make yourself useful," he snapped.

"What do you want me to do, sir?"

Daisy's high-pitched tone bounced in his head. He clenched his teeth and prayed for patience. She'd better not be a chatterbox. By God, he'd teach her not to be a chatterbox, if ever she was one. "Can't you see the cabin needs cleaning? Do that, then tell Blackton he's to give you whatever you need so you can cook our meals here. I'll settle up with him later. You can cook, can't you?"

Daisy nodded. "Shall I—"

"Stop!" He drew a breath. "Not another word, you hear me? Not one bloody word. Just carry out my orders."

Daisy proved a better bargain than Jeremy expected. He couldn't tell if his cabin smelled any sweeter; but it looked cleaner and tidier. Her dinner was hot, and that was the only good thing he could say about it. His appetite remained weak, however, and he didn't finish the meal. Daisy didn't let it go to waste. She licked his plate clean.

Jeremy stared at her for a long moment, then looked away. *What a pig!*

Two weeks later, Daisy became unwell. Worse, she fought him for the use of the chamber pot. He considered sending her back to where she came from, but he was afraid Blackton might refuse to return her when she recovered. He shuddered. No, that was not a risk he was prepared to take.

If only Daisy would recover quickly from whatever was ailing her. He hadn't paid good money to be landed with an inconvenience!

A crash startled him. He turned and saw Daisy sprawled on the deck.

CHAPTER 5

An urgent need to answer nature's call woke Jeremy up the next morning. Reluctantly, he slid off his bed and cursed when his foot landed on Daisy's arm. He shifted his foot, but the scream of pain he expected to hear never came. Was she dead? A rush of fear made him bend low for a closer look. Her harsh breathing was reassuring, but his relief was short lived. She was going to die, and die soon. He was sure of it.

"Be calm," he told himself. "Everything will be all right." He forced himself to walk to the chamber pot. Even as he emptied his bladder, his sense of panic choked him. He had to get rid of Daisy, and quickly. He would not have Blackton blame him for her death.

On shaky legs, he struggled up to the open deck. He squinted into the bright sunshine, searching for Blackton. The deck did a roll. He quickly reached for a pile of stores for support. The urge to return to his cabin was strong, but his problem with Daisy couldn't wait another day. He inched forward, battling the swaying deck and clinging to the rail to keep his balance. Some moments later, he stopped a passing sailor to ask if he'd seen Blackton. The man gave a shrug and walked away.

Insolent dog! If he didn't feel so sick, he'd seek out the captain and lodge a complaint. That would teach the bastard.

A movement at the stern caught his attention. Ah, his quarry was talking to a sailor. Jeremy pulled his shoulders back and moved forward, determined to take the offensive. "Blackton!"

The man looked at him. "Aye, sir?"

Jeremy stabbed his forefinger at him. "Listen you! I won't be foisted with a useless woman."

"Eh? Daisy? What's wrong with her?"

"How should I know? Am I the ship's surgeon?"

Blackton reached for his elbow. "Come, let's go to your cabin, and you can explain it all to me."

Jeremy stared at him in astonishment. The scoundrel was patronising him! Why, he deserved a good kick to teach him some manners, but Jeremy knew he was not the man to do it. At least, not today. The churning in his belly urged him to do as the blackguard suggested.

He raised his voice. "I've been patient, Blackton. But Daisy is no good to me, you hear?" He wanted to rant on, but resisted because he couldn't bear the humiliation if he fell on his face while ranting at the man. He decided to concentrate on making his way down the hatch and along the passageway.

At his open cabin door, he pointed to the figure curled up on the deck. "See? She's useless."

Daisy shifted and moaned. Blackton entered the cabin, hunkered beside her and made a quick examination.

"Damn!" he said. "Another one."

"What? What did you say?"

"Nothing." Blackton got to his feet. "I'll have her removed at once. Sorry sir, looks like you've got to manage by yourself for now."

For a moment, Jeremy gaped at Blackton. He'd been so intent on getting rid of Daisy that he'd forgotten that when he accomplished that, he'd be left to fend for himself. "How the bloody hell am I supposed to do that?"

Blackton shoved his hands into his pockets. "The best you can, I reckon, till Daisy recovers."

The urge to punch Blackton became overpowering, but his

need to use the chamber pot, more compelling. Jeremy closed his eyes, breathed deeply to control his rising nausea. When he opened them, the rascal had disappeared.

Two sailors came and carried Daisy away. A week passed before Jeremy admitted he missed her company. Surely Daisy must have recovered by this time? So why wasn't she back in his cabin? Damn Blackton for a rogue. Obviously he meant Jeremy to become so desperate, he'd happily part with more coins to get Daisy back. Well, the scoundrel would discover he was not so easily fleeced.

Blackton showed up at his cabin early the next morning. He nodded a greeting. "Thought I'd let you know, sir. Daisy passed away two days ago."

"She's dead?" Jeremy cursed. Trust that stupid slut to make life difficult for him. "Well, get me another woman, you hear? If it's more money, I'll pay."

"It'd cost you another fee anyways for a new woman. Now, now. Calm yourself, sir. I'll see what I can do for you." Blackton winked and left.

When the *Merry Mersey* stopped at Santa Cruz harbour in Tenerife, Jeremy spent his time ashore and returned to the ship just hours before she sailed. He found his cabin more foul than he remembered. He tried to clean it, but soon gave up the effort. He'd just have to ignore the filth.

Two weeks later, Blackton showed up again. "Sir, I've a new woman looking for a protector. What do you say?"

"Of course. When can I have her?"

Blackton's eyes gleamed as he rubbed his hands. "Kate O'Neal will be yours sir, when you hand over the cap'n's fee."

Blackton left, pocketing the coins. He came back with a small girl in tow. Jeremy gaped, his gaze riveted to her head, at the uneven stubble covering her scalp. Had the rats gnawed away her hair? He'd heard that rats would eat anything. But hair? He shuddered.

The gargoyle looked at him. She lifted her hand and scratched herself vigorously at the back of her shoulders and under her arms.

He shrank back in revulsion. *Lice!* He could feel an itch starting at his buttocks and spreading to his crotch. *Good God. Can the damn things spread so quickly?*

He turned to Blackton to protest, but the scoundrel had disappeared.

"Damn it!" Jeremy scowled and stepped back into his cabin. "Come on in, then, and cover your head with something, will you? I feel sick enough without having to look at that. And stop staring at me."

"Yes, sir," the girl said and began digging into her small bundle of belongings. She plucked out a woollen cap, put it on, then looked back at him for approval.

He grunted, turned and staggered to his bed. He told himself not to let the girl's hair and her lice bother him. Never mind that she was small and didn't look strong enough to do a good job of cooking his meals and keeping his cabin and clothes clean. Surely, having her around must be better than having no one at all.

Kate stared at her new master who looked a sickly shade of green and waited for her instructions. He surprised her when he climbed into bed and slipped under his blanket without saying a word.

What? No instructions?

Kate wrinkled her nose at the smell of vomit and urine which overpowered the usual smell of stale air of the lower deck. She looked around the cabin, at the splatters of vomit on the deck. Even her cabin, when twenty-six women occupied it, never became this filthy. If this cabin resembled a pigsty, then this lieutenant must be a pig.

She swallowed hard, but the lump in her throat refused to go away. It'd be galling enough for her to rut with any man. Did she have to do it with a pig who'd gush vomit over her?

Kate smoothed down the cap on her head. A pity. She'd rather have her stubble exposed. Oh well. She'd have to scratch herself more frequently and vigorously. Pray God, the ruse would be enough to kill the lieutenant's lust.

She cleared her throat. "Sir, would you like me to tidy up the cabin?"

He turned on his side and faced the wall. "Yes, you do that."

Kate gave the cabin a thorough cleaning. Then she sat on the cabin floor and waited for him to wake. When he did, he looked around, peered at the floor and into the corners of the cabin and gave a nod of approval.

A few hours later, she served him supper. He swallowed a spoonful of gruel, then another, and broke out chuckling. The chuckles became roars of laughter. Confusion and a tinge of fear made Kate wonder if she'd made a mistake. Had she become convict mistress to a mad man?

The lieutenant spluttered. "Bless the black-hearted rogue! He's out-smarted himself, this time. You're a treasure, Kate! I don't know how you do it, but this is the best meal I've had in a long time."

She forced a smile and put aside her doubts. She would wait to see if she'd made a mistake. But mistake or not, she was stuck with this man till the end of the voyage.

After supper, the lieutenant stretched out on his bed again. Kate sat on the deck, wondering when he'd make his move. Would they rut on the floor or on his narrow bed? When nothing happened, she rolled out her sleeping pallet and lay on it. Under the cover of her blanket, she trembled as she waited. She wanted to shout, "What are you waiting for, you pig? Don't torment me like this."

A loud snore that filled the cabin was soon followed by a series of softer ones. Kate's heart raced. Could she be this lucky? She waited. Her eyelids grew heavier.

She woke to the sounds of heavy footfalls passing by the cabin and broke into a smile. The lieutenant hadn't touched her. *Thank you, Holy Mother, I promise to be deserving of this blessing.*

The lieutenant gave no sign he was interested in rutting with her the following days. It looked like the man only wanted her to cook and clean for him, nothing more, but Kate continued to step softly around the lieutenant, all her senses alive, trying to detect the smallest change in his attitude towards her. She never caught him watching her the way Lord Oliver did. Sure, the lieutenant was very demanding. He insisted she stay by his side all the time. She hated giving up both her time spent above deck and the money she earned from her washing. She missed visiting with Fiona and the Petals too, but she'd happily sacrifice more if the lieutenant didn't have rutting on his mind.

One day he asked her to use his given name. She did. When the next storm hit, she was happy to take care of him even though he moaned, vomited and behaved like a fractious child.

Some thirty days after Tenerife, Kate was above deck cleaning out the chamber pot when she sensed excitement in the air. She ran into Fiona who told her they'd be arriving at Rio de Janeiro shortly. She passed on the news to Jeremy.

"We've reached Rio? Thank God!" He climbed out of bed and dragged out his valise and started packing. She could see no sign of his usual discomfort with a shifting deck.

"What are you doing?"

"Getting ready to get off this bloody ship. I'm not staying here one minute more than I have to."

He changed into a fresh set of garments, then looked around as if making sure he'd not missed anything. Apparently satisfied, he picked up the valise and strode to the door.

Kate frowned. How odd that a sick man could recover so quickly. "Jeremy, we've not reached the harbour yet."

"I know that, but I intend to be the first one to disembark." Just outside the door, he stopped. He dug into his pocket and handed Kate several coins. "That should pay for your food while I'm away. Goodbye."

She closed her eyes, delighted to have three, maybe four weeks to herself, to do as she wished.

In the following days, she spent much of her time above deck, soaking up the sun, devouring the fresh air and watching the sailors busy hauling aboard timber and canvas for repairs, food supplies and water for the next leg of the voyage.

She cleaned the cabin and the bedding, over and over. She visited the Petals, cooked for them and shared their meals. Her friends had managed to obtain, through the sailors, a variety of fresh vegetables and meat. Cooking became a real pleasure for Kate, and she set out to dazzle her friends with her skill. She saw less of Fiona, who frequently went ashore with her family.

At the beginning of the third week, Kate returned to her cabin and stopped short at the doorway.

Jeremy was sitting on his bed, drinking from a bottle and peering at her from its length. "Can't trust anyone in this world."

Kate's heart pounded, her mouth dried. Jeremy was drunk. She'd seen her father in this condition, more times than she cared to remember. Da was normally a quiet man, hardworking too. When drunk, he became an unpleasant stranger. Would Jeremy be like Da? Or worse?

Then she spotted an empty bottle lying on its side in the shadows under the bed. Beside it, stood an unopened one. Her impulse to flee became almost overwhelming, but she resisted it, afraid any move she made might provoke Jeremy into violence.

He tilted the bottle, drank another mouthful and glared at her. "Should have stopped before they cleaned me out. Damn!" Suddenly, he pointed a trembling finger at her. "It's your fault. You're my bad luck!"

"What?"

"You brought me bad luck!" He pounced on Kate and dragged her into the cabin. Before she thought to duck, he hit her. The force threw him off balance. He tottered several steps back, cursed when the bottle slipped from his fingers. It hit the deck without breaking, then rolled towards Kate's feet, spilling liquor along the way. She picked it up.

He snatched the bottle from her with one hand and swiped her with the other. She bounced off the bulkhead and crashed to the deck.

"Get up! C'mon, get up, you ungrateful slut." He kicked her.

She swallowed a cry. Her father had taught her not to talk back to a drunken man. Better yet, not to attract his attention. So she stayed very still on the deck.

She heard liquid gurgling down his throat. *Yes. Drink yourself senseless, you bastard!*

He coughed, then cleared his throat. After a while, he said, "Good God, Jeremy. Now see what you've done." The slurring of his words had grown thicker. "You've killed poor Kate. Dumb cow! And you're a stupid sod, Jeremy. Without Kate, who'll take care of you, eh?"

A long silence followed. The snore, when it came, was most welcome.

Kate waited a while longer, then she got to her feet and stared at Jeremy's sleeping form. She was tempted to bash the swine on his head, but the Rustands had taught her a hard lesson. A moment's satisfaction in exacting her revenge on Lord Oliver had cost seven years of her life. She couldn't afford to lose another seven.

She stared at the bottle in Jeremy's hand. That was the source of her problem. Carefully, she pried it from his strong grip, then turned her attention to the unopened one under the bed. Casting caution aside, she dumped the contents of the unopened bottle into the chamber pot. Then for good measure decided to do the same for the half empty bottle. She stopped herself in time. No. She had to leave him something for when he woke. She hesitated, then tipped out half its contents.

Jeremy's snores assured her he slept deeply. Still she approached the bed and poked him in the arm to make sure. He turned over and began snoring again. Thus assured, she picked up the chamber pot and left the cabin.

Jeremy didn't wake till the next morning. She sensed him hovering above her. She saw no point in pretending to be asleep, so she opened her eyes and looked at him. His gaze roamed over her face, then away as he straightened. "Is there any liquor left?"

She handed him the almost empty bottle, fully expecting an argument.

He coughed, tilted the bottle and drained it. He stole another glance at her face, then said loudly, "God! I hate this ship!"

He tossed down the empty bottle and turned to his metal chest. Coins clinked, and the chest lid thudded. Without another word to Kate, he shuffled out of the cabin.

He stayed away four days. Kate had just returned to the cabin after sharing a meal with the Petals, when he walked through the door. He held a valise in one hand and two packages under his arm.

Kate wasn't surprised to see him. The word was out that the *Merry Mersey* would sail with the tide. She didn't think the bastard wanted to be left behind in Rio.

Dropping his valise on the floor, he tossed one bundle onto his bed and offered Kate the other. She accepted the clumsily wrapped package, wondering if he had another beating in store for her.

"Open it. It's something to say I'm sorry I hit you. I was drunk. It won't happen again, Kate. I swear it! Well, go on, open the package."

An apology was the last thing she expected. Indeed, the whole scene seemed unreal to her. She tore open the wrapping, and a colourful shawl fell out. She picked it up. "For me?"

"Who else?"

She smoothed out the fabric. Its rough texture told her this wasn't something Lady Rustand would own, but Kate didn't care. Maybe it was the best Rio de Janeiro had to offer, or the best Jeremy could afford. It was her very first gift.

Perhaps she'd misjudged Jeremy. He must care for her, mustn't he? She looked into his eyes and smiled. "Thank you. This is really lovely." She shook open the colourful wrap and admired it. Suddenly mindful of her manners, she asked, "Did you have better luck this time?"

Jeremy laughed. "Did I ever!" He withdrew a fat bag of coins from his pocket and jingled it before her eyes.

She laughed with him until her gaze fell upon a bottle of liquor peeping out of the package he'd tossed carelessly on the bed. *Oh, no!*

Jeremy brushed past her to the bed. He picked up the bottle. "This is for you as well, Kate. A bottle of woman's wine, or so the man tells me. Shall we give it a try?"

"But I don't drink, Jeremy. Did you get something else for yourself?"

"Oh, no, Kate." He opened the bottle. "I can't control myself when I'm drunk. You know that." He gave her a slow smile.

"But this is different. Let's celebrate! Rio has been very lucky for me."

He filled two cups with wine and offered her one. "To Lady Luck! Come on, Kate. Drink up!"

She took a tentative sip. It tasted foul, but at Jeremy's encouraging nod, she forced herself to swallow another small mouthful. She shuddered. He laughed, then drank from his cup. He choked. With one long stride he reached the chamber pot and spat out the wine.

"Damn! Nothing but rotgut! Bloody foreigners! Here, give me your cup." He emptied the bottle and the cups into the chamber pot, then tossed them aside.

In the next moment, he smiled at Kate and extended his hand. "Come here, sweet."

Kate stared at his hand as she would the devil's cloven hoof. She looked into his light blue eyes, and her heart sank at the familiar gleam she saw there.

CHAPTER 6

The silence in the cabin stretched. Kate blinked but Jeremy's waiting hand didn't disappear.

How could she have been so stupid? Didn't she already know that all men wanted to rut? Why would Jeremy be any different? Did she think she could take a man for her protector and not pay the price?

She forced a smile, stepped forward and reluctantly placed her hand in his. She tried not to pull back when his fingers closed around hers. She forced herself not to flinch when he drew her into his embrace. Her breath caught when he bent to kiss her. She needed air and barely managed to stop herself from pushing him away.

Calm yourself, girl. Breathe!

She made herself accept Jeremy's roaming hands and his insistent tongue. No. She couldn't do it! She couldn't. She tried to concentrate, digging deep into her memory. Nothing. Where had the many tricks the Petals taught her gone?

She leaned into Jeremy while screaming inside her head, "You can do it! Yes, you can. It'll soon be over. You can do it!"

Then Josie's voice whispered in her head, "You've got to be bold, Kate. The men ain't looking for no virgin, not a lump of dead meat, you know? You've got to be bold!"

Thank God for Josie.

A sense of calmness descended on her. She opened her mouth wider to accommodate his exploring tongue. Slipping her hand under his shirt, she tugged at the hair on his chest, gently, then she played with his nipples. His moans of pleasure proved her friends had not misled her.

He released her, unlaced her garment and caressed her breast. Her belly churned. *Don't think about it. It's not Lord Oliver! Remember what Josie said. Just do it!*

He kissed her again. She moaned, the way she'd learned from the Petals. He forced her to step backwards, gently. She obliged till the edge of the bed stopped her. He pulled the gown off her shoulders. She cooperated, freeing her arms from her sleeves. Then anxious for the ordeal to end as soon as possible, she tried to relieve him of his jacket. Her fingers refused to work properly.

"My, my. You *are* impatient." He chuckled. "I'll undress myself. You do the same, sweet."

She whipped off her garments and dropped them to the floor. She scrambled into bed and under the blanket. Her heartbeats thundered in her head. The ghost of Lord Oliver rose before her closed eyes. She tensed, remembering the beating. Her eyes seemed to have a will of their own. They popped open, and she looked at Jeremy. He was down to stripping away his stockings. Naked, he approached the bed. She glanced at his hands, expecting him to hold his belt in one of them. They were empty. *Thank God!*

"We won't need this." He tossed the covers aside and joined her on the narrow bed. His touch, feather-soft and tender, contrasted sharply with the violence and pain she remembered with Lord Oliver. To her surprise, her fears fell away as easily as petals from a faded rose. Her confidence blossomed.

She wriggled beneath his weight and moaned. She nibbled and she bit. She lavished kisses and caresses on him and drove him into a frenzy. With one quick thrust he entered, snug inside her. She urged him on. Faster and faster. Deeper and deeper.

He gave a loud roar and collapsed on top of her like a sack of potatoes.

Finally she understood. The Petals were right. There was no pleasure involved in this, only work. She wanted to giggle, but suppressed the urge, lest she offend Jeremy. She concentrated on his heavy breathing, in rhythm with her own, instead.

He rolled to his side and pulled her close. "You're a wild one all right!"

She smiled. It wasn't hard to deceive a man at all. Thank God for the Petals for showing her the way.

The *Merry Mersey* sailed the next day. Kate heard several sailors wishing aloud for a good blow to get them to Cape Town. She prayed for the opposite and for a little storm now and again to keep Jeremy tame.

After the bedding, she discovered more things about her master. He needed only a nudge to start talking about himself. Kate pretended she couldn't hear enough of his stories. She'd forced an expression of deep interest on her face so often she thought she must look like a rag doll with its painted eyes always rounded in amazement, and her lips forever spread in a daft smile. Occasionally, she would gape in pretended awe just to flatter the fool.

Jeremy claimed to be the younger son of an English baron. *How ridiculous!* She'd worked for the Rustands and seen them and their titled guests on their best behaviour and at their worst. Jeremy's speech did reflect those of the la-di-da who crossed her path, but he often forgot himself, and his speech lapsed to that of the common man. These lapses told their own story. She knew him for a drunk, and now a liar.

Why should she care if he lied? He could claim to be the bastard son of King George, and she'd marvel at the fact. Should he indicate a fondness for rats, she'd rush out to find him one and make a pet of it, even though she hated all rodents.

She'd do anything if it meant she didn't have to share his bed again.

One day, he asked where she came from.

"Kildare, Ireland."

"How did you get here from there?"

Kate almost laughed at his poor effort to express some interest in something other than himself, but he was mistaken if he thought she would confide in him.

"My father's a farmer in Ireland. He put me into service with the Rustands two years ago. I worked as their kitchen maid before they made me 'companion' to his lordship's two little daughters. One day, I took a liking to one of her ladyship's silk handkerchiefs and thought to keep it for myself. They caught me, and that's why I'm here."

He smirked. "Now, let that be a lesson for you. Dishonesty doesn't pay. Still, you can consider yourself lucky. You're to be given a chance at a new life in a new colony. Maybe like me, you'll end up with a fortune too."

Kate knew he'd now talk about some grand vision he had of his future. A fool's dream. She'd be pleased enough to get through the voyage safely, never mind making a 'fortune.' Careful to keep smiling and nodding her head, she stopped listening. There must be some way to keep Jeremy amused, but how, when they were confined to a small cabin in the middle of the sea? She had to find it somehow, for she needed more than bad weather to drive thoughts of rutting from his mind.

One day, Jeremy asked her why she never wore the shawl he'd bought her.

Kate quickly dug out the gift and threw it across her shoulder. She smoothed out the creases on the material. "It's very pretty. I thought I'd wear it on special occasions."

He pulled her down to sit beside him on the bed and then ran a finger down her cheek. "I'll buy you a dozen more when we get to Cape Town, if Lady Luck stays by my side."

"You'll be playing cards again?"

"Of course. I'm rather skilled with cards, I'll have you know. With Lady Luck by my side, no one can beat me."

"But what if Lady Luck . . ."

He shouted, "Never say that to me. Never, never, do you hear?"

"I'm sorry." Kate swallowed hard, telling herself to be more careful. "Jeremy? Would you teach me how to play cards?"

He stared at her, then shook his head. "No. You're a female. It'll be too hard for you to learn."

She ran her hand over his thigh. "With you for my teacher, I might become half as good as you. Think about it, Jeremy. You'd be able to put in more practice. It might be fun."

He stared at her with a gleam in his eye. "Now, why didn't I think of that?"

The card game called *All Fours* presented no great challenge for Kate. She learned the rules quickly. When she became more skilled, she would play to let Jeremy win the crucial hand. This kept his mood sweet. She was careful to stroke his vanity to make certain her occasional win didn't spark his temper.

As the weeks passed, Kate learned that Jeremy was quite the fraud. The sea didn't incapacitate him as much as he'd made out. On six occasions, when they played cards, she'd noticed how a run of good luck often made him ignore a rising storm.

Nor was he unfit when lust reared its ugly head. She learned to submit and feign passion. A woman's lot had never been easy; she'd seen how it was with Ma. Except Ma had been so accepting with what life had handed her—poverty and endless toil. Kate was determined her life would be different. So what if she had to lie and cheat to achieve this? She'd do it, with no regrets.

★   ★   ★   ★   ★

A few days later, Jeremy gave Kate's luscious bottom a light squeeze and a pat. He got out of bed and started to dress. "The sea seems rather calm today. I'm feeling exceptionally well."

Kate sat up. "Indeed. I've not seen you in better spirits."

He watched her draw the bed sheet up to cover herself, and he grinned. *Silly chit.* How could she be so modest when only minutes ago, she'd been utterly shameless and insatiable? And why hide herself from him? Had he not seen, touched or explored every inch of her? "Yes, I think I'll go above deck for a walk. I've been stuck in this cabin for too long."

He emerged from the hatch, momentarily blinded by daylight. A light breeze ruffled his hair, cooling his cheeks. He took a deep breath, then headed for the starboard railing. On his right, he spotted Blackton in deep conversation with a sailor scrubbing the deck. He changed direction. "Mr. Blackton!"

Blackton flashed him a smile. "Lieutenant Kendrick, sir. How very nice to see you above deck! How may I help you?"

"Tell me, Mr. Blackton, what happens to my convict woman when we land at Port Jackson. Is it possible for me to keep her?"

"Ah! You're a right smart one, Lieutenant sir." Blackton wagged a finger at him. "A man should always look ahead, eh? Well, rest assured, sir. I'll be informing the cap'n of your wishes, and we'll see what can be arranged to our mutual benefit."

Jeremy clenched his teeth. "You mean this is going to cost me more money?"

Blackton shrugged. "Well, you know how good things in life must be paid for, sir. 'Tis the way of the world."

Jeremy walked away, muttering curses. He caught sight of the dark clouds looming on the horizon and scowled. Stubbornly, he stood by the starboard rail, challenging the storm to do its worst, determined not to be cowed this time. Fifteen minutes later, when the deck rolled under his feet, he hurried below deck.

The sun was sinking over the horizon when the *Merry Mersey* dropped anchor in Cape Town harbour. Kate followed Jeremy above deck, staying a good distance behind him, lest he spot her and became angry. She wanted to be sure he left the ship. Keeping to the shadows, she watched him make a fuss, demanding he be rowed ashore immediately. Captain Mowat ignored him at first, but finally yielded when Jeremy wouldn't go away.

Kate crossed the deck and walked with very light steps to the bow of the ship, humming a tune, happy to be rid of Jeremy. Of course, he could always return for a quick visit before the ship sailed. That he might beat her again as he did at Rio de Janeiro remained a possibility, but she refused to allow the likelihood to ruin her day.

She spent the first morning standing at the bow, gazing at Cape Town. She could make out a bell tower rising high above the rooftops. Would Port Jackson be even half as big as this? Probably not. Fiona said it was a "Godforsaken land", and Kate had no idea how "Godforsaken" that would be.

A riotous clamour drew her attention. A cow, bound in ropes, mooed plaintively as the sailors hauled it up the side of the ship. It landed on the deck with a loud thud and several sailors fell upon it in a rush.

Kate shook her head. Did the sailors imagine the beast would escape when it lay helpless, bound in ropes?

A light touch on her shoulder made her swing around. "Fiona! Aren't you going ashore?"

"Aye. I'm just waiting for me Jamie and Robbie." She gave Kate a long look. "And how are you?"

"I'm all right." She pointed to the cow. "Why are we taking cattle on board?"

"Cap'n Mowat wouldna carry livestock earlier, lass. He dinna want the trouble of having them die on him on a long voyage. We're about halfway to New South Wales now, and this be our last port of call. We load the beasts here, so they'd have a shorter distance to travel. I suspect this be one of the cap'n's. He likes his livestock aboard before the paying passengers.' "

Fiona touched her hand. "What's wrong, Kate? You dinna look happy."

"I don't want the voyage to end, Fiona. I'm happy enough now. I cannot be sure what awaits me in Port Jackson."

"Mama, Mama!" a young voice called out.

Robbie ran in a circle, flapping his arms. A big man with red hair grabbed him under his arms and tossed him into the air. Above Robbie's screams of delight, Fiona said, "I've got to go Kate. I'll see you later."

Kate stayed above deck a while longer. She watched several sailors help the passengers bring their purchases on board. Jeremy should be doing something similar, but as far as she could tell, the fool thought of nothing but his pleasure, expecting luck to take care of the rest.

She continued her old arrangement with the Petals, cooking for them for a share of their food. They bought baskets of oranges through the sailors, claiming the fruits were so cheap, the farmers must be giving them away. Each day, the five of them gorged themselves, and the cabin smelled of oranges.

At the end of the second week, Jeremy showed up at the cabin, drunk and looking to vent his anger. Kate received swollen cheeks and a painful hip from the beating he gave her. He apologised the next morning and foreswore liquor for the rest of his stay in Cape Town.

She forced her split lips into a smile, then nodded her forgiveness as she squeezed his hand. What else could she do? She had to keep him sweet so he wouldn't think to hurt her again.

He returned six days later and beat her again. Just like before, he looked ashamed when he sobered up, but this time he left without offering her any more false promises.

Kate knew she'd never be safe from Jeremy's fists and boots as long as the *Merry Mersey* remained in harbour. *Please God, let Captain Mowat be ready to set sail soon.* Now, she couldn't wait for the voyage to end, that she might be rid of Jeremy forever. True, she might end up with a worse master, but there was also a chance that he might be a much kinder man.

Jeremy looked out the window of his room at the *Pelican Inn* and watched the red sky turn orange and pink as the sun sank beyond the hills. He fingered his pouch of coins and fought off a feeling of panic. If his luck didn't improve soon, he'd be broke. How could he start a new life in New South Wales then? He might as well slit his throat and save himself the misery.

He rubbed his hands against his trousers. Maybe he should give Lady Luck some help. No, that could be too dangerous. The men he played cards with were strangers, hardened men not young blades right out of the schoolroom and bound by their code of honour. Oh God, he had to win tonight! He just had to!

A few hours later, Jeremy couldn't stop smiling. The pile of coins on the table in front of him continued to grow. The right cards kept coming his way, and he won hand after hand.

His luck held over the next three days, and he won a small fortune. On the fourth night, he counted his coins in his room at the inn. Carefully, he half-filled his coin pouch and tucked it into his pocket. He stuffed the rest into another pouch and hid it on a beam in the ceiling. Win or lose, this would be his last night gaming. The *Merry Mersey* would be sailing soon, and he had every intention of keeping his winnings to give himself a good start in his new life in New South Wales.

The men at the gaming hall were deep into their game when he arrived.

"Back to see if your luck holds, eh?" one of the gamblers greeted him on a sour note.

Jeremy laughed. "If I'm not welcome, I'll leave."

"Jan, give him your chair," said a burly man.

Jan, the thin man with a moustache hesitated. The burly man made a long comment. It sounded like Dutch, but Jeremy understood not a word of it. Jan's expression cleared. He laughed and offered Jeremy his seat. A man from across the room threw in a comment. It raised a few chuckles.

Moments later, the game started anew. An hour passed. The man with his teeth showing through his harelip threw down his cards. He muttered some curses and glared at Jeremy. "You're too lucky, English."

Someone gasped; the men at the table became very still. Jeremy shrugged, gathering in the coins he'd won. "How about a drink? Boy! Give my friend here a—" He turned to the disgruntled loser. "Is rum all right with you?"

The man grunted assent. The tension eased and the game continued.

Jeremy raked in more winnings as the night progressed. Two hours later, he swept his coins on the table into his coin pouch. "Thank you, gentlemen, for a wonderful game. 'Tis late, I'll say goodnight now and see you again tomorrow."

He tucked the pouch into his pocket, flashed a broad smile at the three players at his table and got to his feet. The men didn't return his smile.

Sore losers! Just as well 'twas his last night here. He patted the front of his jacket. The feel of his pistol beneath the fabric was reassuring. Not that he had anything to fear from this lot of cowards. Hadn't he promised to return the following night?

That should keep them happy, dreaming of recovering their losses. *Fools!*

He waved goodbye to the men and threaded his way through the crowded room to the door. A golden crescent hung low in the night sky, and a hundred yards down the road, a scattering of lamplight flickered in the dark, marking the town. The night seemed uneasily quiet. Then a dog howled.

Jeremy straightened his jacket, then stepped into the night. He hadn't covered fifty yards when a strong arm slid under his chin, choking him. Before he could react, other hands dragged him into a side alley.

"Cheating English bastard!" a low voice hissed.

Jeremy gasped. "Here!" he croaked. "I won my money, fair and square."

A hoarse voice said, "We don't care, you bloody sod."

"Hey, he's got a pistol!" someone cried.

"Give it here," shouted another.

Jeremy struggled, kicking out where he could. Suddenly he was free. He landed a few punches, before someone had him in another headlock again, choking him if he so much as twitched. They lay into him, their fists pounding into his belly, his head, his ribs. He fell to his knees and curled up in the dirt. They kicked him. He begged for mercy, but the beating didn't stop.

He woke to a night sky turning silver. He attempted to sit up, but a sharp pain at his side stopped him. After some moments, he tried again and succeeded. His tongue found a loose front tooth. A mere touch, and it dropped onto his tongue. He spat it out.

His belly churned. He took a deep breath, only to choke on the awful stench of garbage and rotting refuse, and vomited. The bastards had left him in a drain, mired in filth and slime. He had to get out of there. When he moved to climb out of the trench, pain hit him like a tidal wave.

When next he woke, the sky was light. Carefully, he crawled out of the ditch. He checked his pockets. Empty. He cursed his attackers roundly. That was it. He was finished with Cape Town.

Kate was enjoying another fine morning above deck when an approaching rowboat caught her attention. *Jeremy!* She frowned. The *Merry Mersey* wouldn't sail for several days yet. Was she to expect another beating? *Please God, no.*

She abandoned the idea of making herself scarce almost as soon as the thought occurred to her. What was the point? She would have to face him eventually. She might as well wait to greet him. Minutes passed, then Jeremy stepped onto the deck. A feeling of delight overwhelmed her as she stared into his battered face. *God.* She hoped he hurt!

Quickly, she covered the sides of her mouth with both hands in feigned horror and cried, "Oh Jeremy! What happened to you?"

Before he could respond, she continued, "You poor dear! Come, let me help you back to the cabin."

She fussed over him, did everything she could think of to make him comfortable. "I'll get the ship's surgeon to look at your injuries. Now, don't try to get up, Jeremy. Rest. I'll be back as soon as I can. Go on, close your eyes!"

She left the cabin in a show of haste, but spent the next hour visiting the Petals. Later, she lingered on the open deck. It was noon when she brought the ship's surgeon back to the cabin.

Jeremy had two cracked ribs and a broken nose. His missing tooth presented a problem for Kate. She had to bite her lip to control her urge to snicker. She pampered him, to show she cared, and he became even more demanding, like a sick child.

The following evening when she handed him his meal, he caught her hand. "Kate, I want you to know you'll be staying with me after we land. You'll like that, won't you?"

73

She smiled and nodded. He could be lying, or indeed be telling the truth. It didn't matter either way. She could very well be better off with another master. Maybe not. Time would tell.

The *Merry Mersey* weighed anchor a few days later. Over the next seven weeks, three monstrous storms hit the ship, and Kate prayed for more just for the joy of seeing Jeremy suffer. Before they could run into another gale, rumours had it that they'd be reaching Port Jackson within days.

One morning, she returned to the cabin to find an excited Jeremy.

"We'll be landing in New South Wales sometime tomorrow, Kate. Blackton just told me. Isn't that wonderful?"

"So soon?"

"Soon? How can you say that? It's been two months of hell since Cape Town. Oh. He also said you're to return to your old cabin by sunset today."

CHAPTER 7

When Kate stepped into the cabin with her arms full with her personal belongings, the Petals waved and called for her to join them. Kate nodded, and as she headed their way, noted that three women had returned to the cabin ahead of her. The others came straggling back in the next few hours. Kate kept count as she sat close to the Petals while listening to their banter. The returning women made no effort to acknowledge the Petals or herself. Kate thought they were merely unhappy to return to the cabin and were sulking. They had never extended a friendly word to her the length of the voyage, and she didn't expect them to change. Why would they bother with the voyage over, and they might not see each other again?

Finally, a guard stepped through the doorway, did a quick tally, then left without saying a word. He closed the door behind him and slammed the bolt home.

Six women had not survived the voyage. Kate shuddered and vowed she'd survive the next six years somehow, to become a free woman—never mind the natives who might want her for a meal, or men like Jeremy who might make a cripple or a common whore out of her. She would endure.

Suddenly she frowned. Something was amiss. Could she be mistaken? In such close quarters it became evident these women were friendly with each other. Only the Petals and she had been given the cold shoulder. Surely not?

The redhead, Flo, tossed her hair, looked at the Petals and

sneered. "Damned whores!"

Kate started. What on earth was wrong with these women that they dared to show their contempt for the Petals? Did these eejits not spread their legs just the same? How could living the entire voyage with one man, not their husband, make them better than the Petals? She stared into their gaunt faces. The Petals looked absolutely in the pink compared to them.

She was about to take these women to task, when she felt Josie's grip on her arm. Josie shook her head at her.

Kate's tension drained away. The Petals could take care of themselves; they didn't need her to defend them. Still, it burned her to accept the injustice of it all. Deliberately, she turned her thoughts to Jeremy.

"I've made special arrangements with Captain Mowat," he'd said before they parted. "Go along with the rest of the women. I'll fetch you after I've reported for duty with the army. You trust me, don't you?"

"Of course," she lied.

"I'll be back quicker than you can blink. You'll see."

She didn't care if she never saw Jeremy again. The man was a drunk and a woman-beater, a liar and arrogant to boot. Her next protector might well be a kinder man.

She bit her lip. But would he put her out to whore for him?

Jeremy stared at Port Jackson, as the *Merry Mersey* approached the harbour, and cursed under his breath. Where was the bustling metropolis of Sydney Town? Had he vomited his way over eight months to reach this—this hellhole? "God rot your soul, Emeline!"

To think he had plans to carve out his fortune in this new colony so he could return home in triumph. He cringed at his foolishness.

His opinion of the new colony didn't improve when he

reached the harbourside. Indeed any village in Yorkshire would look good compared to this primitive colony. He glared at a scattering of brick buildings amongst hovels of crude timber as he marched into town. He sneered at the unpaved road, but after a near tumble, he carefully sidestepped outcropping of rocks and holes he was sure would become large pools of water after the rain.

A hundred yards on, he asked a passerby for directions to the New South Wales Corps' headquarters. He reported to a captain who barely observed the civilities before he ushered Jeremy hastily out of his office and unloaded him onto his sergeant as he would a cartload of manure. Jeremy seethed, but held tightly to his temper. Although unused to military ways, he knew enough not to offend a senior officer.

The sergeant completed the paperwork while he waited. After twenty long minutes, he looked up at Jeremy. "Do you have accommodation, sir?"

"I've just arrived. How would I have accommodation, Sergeant?"

The sergeant stared at him, then shrugged his shoulders. "Very well, sir. You can stay at the Officers' Mess. Here's your key. No doubt you'll find yourself other, more suitable lodgings soon. Now, here's how you get to your quarters . . ."

Half an hour later, Jeremy stood before the Officers' Mess, staring at walls made of slabs of timber. He counted ten doors. How cozy! Ten officers and their families living together under one roof.

He dropped his two valises, unlocked the door and entered his quarters. He thrust open the window shutters, dusted himself of cobwebs and looked around. How gratifying! He now had twice the living space afforded him by the *Merry Mersey.* Luxury indeed. But wait! His Majesty's Army had also seen fit to provide him with a bed, a table and not one, but two chairs!

What generosity.

In a corner, he saw a brazier, a cooking pot and a fry pan. It struck him then that this—this hovel—was to serve him as bedroom, kitchen, dining room and . . . He kicked one of the chairs and watched it skid two feet across the floor, then topple over. Dust swirled into the air.

He sneezed and coughed repeatedly. He backed out of his quarters, snatched up his valises and walked away. What did he care if he'd left the windows and door open? What was there for anyone to steal?

Kate slept in snatches and was wide awake when their guard arrived with the usual two buckets of fresh water. He had a message from Blackton.

"Ladies. Get your things. You be leaving this morning."

The women packed their belongings. Several of them asked around. Should they take their bowls and spoons with them? What about the blankets? Kate didn't care what the others did. She packed everything she could carry with her.

Another guard arrived a short while later. "Hurry up now, ladies. Mr. Blackton, he be expectin' us above deck, and he don't like to be kept waitin'."

The Petals led the way into the corridor, chatting easily amongst themselves as if they didn't have a care in the world. *How fearless,* Kate thought and wished she felt as brave.

On the open deck, sailors scurried to and fro. The guard stopped the women some twenty feet from a group of men in red jackets at the bow of the ship.

"Who are them uniforms?" Kitty asked the guard.

He snickered. "Army officers. They've come a-marketing."

Kate spotted Blackton amongst the officers. His discussion with them soon ended. The men spread out, their interest centred on Kate's group of convict women.

"Gertie!" Blackton shouted. "Take a step forward! Gentlemen, we have here Gertie Seton. The wench be twenty years old. Stole a loaf of bread and got seven years for her trouble. So who'll have her?"

"Damn! She's a skinny one! Don't suppose you'll get much work out of her," one officer commented loudly.

A gust of wind molded Gertie's garment to her form.

"Hey Ted, you see her belly?" another officer called out.

"God's blood! Breeding already?" Ted said. "Well, count me out. I'm not having any fat women or squalling babies."

Kate swallowed hard. Was she to end up with one of these officers?

"Come on, Ted!" another man hollered. "She looks good. Probably has strong legs too. As a matter of fact, you could get her to do the mounting and the riding!"

A burst of guffaws greeted the words.

"Frank's right, Ted! The girl has looks I say. All she needs is a bit of fattening-up. Why, she'd be downright pretty—"

"If she's such a beauty, and the size of her belly doesn't bother you," Ted shouted, "why don't you have her, Buford?"

Buford laughed. "Sorry, Ted! I've got my eye on another. That beauty over there will suit me fine!"

"That one? Why, Buford, her bosom will surely smother you!"

There was another roar of laughter.

"Yes! But what a way to go!"

The men clapped amidst more laughter.

"Well, I'm not a fussy man," a new voice called out. "So, is the wench taken or not? No? All right, Blackton, I'll have her."

Kate stared at Gertie. Had she not boasted last eve that her protector would keep her? Were all men liars? *Dear God, please let Jeremy keep his word to me this time.*

Lewd suggestions and humiliating comments continued amidst bursts of laughter as Blackton presented one convict woman after another. The officers were especially wicked with the six women they'd rejected, four whose bellies were swollen with child and two who looked too skinny and pale to be healthy.

Kate's jaw ached from clenching her teeth as she waited her turn. Then there were just two of them left. Kate closed her eyes as she said another silent prayer. She didn't want to be last and prepared herself to step forward. No call came. Instead the redcoats started to gather and chat amongst themselves.

The guard looked at the pregnant woman beside Kate, then flashed her a wink. "Looks like your men be keeping you for themselves."

Kate blinked away her tears. Jeremy had kept his word.

The pregnant woman beside her sobbed. Kate put an arm around her shoulders. "You're going to be fine," she said.

The deck soon cleared—the officers left taking the twelve convict women, including the Petals, with them.

Blackton waved for the eight remaining women to approach. "Ladies, stay close together. I'll have you taken ashore now. Follow me."

From her seat in the rowboat, Kate feasted her eyes on the green trees and shrubs along the shoreline. After spending eight months on board ship, she yearned to stand on solid ground again. When she did, she was startled. The land seemed to rise and fall beneath her feet. She fought against a giggle at the odd sensation.

A crowd of mostly men soon gathered to gawk at them. *What?* Was this not a penal colony where convicts abound? Why should the arrival of a few more provoke such unseemly interest? Somehow Kate felt intimidated again.

A light wind made her shiver. Didn't Lizzy say Botany Bay was hot and had no winter? *What nonsense.* Kate huddled into her shawl. If late April felt this cold, there'd be winter come December.

The two guards who met the rowboat concluded their business with Blackton, then approached the women.

The older guard looked them over, gave his head a tired shake, then swept his arm wide. "This way, ladies. We're to take you to your new home, and the sooner we git started, the sooner we'll arrive. Then you can all rest them weary bones, and we can get back to our mates."

The guards led them up a long winding road to a large timber building. Three women lounged outside the doorway, their gaze fixed on Kate and her party.

"This be your quarters, ladies," the younger guard said. Without another word, he and the older guard turned and retraced their steps down the road. Kate stared at them in confusion.

Where was the prison? She glanced at her companions to see if they knew what was going on. They looked bewildered.

She turned to the three women outside the building. "We're— convicts. How come they didn't lock us up?"

The woman with dirty blond hair answered, "Nah. They don't do that no more. They just let us be so long as we don't give them no trouble."

Kate frowned. "What's to stop us from running off then?"

The women laughed. Their laughter seemed to draw other women out of the building.

"And where would you go, pray tell?" asked the blonde. "There ain't nothing out there, but death, you fool."

"What do you mean?" the pregnant woman behind Kate asked.

The blonde rolled her eyes. "We get food and shelter here. Out there you get them black fellas who'd kill you with their spears."

The woman leaning against the doorway shouted, "Hey Lily, don't you stop there! Tell them how hunger can kill them too."

Lily ignored the taunt and looked at Kate. "You can try your luck, of course."

"C'mon Lily. Ain't you gonna tell them the soldiers would hunt them down like beasts?"

"Aw, shut up, Gwen!" Lily yelled. Gwen cackled.

"Do we stay here forever, then?" the pregnant woman asked.

Lily sighed. "Don't you know nothing? The government men will find us work. Maybe some free settler will take us for wives or servants—"

"Servants? Whores more like," Gwen said.

The pregnant woman held her belly. "The officers didn't want me 'cause of me babe. You look strong enough. Why—"

Gwen laughed. "Lily's a troublemaker, is what. They've no use for no troublemakers. Sent her back twice already!"

Lily took off a shoe and hurled it at Gwen. "You shut your mouth, you witch!"

Gwen caught the shoe and doubled over, laughing.

Kate suppressed a smile, glad she wouldn't be sharing their lives. Her future would depend only on Jeremy. Hugging her parcel of belongings close, she wandered away from the building. She picked up a dry leaf the wind chased to her feet. It crushed easily in her hand and gave off a sharp but pleasant scent. She strolled to the top of an incline and looked down at the harbour. She had no difficulty picking out the *Merry Mersey* amidst three other ships.

Despite the bird calls drifting down from the trees and the low chatter of the women coming from the building, a sense of peace enfolded Kate. She felt as one with the vastness of this new land.

Approaching footsteps shook her out of her trance. She

glanced over her shoulder. Jeremy stood six paces away, grinning at her.

"Didn't I tell you, I'd be here to get you the first moment I got? Am I not a man of my word?"

"Yes, you are." Kate hugged him.

An hour later, she stared at the shambles that was to be their home. It looked like nobody had lived in this room in a long time. There was dirt at her feet, cobwebs in the corners, a layer of dust everywhere and an upended chair on the floor. "Jeremy, you didn't sleep here last night, did you?"

"Oh, no. I took a room at an inn. This place needs cleaning, and I've got you the cleaning materials. I've also got us food and new sleeping pallets . . ."

She heard no more as she tried to come to terms with her new abode. The two windows would give her plenty of fresh air and sunshine, but she'd happily trade them for a larger room that would better her chances to elude a drunken man's fists.

"This is just temporary," he said. "It's a hovel, I know, but we won't be here for long. You can be sure I didn't travel all this way to end up like this. I'll have a big house with many rooms to share with you one day soon, you'll see."

"Oh I wasn't criticising, Jeremy. This is fine! It's much better than our cabin on the *Merry Mersey* don't you think?"

Jeremy laughed. "You're right. This floor doesn't move!"

She joined in the laughter. *How much better if it did.*

In the following weeks, Jeremy settled into a routine. He'd leave their quarters each morning to attend to his official garrison duties. Often, he'd return home late in the afternoon in a foul mood, complaining about his fellow officers and his lazy soldiers.

One day, Jeremy came home bright-eyed and bursting to share a secret with her. He reminded her of her younger brothers, but Kate knew he was nothing like them.

Somehow, he managed to keep his secret till after they finished supper.

"Kate, do you know how this colony got started?"

"No, Jeremy."

"Well, Captain Arthur Phillip arrived with the First Fleet in February 1788 to establish this colony. The fool was here to start a settlement, but he didn't bring along any farmers, and certainly not enough farming tools to open up the land. Can you believe that? I could have done a better job, I promise you. I wouldn't have ended up with the settlement depending on imports to survive. I'd have fields of wheat and corn to feed the settlers . . ."

Kate didn't dare laugh. The man knew nothing about farming, but that didn't stop him from thinking he could do better than Governor Phillip. She kept smiling and nodding her head as he continued to talk.

"As governor, he offered free settlers land grants of thirty to sixty acres each and the services of two convicts at government expense to start them farming. He also opened up over a thousand acres as public farms."

She could hardly believe what she'd heard. "Sixty acres! He gives sixty acres of land away for free?" Her father farmed a land no bigger than three acres, and he paid rent to do it. And here, the governor gave away huge tracts of land for nothing? She stared at Jeremy and swallowed hard. "Can you get a land grant too?"

"It's been the standing government policy that no serving army officer is eligible for land grants in a Crown colony, Kate. Yes, that's not fair, is it? So the army officers persuaded Governor Phillip to apply to London for permission to change the rules here."

"And?" Kate said.

"London has approved the change, and lucky for us this decision came after Governor Phillip resigned, leaving our present commanding officer, Major Grose, in charge."

"Why lucky?"

"Because the major knows how to take care of his officers. We get one hundred acres of land each and the free services of ten convicts to boot!"

"One hundred acres!"

Jeremy sipped some water from his glass. "Yes, but we don't have to do the farming ourselves. The convict workers will do that, and for free."

"Will you be getting a land grant then?"

"Of course." He winked at Kate. "I'll have the choicest piece of property yet."

Kate nodded, but didn't see how that could be.

"The Hawkesbury area, the richest farming land in this colony, has just been opened for settlement, and that's where I'll have my farm." He leaned back in his chair. "Well, Kate, don't you see? This is only the beginning."

Kate reached out and cleared the table. "Is the Hawkesbury far from here?"

"It's somewhere north of Sydney Town and Parramatta, but what do I care about the distance? We're talking about establishing my personal empire!"

"Yes, of course."

"I'll be going to the Hawkesbury this weekend," he told Kate four days later. "I need to put in my claim before some bastard beats me to the best hundred acres."

"Be sure you have the river—"

He turned on her. "I don't need you to remind me I need water for the crops. I'm not a fool, you know?"

"Of course not. I'm sorry."

"I know what I'm doing."

"Yes, of course."

He set forth that Saturday morning and returned on Sunday night, with sunken eyes and a faceful of whiskers, complaining about the mosquitoes and the crawlies who wanted to share his bed.

Jeremy was a man who liked his comforts. Kate thought his interest in owning land might wane, but he proved more determined than she had expected. Weekend after weekend he set out for the Hawkesbury, and it was not until his sixth outing that he returned brimming with excitement. "Kate. I've found it. I've found what I wanted!"

"How marvelous!" she said. *Thank goodness. Maybe now he'll stop complaining about his aches, the mosquito bites and one miserable bee sting.*

He couldn't stop talking of his future, not even when they settled into bed. "We're on our way, Kate. To a ready fortune and an easy life. You should see the land I've picked for my own, right next to the Hawkesbury River . . ."

Kate nodded, thinking she wouldn't mind at all if this excitement sustained him for another six years. He would have no reason to drink heavily, and she'd have no cause to fear another beating.

". . . I'm going to name the property, 'Red Roo'—after, you know, the strange, rather large animal that would hop on two legs rather than run on four . . ."

He shook her awake. "Think, Kate. I'll not be out of pocket for anything! Not even on tools or seeds . . ."

Kate did not think a man like Jeremy would change. He did not believe in working hard, and a farm could not prosper without it. She could see more trouble ahead for her.

CHAPTER 8

The morning after he received the approval of his application for a land grant, Jeremy presented himself to Lieutenant Price, the officer in charge of convict workers.

Price introduced him to Sergeant Riley. "I'll leave you in my sergeant's very capable hands," he said and left.

Jeremy glared at his colleague's retreating back. *Damned bastard. Too important to attend to me, eh? Am I not a lieutenant too? Ill-mannered oaf!*

Riley cleared his throat. "Sir? If you'll follow me?"

Jeremy gave a curt nod and followed the sergeant out of the building. They stopped before a group of ten convicts lounging under a huge eucalyptus tree.

"I hope you don't mind sir," Riley said. "I took the liberty of picking your workers for you. I think you'll be right pleased with me choice."

Jeremy inspected the convicts. He'd seen dead fish with livelier expressions. The convicts' oversized clothes couldn't hide their skeletal frames. Their sunken cheeks and dark-ringed eyes gave him the shivers. Then he noticed a female amongst the men. Did Riley think he was blind? Or stupid not to notice a useless woman he had included amongst this lot of ten convict workers?

He took a deep breath, ready to blast the sergeant for his impertinence, when he suddenly gasped. *Price!* Why, that damned bastard meant to cheat him, through his sergeant.

Well, two could play the same game. He frosted his tone. "Is this your idea of a joke, Sergeant?"

"Sir?"

Riley's fake confusion didn't deceive him. "You have the bloody gall to tell me I'd be pleased with this lot? Why, I'll have you flogged, you scoundrel!"

He swung around and headed back into the building. His temper flared when he caught sight of Price, seemingly preoccupied with a stack of paper on his desk.

"Lieutenant Price," he called out. "This is intolerable! I'll have you know your sergeant here is insolent."

Price flashed his sergeant a glance. "Surely not, Lieutenant."

"See for yourself!" Jeremy strode off. After taking ten paces, he looked over his shoulder. Assured Price was following, albeit slowly, he continued his way into the morning sunshine. He stopped before the convicts and waited for Price and Riley to join him.

Price surveyed the ten convicts. Jeremy resented his careless attitude.

Price cocked an eyebrow. "Well?"

Jeremy resisted the urge to punch him. "Sergeant Riley says these are my convict workers, pick of the lot. Well, look at them! They're ready for the grave, and he'd have me believe he's done me a bloody favour?"

Price's eyes narrowed, his lips thinned. "Lieutenant Kendrick, follow me. This way." He strode off, making no effort to see if Jeremy followed.

Jeremy stared at Price's fast-receding figure, then scurried after the lieutenant. They'd covered a good distance before he wondered why he was following the bastard like an eager pup. He was about to stop when they rounded another bend, and Price came to a halt. Jeremy stumbled into him. "I'm sorry—"

Price stepped away. "It seems our best effort hasn't met with your approval, Lieutenant Kendrick. Why don't you step inside this building and take your pick?"

Jeremy took a deep breath. *Why the hell not?* He approached the large timber building, sneered at the bold picture of a skull and crossed bones on one wall, and ducked inside.

The sight of men on pallets, bare-chested and displaying rows of ribs made his skin crawl. The low moans of pain and the sickly odour of death sent him scrambling back outside.

"That was quick," Price said. "If you'll let me have their names—"

Jeremy flushed. He cleared his throat. "Perhaps I've been hasty. I'll accept Riley's selection."

"Yes. That will please my sergeant, I'm sure. Good-day." A curt nod, and Price was gone.

"Bastard!" Jeremy muttered.

Riley's manner remained respectful, but he kept his distance. He completed the paperwork, then handed over the documents. Jeremy studied their content.

"Must I have the woman?"

"No, sir. You can trade the woman for another man."

Jeremy hesitated. He needed strong men to open up his land and cultivate his farm. What could a weak woman do but take up space and likely cause chaos amongst the men? *Don't be hasty now, Jeremy. Riley must have good reasons for including the woman.*

He stared at the sergeant, who stared right back. "No. Leave it. I'll not waste more time on this matter." He walked away.

His convict workers looked no better than before. He proceeded to match names in the documents to faces. When questioned, seven of them claimed to be city-born and -bred and to have never been on a farm. Three had tilled the land for the government, but Jeremy didn't think three to four months at the job counted for much. He'd been saddled with ten useless convicts to work his farm, and there was nothing he could do about it.

He glanced at his hired vehicle and scrapped his plan to have the wagon haul the goods and the convicts walk the distance to Red Roo. In their present weak condition, they'd take forever to reach his Hawkesbury property. He'd have to hire another wagon.

"You, Hickson! Can you drive a wagon?"

The tallest of the convicts nodded.

"Well, drive this one and follow me." He looked at the rest of the convicts. "And what are you all waiting for? Get into the wagon!"

He hired another vehicle with a driver, then made his way to the Commissariat Store to collect his entitlements. He ordered the men to wait for him in the wagons, then made his way to the store front, only to come to an abrupt halt. Lieutenant Price was seated at a desk with another officer. They appeared to be deep in conversation.

What is that bastard doing here?

Price looked up then and stared at Jeremy. He leaned towards the other officer, said something, then got to his feet. As he passed Jeremy on his way out, he dipped his head in a greeting. Jeremy ignored him. He walked into the Commissariat Store and introduced himself to the officer there.

The fat man in his forties gave a nod. "Lieutenant Andrew Crawford. How may I help you, Kendrick?"

Jeremy read his requirements from the list in his hand. Crawford listened. He nodded and smiled now and again until Jeremy came to the end of his list. Crawford then put up one finger and using his other hand, pulled open a drawer. He withdrew a sheet of paper and waved it. "Surprise, surprise! I believe it's the same list you have there."

Jeremy glared at him. *Bloody bastard!*

Crawford grinned. "Why don't you look around, Kendrick? Take your pick. Give me a shout after you're done, and we'll deal with the paperwork."

A variety of goods lay in small piles on the floor. They had little pieces of paper attached to them, declaring ownership. Jeremy sifted through the unclaimed farming tools. He picked up a bent shovel, scraped off the rust with his fingernail and tossed it down. Half an hour later, he started to fume. How was it possible that all the farming implements were rusted, and so many of them bent or broken?

He marched up to Crawford. "Lieutenant, are you sure there're no better tools than what I see here?"

"To be sure there are, Kendrick." Crawford chuckled. "In London or Cape Town, maybe in Bombay or Madras, but certainly not here or they'd be out on display."

Jeremy held back his temper. "There's nothing here but mere rubbish. The tools are almost rusted through. They wouldn't last a week of hard work."

"Tell me about it, lad! But these are all I have on hand." He lowered his voice. "I tell you what. If you're prepared to wait, I may have better tools to offer you soon."

Jeremy's heart skipped a beat. An improvement, and all it took was some pushing! "When?"

"Well . . ." Crawford stroked his moustache and flashed Jeremy a broad grin. "When the next shipment arrives. There'll be plenty of choice then."

"When do you expect the next shipment?"

"Oh any day now, I'm sure." Crawford paused and shook his head slowly. " 'Tis strange though, come to think of it. I've been telling everybody this for the past two months." He gave a loud sigh. "Truth to tell, it may take another month. Who knows with these ships' captains? Damned unreliable bastards, all of them, and they've been making a bloody liar out of me."

"Wonderful! What are my workers supposed to use while I wait for this next shipment of farming tools?"

Crawford's expression froze. "Lieutenant Kendrick, that's your problem, sir. You deal with it. Take what's available here or wait for the next shipment. I don't care which. I'll have my men bring out your convicts' rations." He gave Jeremy a nod and strolled away.

With shaking hands, Jeremy made his selections, then approached Crawford again. "What about livestock?"

"What about it?"

"The list says I'm entitled to some livestock."

"Of course. Those livestock. Well, there's none on hand."

"When do you expect to get new stock?"

Crawford shrugged. "I'd like to know the answer myself."

Jeremy wanted to hit the man, but he needed a favour. "Can you get your men to load these goods onto my wagon?"

"Sure, and if you'll sign this, we'll be done for now."

Jeremy had the goods loaded into the hired wagon. He mounted his horse, then waved to the two drivers to get their wagons rolling.

When they reached the outskirts of Sydney Town, he led the way. Very soon his patience began to fray. The wagons, creaking under their loads, moved along slowly, and he resented the need to match their pace.

He scowled at the tall eucalyptus trees, crowding him from both sides of the dirt road. He detested the small grey kangaroos, which hopped away at speed only to stop and stare at him from a safe distance. They were as vain as any woman— bouncing around on two legs to avoid sullying their dainty little hands. If he had time to spare, he'd shoot the bastards. He'd shoot the bloody birds too. Why couldn't they stop their twitting? He had enough problems of his own. Did he have to listen to theirs?

He dug a canister from his pocket and swallowed a mouthful of rum. *Damn Emeline.* The gift of her trinkets and some gold coins couldn't make up for the misery she'd unleashed on him. If only he could make some quick money in this new land, he'd be on the first ship back to London. All he wanted was a modest fortune to repair his reputation. Was that too much to ask?

He looked around him. The area appeared familiar. He made a turn. Half an hour later, he led his party out again. Damned place looked the same everywhere. Why couldn't someone put up signposts? At this rate, it'd be dark before they got to Red Roo. He made two more wrong turns and seethed over his mistakes. *Damned convicts must be sniggering at me. Just don't let me catch them at it!* Forty yards down the next turning, he smiled. Thank goodness, he finally got it right. He stopped at a natural clearing. The wagons rolled to a stop. No one moved.

"Get off the wagon and unload the goods, you fools," he shouted. "What are you all waiting for?"

He sat in his saddle and watched his convicts work, ground his teeth when he saw two of them struggle to shift a small bag of flour and three others wrestle with a bag of potatoes. *Patience, Jeremy. For the walking dead, they're probably doing a good job.*

When the hired wagon was empty, the convicts stood in a loose circle around him. Someone coughed. A few others joined in. Still they wouldn't look at him, only at their feet.

"Listen up, all of you!" he yelled in a burst of fury. "I'll have you know this is my land here, one hundred acres of it. It is your job to beat back the wilderness and turn this lot into a farm. You're to clear the land for me, you hear? Chop down those trees and those bushes. I've got you tools to do it."

He took a deep breath and decided to soften his stand. "Now, that shouldn't be too hard to do. Right?"

The convicts didn't respond, and Jeremy didn't know how to proceed with more instructions. What did he know about farming a land, much less how to carve a farm out of the wilderness? He wanted to bash the heads of his workers for not knowing more and for making him feel such a fool.

He pressed on. "Now, I'm an easy man, not demanding at all. I won't tell you how to do your job, when to do it or where to do it. Just clear the land and you'll get no trouble from me. Work hard, and I'll deliver your food rations. What can be fairer than that eh? All you have to do is clear the land. All right?"

The men looked at him. The blank looks in their eyes didn't change. Jeremy scowled and barked, "Do you all understand me?"

The piebald whinnied and pranced around. Jeremy pulled on his reins and quickly brought the beast under control. "Let's get one thing straight. You're here to work my land. Cross me, and I'll have you flogged. Do you understand me?"

A few of the convicts nodded.

"Another thing! Just clear up the land around here. I don't want you clearing too far in any one direction. You're working my land, not somebody else's. And let me warn you. Don't try to escape. I'll have the army hunt you down like vermin, and you'll hang for runaways. Is this clear?"

More nods.

"I'll be back next month, and there had better be a sizeable area cleared. Don't disappoint me, or you'll regret it."

CHAPTER 9

The sound of squeaking wheels faded into silence as the two wagons disappeared into the distance. Rory O'Connell heaved a sigh, glad to be rid of the lieutenant, a fool who loved the sound of his own voice.

It'd be a month before they saw him again. Time enough to decide whether they, as a group, should work to please the lieutenant. Or ignore his orders and take the consequences.

Someone gave his back a nudge. "What a bastard, eh?"

Rory looked at Peter Coxley and nodded. All ten of them had exchanged names and a little history earlier that morning. Rory was about to add his own comments when he became distracted by a soft humming. The sound came from Nellie Swift a short distance away. She seemed intent on picking wild flowers to add to the bunch in her hand.

Rory looked away quickly, hoping Peter had not noticed his sudden interest. A woman didn't have to be young or pretty to be a tasty bit of morsel. He'd wager his last penny, if he still had it, that it'd been longer than six months since any of the fellas had felt the softness of a woman's skin. There'd probably be a fight to claim Nellie for his own. Maybe he should leave it to the others to fight it out. He hated violence of any kind and would avoid it if he could.

"There had better be a sizeable area cleared, do you hear me?" Lieutenant Kendrick's voice thundered in his ears.

Rory swung around. *What the devil!* How had the lieutenant sneaked back—

Roger Hardie stood on one leg while his hands held imaginary reins in a pose of a man riding a horse. He had his nose stuck up in the air, and his lips twisted in a sneer. "You hear me?" he repeated, then grinned broadly.

Rory laughed. The others did too—a few looked relieved, and some embarrassed.

Roger discarded his pose. "Did the damned fool think to frighten us? Scare us into working hard for him? Whatever for? Government rations? We'd do better working for the government—in a chain gang."

"Thought we was ready for the grave, didn't he, Sam?" Tom Baines said. "Told the other officer as much, this morning."

Sam Appleby chuckled. "And didn't we oblige him, though?"

"Aye!" Tom crowed. "I almost pissed meself when you three dropped that bag of potatoes like 'twas much too heavy for the likes of us."

Rory beamed, then looked at Sam and Peter, glad their efforts had been noted.

"And didn't he look furious?" David Hickson asked. "Like he wanted to jump off his horse and thrash us."

"Settle down, fellas. Best we check out the stuff the lieutenant left behind," Ben Morgan said as he brushed past Rory to examine one of the several piles of goods on the ground.

The others followed his lead and began opening up bags and packages to check their contents. Then Roger knocked over a bag of flour.

Ben cried, "Careful there! The food has to last us a month, at least. We can't trust that fool to keep his word."

"Nah, he'll be back. He want us to work for him," Roger said. "And why not? Our hard work can only mean more coins in his pockets. That bastard can't be trusted to be fair. Sod him, I say."

"Aye," Tom said. "Wouldn't hurt me none if he'd got lost on his way here again. Silly bugger."

Rory chuckled with the rest of the men. He looked at the rations: the usual assortment of flour, potatoes, salt pork and beef. The food wouldn't last them two weeks, not if they ate heartily, and surely not above four, if they didn't.

Ben sifted through the clothing pile. "Jackets, frocks, trousers, shoes—"

"Hello, fellas," a woman's voice called out.

Startled, Rory whirled around. Roger had a woman's shift pressed to his front. He turned this way and that, batting his eyelashes, then continued in a falsetto tone, "Oh my, ain't you fellas a good-looking bunch?"

Laughter broke out again. Rory frowned when he noticed Nellie had disappeared. "Anyone see where Nellie went?"

"Not me," David said in the sudden silence.

Artie Wolfe shook his head. "I was laughing."

Roger waved a hand. "Don't trouble yourselves, fellas. If she ain't back by dusk, I'll go look for her."

"We'll do that together!" Ben said, glaring at Roger, who grinned.

"Where shall we sleep?" Harry asked.

Ben looked around. "In bough humpies, I guess, and we better build them while there's still light. But not here—"

"How about next to the river?" Tom pointed to his left.

"No. If the river swelled, we'd be washed away."

"Not too far from the river then," Tom said. "It's stupid to track a mile just to fetch water."

Rory picked up a small packet from under a collection of bowls and platters. He opened it. Unable to make sense of the tiny metal objects, he held them out. "What are these?"

"Fish hooks!" Peter cried. "Me friend had one. Where did you find them?" Without waiting for an answer, he pushed aside the sleeping pallets and a small bale of canvas. He knocked away the camp kettle and an iron pot and came up with a spool of cotton. "And you tie these fish hooks to these lines and—"

"Do you know how to fish, Peter?" Ben asked.

"No. But me friend told me there be nothing to it."

"Good. You can be in charge of fishing then. We ain't gonna starve now, fellas. Thanks to Peter here!"

They all grinned, except Peter, who tugged at his ear, looking somewhat uncertain.

Ben picked up a felling axe. "Come on then, fellas, we'd best get started on them humpies before we lose the light."

The men grabbed a cutting tool each and followed Ben into the trees. Ben picked a likely spot, then directed the men to cut down the smaller trees and the thick branches of the bigger ones.

Rory put his hatchet to good use, but soon his arm began to tire. A short distance away, Sam and David stopped chipping at the trunk of a small tree. They wiped off sweat running down their faces and watched Ben cut down a thick branch with two blows of his axe.

Sam called out, "Damn. You sure make that look easy, Ben."

"With practice, you will too, Sam."

David held up his hands. "Look at them blisters. They sure hurt, and I ain't—"

"Will you stop your blathering," Harry shouted from a dozen yards' distance. "Words ain't gonna get no humpy built! We all got blisters. Do you see the rest of us complaining?"

Sheepishly, David and Sam picked up their axes and started hacking at their tree.

Like Ben and Peter, Rory had lived in a self-built humpy. This way they saved on rent on accommodation provided by the free settlers they'd been assigned to serve. Now the three of them showed the others how to build their humpies. They worked hard at their tasks till the sun sank low in the sky and the day turned a little cooler. The humpies took shape, a simple structure of leaves and bark supported by strong tree limbs. The careful interweaving of the leaves and bark, and the use of twines secured the humpies from the wind and rain.

Ben then assigned a humpy to each man so they could add their own personal touches. They worked on for an hour more.

"That'll do me for today," Ben said. The others stood back and admired their handiwork.

Ben clapped his hands. "C'mon fellas, before you get too lazy. We'd best haul the foodstuff under shelter. We don't want the rain ruining—"

Rory coughed. "Ben, what about Nellie?"

Ben became very still, then he cursed.

"No need for fuss, fellas. She's welcome to share me humpy with me." Roger grinned.

Ben frowned. "Don't you start that again. It shouldn't take nine of us long to build her a humpy. Right. Get to work fellas. Before it gets too dark."

Tom offered to do the cooking, which left eight men to build the tenth humpy which they did in short time. They then settled down to have their supper—a thick soup with bits of salt beef. They had just finished when Nellie came strolling up to join them. Rory thought it kind of Tom to save a bowl of soup for her. They watched her till she finished eating. When Tom got off the table, she did too, took his hand and accompanied him to his humpy.

Rory gaped, stunned. It had happened too quickly. The others cursed.

"Enough," Ben said. "Look on the bright side. We don't have to fight each other over Nellie no more."

"But Tom cheated!" Peter cried. "He bribed her—"

"You could have done the same," Ben said.

"What if she choose me tomorrow?" Roger asked.

Ben bit on his fingernail. It looked like he was in no hurry to cut himself or any of the others out of a share of Nellie. "If she pick you, then you're one lucky fella. But be sure you don't force Nellie none. I ain't standing for that. Persuade her, bribe her, if you want. You use force, and the others would too. We'd be at each others' throats then, and we don't want that."

Rory looked forward to the next day and thought of ways to win Nellie's favour. He'd be extra sweet to her. Maybe offer her bribe. He'd seen how much she liked flowers—

A roar broke the silence of the night, then a series of moans followed. Rory clapped his hands over his ears, then turned over in his pallet, all his plans for tomorrow forgotten. Bloody Tom. Did he have to be so loud? The bastard!

The second night, right after supper, Rory saw Tom head for the river for a wash. Not long afterwards, he saw Peter leading Nellie to his humpy. *Oh-oh. Tom ain't gonna like this.*

Roger sniggered when Tom stepped out of the shadows into the clearing. Tom stared at him, then at the rest of the fellas. He frowned, then, with a curse, he ran straight to Peter's humpy.

"She's mine, you scoundrel!" He hauled a half-naked Peter out into the open and threw a couple of punches at him. Peter ducked, then took a few swipes of his own.

Nellie ran out of the hut, the bodice of her garment unlaced. "Don't! Don't hurt Peter," she shrieked. She tried to get between the combatants and got flung away to the ground for her effort.

Concern for Nellie had Rory rush to her side, but Roger had reached her first. So Rory joined the others to break up the fight.

"Damn bastard," Tom shouted, as he struggled to free himself from two pairs of hands holding him back. "How dare you steal me woman."

"One night, and she's your woman?" Peter sneered between gasps. "She came to me. Ask her."

"What does she know? She's a halfwit! And don't think I didn't see you giving her flowers—"

"Stop it, both of you," Ben roared.

"Look," Rory said, pointing with his chin.

A short distance away, Roger held the weeping Nellie close. He was saying something while he stroked her hair. Peter shook himself free from Rory and David and strode up to Nellie, his arm outstretched. She pushed him away. Tom smiled and reached for her next.

She shrank from him. "Go away. I don't like you!"

Tom cursed and stormed into the trees. Roger led Nellie into his hut. The men withdrew to their beds. Not Peter. He stayed in the shadows, his gaze fixed on Roger's humpy.

Poor bastard, Rory thought. To have the prize within his grasp, only to lose it to another. The night's happening gave Rory hope. Maybe, if he was lucky, Nellie would be sharing his bed one of these nights.

Morning came, and after Nellie had wandered into the bush, Ben laid down the law: there was to be no more fighting over Nellie. They had to respect Nellie's choice of a lover every time, no matter how unfair it seemed.

Rory expected Roger to object, but after a moment's hesitation, he nodded. They would all follow the rule Ben had set, even Artie who, like Nellie, was simple-minded too.

At the end of their first week, Rory came back from a swim in the river to find the men gathered in a group, deep in a discussion.

"I still say we run and forget about Kendrick," Tom said. "We'll have at least two weeks' start before he finds out."

Rory sighed. Why would anyone want to run away from Red Roo? Kendrick hadn't been around to bother them. They ate well, and they had Nellie. Life was good, and he, for one, wouldn't tempt Fate to ask for more.

"Two weeks could see us far away from here," Roger said.

"Do you fancy working for that bastard?" Tom looked at each of the men in turn. "Well, do you?"

"Tom—" Ben said.

"I know his kind," Roger said. "All he want is take, take, take. He don't care for nobody but himself. To hell with him, I say."

"And be on the run for the rest of our lives?" Ben asked. "Hunted by the soldiers and the black fellas? You do it, if you want to, Tom. You, too, Roger. I say we tough it out till Kendrick send us back to the government. If we refuse to work for him, likely he'll get rid of us—"

Roger objected, "Not before he flog us—"

"A little flogging ain't gonna kill us. He's just one man," Peter said. "His arms will drop off before he can finish flogging all nine of us."

"I doubt he wants to travel all that way from Sydney Town to check on us very often—at best, once a month—to bring the rations," Rory said. "He'd get here, say around noon. He won't stay long, else he won't get home before dark—"

Ben nodded. "Rory's got it right. He won't have much time to give all of us a good flogging, and as Peter say, the bastard don't want to tire himself out neither. Well, 'tis up to you men. I'm staying."

"I say we stay," Rory said. "You know what'll happen when you get caught if you run. They'll increase your sentence, if they don't hang you first."

CHAPTER 10

In July, a month after he set his convicts to work clearing his land, Jeremy journeyed forth to the Hawkesbury to check on their progress and to deliver their food rations. His spirits were high. He had joined the ranks of the landed gentry and soon would have more money than he could spend, at least in this Godforsaken backwater. Why, he might even consider giving up the idea of going home to England.

His optimism turned to outrage within moments of reaching Red Roo. His convict workers had not done a lick of work. As he travelled farther down the track, he saw the men had cleared a small area of land for themselves, to build ten bough humpies, but nothing for him.

He stopped his wagon when he saw his workers, just three of them, standing under the shady trees, watching him.

What? Did they think he just happened to drive by—to admire the view, perhaps? Bastards! And damn me for a fool for bringing them their food rations.

"You there!" he shouted. "Come here!"

They didn't move. He withdrew his pistol from his jacket pocket, cocked it and pointed it at them. That got them moving all right. They came to him at a run.

"Fetch the rest of the men. Go on! I haven't got all day to waste like you lazy buggers!"

They scurried away in different directions. He returned his

pistol to his jacket pocket and leapt from the wagon. He stared at the ten humpies before him. *How cozy.* He strode up to the first one and kicked at the supporting structure, leaping back quickly when it crashed to the ground. The next humpy received the same treatment, then another.

A whisper of a sound made him look over his shoulder. His convict workers stood behind him. Determined to show them he meant business, he stepped up to the fourth humpy and destroyed that too.

Then panting from his exertion, he turned to face them. "This is just a small measure of what I'll do if you ever cross me again. You're here to work. Work! So what have you done for me in four weeks?" He glared at the men. "Nothing! And why not? Huh? Huh? Why not, you lazy lot of scoundrels . . ."

He might as well be a dog barking at a tree for all the interest they showed him. Nor did their expressions change when he threatened to flog them. He realised he couldn't keep shouting at these idiots. It was too tiring. He calmed himself. "I'm a reasonable man. We'll start over. I want to see some real progress come August."

They looked at him as if he spoke a foreign tongue.

He felt his anger stir again. "Clear the land," he said. "I'm warning you for the last time."

"Shall we unload the wagon, sir?" one of the men asked.

"Yes, you'd like that, wouldn't you? No! You're not getting these rations. Why should I reward you for doing nothing? You don't work, you don't eat."

The man shrugged and stepped back. Jeremy wanted to punch him, but controlled his impulse. He told himself that they wouldn't be as nonchalant in the coming weeks.

Jeremy set out the following month, convinced his workers would be chastened by their hunger. No, he didn't think they would cross him again. They wouldn't risk his displeasure, or the loss of another month's rations.

He couldn't believe his eyes. The scoundrels had ignored his orders again. He found a handful of them hanging around outside one of the humpies, calmly watching him as he drove to a stop before them. It galled him to note that they had rebuilt the humpies he'd destroyed. Worse. They had even put on weight despite his effort to starve them. He wouldn't be surprised if they had dined on snakes or grubs or some such, like the natives. *Goddammit.* He would teach them to obey him if it was the last thing he did.

Pointing to two men, he snapped, "Go fetch the others and be quick about it!"

He jumped off the wagon and squished his way through mud, the result of continuous rain over the past two days, to a clump of shrubs. He broke several branches off a wattle tree. With economical movements, he stripped off the leaves, then flexed each one to test its length for suppleness before slicing it through the air with clean sweeps of his arm.

Next, he retrieved two lengths of ropes from amongst the sacks of food. When he counted ten people before him, he ordered two men to tie a third to the back of the wagon. All three men baulked.

"Do it," he glared at the first two men, "or do you want to take his place? I don't give a damn who gets flogged. Well?"

Once the man was secured, Jeremy handed the two men a stripped branch each. He faced the seven other convicts. "I'll be forgiving, this time. I'm calling for twenty, not the usual two hundred lashes."

He expected to see relief on the men's faces. Nothing. "I mean to be obeyed! Do you hear me?"

The horses moved at his raised voice. Jeremy frowned. *Damn.* He should've considered the horses might bolt from any sudden movement or noise from the flogging. He could easily have laid waste the rations he had brought with him. Before he could issue a new order, one of the men had moved out from the crowd to control the beasts.

He glared at each of his workers in turn. *Ungrateful brutes.* His fury mounted. He turned to the two men with the stripped branches. "You will deliver ten lashes each. If I see a lack of strength behind any of the strokes, I'll call for fifty more. Is that clear?"

The two men nodded. The others shifted restlessly, muttering.

Jeremy sneered at them. "You men aren't just lazy, but stupid. You are convicts, serving your sentences. You must work for me. Can't you understand that? The law says so. If you cross me, I can have you flogged. Try to harm me, and you'll hang. Why can't you understand I'm a better master than many others in this hellhole? Well?"

They stared at him.

He cursed. "Start the flogging!"

The bound man jerked and gasped at the first two strokes. On the third, he began to howl. The horses whinnied and stepped about in alarm.

The convict woman screamed, "No, no. Don't hurt Roger!"

Two men held her back when she tried to rush forward. She struggled and shrieked. On the fifth stroke, she swooned. Five men crowded around her, their brows furrowed in concern. Jeremy ordered them away from the woman. He wanted their attention focused on the flogging, nothing else.

The twentieth stroke fell with a dull thud.

"You, untie him, then hand me the ropes," Jeremy ordered. He retied the sacks of food with the ropes, then faced the men. "Let this be your lesson. Continue to defy me and I'll have two or more of you flogged. You hear me? You want a battle? Fine. I'll give you one."

★   ★   ★   ★   ★

Kate gave the pot a stir. It'd take a few minutes more, and the stew would be ready. She sighed heavily. Jeremy was such a fool. She thought it a simple enough task, but he'd not been able to get his workers to clear his land, not one miserable acre in two months. Wrecking their humpies to teach them a lesson hadn't worked. She doubted flogging one of the workers would work either. What did he plan to do next? Flog all of them? And then what? Come home and beat her too? Why not? Had he not taken to beating her at his whim already?

She was glad to be done with his lies, relieved he'd stopped blaming liquor for his brutality and ceased offering her false promises to do better. He continued to be very sweet to her the morning after each beating. He obviously believed a show of remorse was enough to earn him forgiveness for hurting her.

It became clearer by the day that she had to get away from him, and soon before he strangled her soul, or killed her.

"Yoo hoo!" a voice called out. "Is it ready?"

Kate looked over her shoulder and smiled at a plump woman in her thirties. "Just about, Mabel!"

"Here's me bowl. God, I hope George never catch me eating your food and feeding him me leftovers! He'd kill me!"

Another voice called out, "Keep some of the good bits for me, Kate!"

"Don't you worry, Annie. There's plenty to go around." Kate gave the pot a final stir and filled Mabel's bowl.

She'd become friends with Mabel her first week at the Officers' Mess, and Mabel had introduced her to Annie. As neighbours and convict mistresses, they had plenty in common. When they tasted Kate's stew that first time, they couldn't stop marvelling at her cooking skill. They begged her to cook for them. They'd pay her of course, they said, and she'd agreed.

Kate handed Mabel her bowl of stew. "Add some salt and

hot water for more gravy."

Mabel laughed. "Aye Kate, only after I've had me fill. George reckons I'm getting to be a good cook. Ain't that a scream?"

"Be careful, Mabel," Kate said.

"Don't you worry none." Mabel waved a hand. "George, he's having a fine time, laughing at your Jeremy."

"Why?"

Mabel plucked a piece of meat from her bowl and popped it into her mouth. "George thinks your Jeremy's a dolt, trying to get into the Trading Officers' Fraternity and all. They ain't going to make him a member. Never. George says finer men have been turned away."

Kate's heart sank.

Mabel gave her a thoughtful look. "I'll tell you something else. Them officers must hate your Jeremy very much. Why else would they give him this for his quarters?"

"What's wrong with our quarters?" Kate asked.

"Well, the roof leaks. Ain't that so? Nobody has bothered to fix that. There's been murder done here too. 'Tis why the army don't care for this place no more."

Kate knew the roof leaked, but she didn't know about the murder. She shuddered.

Mabel shook her head. "Me George says your Jeremy could have the pick of two nicer places, but they gave him this one. What does that tell you?"

One evening, Jeremy came home cursing loudly. "They can't do this to me. My gold's as good as any man's."

Kate said nothing, but braced herself for trouble.

"It's an officers' trading fraternity, isn't it? I'm an officer. Why won't they let me be a member, eh? They have so much. I'm only asking for a little, a chance to do some trading. Import, wholesale, even retail—it wouldn't matter which. What have they got against me?" He was quiet for a minute then he began cursing. "Of course! How could I have forgotten? I know who's to blame for my trouble."

Kate took a few hurried steps backwards.

"Price and Crawford. They're keeping me out. Bloody bastards!"

It was the last day of September. Kate waited up for Jeremy to come home from Red Roo, fully expecting him to be in a bad mood. She didn't think flogging his farm workers would change their minds about clearing the land for him. He surprised her by storming into the house, whooping loudly, then grabbing her at her waist and swinging her around. "I did it, Kate!"

"What?"

"The flogging worked! They've started to clear the land!" He put Kate down and started to laugh. "And all it took was a bloody flogging! I know how to control them now. Not with kindness, but with the lash!"

Can it be that easy? "You're pleased then?"

"Yes. But I took care not to show my satisfaction. The scoundrels would only take advantage of that. So I roared at them: 'Four weeks! Is this the best you can do?'" Jeremy smiled at her. "Soon, we'll be out of this hovel, Kate. I'll get my farm, then my house. You'll see."

But five weeks later, in early November, he came home cursing and ranting. "Damned bastards! They idled a whole month away! I felt such a fool bringing them their food rations thinking to reward them for more good work, when they deserved a hanging! I had four of them flogged, and they mocked me. God rot them all!"

Kate frowned. "Mocked you?"

"Yes. Mocked me. I had two of them do the flogging, but they put no strength behind their strokes. Bastards! They made a farce of my punishment. God, why am I beset by scoundrels at every turn?"

He kicked a chair. "If I could, I'd return them to the government and get a new lot of workers. But I don't trust Price not to accuse me of some nefarious deed. Damn!"

Kate hauled her basket of dirty laundry onto her hip and stepped out the door. She bumped into Mabel.

"Oooh. You've got a real shiner there, Kate."

Kate tried a small smile, careful not to stretch her split lip. Then Annie strolled up to join them. She looked at Kate, then began to unlace her bodice. Kate stared, appalled at such brazen behaviour. She gasped and turned her face away from the sight of angry colours on Annie's breast and shoulders. They reminded her of her own bruises from Lord Oliver.

Perhaps she should count her blessings that Jeremy wasn't as bad as Lord Oliver, but she couldn't. She had to get away from him. She must before she didn't care what happened to herself anymore.

Later, she stood looking out the window, her hand resting on the swelling on her left cheek. If only she could get Jeremy to send her away, she didn't care where, just so long as it was away from him. She decided to catch him in a good mood and then persuade him to send her to Red Roo. He wanted a farm. She would convince him that she could make that happen, if he sent her there.

Her chance came when he came home several evenings later, looking pleased with himself. Without doubt, she knew he'd won at cards.

She waited till after they'd celebrated his success. When he rolled off her, she turned on her side and stroked his chest. "Jeremy? Do you remember I told you I grew up on a farm?"

"Yes. What about it?"

"I've been thinking. Perhaps the convicts at Red Roo aren't working because they don't really know what to do—"

"Don't be silly. They only had to cut down the bloody trees and shrubs. The lazy bastards just won't do it."

"Perhaps they need someone to push them, see they do things right—"

Jeremy glared at her. "Are you saying I should stay in that Godforsaken wilderness and supervise them?"

"No, no! Of course not. But I could do it for you. I'll make sure—"

Jeremy laughed. He climbed over her and got off the bed. "Will you listen to yourself? You're going to supervise them? And of course, they're going to listen to you, take your orders, right?"

He reached for a drink. She sat up and pulled the blanket to cover herself. "Why not? I know how to farm a piece of land— 'twas all I ever did when I was young. I could teach those men—"

"Kate, Kate! Listen to me. Those bastards won't take orders from you—"

"Why not, if I told them I speak for you—"

"They defy me at every turn, but they'd listen to you because you tell them you speak for me? Don't be stupid. I'm not wasting any more time on those buggers! Let them rot!"

"We could try—"

Jeremy's face turned ruddy. "What makes my orders better coming from you, eh? You're a bloody woman. Men don't take orders from a woman. The sky will surely fall when men take orders from a woman! And you're nothing but a green girl. A convict too. No better than them. Why would they take orders from you? Enough! Go to sleep. Damned witless woman!"

Kate retreated into silence, telling herself she could try again another day. She must succeed in this somehow. She must.

A few days later, Kate tugged at her garment to stretch it, so she could breathe. New South Wales was an odd place. January was so hot! And July had been so cold. Her world had turned topsy-turvy.

She loosened the lacing on her gown, and one look down her exposed breasts had her closing her eyes. She could no longer deny it: she was carrying Jeremy's baby.

But how could she have Jeremy's baby? How could she look at her baby and not think of his loathsome father? And sinful or not she wanted to be rid of it. She turned to her friends for help. Annie suggested frequent cold baths. She swore they got her out of trouble, twice. Mabel claimed hard exercise, like jumping up and down, had served her well. Kate took long freezing baths. She jumped up and down for hours. A week passed. Nothing happened. Kate took hot baths too and continued to exercise vigorously, without success. The baby remained stubbornly lodged in her womb. With great reluctance, she informed Jeremy of her condition.

"A baby!" he snarled. "What would I do with a bloody baby?"

Kate had no answer.

"Goddammit! As if I didn't have enough problems . . ." Jeremy ranted.

Four evenings later, he came home and jingled a bag of coins before Kate's eyes and bragged, "For little Jeremy! He brought me luck."

The following night, Kate saw him stumbling through the door, roaring drunk. She couldn't move away fast enough before he gave her another beating. It seemed Kate and a baby not yet born were the cause of his losses that night.

Jeremy had left for work when Kate woke the next morning. She got out of bed with the words Red Roo, Red Roo drumming inside her head, but she didn't have a clue how to get there. Absently, she ran her hands over the swell of her belly, gasped when a flutter of movements startled her. Then a sudden bolt of pain doubled her over. She held her breath when something wet and warm trickled down her thighs.

CHAPTER 11

Kate knew she was losing her baby. She had acted as Ma's midwife since she was barely eleven, and she recognised the signs in herself. Like her mother before her, she would try to save her baby. Rest. Rest could do the trick. She took to her bed at once, just as Ma did.

A short while later, she shook her head in confusion. Wasn't she trying to lose the baby just weeks ago? Shouldn't she be rejoicing now, instead of weeping? Why was she staying so very still in bed, wishing the bleeding would stop? No matter how she tried, she couldn't make herself get out of bed. She was an eejit!

She woke to a room in shadows. She looked out the window and decided Jeremy wouldn't be home for a while yet. On Fridays, he usually went straight from work to chance his luck at the Officers' Club. Kate was glad he was out. He would only add to her confusion.

She lit the oil lamp and checked her bleeding. It had stopped. She ran a hand over her belly and smiled. The rest had done her good; her baby was safe. She made herself a cup of tea. The steam swirled past her nose. She took a small sip and then another, when hurried footsteps sounded outside the door. She listened for a moment. It couldn't be Jeremy. She'd never known him to come home before midnight.

The door crashed open, then slammed shut. Jeremy slumped against it, his breathing, ragged. Striving for a calm she didn't feel, she set her cup down and ignoring the hot tea splashing onto her fingers, slowly got to her feet. She knew she was in for another beating, perhaps the worst ever.

He took one shuddering breath and stepped away from the door. He groped under the bed for a bottle of rum and opened it. "I'm in terrible trouble, Kate."

"What is it?"

He gulped back the rum, then began to pace the floor. Kate took several steps away and watched him carefully, ready to jump out of his reach. He stumbled against a chair twice before he kicked it away, sending it crashing into the wall. He tipped more liquor down his throat, then hurled the bottle at the wall. "Damn them all to hell!"

The glass shattered, spewing shards across the floor. He swung around. "They dared question my honour! Accused me of cheating. The bloody nerve, I say! Would I cheat, I ask you? Would I?"

She shook her head firmly, but knew however she answered, he'd do whatever he pleased.

He stared at her for a moment, his eyes narrowing. "Why, you slut! You think I cheated too! How dare you!"

He lunged. She dodged to the right. He followed. Too late. The wall and the bed had her trapped in a corner. His backhand slammed her head into the wall. Dazed, she slid to the floor.

He kicked her. "You're nothing! Just a convict slut!"

Somehow she broke free. She scrambled away across the bed and tumbled to the floor. Broken glass bit into her arm and bottom. She ignored the pain. As she staggered to her feet, he yanked her up, spinning her to face him. He grabbed her hair with both hands, then banged her head against the wall. "That's for looking down your nose at me, you ungrateful strumpet!"

Ungrateful! In that moment, Kate threw caution away. She pried her hair free from his grip and hammered his chest. She gave him a mighty push and then another and another. "Yes! I'm a slut. I'm a whore. I'm your bad luck. So throw me out, Jeremy! Why don't you?"

He rocked from each thrust, even stumbled back a few steps.

"Go on! Send me away! Send me to Red Roo. Then you'll be rid of your no-good slut, your bad luck. You'll get your fortune back then, won't you? You'll be rich as a king then, won't you?"

Jeremy blinked his bloodshot eyes, as if he couldn't believe what he was hearing. Then without warning, he punched her in the mouth.

Kate staggered, biting back the pain. "Go on, hit me! Hit your useless convict slut! Come on, a brave and powerful man like you can hit better than that, surely?"

The blows came from all directions. "Is that the best you can do?" she screamed. *Go on, kill your baby. See if I care, you bloody bastard!*

Even as she invited the punches, Kate tried to evade the blows to her belly by hunching over, turning away, when she could, and shielding her baby with her hands and arms, when she couldn't. But a powerful blow finally landed. She screamed in anguish, as the pain brought her to her knees. He kicked her several times in her belly.

An agonizing spasm woke her. Vaguely, she heard the sound of snores. The pain passed, only to return again and again, turning sharper and lasting longer. She wept. Her baby was lost.

Eejit! She should rejoice. 'Twas only the pain making her weep. Losing her baby had nothing to do with it.

She closed her eyes. *I could have avoided this.* True. The Petals had shown her how to use a piece of sponge soaked in vinegar. Why hadn't she put that to good use? But the mere thought of pushing anything so foul inside herself revolted her.

Another wave of pain pierced into her bones. She bit down on her lip and tasted blood. *This is no time for regrets.*

"No," she cried. " 'Tis the best time for it." Could that loathsome scrap be more repulsive than letting Jeremy inside? She moved her head from side to side in denial, and pressed her hands down on her swollen belly in an effort to contain her pain. *Oh God, please let me die.*

The pain attacked in waves, and when she thought she could take no more, her baby came sliding forth, and the pain stopped.

She waited a while to catch her breath and gather her strength. Her baby, still attached to a white cord, filled her hand. He looked almost human. She cried softly. *My firstborn.* Then the pain started again, stopped after the afterbirth came.

She lay there, oblivious to time. Slowly, she became aware of the cold baby beside her. She told herself to be sensible, to be practical. First, she must clean herself, then the mess the miscarriage had caused. She glanced over at the bed. The wretch, the cause of all her trouble, slept peacefully on. *Bastard!*

An idea took root in her head. It grew more appealing by the moment.

Calmly, she fetched a bucket of water. She wet the rags and cleaned herself. Then she soaked the rag and squeezed the bloody water to the floor. She did this several times, then soaked the rags again and scattered them around her. Next, she placed her dead baby within Jeremy's unobstructed view. Satisfied that everything couldn't be better arranged, she curled up beside her baby and waited for morning.

Jeremy opened his eyes and saw blood on the floor. Blood? How could that be? He sat up to take a better look and swallowed hard. Even if he couldn't believe his eyes, he couldn't ignore his nose. The smell of blood was overwhelming, and when he noticed a grey, unmoving lump beside Kate, he couldn't tear his gaze away. Terror tore through him. His belly churned. He vomited.

Oh God, what have I done? He stared at the grey lump, which had to be his baby. He vomited again. The stench of sour alcohol filled the room. He welcomed it. Better that than the smell of blood.

Trembling, as if from the cold, he forced himself out of bed. He pulled off the bed sheet and wiped his mouth, then hastily used it to cover the grey lump. Was Kate dead too? Had he killed her? Much as he disliked it, he lowered himself to the floor beside her. He reached out and poked her in the arm with his forefinger. "Kate! Kate! Are you all right?"

When she didn't respond, he wanted to flee. Then he saw her chest moving, and the tightness in his own eased. *She's alive. Thank God!*

He poured himself a drink. Could he trust her not to die? Would Price give him trouble if she did? He couldn't trust that damned scoundrel. He'd better get rid of Kate quickly. If she had to die, let her die some place else. He couldn't be held responsible then.

The answer came at once.

He brushed his hair back with a trembling hand, then bending low, close to Kate's ear, he whispered, "You want to go to Red Roo, don't you, Kate? I'll take you there. So don't die. Don't die. Not yet."

CHAPTER 12

Rory hauled in his third fishing line. As with his other two, the metal hook was bare. He plucked a worm from a small ragbag tied to his waist and threaded the hook through it. He spat on the wriggling creature for luck and cast the line back into the water.

Three small fishes lay at his feet. They gave him no pleasure. Still, when one of them flapped its tail, he quickly splashed water over all three of them to keep them alive. He was determined to catch a big fish. Maybe he'd be lucky today.

A loud squawk and cackle broke the silence. It echoed through the treetops. Rory looked up at a white cockatoo perched on a high branch. "Get out of here, you stupid parrot! Stop frightening off me fish."

He frowned. His best effort so far remained the seven baby fish he'd caught last week, which Ben made him throw back into the river. It was all right for Ben to be so careless with other people's precious catch. He had the magic touch. Big fat fishes just hooked themselves to Ben's lines.

But it hadn't always been that way.

No one knew how to fish that first week. They depended on Peter to teach them. After all he was the only one who knew anything about it. They pressed him into repeating all he remembered of his friend's words about fishing. They'd put those ideas into practice, but nobody caught no fish. Not one fish in five days of trying.

"We're wasting our time," Harry said. "I ain't listening to Peter no more. He's got it all wrong, or his friend lied to him."

Peter's face turned a darker shade of red. "I never said I knew how to fish. And me friend's no liar. Maybe I ain't remembering all that he told me. Maybe there ain't no fish in this river."

"I've seen them bloody fish. What about them rippling circles?" Harry pointed to the river. "Fish coming up to take a peek at the sky, is what!"

"Listen," Ben said. "We better learn to catch some fish soon. You know Kendrick won't be doing us no favours."

"Well, don't look at me!" Peter cried. "I told you what me friend said. Leave the hook in the water and the fish will swallow it. Fish be curious creatures, he said. They'd eat anything. Well, maybe Harry's right. Maybe the bastard be lying through his teeth!"

The next day, Ben caught their first lot of fish—six of them. He'd baited the hook with worms.

"What made you think to use them worms?" Peter asked.

"I figured if birds like worms, fish might too."

A daily diet of fish didn't satisfy the men for long. They began to talk about sinking their teeth into a thick slab of juicy meat and started eyeing the kangaroos.

"We could dig a pit and maybe one of them bastards would hop into it." Peter said.

Sam shook his head. "He'd just hop right out again, unless we make it a very deep hole."

"So let's dig a very deep hole!"

Roger snickered. "Aye, with all this vast land, they'll come hopping into our pit. Maybe if we're lucky, they'll hop right into our cooking pot!"

Peter glared at him. "We could dig a number of pits. What do you say, Ben?"

Roger shrugged. "I don't know about you, Ben, but I think we'd have better luck hunting the roos with spears like the black fellas do."

"Roger's right," Ben said.

They spent a week fashioning spears out of branches, then practised throwing their new weapons. Rory envied Peter and Sam the strength of their arms and the accuracy of their throws. If anybody could hunt down the kangaroos, those two might just do it.

They came home, after a day of hunting, empty-handed. They set out again and again in the days that followed, but with no better result. A week later, Roger announced he was not wasting another day hunting the kangaroos. A few others muttered agreement.

"C'mon, fellas. A week's hardly any time. Give it another week, what do you say?" Ben said.

Some of the others gave suggestions.

Peter snarled at David. "Creep up on the sleeping kangaroos and bash them on their heads with a big rock? Right! You do it, if you think it can be done."

"You don't have to bite me head off. I was only trying to help."

They would all be living on fish forever more, too, Rory thought, if it hadn't been for Artie.

Artie was simple-minded. They all treated him kindly, never asked him to do anything difficult lest he got confused and did things wrong. They gave him small tasks to perform and never pressed him to do anything he didn't like.

All that changed three months ago.

Rory had been checking the remaining food rations when Sam came rushing up to him.

"You've got to come with me," Sam said between gasps. "Else you won't bloody believe it!"

"What is it?"

"Never you mind. Just come with me. Hurry!"

He followed Sam at a run to the south end of the property. There they crept a short distance to a leafy glade. From behind a shrub, Rory watched Artie mingling with a mob of kangaroos.

"How is this possible, Rory?" Sam asked in a low voice. "Why ain't the bloody kangaroos scattering like they usually do? You'd think they see Artie as one of them!"

Rory couldn't tear his gaze away from their half-witted friend. "Sam, do you realise we've got our kangaroo meat? Tender, juicy meat, and we don't even have to hunt for it."

They all took turns teaching Artie how to rope a baby kangaroo. They told him it was a game: that he had to rope the joey without frightening him.

"Why should that frighten him?" Artie asked.

No one answered, and they made sure they didn't kill the animal in front of him. The first time Artie saw the meat on his supper plate, he shrank back in his seat, his eyes wide in shock. Rory felt sorry for the poor fella, just not enough to sacrifice his dinners of tender juicy meat.

Roger threw his arm over Artie's shoulder. "Don't upset yourself, Artie. Didn't you know? God put them roos here so we wouldn't starve."

"We didn't hurt the joey, Artie." Tom swallowed a piece of the meat and smiled. "He went, peaceful like, to God."

"Look, Nellie's enjoying her supper," Rory said, then called out to Nellie, "Do you like your roo, Nellie?"

Nellie nodded. "Can I have some more?"

"There you go, Artie," Ben said. "You want to make Nellie happy, don't you? Of course, you do."

A few weeks later, Rory took out a shovel and a hoe and began digging up a small patch of land, not too far from the river. A large rock refused to budge, and Rory sweated to remove it.

A voice from the back of him demanded, "Have you turned bootlicker, Rory, the lieutenant's bootlicker?"

Rory looked over his shoulder at Tom. " 'Course not. I just thought some carrots, maybe cabbages would go very nicely with our roo and fish."

"Do you know how to raise them vegetables?"

"Seen it done before. Turn the soil over, bury some of the seeds and water them. Can't be that hard. How about giving me some help?"

Tom snickered. "I ain't no farmer. But I tell you what—I'll cook your vegetables for you, even help you eat them."

The seeds sprouted after two weeks, and Rory was pleased. A week later, most of the seedlings had lost their young leaves. The rest wilted away, no matter how hard he watered them.

The men had laughed at him. Well, perhaps he was no farmer, but by God, he'd show them he could catch one big fat fish. He glanced over at David who was fishing a short distance away. As usual, not a man to waste his time, he was weaving a hat out of the leaves of the cabbage tree while he waited for a fish to bite. David had quite a collection of his misshapen hats which he wore proudly, hats that no one would accept for a gift. Harry told him he'd rather go bareheaded, no matter how hot the day, than look ridiculous as David did.

"Yo, Rory!" a voice hailed him.

He turned.

Ben held aloft a bunch of fish strung on a piece of twine, each fish about twice the length of Rory's hand. "Look at me beauties!"

"Damn! How do you do it?" Rory stared at the fish. "Never mind. Who's cooking tonight?"

Ben laughed. "Not you, for sure. Not them neither," he said, pointing to Peter, Harry and Sam, heading their way.

Sam held up two large bunches of wild onions and shook them in triumph.

Ben lifted his fish in response, shouting, "Tom will cook us a fine dinner tonight!"

The men gathered, even David, then settled themselves on a grassy patch by the riverbank.

Ben looked at David. "What did you catch?"

Rory wished he'd thought to cover his three baby fishes with leaves or something to hide them from curious eyes, but it was too late to do anything about it now. In desperation, he tried to nudge them out of sight with his foot.

"Threw back four baby ones," David said, then sniggered, pointing at Rory's meagre catch. "Are you planning to raise those, mate?"

Rory grabbed a handful of dirt and threw it at him. David ducked, laughed so hard he almost lost his balance.

Ben looked at Peter. "Where's Roger. Didn't he go with you?"

"He's with Artie, hoping to rope us a roo."

The others grunted. Roger made no secret of his fondness for meat.

They chatted on for a short while, then Sam got to his feet. "Come on Ben, I'll help you clean your fish."

Peter looked at the others. "We'll get them firewood."

Rory picked up his catch and threw them back into the river. If it weren't for Ben, he didn't think anyone would sneer at the size of his fishes. No, they'd be glad to sup on his little offering.

He lingered for a moment by the riverbank, staring out at the trees around him. Though they all waited for Kendrick to send them back to the government, Rory knew he would miss Red Roo when they left.

"Rory!" The shout startled him.

In a moment, Harry came panting up to him. "'Tis the

bloody bastard. He's here. We've got to find Nellie."

Harry whirled and disappeared into the trees. Rory had no trouble identifying the "bloody bastard". He started running in the opposite direction. One of them had to find Nellie, make sure she was hidden away till Kendrick had left again. They didn't fear a flogging, but they couldn't risk having Nellie around. She'd fainted when Roger was flogged that first time. They wouldn't have her upset again, not if they could help it. Besides they couldn't risk Kendrick finding out how much they cared for Nellie. They couldn't trust the bastard not to flog her to get them to do his bidding.

They'd learned their lesson well. Didn't they work their hearts out on a clearing to please Kendrick after Roger's flogging in August? They thought if they worked as hard as he demanded, he would treat them proper, and Nellie would be spared the torment of seeing any one of them flogged again. But Kendrick had ranted at them in September, demanding better results come October.

Rory knew there'd be no pleasing the lieutenant, no matter how hard they worked. The fellas thought the same, and they all decided they'd not lift another finger to do any of his bidding. If Kendrick wanted better results, he would've to do the work himself.

They'd sent Nellie out every day around the time they expected Kendrick to call, which was about every four weeks. But he'd not bothered to check on them since early November when he had four of the fellas flogged. They thought he'd lost interest in them, but to be safe, had kept a constant lookout for him.

And now *he* was here. Rory decided to search the area east and hoped the others would cover the other spots. He also prayed that Nellie had not chosen today of all days to go some place new. He called out her name as he tried to track her down but soon admitted she was not around. Trusting that one of the fellas had found her, Rory headed back home. He joined the other fellas who stood together outside the cookhouse, staring down the approach path.

Rory could see Kendrick driving up in his wagon; he would reach them within minutes. He gave Peter a nudge. "Is Nellie all right?"

"Aye. Harry took care of her."

"Why is the bastard bothering with the wagon this time?" David asked.

Roger sniggered. "You think he's bringing us our rations? Out of the goodness of his heart? Don't you be a fool."

Harry turned around and glared at Roger. "Perhaps he's showing us what we're missing, then he'd take them rations home again. See if I ain't right. The bastard! Them be our rations, not his!"

No one said another word, then Rory gasped in disbelief. "He's got someone riding at the back of the wagon!"

"I see her." Then in a note of warning to the others who had begun to speak, Ben added, "Let's wait to hear what he has to say."

The wagon drew to a stop. Kendrick rose to his feet and glared down at the men. "God curse you all. Is this—"

The woman groaned loudly. "Jeremy . . ."

Kendrick twisted to look behind him. Rory never thought the man knew anything but to shout abuse of one kind or another, but there was a definite note of concern and uncertainty in Kendrick's voice when he said, "Kate? Are you all right?"

The woman moaned in answer. She sounded weak and ill. Rory craned his neck to get a better look at her, but he could see only long dark hair. *Why did the bastard bring her?*

"Don't just stand there," Kendrick yelled. "Help her down. Can't you fools see she's not well?"

The moan came again.

"Are you all deaf?" Kendrick demanded. "Find her a bed."

Rory and David stepped forward as one. They made their way to the back of the wagon. The moment they came within sight of the woman, David faltered, turned to look at Rory. Rory shook his head, silencing him.

The woman's face was a shocker—swollen and bruised—and yet Rory could swear she was trying to smile at him. *With all the marks of a beating, what had she to smile about?*

Kendrick continued, "And she'll be staying with you lot from. . . ." The woman jerked her head to look at the lieutenant. She narrowed her eyes, and Rory fancied he saw a flash of annoyance. *How curious.*

David placed a hand under her arm. "Let me help you down, missus."

She flinched at David's touch. "Wait." She picked up a bundle and, holding it close, allowed David to help her off the wagon. On her feet, she hardly came up to David's chest. Rory shook his head. They had thought Nellie small. This woman was smaller.

She stumbled.

"Damn it!" Kendrick roared. "Be gentle with her!"

Together, David and Rory helped the woman to the nearest humpy: Sam's. Behind them, Rory heard the lieutenant sneer.

"Yes. Watch. That's all you ever do, you bastards. Well, I won't tolerate your laziness anymore! You're going to work on this land from now on . . ."

"Will you be all right, missus?" Rory asked. "We'll fetch your belongings later and take away whatever else you don't need here."

"Thank you. My name is Kate, Kate O'Neal."

Rory nodded, turned and headed back to join the other fellas.

David followed and in a low voice asked, "Why is she staying here with us?"

Rory shrugged.

"Six months!" Kendrick screamed. "Six bloody months and you've got nothing to show for your time here! I'm putting Kate in charge. By God, she'll see that you buggers behave yourselves and do the work you're supposed to do. Kate knows all about farming. She'll get you lazy lot working!"

David turned to Rory again. "She's here to whip us all into shape? That *little girl?*"

CHAPTER 13

Careful to keep to the shadows, Kate watched Jeremy from the doorway of the bough humpy and listened to him ranting away. The stupid, stupid man! He was only setting them against him and making her task so much harder.

Go! Just go, Jeremy. I don't want you here—nor do your workers.

Finally, he ran out of words. A moment later, he uttered a foul curse, then turned the wagon around. Kate held her breath, afraid he'd stop any moment and call out for her to get back into the wagon with him. He didn't, and Kate began to feel safer as he started the horses moving. *That's right, Jeremy. Go!* He was fifty yards away when she recalled the sacks of food at the back of the wagon—her rations for the month. Too bad he was taking them back with him, no doubt to sell them—as he'd done with his workers' rations—to pay for his various pleasures.

Then Jeremy swung the wagon around and came driving back. Her breath caught and she almost wept. She should have known her good luck wouldn't last.

Jeremy drew the horses to a halt and shouted at the men. "You forgot to unload Kate's rations, you fools. Well, be quick about it. I don't have all day!"

Kate closed her eyes and whispered a prayer of thanks. She then watched the men unload her rations, and minutes later, Jeremy was gone. Her relief was so intense she trembled. She was free! Free of him at last! She could have danced if she knew how. There was no need for her to hide in the shadows anymore.

She inhaled sharply as she blinked away tears of joy. Her gaze fell on Jeremy's workers and her elation shrivelled and died. They were looking at her as if they wanted to bury her carcass before her stench fouled up their lives.

She had to do something, and quickly, before they believed Jeremy's exaggerated claims. She picked up the bundle at her feet and threw off her shawl. With luck, the display of her bruises would persuade them she had every reason to hate Jeremy as much as they did.

Some of the men had begun to move away when she stepped out of the humpy. They stopped and stared at her, presenting her with a wall of silence. Her belly churned as she forced her feet to move forward. They all looked her over. Her mouth became very dry. She hugged her bundle closer. Their gaze slid from her face to her neck, shoulders and arms. She hated being the object of their intense interest, but she needed to gain their sympathy. Several of the men very quickly averted their gazes, as if embarrassed. She was not sure if the few curses she heard were directed at her or Jeremy.

She searched for a friendly face, stopped when she spotted the tallest man, the one who'd helped her off the wagon. She offered him the bundle. "Will you help me? Please?"

The man hesitated.

"Please?" she pressed.

"What is it?" he asked.

"My baby."

He shrank back.

A mistake. She should have picked another man. She swallowed hard as she clung to her flagging courage. "Lieutenant Kendrick kicked him out of me last night in a drunken rage. Please. Will you bury him for me?"

"M—me?" the tall man rasped. His Adam's apple bobbed.

Another man stepped forward and took the bundle from

Kate. "It's all right, David. I'll take care of this."

"Th—thank you, Tom."

Kate stared at the bundle now in Tom's hands. She trembled, then doubled over in pain. Her dead baby had not been real to her, not until this moment. No. She couldn't stay before these strangers and let them see her bawl like a baby, but her feet seemed nailed to the ground. Her vision blurred.

Run, you eejit, run! And Kate ran back to the humpy.

By the time she recovered from a fit of sobbing, it was dark. Her eyelids were heavy, and it was hard breathing through her nose. Finally, she understood why her mother had grieved over each of her miscarriages, even though the family couldn't afford more mouths to feed.

Kate had not wanted Jeremy's baby, but she'd forgotten it was her baby too—a mistake she'd not repeat. For now, she must put aside her pain. She dried her eyes and thought of her wasted opportunity. The bruises Jeremy had left on her body and her dead baby had gained her some sympathy. She should have turned this to her advantage.

She blew her nose and stared at the branches with dried leaves and the bark of trees that made up the roof and walls of the humpy. These men had done a good job building their shelters. She was sure they could easily turn this wilderness into a thriving farm. The problem was how to persuade them to do this. More, she had to get them to produce stunning results that would impress Jeremy, so he'd let her remain at Red Roo. She had less than four weeks to accomplish it. It seemed like an impossible task, but she had to do it. She must.

A cough woke her. She saw a shadow hovering in the doorway and quickly got to her feet.

"Your supper, missus."

She accepted the platter bearing a chunk of blackened meat and a cup of water. "Thank you. Please, call me Kate. And

131

you're . . . David?"

"Aye."

She touched his arm. "Will you sit a spell with me, David?"

"I can't stay—"

"A spell?"

He hesitated, and Kate rushed on, "You don't like the lieutenant."

He shrugged.

"I hate him too."

He shrugged again. Kate's heart sank. Were they all like him? "Listen. Jeremy Kendrick's a liar. Why would I wish him anything good? He beat me up! If I had a choice—"

"Why are you telling me this? I only brought you supper. I gotta go."

Kate stared at the empty doorway. What remained of her appetite disappeared. She'd been too impatient, she told herself, but how could she help it? Time was fleeting. Jeremy would be here, perhaps in less than a month, and once he saw she'd recovered from the beating, he'd drag her back to Sydney Town . . . No! She couldn't let that happen.

David brought her breakfast the next morning. He jumped when she greeted him and rushed away before she could say another word. For all his great size, Kate didn't think him the leader. Who then? She needed to seek him out, to appeal to his good nature—if he had one—and persuade him to work with her.

She stared at her meal, another piece of charred meat. Perhaps she could cook for them? She'd traded her cooking skill for a benefit, first with the Petals, then with Mabel and Annie. Maybe she could do it again?

She finished her meal and headed for the humpy she'd seen the men use as a kitchen. A stack of dirty dishes lay on the ground, close to the doorway.

"What are you doing?" a gruff voice demanded.

"I thought—"

"Leave them dirty dishes alone. One of us can do the washing-up later."

"All right. I'm Kate."

"Harry. We don't need no help, see?"

"All right." She stared into unfriendly grey eyes in a broad face dominated by a large nose. A massive bush of moustache and beard hid all else.

Harry gave a nod and marched away. She stuck a quick tongue at the receding figure and set down the dishes. She headed in the opposite direction, to avoid the ill-mannered oaf. A short while later, she came upon a river. A flash of colour caught her eye. A red parrot with green wings and a deep blue tail stopped to perch on a low branch hanging over the water. It uttered a shrill, grating "eek-eek-eek" and was joined by a second bird with greener feathers. Kate took a step closer, and the two birds flew off. No one, it seemed, would be her friend, not even the birds.

She walked on, stopping now and again to dig the soil with a stick. Each handful of dirt she sifted through her fingers felt rich and loamy. Jeremy had done well, chosen a good piece of farming land.

A hundred yards down the track, by the riverbank, she caught sight of a familiar figure. He turned as she approached. She smiled. "I'm Kate O'Neal. Thank you for taking care of my baby."

He nodded. "I'm Tom." He hauled in his fishing line. A small fish wriggled at the end of it, flashing silver in the sunlight. He freed it and tossed it back into the water.

Throw away a good fish? These men obviously did very well for themselves, living off the land. No wonder they showed no concern about losing their rations.

Tom dropped the fishing line on a patch of grass. "You want to visit your baby, I suppose?"

"Yes, please."

"Follow me."

He brushed past her. Kate ran to catch up. They covered a hundred yards without exchanging a word, although she often sensed his gaze upon her. This was her chance, but she couldn't find the words to win him to her cause. She started when she realised he'd said something to her. "What?"

"You've been the lieutenant's woman a long time, eh?" he repeated.

"Yes."

"He must think a lot of you."

Kate hated the way his lips curled in a smirk. She looked around at the trees. "Do you like living in these parts?"

"Sure. Nothing to dislike."

"Do you know what I like best about this place?"

"What?"

"Jeremy Kendrick's sweet absence."

He laughed. Encouraged, she stopped and faced him. "Will you help me?"

He gave her a smile that sent goose bumps chasing up her arms. "How can I do that?"

"I want to stay here, away from Jeremy, and I can if you and your friends would help me—"

"How?"

"Open up this land, turn it into a farm. Jeremy would be pleased, and he'd be persuaded to let me stay, to carry on the good work."

"Ah. Thought me as much." He laughed. "Aye, the lieutenant would be right pleased to have himself a working farm, I'm sure, and you'd be his clever little woman. What do we get for all the hard work we have to do, hey?"

"Wouldn't you like to spend the rest of your sentence here? If we all worked together, Jeremy would leave us alone. There'd be no more flogging."

Tom shook his head. "Kendrick can flog us all he want, or send us back to the government. We don't care."

"Why? What's so hard about putting a little work into this place? Just enough to keep Jeremy happy—"

"Here's what we think. The lieutenant ain't gonna be satisfied whatever we do for him. He'll just want more and more—"

"You're wrong!"

"You believe what you want, missus. No doubt we'll be parting company soon. Perhaps the lieutenant will be happier with his next lot of workers. Good luck to him, I say." He stopped and pointed to a spot a short distance ahead. "The grave's just over there."

Kate fretted as another day passed. She wanted to scream, if only to get their attention. She wanted to bash them on their heads to get them to listen to her, but all she did was stare at them.

She knew all their names now, but still had no idea who their leader was. On five separate occasions, and to a different man each time, she offered to cook their meals. They all turned her down.

She said good morning, they said good morning. If she said more, they excused themselves. If she asked questions, they answered, then hurried away. She refused to despair. *I'll change their minds somehow. I must!*

Nellie intrigued her. She thought to find a kindred spirit in the only other woman at Red Roo, but Nellie showed no interest in becoming acquainted. She did no work that Kate could see and was only around when it was time to eat or sleep.

It took her four days to be certain of Nellie's strange sleeping arrangement. Nellie's wanton behaviour shocked her. The men's protective attitude towards Nellie showed they cared, and Kate took heart from this. If she could win Nellie for her friend, the men would surely soften their attitude towards her.

The two times Kate tried to approach Nellie, several of the men came to her side with excuses and bore her away.

In desperation Kate considered rutting with the leader, if only she knew who he was. Rut with nine men? Well, if Nellie could do it, why couldn't she? She could pretend they were all Jeremy. She closed her eyes and shuddered. No, she couldn't do it.

On her eighth morning Kate made her way to the river. She looked at the almost cloudless sky and knew it would be another fine day. It brought her no joy, for she still had no success in befriending any of the men. She soaked her dirty clothes in the shallow water, then began to give them a scrub. After a while, she thought she heard a cry. She paused to listen and heard it again. She got to her feet and looked in the direction of the sound.

David approached at a run. He halted by the riverbank, panting heavily and looking pale. "Nellie's sick. Can you come, Kate? Can you help her?"

"I'll come." She then bent low and scooped up the wet clothes and tossed them on the riverbank. She ran after David who waved for her to catch up.

Kate found herself trembling with every step she took. The barrier these men had built to keep her out had cracked. Nellie had given her the opportunity she needed. She must not waste it.

Seven men lingered outside a humpy. They stepped back from the doorway as she and David approached. She heard some murmured exchange, then Peter emerged from the humpy. Kate's footsteps never faltered. She gave the men a quick nod, then ducked inside.

"Will Nellie be all right?" David asked.

"Let me find out what is wrong with her first, David. Can you fellas not crowd the doorway?"

In a moment, the shadows shifted.

The smell of vomit was strong inside the humpy. "David, can you fetch me some warm water and rags? Nellie needs a wash."

David left her side. She heard a short murmured conversation he had with the men outside, then hurried footsteps fading into different directions.

Kate laid a hand on Nellie's forehead. It didn't feel hot to her. She rubbed Nellie's shoulders. "Are you with babe, Nellie?"

"I had a babe once. They took him away."

Kate froze at the childish tone, then tried again, "When did you last bleed, do you remember?"

"I haven't cut meself in the longest time."

"No. I mean your woman's flow—"

"I don't like being sick. Will I get better soon?"

Kate brushed back Nellie's hair from her face. "Yes, love. Of course, you will."

The woman was simple-minded and likely, pregnant. It wouldn't matter if she wasn't. The possibility was good enough for Kate's purposes. The men would need her help unless they meant to deliver the baby themselves. And should they not see the obvious, she would gladly make it very plain to them.

She smiled. A load of worries had rolled off her shoulders. She cleaned Nellie and settled her down to sleep. Then she stepped out of the humpy. The men looked at her—their faces anxious. "Nellie's fine. She's going to have a baby."

"A baby!" a voice said.

"I told you!" said another.

Kate suppressed a smile. *How nice that the possibility had oc-*

curred to some of them already.

Someone touched her arm. "Thank you for your help," Ben said.

She gave him a nod and walked away, her footsteps so light she thought she floated. She washed her clothes, hung them out to dry and then returned to her humpy and waited for the men to show. The afternoon wore on. She began to fret. David brought her fish for dinner, but he didn't linger. He came with another fish for supper and disappeared just as quickly.

She'd like to give the fools a good shake, tell them what they should have realised by now: they needed her. Were all men thickheaded?

"Kate, can I have a word with you?" a voice said.

She jumped. Rory stood in the doorway.

"Of course." She stepped outside to join him. "What is it?"

Rory hesitated, as if choosing his words. She rubbed her clammy hands on her skirts and waited.

"Tom says you'd like to stay with us—"

"Yes. I would."

"We've been talking—Nellie, she'll need a woman's help with the baby when the time comes, and we'd like it too if we can stay here together with Nellie and the baby. So. If you can help us, we'll work as hard as we can for you."

Kate looked down at her feet and closed her eyes. *Holy Mary Mother of God, thank you, thank you.*

The next day, she tested their resolve. She picked an area close to the river, but not too far from the approach road, and told them to clear the area of trees and bushes. Without a hint of protest, the men went about their task.

She helped them in every way she could: gathering the branches the men sent tumbling to the ground and piling them high for burning. Hard work had never frightened her, and quick results remained her purpose. More importantly, she wanted to show her new friends that she was one of them and would work as hard as they did.

"Ben!" Harry yelled. "Will you get her out of here!"

Everybody stopped work. Some of the men, their faces sweaty and red, looked from Harry to Kate, then quickly away.

Kate glared at Harry. He didn't even spare her a glance. He marched up to Ben some distance away instead. She couldn't see how she'd upset him. Damn Harry. Not only was he rude, he was a troublemaker too! Kate strained to listen to his complaint, but couldn't make out the words. The rest of the men gathered around him, and they too had something to say. After a while they all approached her.

"Kate," Ben said. "We'd all like it better if you leave the clearing of the land to us. Tell us what you want done, then keep your distance. We can't be looking out for you all the time."

"What? Look, I'm not Nellie."

"No. But you're a woman."

She saw no point in arguing. "All right, then. I'll look after the cooking. I'll clean your huts, do your washing—"

"Cook all you want, Kate," Ben said. "Just leave our huts and our washing be. Good heavens! You're not our maid."

"Hey, wait up," Tom said. "That's a good idea—" Ben gave him an elbow; he yelped.

"I don't mind the housework, Ben. Really. You all work the fields, and I'll take care of the rest. We don't have much time. Jeremy could be here next week, to check on me, and we need to dazzle him with our progress."

She retreated from the field, went into the kitchen humpy and examined the food supplies there. The fellas hadn't touched the rations that came with her over a week ago. She found fresh meat, sprouting potatoes and what looked like onions. That should serve for stew.

She dug a pit, filled it with dry branches and started a fire. She waited till the wood was burning before she tossed in several logs. For the next half hour, she worked to produce a dough made of flour, salt and water. She formed a dozen balls, then flattened them into rounds, two inches thick. Braving the heat, she shoveled out some of the burning wood in the pit and gave the rest a stir to kill the flames and shake off the ashes. Then she placed the dough rounds on top of the glowing wood. Carefully, she buried them with the embers. The dampers should be ready in half an hour or so.

The meal was ready when the men came in from the fields and settled down on a grass patch outside the kitchen humpy. An oil lamp Kate had lit pushed back the shadows. She handed out the food.

"God!" Peter said after swallowing a mouthful of food. "To think we could be feasting on food like this for eight bloody days and didn't! Why, 'tis enough to make a fella cry!"

He turned on David. "You silly bugger! Why didn't you say something?"

David's face turned scarlet, his eyes aflame. "Oh, do you dare to say that to me face, you damned rascal you." He glared at the others. "Didn't I tell you all till I was blue in me face? I said Kate was all right that first morning. That she was no spy for that sod, Kendrick. But no, you had your doubts."

Peter laughed. "You didn't try hard enough, mate!"

"I'll sock you one, you bloody swine! Don't think—"

"David," Ben said. "Don't you get hot and bothered for nothing. Don't let Peter goad you. Eat! Before your stew get cold."

David reached for the last damper.

Artie snatched it away. "No! That's for Kate. Here you are, Kate."

"Thank you, Artie. Nellie, would you share this with me?"

Nellie smiled and nodded. Kate tore the damper in two and

handed Nellie half. "So, who's getting the fish tomorrow?" she asked.

"Roger," Sam said. "It's about time that bugger did some fishing. Someone else can help Artie with the joey, next time."

"But I hate fishing," Roger said. "Ben, you're a better fisherman. You fish. I'll have a go at them trees."

"All right."

Sam looked around and sighed. "Ain't life wonderful? Me family back in London never got enough to eat. 'Twas hard to listen to me babies crying . . ."

"You've got children, Sam?" Kate asked.

"Aye. Three small ones. One of them got real sick one day and I couldn't pay for no doctor. So I tried to steal from a merchant. 'Tis how I ended up here."

Roger nodded. "Aye. They said I stole ten bob."

Artie smiled. "They said I stole ten bob too!"

Roger wagged a finger at Artie. "Ah. But I didn't steal no ten bob. I lifted a whole coin pouch! A heavy one too! A pity they caught me."

This started the others confessing to their crimes, and Kate wondered if she could believe them. Were they all thieves? She knew she was not a thief, but she had no problem claiming she had stolen Lady Rustand's lace handkerchief.

She looked at Sam. "Do you know if your sick child recovered?"

"Me Sally's brother came to see me before I sailed. Told me the babe died. Sally and our two boys followed soon after."

"I'm sorry, Sam."

Nellie snuggled up close to Ben. David picked up a wet rag and wiped Nellie's hands. Nellie, a halfwit who did no work for the men, was beloved by them all. For the first time in her life, Kate tasted envy, but for now, she was also content. She was amongst people she could call "friends".

CHAPTER 14

The change in the fellas' attitude towards her in the week that followed was marked, and Kate wanted to pinch herself to be convinced she was not dreaming. Their greetings each morning, sometimes accompanied by nods, sometimes by smiles, warmed her heart. She would feed them breakfast and then watched them head for the fields with their farm tool of choice slung over their shoulders.

Then she'd pile the dirty plates and the men's dirty clothes onto the sled that she'd fashioned and haul them to the river to wash. Next she'd prepare the two main meals for the day. This morning, she decided to do more—she would bake Nellie her favourite biscuits.

She started a fire in her ground oven, then worked quickly on the dough for the biscuits. When she returned to the ground oven, the fire was burning well. Using a long stick, she stirred the burning logs, killing the flames. The oven was ready for her biscuits.

She turned when she heard footsteps behind her.

"Kate, we're going to build you a new cookhouse," Ben announced.

"Oh, no! I don't need a new cookhouse, Ben. This one suits me fine." *Damn.* What could the fellas be thinking of—squandering precious time on unimportant things when Jeremy could show in another two weeks?

Ben raised a hand. "Let's not argue, Kate. The fellas and I

just don't want to run for our humpies again should it start raining next time we sit down to eat. We might as well build a new cookhouse with a kitchen and a room at the back for you. Patching on a shade to this here humpy would take us just as long, we reckon. Besides, think of Sam—he'll be glad to have his humpy back too."

"But Ben, can't you do this after Jeremy's visit? He'll be here—"

"Don't worry, Kate. We've plenty of time. Kendrick won't be here so soon. Why would he even come? To bring us our rations? He cares nothing for us. To see how much work we done for him? Nah. He knows better. He couldn't make us work with the flogging and the ranting. Why would he think we'd work for you?"

Kate knew it would be useless to argue. Unhappily she watched the men work on the new building. When she thought the cookhouse finished, the men spent time fashioning a long table and two benches to seat ten people, and then used two fat tree stumps for seats at the table ends.

"Now, can we get back to clearing the land?" she asked.

Artie tugged at her sleeve. "Don't you like your cookhouse, Kate?"

"I do, Artie. It's just that—" She took a deep breath. "Thank you all for my wonderful cookhouse."

"You're welcome, Kate," Peter said.

Artie smiled, and Kate felt her heart soften. She had a special fondness for Artie. Although younger than he, she felt much like his older sister. Artie provided her welcome company too, especially when Tom happened to be near. She didn't trust the sly looks Tom sent her way.

With Nellie, Kate felt protective. Unlike Artie, Nellie stayed close to her when she baked biscuits. At other times, after she was over her morning discomforts, she'd stay out in the bush, coming home only to eat and sleep.

One day, Nellie didn't show up for dinner. Kate worried as the shadows lengthened. She sought out the men in the fields.

"Roger! Have you seen Nellie?"

"No. Why?"

"She didn't come back for her dinner. Where is she?"

The other men working farther out in the field looked her way. Kate waved for them to approach. They dropped their tools and picked their way through fallen tree trunks and branches to reach her.

"What's wrong?" Sam asked.

"Nellie didn't come home for dinner," Roger said, "and Kate thinks she's lost."

The fellas chuckled.

"Don't worry, Kate," Ben said with a smile. "She'll be back for supper."

Kate glared at them. "Nellie's pregnant. She's lost somewhere out there in the wild, and—"

"Nellie's not lost," Artie said. "She's with her friends—"

"Friends? What friends?"

Sam touched her arm. "Nellie's black fella friends—"

"What? You mean the natives? No! Say you're jesting."

Sam chuckled. "They're her friends, Kate. They'll be feeding her and taking care of her. There's nothing for you to fret about. She'll be back soon enough."

"Holy Mother of God! Don't you know that these . . ." She swallowed hard. ". . . these natives eat people? We've got to look for Nellie right away!"

Rory rubbed her shoulders. "Calm yourself, Kate. The black fellas ain't dangerous. Who told you they eat people?"

She suddenly felt uncertain. "Have you forgotten that Nellie's pregnant?"

He laughed. "I don't see what one has to do with the other!

But no, Kate, we ain't forgetting nothing. Nellie likes to roam. We don't mind. She's safe enough in these parts."

Kate took a deep breath. "You men can be downright foolish! She could be out there somewhere, hurt, and you don't even care."

"Don't be silly," Ben said. "You know we all care for our Nellie."

"Come on, you're getting all worked up for nothing," Rory said. "Nellie knows her way around this property. God knows she's roamed every inch of it. As for dangerous black fellas? Ask Ben. He knows some pretty nasty ones."

Ben's face turned scarlet. "I thought them black fellas dangerous too, Kate. I was wrong. Them around here be right friendly."

Nellie came home later that day, unharmed, and Kate forced herself to accept Nellie's occasional long absences in the days that followed. There were days when Nellie came home with gifts for Kate. These were usually an assortment of berries, mushrooms and fat roots. Kate would smile agreeably when Nellie insisted they were good to eat, but throw them all away when Nellie wasn't looking.

The men worked hard clearing the land. Kate knew they were trying to please her, to make up for the two days they spent on the new cookhouse. One evening at supper, she found herself studying the silver threads in Ben's hair. Here was a man whose sense of fairness had made him leader. Next to him sat Harry with his perpetual scowl. For all his gruff and rude manner, Harry could be very kind . . .

Her heart ached. Somehow, all these people had replaced the brothers and sister lost to her over three years ago. Still, she was under no illusion. But for Nellie, these men would've had nothing to do with her. But for Jeremy's rank and the knowledge she was his woman, they would've treated her differently. Now, they looked upon her as a sister, and as a group, kept her safe.

The sun blazed down a searing heat on Red Roo as the days moved into February. Kate wondered if it could get any hotter.

" 'Tis strange, isn't it?" Kate said. "It's so hot here in winter and ever so cool in summer. Takes some getting used to."

There was a sudden silence.

Rory cleared his throat. "Kate, 'tis summer now. Winter comes in June."

"Oh." Kate felt the heat in her face. "You're right. How stupid of me to think winter must always be in December, and Christmas comes with snow."

"You're not stupid, Kate," Harry said. "And you're a great cook. I don't care what Ben thinks, but I know Kendrick will come for you. He'll want you back for the meals you cook."

"And for other comforts," Tom said with a smirk.

Ben shook his head. "No. He won't come anytime soon. He'd think it'd be just like before with us—no work done on the farm—and fear he'd be thrown into a passion again."

"Are you sure Ben?" Artie asked.

Ben hooked an arm around Artie's neck. "Of course."

Artie's eyes rounded. "Really?"

Ben winked. "He thinks our Kate's dead."

"She be the liveliest piece of dead meat in this here land then," Roger said, and minced about, mimicking Kate. They all laughed, even Nellie.

Perhaps speaking of the devil brought him around. Jeremy showed up the next day in a wagon half-loaded with food rations. He jumped lightly off the wagon and greeted Kate with a broad grin. "Goddammit, Kate! You're a bloody marvel!"

She smiled into his eyes. *You haven't changed at all, you toad.* His interest lay in the progress of the farm. He cared nothing for her.

As if he'd read her mind, Jeremy's smile died. He looked somewhat ashamed. "How are you, Kate?" He framed her face with his hands and kissed her. "Did you miss me, sweet?"

She took a step back. "I've been busy, Jeremy. Don't you think the fellas have done a good job?"

"Indeed. When will you start planting?"

"Soon, after we clear a little more land towards the east." Kate kept her voice low and hid her clenched fists in the folds of her skirts. "Will you be staying the night, Jeremy?"

"Yes, of course." He stared at the clearing and the surrounding trees and reached for her hand. "Truth to tell, I didn't expect any progress. It's a wonderful surprise."

Kate glanced over at her friends who stood just out of hearing range. She slipped free her hand and beckoned for Ben to approach. "Why don't you let Ben show you around, answer all your questions?"

She watched the two men walk away, then waved the rest of her friends back to work. Jeremy's presence stifled her; the very thought of spending the night with him sickened her. She retreated to her room and sank onto her pallet. Impatiently, she dashed away her tears.

'Tis time to be practical.

She dug into a bundle of her personal belongings until she found the sponge, a gift from the Petals. She needed to be at her persuasive best, but she wouldn't risk having another baby.

Kate felt no particular triumph the next morning. Jeremy left the way he came: alone. She got what she wanted, but not without feeling like a whore in the process. Her cheeks burned when Tom winked and smirked at her. The others simply avoided her eyes, but as she busied herself with the cleaning and the cooking, she put her shame where it belonged: in the past.

With Kate at Red Roo, Jeremy found staying in his quarters a lonely experience. He took to spending his hours after work at the Officers' Club. Low on funds, he forced himself to be content with two drinks each night and occupied himself watching his fellow officers gamble. He was biding his time, waiting for Lady Luck to come calling again, and he thought it could be happening soon. Indeed change was in the air. Had his convict workers not turned tame and were now working hard for him?

That evening, he arrived early at the Club. On his way to the bar, he glanced at the three empty gaming tables and, as before, heard and resisted their siren call. *Not too long, now,* he promised himself as he bought his first drink for the night.

The rum warmed his blood and lifted his spirits. The Club slowly filled. While many officers drifted to the bar, a few regulars headed for the gaming tables and play started very quickly. Jeremy followed the officers' game, often moving back and forth from table to table. Eventually, his glass emptied. He bought a refill.

A player at the third table announced his early retirement. His wife was waiting up for him, he said. The remaining three invited Jeremy to make up the fourth. He hesitated, then told himself fate had called. Who was he to deny fate? Besides, both his palms itched, a sure sign he'd win.

Two hands later, Jeremy grinned his delight. He judged the three officers at his table as foolish as the young bucks he'd fleeced in London. His hands trembled, as he marked two cards with his fingernails. A few hands later, he could identify enough cards to begin plucking his three unsuspecting pigeons.

One of the men remarked on Jeremy's winning streak. He responded by forcing himself to lose that hand, then chided the man for driving his "good" luck away. He lost another hand before he started to bleed his victims again.

An hour later, two officers at Jeremy's table declared they'd lost all they were prepared to lose that night. One grumbled about his misfortune; the other laughed and slapped his friend on his back. They left the Club together.

Colby, the remaining player, looked across at Jeremy. "It's just the two of us, now. How about a fast game? Let's raise the stakes."

Jeremy's heart leapt at the suggestion. He pretended to consider, then shook his head. "I'm on a winning streak. Four players reduced to two can affect my good luck already. Why would I want to change anything else?"

Colby shrugged. "A man's luck can change for any number of reasons, but higher stakes would allow me to recover my losses more quickly. On the other hand, I could as easily lose what remains in my pocket. What do you say?"

Jeremy took a sip of his rum. "All right."

"May we be allowed to join you?" a voice said.

"Of course." Colby smiled at the newcomers and indicated the empty chairs. "Take a seat, gentlemen. Have you met Lieutenant Kendrick?"

Jeremy knew Lieutenant Hudson, by sight, as one of the trading officers. He'd seen the man play a couple of times at the Club and judged him, at best, an indifferent player. It'd be his pleasure to pick Hudson's deep pockets—compensation for being denied the opportunity to join the trading fraternity.

Captain Spencer was a stranger to him. The name seemed familiar, but he couldn't recall where or when he'd heard it. Colby mentioned the new stakes. Spencer leaned back in his chair and arched an eyebrow.

"Too rich for your blood, Captain?" Jeremy sneered, then turned to Colby. "Perhaps we can accommodate—"

"That's not necessary." Spencer faced Hudson. "Bill?"

"Fine by me." Hudson rubbed his hands and grinned. "I feel lucky tonight."

Jeremy dealt out six cards each, in two rounds, and play began after Hudson, the "eldest" for the hand, settled the question of trumps. For a half hour, Jeremy resisted his secret advantage and played a straight game. He used the time to observe Spencer.

The captain's every movement seemed slow, if deliberate, as was his speech. Jeremy judged him a man of indolence and took him for another pigeon. His luck had certainly turned.

When Colby came back after excusing himself for a few minutes, Jeremy made his move. Slowly, the pile of coins in front of him began to grow. Twice when he turned unexpectedly, he caught Spencer staring at him. A chill shot down his back.

Perhaps he should stop giving luck a helping hand. Why risk discovery? Then he chided himself for being foolish. Captain Spencer looked a dullard; not someone to be feared.

A half hour later, Jeremy misread a card. When it happened again, he trembled at the implication. Someone had messed with his markings. He looked into Colby's smiling face and noted the healthy pile of coins before him. Was Colby the one? No. He'd fleeced the fool earlier. Still, Colby had raised the stakes. No, no. It couldn't be him. Hudson was the more likely suspect, but the man had not won significantly. Neither had Spencer.

Jeremy flinched when he lost another hand. His anxiety mounted as his earlier winnings dwindled. He tried to go slow on the liquor, but he couldn't seem to stop his hand from reaching out for his glass again and again and then shouting for a refill when his glass emptied. His fingers wouldn't stay still, either. They snapped the cards in his hand or drummed the table as he waited his turn.

"Odd, how quickly my luck has plummeted," he said. "Yours seems to have improved considerably, Colby."

Colby stiffened; his face paled.

"It's only a game, gentlemen," Spencer said. "Let's keep it friendly."

At the end of another winning round, Colby pushed back his chair. "It's late and I'm tired. If you gentlemen will excuse me, I shall retire."

Fury tightened its hold on Jeremy. "Running off with the winnings, Colby? How very sporting of you, dear sir."

Colby's hand froze in the middle of sweeping his winnings into his coin pouch. Spencer cut in before Colby could say anything. "Lieutenant Kendrick, if you're determined to play, I'll be happy to accommodate you. We shouldn't deter the others if they wish to withdraw."

Hudson got to his feet. "Well, if nobody minds, I'll retire too. I'll watch you play, Nicholas. Maybe I'll learn something new and improve my skill."

Spencer nodded. Jeremy shrugged, averted his eyes and drained his glass. He called out to the convict bartender for a refill.

Officers around the room looked his way. When the bartender came forward with his drink, they strolled up to surround the table. Jeremy glared at them. If he could, he'd chase them all away.

He'd ignore them, he decided. After taking another small sip of rum, Jeremy put down his glass, but it slipped from his fingers, hit the floor and shattered. The tension in the room increased. The bartender came running to clear the mess.

Jeremy looked across at Spencer. "Shall I deal?"

"It's getting late. Let's raise the stakes," Spencer said. "Five pounds?"

Someone gasped. "That's what I used to earn in a month!"

Laughter rippled through the crowd. Jeremy licked his lips. "Fine. Can I deal now?"

Spencer stared at him, then called out, "Bartender! Can we

have a new pack of cards here?"

The bartender handed him a pack. Spencer looked around. "Would someone do us a favour, deal for us?"

"It'll be my pleasure," a voice said.

Spencer smiled. "Lieutenant Hathaway, how kind of you. Lieutenant Kendrick, do you object?"

Jeremy shrugged. "I don't care. Can we begin now?"

Hathaway opened the new pack of cards and, after the courtesies, dealt them out. Play continued. Jeremy clung to his waning hopes, unable to believe Lady Luck had turned her back on him again.

Then he was down to the turn of the last card. His heart sank when the five of diamonds showed. He carefully laid his cards, face down, on the table, when he wanted to hurl them into Spencer's face.

"Captain Spencer?"

"Yes?"

"Listen," Jeremy stammered. "I'm cleaned out, but I have this land grant at the Hawkesbury—"

"How much?"

"Two hundred pounds?"

Loud guffaws shattered the tense mood around the table. Jeremy glared at the fools. "My farm is worth every penny of two hundred pounds," he cried.

"What does your farm yield? Gold dust?" a voice demanded.

"If it's so wonderful, why don't you keep it?" another asked.

Damned meddlers! He looked into Spencer's grey eyes. "All right, maybe it's not worth that much yet, Captain, but near enough. You've only to see my farm to know it's no lie."

Spencer said nothing, just looked at him with his hooded eyes.

Jeremy swallowed. "One hundred pounds?"

Spencer nodded and began counting out the coins. Lieutenant Hathaway shuffled the cards and waited. Spencer pushed the coins across to Jeremy, and Hathaway started dealing out the cards once more. Three cards each, then another three before Spencer called the trumps.

Jeremy lost the hand again, and a new one started. He licked his lips, took a deep breath and silently begged for divine intervention.

Some minutes later, the hooded eyes stared at him. "Are we finished here or is there anything else you'd like to stake?"

Jeremy read mockery in the question and, for a moment, pictured his fist smashing into the bastard's face. Someone tittered. Jeremy jerked back into reality. "I have this convict woman—"

Spencer's eyes narrowed into slits, his voice turned chilly. "A—convict—woman?"

Behind him, a titter started. A barely suppressed chuckle followed. Then the room rocked with ribald laughter.

Jeremy glared at the officers. *Goddamn bastards!* He forced the sincerest note he could muster into his voice. "She's no ordinary convict woman, Captain. She's a gem. A gem really! Knows a lot about farming. She's a great housekeeper, a divine cook—"

"A beauty to be sure!" a voice behind him sneered.

"A rare bed sport, I'll bet!" another added.

"How many ways can she do it? On her head?" someone demanded.

"Let's not quibble," Spencer snapped, and the loud hoots and laughter trailed into silence. "It's getting late. I've no wish to spend the rest of my night here. A hundred pounds? Here, count it! Please deal, Lieutenant Hathaway."

Time seemed to fly and the coins on the table in front of Jeremy refused to stay put. Then he was down to his last hand, the best one so far this horrible night. He stood a good chance of breaking his losing streak, finally. He needed to secure the two of spades and the game was his. He used his last trump.

Spencer beat it with a queen. Jeremy stared at the cards in his trembling hand for a moment, then tossed them down. A collective sigh broke the sudden silence.

Jeremy cleared his throat. He couldn't control his stammer. "I don't have the papers with me now, Captain. Where can I reach you tomorrow?"

"I'll be at Lieutenant Hudson's residence till noon."

Spencer swept his coins into his pouch and rose to his feet. He straightened his jacket and gave Hathaway a nod. "Well, gentlemen, I'll say my goodnight now. It's been an interesting evening."

Jeremy didn't wait to hear more. He sidled out the door while everyone's attention remained with the victor. As he stumbled his way home, he wondered if he should not kill himself. Stripped of all he owned, he didn't have a future left.

The next day, he searched through his papers and tucked a selection of them—the title to Red Roo and the documentation of the convicts assigned to him—into his pocket. No matter how it hurt, he had to hand them over to Captain-bloody-Spencer.

Telling himself he'd be well rid of his troublesome convict workers didn't lessen his regret for the loss of his land grant, and, for now, the money he'd been getting from the sale of the convict rations. Yes, he was sorry to lose Kate too.

He came storming home after seeing Spencer. He poured himself a drink and swallowed it in one gulp. It burned him that the captain had treated him like dirt. His rage billowed, and he booted the chair in front of him and watched it fall against the table, dislodging a stack of papers. He swung his leg to kick the papers on the floor and froze, his gaze fixed on one document.

Kate's paper! He must have missed it earlier this morning.

Wicked thoughts spun in his head, and suddenly he laughed.

"By God, yes! Spencer, you bastard, we'll see who has the last laugh now!"

CHAPTER 15

The sound of running footsteps made Kate look up. It never failed to amuse her how Nellie, a grown woman, could look so much like an excited child. She smiled at her approaching friend.

"Ain't them biscuits ready yet?" Nellie demanded, a little short of breath.

"Not ye—et," Kate said for the third time that morning.

" 'Tis taking too long," Nellie wailed.

"It'd be ready soon, I promise."

"Can I take a peek? Please?"

"You can't. The biscuits would turn as hard as stones, and then you wouldn't be able to eat them. You could break your teeth. Then the fellas will say, 'Here comes Nellie with no teeth!' "

Nellie giggled, turned and, avoiding the pools of rain water, ran for the trees.

"Nellie, be careful!" Kate shouted. "The ground's slippery."

Nellie paid her no heed, and Kate only shook her head. She didn't fear for Nellie's safety for Nellie was as sure-footed as a sailor on a rolling deck. A short while later, Kate took out the baked biscuits from the ground oven. With the mouth-watering smell filling the air, she expected Nellie to show up at once. The dear girl would surely grab a hot biscuit and nibble on it, but there was no sign of her. Later on, the men came back for their dinner and left. Still there was no sign of Nellie. When the sun sank lower in the sky, Kate's sense of unease increased.

No, she couldn't bear the uncertainty anymore. She lifted her skirts some inches off the ground and stepped out of the cookhouse. She squished her way over ground made wet and slippery by several days of rain, to the fields. Soon the fellas, busy clearing the land, came into view. She waved at them and then shouted, "Ben! Peter! Have you seen Nellie?"

Ben must have heard her. He said something to the others and then they all dropped their tools and moved as one to meet her. When they came within hearing distance, she called out again, "Nellie didn't come home for her biscuits, and she missed dinner. I'm worried."

"Oh, no. Not again!" Roger groaned. "Kate, you know—"

"Something's wrong, I tell you. You've got to look for her."

Peter shook his head. "Kate, you've got to stop fretting like this."

"Please?"

Ben sighed. "Looks like Kate here ain't gonna stop worrying, and we'll be getting no peace from her. Best we fetch our Nellie home. Come on, fellas. Let's go."

Kate waited outside the cookhouse for the fellas to return. She paced the ground and bit her nails. The slightest noise made her search the distance, in every direction. Nothing. The shadows grew darker, and her sense of dread deepened. *Please God, let the fellas find Nellie before it gets too dark to see.*

"Coo-ee! Coo-ee!"

Kate's heart leapt at the call from a distance to her left. She saw a group at first, then she could make out David with a lifeless-looking Nellie in his arms. She gasped when David stumbled. The fellas cried out in alarm. This convinced Kate that Nellie was still alive. Why else would they fear if David dropped Nellie? After a while, the fellas started moving again, this time it was Sam carrying Nellie.

Kate hurried forward to meet them. She hadn't covered

twenty yards when she slipped on a slippery patch and almost fell. She took a moment to recover her breath and then started running again. Rory and Peter, who had raced ahead, met her halfway.

Rory cried. "Nellie's bleeding bad, Kate. Sam thinks she's losing the baby."

Damn. "Come with me!" She whirled and headed back to the cookhouse. Within moments, the two fellas were by her side, keeping pace with her. Already thinking of what must be done, she raised her voice. "Boil water for me, Rory; and Peter, get me all the clean rags you can find! Hurry!"

She cleared up her room as best she could, and all too quickly, Sam was at the doorway with Nellie in his arms.

"Set her on my pallet, Sam. The rest of you, stay outside. You too, Sam. I'll take care of our Nellie now. If I need help, I'll call out."

There was nothing much Kate could do except see to Nellie's comfort. She stared into Nellie's pale face and wished for Nellie to wake up and for her bleeding to stop.

She could see the fellas were worried, eager to help in any way they could. Before night fell, they had lit the room with several oil lamps and kept three torches burning outside. No one thought about food, and Kate didn't think to remind them.

The hours dragged by. Kate kept a close watch on Nellie, and each time she checked, the rag between her legs came away soaked in blood. It reminded her of the time when her mother lost her last baby, and she knew Nellie's baby was lost too. A coldness wrapped itself around Kate's heart. She trembled as she tightened her hold on Nellie's hand. *But you're going to be all right, Nellie. You must!*

"How's Nellie?" Peter asked from the doorway.

When she shook her head, Peter went away, but she knew David or Ben or another would be at the door next to ask the same question. It had been that way the past several hours. She wanted to scream for them to leave her and Nellie alone, but resisted. The fellas had a right to know about Nellie and the baby.

Then Nellie stirred and whimpered. "It hurts, Kate. Make the pain go away . . ."

The men, who must have heard Nellie's soft words, crowded the doorway. "Is Nellie all right?" several voices demanded.

"Is there anything we can do to help, Kate?" Ben asked.

"I'll let you know if I think of anything." She waved them away. So far all they'd done was strain her patience. Suddenly an idea struck her. Without stopping to give it further thought, she moved to the doorway, calling out, "Wait a minute, Ben. I've just thought of something. Yes, you and the fellas can help."

"What is it?" Ben asked even as the other fellas crowded around him to hear what she had to say.

"I'm going to need more hot water for Nellie shortly. Can you boil the water for me?"

"How much do you need, Kate?" David asked.

After a moment's hesitation, she said, "I'm going to need plenty."

"You'll get your hot water, Kate," Ben promised. "As much as you want." He moved away from the doorway with purpose in his stride. "Harry, you and Sam gather more firewood. Tom, you and Peter can help Roger and me haul water from the river. The rest of you keep us supplied with torches to light the way."

Kate smiled as she listened to the fellas hurrying this way and that, shouting instructions to each other as they went about their tasks. The men were now so busy, they had no time to pester her about Nellie anymore.

"I said we should build our huts next to the river, but you wouldn't listen," she heard Tom shout. "If you did, we wouldn't have to worry about walking that distance to get some water now, would we?"

"Stop complaining," Ben said. "Fetch more water. Go!"

Nellie writhed on the pallet, making mewling noises. After a while she fell into a restless sleep. Kate decided to snatch some sleep herself. She jerked awake and saw David at the doorway holding a bucket.

"Here's your hot water, Kate. How's Nellie?"

She accepted the bucket. "Resting. I think she's feeling better. Thanks for the water. You'll keep more coming?"

"You need some more?" He sounded surprised.

"Oh yes, plenty more."

After David left, Kate studied the bucket of water, then using her body to shield the bucket from the doorway, dug up a handful of dirt and dropped it into the water. She scooped in another handful, then pressed a hand over her mouth to stifle the sound of her giggles. God, wouldn't they half-kill her, if they discovered how she was wasting their hard work.

All night long two buckets journeyed back and forth between the men and Kate: the water coming to her hot and clean and leaving slightly colder and muddier.

She watched over Nellie as she listened to the men.

"Why does Kate need so much hot water?" David asked.

"How should I know? Just give it to her," Harry said.

"Does the water look muddy to you?" Rory asked a while later.

"You think Nellie's bleeding mud?" Ben demanded.

"No, no. It looked muddy to me, that's all."

"It's the light. The bloody torches are giving out too much smoke," Sam said and coughed.

"Well, don't just stand there. We're running out of dry wood," Rory snapped.

"What's Kate doing with so much water? You'd think she'd

have enough by now." Tom said. "Do you think Nellie's getting a bath?"

"What's that?" Rory asked.

"A scratch. I slipped on the bloody path. 'Tis just good luck I didn't tumble into the river. Damn treacherous path."

Inside her room, Kate choked on more laughter. *Tom will kill me for this!*

Then Nellie screamed. Kate sobered. Minutes later, choking on her tears, she called out, "It's the baby. Nellie's losing the baby."

After she'd attended to Nellie, made sure she was clean, comfortable and asleep once more, Kate turned her attention to the baby. The water the men had provided her all night long proved very useful now. After she cleaned the baby, she wrapped it in calico. Then cradling the tiny body, she took a deep breath and stepped out of the cookhouse. The night sky had turned lighter. She faced the men. They were all staring at the bundle she carried.

She saw the gleam of tears in Ben's eyes and felt the sting in her own. "I'd rather you didn't look at this." She turned to Tom. "Can I leave this with you?"

Tom nodded.

"Nellie's sleeping. You can take turns to sit with her. She wanted this baby very much, you know . . ." Kate's voice wobbled, and she turned her face away. Rory put his arms around her. She wept into his chest. Two babies lost in six weeks: hers and now, Nellie's.

No one had supper, so Kate decided to prepare breakfast. When the meal was cooked, she called the men over to eat, but no one had an appetite.

"Look, you're not doing Nellie any good just hanging around here. Go on. Go hack down some trees! Do something!"

The fellas sat around the table with their heads bowed. Later, they drifted back to the fields, leaving Rory to sit his turn with Nellie. Kate retreated to Sam's humpy to rest. Her grief refused to loosen its grip on her and seemed to keep sleep at bay.

A loud pounding in her head woke her up. It grew stronger and louder till she recognised it for the rhythmic sound of hoof beats. Jeremy wouldn't visit for another fortnight at least, and she was sure he'd come in a wagon to carry their food rations, not on horseback. Who could their visitor be?

She stepped outside the humpy. The afternoon sun shone into her eyes. She hurried over to the cookhouse. Rory grabbed her arm and pulled her into the room. "Stay here with Nellie. I'll see who comes."

He returned some minutes later with a frown on his face. "It's Kendrick."

Kate's heart sank.

Jeremy, mud-splattered and pale, rode up to the cookhouse. He swung down from his horse.

"Did you forget something, Jeremy?"

"Never mind the questions."

She caught a whiff of stale liquor on his breath.

"Get your things! We're leaving."

"Why?"

"Get your belongings! You're coming back to Sydney Town with me."

"Why? What's happening?"

"You and your infernal questions!" He gave her a shove.

She stumbled and landed on the soft ground. Keeping her gaze on Jeremy, she struggled to her feet, then brushed off the mud on her arms and skirts. A movement on her right caught her eye. Her friends had come in from the fields, stopping some ten yards away. They stared at Jeremy, their bodies still and tense, their expressions, hostile.

Kate's heart pounded. *Oh God, don't let them interfere. They don't need more trouble.* She gave them a fierce look and shook her head in warning.

"Dammit! Do as you're told," Jeremy shouted at her. "Get your things!"

She backed her way to the cookhouse, pleading with him with each step she took. "I'm doing good work here, Jeremy. We've already started some planting. Take a look at the fields. Please, Jeremy. Please, let me stay."

"Get your bloody stuff. I won't tell you again!"

"Jeremy, just look around—"

"I don't give a damn! This place has been nothing but trouble. Good riddance, I say!"

"It's not yours—"

When he raised his hand to hit her, she backed away. She hurried past Rory into the room, grabbed her belongings and stuffed them into a bag. She wiped the tears from her eyes. On her way out, she stopped in front of Rory. "Keep Nellie clean," she told him. "See that she eats well."

She rested her hand on his arm for a moment. "Goodbye, Rory. Take care."

She walked up to Jeremy and handed him her bag. Then, ignoring his bellows, she strode up to the eight fellas to say goodbye. With her head held high, she walked back to Jeremy, not caring if he should hit her for her defiance. He didn't. Without a word, he lifted her onto the horse's back, then he swung himself into the saddle behind her. With a kick, he sent the piebald into a gallop. After a while, he slowed the horse to a steady trot.

He cleared his throat. "I know you did a fine job at Red Roo, Kate. It's just rotten luck I lost the property. But we'll come about again. You'll see."

She stared into the distance, unable to believe her own bad luck. A gurgle of laughter welled up inside. It emerged as a sob.

When Jeremy tightened his hold on her, she leaned into him and wept. Would she never be free of this monster, ever?

CHAPTER 16

Nicholas Spencer tossed his leather bag to the ground and swung down from his horse. He looked around him to study the neighbourhood. The land to his right, vacant only three weeks ago, now supported a double-story structure of timber frames. Fresh landfill covered the land to his left, hinting of more buildings to come. Sydney Town seemed to have grown bigger in just three weeks. Soon it would bear the hallmarks of a great metropolis. No doubt Parramatta, his hometown was developing just as fast, but the changes there did not strike him as marked.

He picked up his bag, walked up to the door and rapped it with his riding crop.

After some moments the door opened, and he looked down into Hudson's chubby face.

"Why, Nicholas," Hudson exclaimed with pleasure.

Spencer smiled. He was fond of his young friend and often laughed at the shameless way he traded on his harmless looks to deceive others into under-estimating his character.

Hudson grinned. "Gad, this is indeed a splendid surprise! I never see you for months on end and now twice in three weeks?" He urged him through the doorway. "Come on in. Leave your valise. Jim will take care of that for you."

They moved into the drawing room. Spencer eased himself into the familiar deep-seated chair and looked at the painting Bill had won from him in one of their card games. Losing the painting had been one of his better ideas. Bill had been so pleased, he couldn't stop crowing at his unexpected "luck". Spencer smiled as he noted how the painting still held pride of place over Bill's mantelpiece.

Hudson passed him a brandy. "I don't suppose this is a social visit?"

"Social visit?" He arched a brow. "Count yourself lucky, Bill, that I haven't bloodied your nose yet."

"Eh? How have I offended?"

"Doing it much too brown, you rogue." He gave Hudson a stern look. "I received a note from Anders two days ago."

Hudson shrugged. "Oh that."

"Yes, that! Been rather free with my services, haven't you?"

"But Nicholas! You're the best man for the job."

"Flattery won't do it. You should know that."

"Upon my word. 'Tis not flattery. I swear you'll have no trouble from Captain Perkins of the *Seventh Cross*. How could he fail to recognise your quality? He'd be falling over himself to accommodate your wishes, and the errand would be completed in ten minutes. Trust me."

Spencer choked on a laugh. "You're a scoundrel, all right!"

"You mean to humiliate me, don't you? Say *I* called on Captain Perkins. What kind of reception do you think I'll get? The man will take one look at this face, and I'd be lucky if he didn't send for my mother to fetch me away!"

Spencer spluttered into laughter. "Bill, you know I don't like getting involved in the Fraternity's activities. I didn't mind putting up the gold, but—"

"We're hard-pressed, Nicholas. All the ships' captains are demanding payment and growing more impatient—"

Spencer frowned. "How long have they waited?"

"Some more than four weeks. Dammit. The market is glutted, and it'll take a little longer for us to convert the goods into coins to pay for their cargo—"

"Maybe the Fraternity should take in more 'contributors'—"

"No, no. This is just a temporary situation. Things will improve soon. Till then, we need to smooth out a few ruffled feathers—"

"Hmmm."

"Those of us who usually deal with the sea captains have been making, in retrospect, rather rash promises. How were we to know the economy would languish in just a matter of weeks? Naturally, we're somewhat embarrassed and need a few new faces to—You know how it is, Nicholas—"

"Indeed, I begin to."

"You recall Lieutenant Taylor?"

"That blubber head? Spare me, please."

Hudson grinned. "He's suggesting we get tough with all the ships' captains. Don't pay them, he said, and see what they can do. They're at our mercy. We can put all those bastards into chains if we wished."

Spencer shuddered. "Did he say what he'd do when news travels, and foreign ships stop calling here?"

Hudson cursed. "We wouldn't have a problem if the East India Company would be reasonable. Not interested in trading with us, yet they'd invoke their Royal Charter to disallow us to use our own ships to conduct our trade."

"Enough of your moans. I don't wish to be disobliging, Bill, but from the start I've made it clear I wanted no hand in the running of the organisation, nor in the merchandising of the goods."

"I know, Nicholas. Don't think we're not grateful for your decision to stay away from managing the Fraternity—as it is, we're all jealous of what little authority we possess."

Spencer snorted. "Not grateful enough, obviously. Didn't Anders promise not to trouble me with commerce? Did he not then dump my share of the cargo at my doorstep six months later?"

"Come on, Nicholas. It's not as if you have to do any selling yourself—"

"That's because I found Sergeants Cross and Latham to do it for me. Yes, they're excellent fellows and all that, but that's beside the point. I should never have been required to use their services. Hell! I've become a damned colonial merchant. Bill, I assure you, had I wished to engage in trade, I'd have done so in England, and with better results."

"Must you hark back to over two years ago?"

He gave Hudson a stern look. "You brought the subject up."

Hudson raised both hands in surrender. "All right, all right. See Captain Perkins for us, and we won't trouble you again. You have my word on it."

After dinner, Hudson suggested they call on Lieutenant Irving.

Spencer's lips twitched. "Ah. I'm not sure if I can bear an entire evening watching you make calf-eyes at the lovely Mistress Irving, Bill."

Hudson choked on his drink. "Oh, this is famous! Do you mean to go to the Officers' Club again?"

Spencer looked away. If he could, he'd rather forget the entire episode. His impulse to teach a cheat a lesson had ended in his extreme mortification: gambling over a female, a convict female, no less.

"Tell me, have you inspected Kendrick's property yet?" Hudson asked.

"No. I haven't seen a penny's profit from my Parramatta farm. It'd be no different with Red Roo, no matter what Kendrick may have claimed for his farm."

"And the woman?"

He glared at Hudson, who laughed. He sighed, finding it

hard to stay annoyed with the younger man. It had always been so, from the first day they'd met, almost three years ago. He'd just reported at the Corps headquarters, right after landing, and was waiting for the paperwork to be done, when Hudson engaged him in conversation.

"Are you always this impulsive, Bill?" He'd asked a week later. "Do you usually offer strangers accommodation?"

Hudson chuckled. "You must think me a rustic!"

"Well, perhaps you could be a little less trusting—"

The chuckles grew louder. "I'm not as foolish as you think, Nicholas. What did I have to fear from a man who outranks me? Captains don't grow on trees, you know, and I do have a knack for spotting quality."

Spencer admitted there was more to Bill than the immature youth most people saw. A friendship begun so simply had strengthened over the months. Their paths had diverged six months later when he moved into his own residence at Parramatta. Distance, duties and new interests impeded frequent meetings, but their bond remained as strong as ever.

"So is it to be the Officers' Club again tonight?" Hudson's words interrupted his reverie.

He winked. "On second thought, I feel it's my duty to assist my wily young friend dangle after the beautiful Mistress Irving."

A week later, Spencer drove up to the Commissariat Store.

Lieutenant Crawford called out a greeting. "Heard you took over Kendrick's Hawkesbury property, sir."

Spencer winced. *You and everybody else.* "Indeed. I'm on my way there this morning. Let me have the rations for Red Roo and anything else you can spare, Crawford. New tools or seeds, whatever."

"Of course, Captain." He turned away and shouted, "Sergeant! Get the Red Roo convicts' rations for the captain, will you? Fetch some of those new tools I keep in the back room. Some bags of seeds too."

He turned to Spencer. "Anything else I can do for you, Captain?"

"Can I buy six bottles of rum and four packets of tobacco off you?"

Crawford grinned. "My pleasure, sir. Anything else?"

"Some frippery for a woman?"

"I have some green and gold ribbons that are selling very quickly."

"Fine. Give me two lengths each."

Spencer left with a lighter coin pouch and the assurance he'd established a friendly connection with Crawford.

Two hours into the journey, he glanced up at the intermittent low clouds and shifted uncomfortably in his hard wagon seat. Three hours later, he took a wrong turn and his temper frayed. He swore at Kendrick for landing him in his predicament and cursed himself for not handing the property back to Kendrick, in a gesture of contempt. He sighed. No matter how much he loathed the scoundrel, he couldn't humiliate him thus, certainly not a man who had nothing left, but his pride.

As he'd told Bill, he didn't expect Red Roo to do any better than his farm, Random. The problem as he saw it was that, while he felt he owed his convict workers a duty to see them clothed and fed, they didn't seem to think they owed him anything. Why would Kendrick's workers be any different?

He was stretching his neck and rotating his shoulders to shake off the stiffness when he detected a movement beneath a clump of trees. A man, dressed in convict clothing, stood watching him.

Spencer stopped the horses and beckoned the man to approach. "Can you show me the way to Red Roo?"

"This is Red Roo."

"Do you work here?"

The man nodded. Spencer gave him a long look. A man of few words. He liked that. "I'm Captain Spencer, the new owner of Red Roo. What's your name?"

The man stared at him, his expression turning wary. "Rory, sir. Rory O'Connell."

"Climb aboard, Rory O'Connell," he said. "You can guide me to your camp." He waited till O'Connell was seated, then flicked the reins. The horses snorted and started moving. He looked at Rory. "Turn here?"

"Aye."

They passed by a large area showing signs of land clearing. Farther along, he saw a scattering of humpies. At the largest building, complete with a shade, he counted five men sitting at a long table. He stopped the horses. "Rory, would you like to fetch the others?"

He watched Rory take off into the trees, then he approached the five men and introduced himself, before suggesting they unload the wagon. He was pleasantly engaged in idle conversation with them when Rory returned in the company of three men. He looked the newcomers over. "Introduce yourselves, gentlemen."

As the men did so, he committed their names to memory. "And I'm Nicholas Spencer, captain of the New South Wales Corps and the new owner of Red Roo."

Nine men? One of their number was missing. *Had Kendrick used a non-existent woman to stake his game?* He should have checked the documents Kendrick had given him. But why would he, when he didn't plan to have much more to do with his new workers or the farm?

"I hope you'll work as hard for me as you did for Lieutenant Kendrick. How do I know you're hard workers? Because the lieutenant told me so. Now, I've no quarrel with hard work.

Indeed, if you continue to work hard, I promise, you won't go unrewarded."

The men didn't react. He wasn't surprised. "Here's what I'm going to do. I'll let you keep a quarter of the value of whatever you produce from this farm. As a sign of my good faith, I've brought along some gifts." He turned to Rory, "I have liquor and tobacco under the wagon seat. Can you fetch them, please?"

The men watched Rory as he made his way to the wagon. They sighed as one when he came back with the bottles and a package. Spencer suppressed a smile. He'd not come across a man who didn't appreciate a taste of rum or a spot of tobacco. "Tell me, do you have a leader?"

"Ben's our leader," Tom said above the low buzz as the men exchanged some words.

"Step forward, Ben." He gave the stout man a long look. "Tell me, isn't there a woman missing here?"

The sudden hush took him by surprise. Smiles at the promise of rum and tobacco vanished. The men glared at him.

He frowned. *What? Have I suddenly sprouted horns and a tail?* "Well?"

"Nellie's out bushwalking," Ben said. "She should be back before supper."

"Oh? She cooks for all of you then?"

Ben looked away. "We takes our turn cooking."

A great cook? Damn Kendrick for a liar. "What does Nellie do then?"

"She looks after us. And we look out for her."

He waited, but Ben looked down at his feet and seemed to have run out of words. *How curious. The woman must mean a lot to them.* "I'll be staying the night. Is there a bed you can let me have?"

Ben pointed to the back of the cookhouse. "You can use the room back there. I'll have some water fetched so you can freshen up. If you want to rest, we'll call you when supper's ready."

A refreshing wash later, Spencer emerged from the back room to find no sign of his workers. He looked around, saw a well-worn path and decided to follow it. He would inspect Kendrick's *wonderful* farm.

He found nothing remarkable about Red Roo. A little more than seven acres had been cleared, and less than a quarter of that planted. If Kendrick saw this as spectacular progress over nine months, he was a fool. Spencer shook his head. Kendrick was a cheat at cards. Why wouldn't he lie and cheat in all else?

He strolled on, his boots snapping twigs and crunching dried leaves. A half hour later, he caught sight of a river. He wondered if it offered good fishing and decided to explore.

A loud curse startled him.

He reached inside his jacket pocket for his firearm. He armed it and then, with his finger resting lightly on the trigger, moved forward to investigate. Hunching low and using the tree trunks and shrubs for cover, he moved silently, deeper into the trees.

His nine convict workers stood twenty yards away, engrossed in a heated argument. Assured no danger threatened, he disarmed the pistol and put it away. He strained to listen, to discover what troubled them. Distance and the wind garbled the words. He moved closer.

"He's worse than Kendrick," Roger said.

Sam waved his hand. "Never mind that now. I tell you, he's after Nellie."

After Nellie? Spencer blinked. He'd not even seen the woman.

"Sam's right," David said. "He can have any bloody woman in this entire colony, but he wants our Nellie."

Rory brushed back his hair. "Come on, fellas. He was only asking—"

"Asking, me foot," Sam said. "He's come to take her away, I tell you."

173

"Can't we just hide Nellie like we did with the lieutenant?" Artie asked.

"Maybe Artie's right, Ben," David said. "We could hide Nellie till—"

"No, we can't," Ben said. "The cap'n already asked after Nellie. Funny that he should think Nellie's been cooking for us."

"No," Harry said, "Let's kill him and bury him so deep nobody would find—"

Ben laughed. "Don't be foolish—"

"Cap'n Spencer!" Rory called out, walking away from his friends as he moved forward. "What are you doing here? Not lost, are you?"

The silence was absolute for several moments as the others gaped at him.

Damn. What a shame that Rory had spotted him, just when things were getting more interesting. He raised his hand in a friendly wave, and stepped forward to meet Rory. "The river back there. Does it offer good fishing?" He stopped and assumed an expression of confusion. "What's the matter? You all look troubled. Is there a problem?"

"Oh, no, Cap'n." Ben approached him with a smile. "Just a silly quarrel. Can I show you around?"

Spencer allowed himself to be led away. Discreetly, he studied Ben as he ran the conversation he'd overheard in his head. These men were certainly sharper than he'd supposed. Somehow, they'd been playing Kendrick for a fool. But why did they hide Nellie from him? And if he saw so little of the woman, how was it that he could speak so glowingly of her? *Damn.* Nothing made sense, and he couldn't ask them any questions without revealing the fact that he'd spied on them.

Ben showed him various spots along the river that yielded good fishing. Before Spencer realised it, he found they'd made a circle and was back at the camp. He caught a glimpse of a figure in skirts amongst the men waiting for them by the cookhouse.

"I believe supper's ready, Cap'n," Ben said.

"Good. I'm famished."

Ben led the way to the cookhouse and stopped at the far end of the table. Spencer tried to keep track of the female, without being obvious, but the men moved, cleverly obstructing his view every time. Once they were all seated, he couldn't see anything of her at all. The situation amused him, and the impulse to stir a little alarm proved irresistible.

Just then the smell of mouthwatering food distracted him. Tom plopped two large plates bearing thick slices of cooked meat on the table. All at once, hands hovered over the plates, and as Spencer blinked, only two pieces of the meat were left.

What appalling table manners. Well, what did he expect? These men lived a hard life. They had no time for refinements.

Spencer leaned back and watched Ben reach for the meat, the larger piece. He surprised Spencer by placing it gently on Spencer's plate, then took the last piece for himself.

"Thank you." Before Spencer could say more, Tom arrived with a stack of damper which he tossed out to the men, then retreated, to return with his own platter of food. He took his seat and like the others, tore into his meal like he'd not eaten in a month.

Spencer took a cautious first bite. His teeth sank easily into the tender and juicy meat. He chewed slowly and closed his eyes in bliss. Perhaps he should consider taking Tom back with him to Parramatta. It'd be good to dine on excellent fare again.

When he opened his eyes, he was surprised to note the other men were looking at him with suspicion. *God.* What was wrong with them? How did they get the idea he was hungry for their Nellie? Perhaps he should take a closer look at this jewel of a woman.

He cleared his throat. "Can we have the young lady sit here, next to me, please? I'd be grateful for some female conversation."

Silence fell and all movement ceased. Then Ben stood and walked to the other end of the table. The men turned their heads, following his progress.

"Nellie," Ben said, "the cap'n wants you to sit next to him. Come along, dear. Don't be afraid."

Smears of dirt and grime that covered the woman's face made it impossible for Spencer to gauge the woman's attractions. In another moment, he wished he'd left well enough alone. The woman came with a peculiar scent, a ripe smell that forced him to take shallow breaths.

This is Kendrick's divine cook and great housekeeper? How did he stand her? How could she be worth one hundred pounds? Damned swindler.

Ben helped Nellie settle into his seat, placed her plate before her, then grabbed his own plate and moved away to take a seat at the other end of the table.

Spencer decided it wasn't Nellie's fault that she fell so far short of Kendrick's glowing description. He smiled at her and reached into his pocket. "I've a present for you."

Nellie gave a squeal of delight at the green and gold ribbons he handed her. She began to fix her hair. Surprised by this somewhat childish behaviour, Spencer glanced at the men. They glared at him.

He shrugged away the men's hostility and tried to draw Nellie into a conversation. She made no attempt to answer his questions, but giggled at his words. Apparently, he was the only one to find her half-witted and unappealing.

The settlement had one white unattached woman to four or five unmarried men. He could understand how these men would be possessive with the one woman in their midst. But Kendrick?

How had this woman managed to snare her faithful band of admirers? A short while later, he lost all interest to know.

He swallowed his last bite and gave a satisfied sigh. "I enjoyed that. It's the best meal I've had in a long time. Thank you—Tom—isn't it?"

Tom smirked. "Aye sir, and thank you kindly. I've always had a knack with cooking."

Artie jumped to his feet. "Don't you boast, you rascal! You learned from our Kate. You watched and you learned from her."

Rory held on to Artie's arm, forcing him back to his seat. "Artie, leave it. 'Tis all right."

"But 'tis not all right!" He faced Spencer. "Kate could cook better, much better. Isn't that so, Ben?"

Spencer turned to the woman at his side. "Isn't your name Nellie?"

She giggled, then surprised him by answering, "I'm Nellie."

"Who's Kate?"

No one said a word.

Spencer fixed his gaze on Ben. "Who—is—Kate?"

Ben shrugged. "Kate O'Neal. Lieutenant Kendrick's woman."

Spencer blinked. "So where is she?"

"With the lieutenant, I reckon."

"Kate's our friend," Artie said. "She looks after us. We likes it when she's here. Can we have her back?"

Spencer looked at Ben. "What's he talking about now?"

Ben took a deep breath, then gave a brief account of Kate's arrival at Red Roo, her short stay and her hasty departure.

Spencer couldn't remember when he'd been angrier. *Damn Kendrick! The bastard shall pay for this.*

Kate planted the empty laundry basket on her hip and headed back home. She rounded the corner and crashed into a hard body. The basket flew from her grasp while she staggered for balance. Two strong hands reached out to steady her. She looked a long way up, into a pair of grey eyes in a clean-shaven face.

The man apologised. "Are you all right?"

"Yes, sir." She freed herself from his hold.

"I'm looking for Lieutenant Kendrick. Do you—"

"The fourth door, that way."

"Can you do me a favour? Tell him Captain Spencer is here to see him?"

Spencer? The object of Jeremy's bitterness these days? The captain didn't strike her as Satan. She nodded, picked up the laundry basket and walked on.

Kendrick was still abed. She gave him a good shake. "You have a visitor."

"Tell whoever it is to come back later."

"He says he's Captain Spencer."

Jeremy sat up. "Spencer?"

"Yes."

"Damn! He must have found out. How?"

"What?"

"Quiet! Let me think. Damn! You've got to go, but don't you worry, Kate. This is just another temporary setback. Give it a few months, and I'll have you back, you'll see."

"What are you saying?" Her hands turned clammy. She didn't like the way Jeremy avoided her eyes.

"Pack your things. I'll see to Spencer. Damn."

"Pack?" Her heart thumped wildly

"Yes, pack. Are you deaf?" he shouted. "You'll be leaving with Spencer."

"Am I being re-assigned, Jeremy?" she asked, but Jeremy had left.

Kate started packing. Her hands shook as she thrust her clothes and other possessions into a pillow case. After her experience of freedom to do as she wished in Red Roo, life with

Jeremy became almost unbearable. There was no respite. Before, he'd taken to spending time at the Officers' Club after his garrison duties. Now, he stayed home and took his temper out on her. She started praying for a new protector. With a new master, she could hope for a kinder man, but she hadn't counted on God answering her prayers quite so promptly.

Jeremy came back cursing. He searched through some papers in his valise, selected a document and thrust it at her. "Give that to him. Go on. Damned sarcastic bastard is waiting for you."

Kate accepted the paper and headed for the door.

"Now, don't you worry, sweet. This is only temporary—"

She closed the door behind her, cutting out the rest of his words. She approached the man who'd almost knocked her down. "Captain Spencer? I'm Kate O'Neal."

He ignored the document she extended. He gripped her wrist and pulled her closer. With his other hand, he gently turned her face left, then right.

Kate resisted the urge to jerk her head away. She closed her eyes and fought back tears of humiliation and rising despair. *What now?*

Chapter 17

Nicholas Spencer noted the dark clouds gathering on the western horizon. At a road junction, he pulled on the reins and guided his horses into making a left turn. He held the reins lightly as he settled down for the long drive to Red Roo. He didn't think it'd be long before the woman by his side made a move on him. It was his experience that women, whether rich or poor, would use a man to ease her way in the world. He didn't think Kate O'Neal would be any different. The journey north should prove interesting.

Minutes lengthened into the half hour, by which time, it struck Spencer that he might as well not be there for all the interest she showed in him. He was not used to being ignored, and he didn't like the feeling.

He turned to stare at her. His stare had been known to cause his subordinates to shiver in their boots, but it didn't work on the woman. She had her gaze fixed on the road ahead, and he didn't think she would shift that gaze unless he made her. He noted her clenched hands with the knuckles showing white. Her bruises could not hide the pallor on her face. No, he didn't think her a beauty, and it was a pity she was so small for he liked his women big.

She was a puzzle. That was all she was to him: a puzzle. Did she give Kendrick cause to beat her? And why would he go to such lengths to keep her, if she gave him problems? What about the men at the farm? They wanted her back too.

Questions and more questions, and he knew he'd have to work to get the answers from her.

They'd travelled an hour before Spencer decided he would break their silence. "Aren't you curious to know where we're going?"

"You'll tell me when you're ready."

"I'm taking you to Red Roo."

She turned to look at him finally, but just as quickly, she looked away, but not before he saw a glow of pleasure in her eyes.

Ah, a reaction at last. "No questions?" he asked.

She faced him. "What do you want me to say?"

Spencer laughed softly. "I'm not sure."

She held his gaze for a moment, then she was back to staring at the road ahead.

Lightning flashed in the distance, and a low rumble of thunder swooped past them. He heard a muffled gurgle of laughter.

"It's a beautiful day," she said.

A beautiful day? With a storm about to overtake them? Kate O'Neal was not what he'd expected, but she was certainly an interesting woman.

The wind shifted and took the rain clouds with it. Fifty yards into Red Roo, a voice burst from the trees, "It's Kate. Hey, fellas! It's Kate!"

They came hurrying out of the woods. Ben, Rory, Harry . . . Spencer named them all in his mind without hesitation. He stopped the horses, watched the approaching men for a moment more, then nodded at Kate.

She jumped lightly to the ground, picked up her skirts and ran headlong into Sam's arms, and then Ben's. The men closed around her, and laughter filled the air. It looked to him like a beloved member of the family returned to its fold, not a harlot reunited with her lovers. Spencer shook his head. He was no nearer to solving the puzzle that was Kate O'Neal.

Kate could see curiosity reflected in Captain Spencer's eyes whenever he looked at her. She searched for that glimmer of lust in them, but couldn't find any, and for this she was grateful. Sam gave up his humpy for her while the captain stayed at the cookhouse. When Spencer took his leave the next morning, life at the farm returned to what it was before Jeremy took her away.

The fellas told her they liked Spencer well enough. He was easier to get along with than Jeremy. And if he kept his word to give them a share of the harvest, they might, if they were careful, be able to save a little nest egg for their future.

"I don't believe in no gifts," Harry said. "I tell you, he's just softening us up so we'll work our hearts out for him. Then after we've done it, wham!" He slammed a fist into his palm. "We'll see his true self then."

"What about the grog and the tobacco? He didn't have to give them to us," Peter said.

Harry snorted. "Don't you know nothing? You catch more flies with honey."

"Aw, Harry, you and your suspicions!" Sam said. "He brought Kate back to us, didn't he? And he ain't showing no interest in Nellie neither. And if we want to stay together, we got to work the land anyways, be it for bloody Kendrick or your tricky Spencer."

Ben held up a hand. "We work as usual. If he hand us coins after we sell the harvest, then we work harder. Otherwise, we don't."

"Maybe we should test him," Kate said. "See if his word is any good."

"Aye," Harry said. "Let's test the damned bastard! You'll see I'm right."

"How?" Ben asked.

They would cultivate cabbages, Kate decided. She made the men take turns to water the seeds they planted. When the weeds grew faster than the cabbage seedlings, she made them help her remove the weeds and squash the snails and slugs. The men grumbled—they still had a lot of land to clear, they protested—but did as she bade them.

Summer lingered through early fall. Occasionally, Kate spent the day with Nellie. The two of them would roam the vast property. The first time they went out together, Nellie helped her pick mushrooms for fun.

"No!" Nellie cried and knocked the mushrooms off Kate's hands. "Bad mushrooms. They make you sick."

"What?" Kate pretended to frown. "Mushrooms are bad?"

Nellie giggled and shook her head. "I find good mushrooms for you, Kate." She ran off into the trees, came back a while later, with a handful of mushrooms. Kate couldn't see the difference between these and those she'd thrown away. She got rid of these too, when Nellie wasn't looking. She wouldn't risk poisoning the fellas, not on Nellie's word.

On another day, Nellie took her to the northeastern corner of the property, where two low trees sagged under a burden of yellow berries.

"We can eat these! See?"

Before Kate could stop her, Nellie had popped a handful of berries into her mouth. She chewed, spat out the pips and swallowed the rest. Then she looked at Kate like a child seeking approval. Kate was looking for words to caution her, when Nellie broke into peals of laughter. "It's all right! It's good. Have some!" She held out her other hand cupping berries.

Kate grabbed her wrist. "Listen Nellie, you mustn't eat these berries. It's—"

Nellie wrenched herself free, then began waving and calling out to someone a distance away. In a flash, Nellie raced away from her.

"Nellie, you come back here!" she shouted, but Nellie ignored her. Kate's belly knotted. Was Nellie running to meet her black fella friends? But how could she tell they weren't strangers at this distance? *Damn.* She needed to have a serious talk with the fellas. Somehow, Nellie must be protected from her trusting ways.

Kate gave chase, then stumbled to a stop. Two black figures had emerged from the trees to intercept Nellie. One held a long spear. Kate's instinct told her to flee, but she couldn't abandon Nellie. She started running again. She had to protect her friend, fight the natives with her bare hands, if she had to.

Kate gasped when Nellie slammed into one black figure, but laughter rang out, not the screams of terror she'd expected. Relief washed over her. She took in large gulps of air, then slowly approached the group of three. At closer range, she froze in astonishment. The strange clothes she thought the black fellas wore, were nothing but paint on black skin.

Holy Mary, Mother of God! How dared anybody walk around in broad daylight, naked! A grown man and woman too. Did they have no shame? She averted her gaze, fixing it to their black faces, and suffered another shock: the broad features and dark curly hair were foreign and frightening. Only the sight of the native woman stroking Nellie's hair in a motherly way assured Kate she had nothing to fear.

Nellie broke away from the woman. She ran to Kate and dragged her to meet her friends. She insisted Kate and the native woman hug each other, then laughed when they did so. Nellie then turned to the man and offered him her clutch of berries. He popped them into his mouth, smiled at Nellie and made some foreign sounds. Nellie responded with sounds of her own. They seemed to understand each other.

Before Kate could close her gaping mouth, the two black fellas said their farewells and went on their way.

The encounter settled Kate's fears about hostile natives. It also persuaded her to try Nellie's mushrooms and berries to spice up her cooking.

A week afterwards, Kate was preparing to go to bed when she heard a noise.

"Are you still awake, Kate?" Rory asked.

She came forward to greet him. "What's wrong?"

"Can we talk?"

"Of course."

"Just hear me out, all right? The fellas and I—we've been talking. We love Nellie, we care for her and all that . . . but . . . You're no longer Kendrick's woman, Kate, and we wondered . . . I wonder if you'd be me woman? I promise I'll be taking good care of you."

Kate's palms became sweaty. "Oh—Will the others be asking me too?"

"We drew straws to see who gets to ask first. It ain't right that you should be alone when you can be with us, one of us at least—"

"Rory, I don't know about it being right or not. I just know I like being by myself for now. Jeremy hurt me, and I think I have to get over him for a bit first before I go with another man. You know I like you very much. If I had to choose a man to be with, it'd be you, but I don't want to be with another man. At least, not yet. Can't we stay as friends? Good friends?"

"Oh Kate—"

She stretched out both her hands to Rory. "Please?"

He sighed, then clasped her hands in his.

"Will you tell the others? I'd like us all to carry on as before. For now?"

Kate feared to face the men the next day, but they treated her no differently from before. She knew the question would come up again, but for now, she refused to look too far into the future.

The days in May grew shorter and colder. One day, Kate helped Roger butcher a joey behind the cookhouse. She was directing him to chop up the bones for her pot of soup when she heard Sam call out, "Kate! Where are you?"

Alarmed by the urgent tone, she hurried to the front of the cookhouse. She stopped and gaped. David stood holding an unconscious Ben in his arms. "On your bed?" David asked.

She nodded. "What happened?"

"He got bit by a snake."

"By this bloody viper!" Sam held up a cloth bag and shook it. A dead snake fell out. He stomped on it. "I'm gonna chop it up into tiny bits and feed them to the fishes, if Ben dies. No. I'm gonna chop it up anyways."

David looked at Kate. "Please, don't let Ben die."

Kate hoped her fear didn't show. "Damn! I don't know anything about a snake bite, David. I'll certainly do my best."

She cleaned the wound, then sat by Ben's side. Later when he began to shift restlessly, she felt his forehead and found it unusually warm. She used rags soaked in water to cool him down, but they only worked for a little while. Ben groaned and tossed around on the pallet, and Kate chafed at her helplessness. As when she feared for her mother's life, she got on her knees and started to pray, "Holy Mary, Mother of God, pray for us sinners . . . Our Father who art in heaven . . ."

Nellie's scream startled her. In the next instant, a whirlwind came through the door.

"Ben, Ben," Nellie cried.

"Don't, Nellie!" Kate shouted, but Nellie had thrown herself on top of Ben. Quickly, she peeled Nellie off.

David, who had followed hard on Nellie's heels, picked up the snake. "Look, Nellie, let's bury the bad snake that bit Ben. Come along. Ben needs his rest to get better. You want him to get better, don't you?"

Nellie froze, her gaze fixed on the snake dangling from David's hand. Then she gasped, broke free and dashed out of the hut.

"David! Go after her!" Kate cried. "She's upset, see she doesn't hurt herself."

David hurried after Nellie, and Kate returned to Ben's side. Poor Ben was burning up, yet shivered as if from a chill. She covered him with another blanket. More time passed. Her prayers and her efforts to cool him down didn't seem to work. She feared Ben would die, and soon. The fellas must have sensed her fears. Why else did they seem to be already in mourning?

Damn, damn, damn! She wished Ben would open his eyes and laugh. Let him claim he was just playing a trick on them all. She wouldn't care about being frightened needlessly. She just wanted him well. Then she heard loud, angry voices outside the cookhouse. Curious, she left Ben's side to see what was happening. Nellie and Roger appeared to be fighting over a black fella: Nellie pulling him towards the cookhouse by one arm, and Roger holding him back by his other. The black fella carried no weapon, only a dilly bag of woven reeds he wore on a twine at his waist.

Peter shouted, "Roger, let the black fella take a look at Ben."

Tom turned on him. "Are you daft?. What can he do that Kate's not already done for Ben? Well, I ain't having him near Ben! He's nothing but a savage!"

"Tom's right. Look at him," Roger cried. "What can he know of healing? Likely, the ignorant sod will kill Ben with his poison.

187

Is that what you want?"

Artie tugged at Roger's arm. "You're making Nellie cry."

"You silly bugger." Sam gave David a push. "Why couldn't you have stopped Nellie before she got to him?"

"Never mind that," David said. "If Ben's going to die, how can the black fella hurt him any more?"

"Don't be stupid," Tom said. "Ben should die in peace, if he's to die. I don't want no ignorant savage killing him with no poison."

"Stupid? Are you calling me stupid?" David took a threatening step towards Tom.

"Quiet," Rory yelled. "Let the black fella go, Roger! Watch him closely, if you must, to see he does Ben no harm. But just you remember, he's Nellie's friend."

"Rory, the savage is naked," Harry said as Roger released the black fella. "I don't think it's proper to have him around the women—"

"Not now, Harry," Rory said.

"But—"

Rory and the others hurried after Nellie as she towed her friend past Kate. She babbled gibberish as she pointed to the dead snake on the floor.

Tom roared, "Damned bastard has turned our Nellie native!"

David grabbed him before he could punch the black fella.

"Enough!" Kate shouted. "I will not wait for Ben to die! And that's what we've been doing all this time: waiting for him to die, but no more! Tom, Roger, you leave the black fella alone. Let him help Ben. Don't you think he'd know how to deal with a snake bite? For God's sake, he grew up with snakes. Now, all of you, out!"

"I don't want nobody killing our Ben," Tom insisted. "Ben would do the same for me."

"Out!" Kate pointed to the door.

Tom hesitated, then obeyed.

Kate kissed Nellie. "Thank you, Nellie. Will you wait outside so your friend and I can help Ben?"

The black fella made a poultice out of the contents of his dilly bag and put it over the snake bite. He changed the pack every few hours. By early morning, Kate fancied Ben's sleep had become easier; his brow felt cool to her touch.

"Kate?" a voice said.

She turned and smiled at Rory. "I think Ben's going to be all right now."

"Good. I'll tell the others."

With Ben on the road to recovery, the men embraced the black fella for their best mate. They christened him "Johnnie" and shared what was left of their grog with him. Kate shook her head at the change in their attitude. Only Harry remained vexed. He continued to press a pair of his pants on Johnnie, but the black fella only laughed, rejecting the garment.

A day after Ben refused to stay in bed, Johnnie announced he was leaving. The men tried to dissuade him. They hadn't perfected their new skill in fashioning a boomerang or throwing it yet. Johnnie only smiled. The next morning he was gone, and Kate never saw him again.

Spencer was in a foul mood. Nothing seemed to please him these days—not even the knowledge that Kendrick was on his way to Norfolk Island, to take up his new posting there, where he'd have little hope of advancing his career in His Majesty's Army and even less opportunity of making a fortune.

He'd known from the start that Kendrick's property would be a burden. Now that he'd arranged for his sergeant to deliver the workers there their monthly food rations, Spencer considered himself free of his obligations, free to resume the life he'd led before he ever set eyes on Kendrick. But questions about Kate

O'Neal gave him no peace. He could not forget her striking green eyes either.

So, much to his chagrin, he took upon himself the task of delivering the food rations to Red Roo in July. He berated himself for a fool. He could be indoors enjoying a good fire instead of undertaking a long journey in winter's cold to deliver supplies to a bunch of convicts.

David, Peter and Roger met him not far from their dwellings. They offered him muttered greetings, then followed him on foot to the cookhouse.

"Unload the wagon, Cap'n?" David asked.

He nodded. "Where are the women?"

The men looked at each other.

"Kate's down by the river," David said.

Spencer barely heard the words, for he'd seen her emerge from a shaded glade. Ben and Rory walked beside her. The picture of Kate O'Neal laughing with the men didn't sit well with him. Not at all.

She glanced his way and came to a stop. Her companions did the same, and their laughter died. Slowly, they walked towards him. All three murmured a greeting. He gave them a nodbut kept his gaze on Kate.

She'd cleaned up very nicely. No longer sporting signs of Kendrick's brutality, she looked a tasty morsel. And he hadn't been mistaken about her green eyes. They were indeed magnificent.

Her expression changed, turned wary, and he realised he'd been staring.

"Cap'n," Rory said. "Can I show you around the farm?"

He was glad for the interruption, but only for a moment. He didn't like the expression on Rory's face, as if he had a claim on Kate, and resented Spencer's interest.

"Perhaps later," he said dismissively, then turned to Kate.

"Can I have a cup of water? It's been a long drive."

She lowered her gaze. "Of course."

He followed her to the cookhouse. She told him to take a seat and went to fetch his drink.

She came back with a cup of water. He thanked her, waited till she was seated, then sat next to her. He drank from the cup, while he watched Ben, Sam and Peter carry the food rations he'd brought with him into the cookhouse and stack them against the wall. When the wagon was empty, he suggested they return to what they were doing.

At last, he had the privacy he craved. He wrapped his hands around the cup and pretended to be lost in his thoughts.

"Excuse me," Kate said, getting to her feet.

He placed his hand over hers on the table. "Don't go."

She sat down again. He moved his legs casually so his knees nudged hers. She shifted her legs away.

He looked at her as he drained the cup and placed it on the table. "So what's been happening here?"

"Um . . . Er . . . the other day, Ben was bitten by a snake and—" She stopped, took a deep breath and began again without the stammers.

He remembered her composure when they first met. There was little of it in evidence now. He watched her mouth move as she shaped her words and found himself enchanted. She was relating an incident—something about an aborigine helping Ben with a snake bite. The tale didn't particularly interest him. Leisurely, he got to his feet and walked to the other side of the table so he could face her. He sat down and stretched out his legs till his boot leaned against her foot.

"I'm sorry," she said, moving her legs aside before returning to her tale.

He waited a short while before he moved his legs again, in search of hers. The colour came and went on her face. She kept shifting her legs away, and her words became disjointed. He smiled into her eyes, then returned his gaze to her lips. She lifted her hand and nervously brushed the corners of her mouth, as if to remove food crumbs lodged there. He couldn't help it; he laughed. Her expression became alarmed. He stopped laughing, looked away, to allow her time to recover.

". . . and Ben's fine now," she said, jumping to her feet. "Here's Rory to show you around the farm. Please excuse me. Supper won't get cooked by itself."

Kate waited till the captain and Rory disappeared from view before she hurried into the back room and quickly cleared it of her possessions. The captain could have her bed all to himself, with her blessing. She moved into Harry's humpy, the one farthest from the cookhouse. She was sure Harry wouldn't mind bedding down elsewhere that night.

She had a word with Ben. "At supper, keep the seat next to you for me, and make sure you sit as far from the captain as you can."

He gave her a long look, then shook his head. "Kate, he'll only ask very nicely for you to sit next to him."

"Never mind that. Just do as I ask. Please?"

She served supper, then quickly took her seat beside Ben. The captain didn't object, as Ben had suggested he would do. In fact he ignored her all through the meal while he concentrated his efforts on the men, charming them. He insisted on opening four bottles of rum he'd brought with him. The men didn't talk very much at first, but the liquor soon loosened their tongues. They began trading stories, even laughed with the captain as if they were the greatest of mates. She felt let down, as if her friends had deserted her for the enemy.

Then the plates were clean and the rum bottles empty. Ben said it was late and suggested it was time they retired. The men, still laughing, pushed the bench back and got to their feet. She did the same, eager to be gone.

"Kate. Please stay," Spencer said.

She froze. She didn't think it likely the fellas would mistake the captain's words for anything but a command. In another instant the fellas and Nellie were gone, and she was alone with the captain.

He extended a hand. "Come. We'll be more private in the back room."

CHAPTER 18

Kate was barely aware of the trees that drifted past her, or of the wagon wheels rumbling on. A display of the most spectacular views could not have commanded her attention. She was so angry with herself she could have wept.

If only she'd used her head, she'd not be in this pickle. She'd still be with the fellas at Red Roo—safe—not on her way to God knows where, facing an uncertain future again. She was a bloody eejit!

How could she have forgotten what Josie said—that not even a desperate man would rut with a slab of dead meat? She could have pretended to be just that, and Captain Spencer would've been disgusted. He'd toss her out of his bed and never look at her again.

But she'd acted the wanton. She hadn't just welcomed his bloody advances; she'd attacked and devoured him like a ravening beast! *Eejit!*

Night had fallen when the captain drew the wagon to a stop before a large house. He helped her to the ground, grabbed her small bag of belongings and led her to the front door. "This is my home, Dunover. Welcome, my sweet, I hope you'll be very happy here with me."

Inside the house, he lit two oil lamps. "Wait here," he said and moved away, taking one lamp with him. He returned some minutes later and guided her up the stairs. Exhaustion weighed her down. She stumbled.

He steadied her with one hand. "Careful!"

Her eyes teared at his concerned tone. They entered a room. She saw a huge four-poster bed, and it blinded her to all else. A fitting place for a trollop, she thought and cringed in shame.

He indicated the pitcher on the dresser. "You'll find towels in the top drawer, if you'd like a wash. Rest yourself, my dear, while I fetch us something to eat. A cup of tea for you?"

Kate nodded, then waited till he left before she helped herself to some water. She sponged off the dirt and sweat, shed off all but her underclothes and crept into bed.

It was morning when she woke. The captain lay beside her, still asleep. She studied the fine lines on his face in the morning light. Nicholas Spencer was better looking than Jeremy and was likely six to ten years older. Suddenly he stirred. Kate quickly closed her eyes, feigning sleep. She tensed when she felt him playing with her hair. Her heart raced when he nibbled on her ear, then his lips were upon her mouth, his tongue seeking entrance. A warmth started in the pit of her belly. It spread outward, heightening her senses, making her forget all but a rising need for fulfillment. She wrapped her arms around his neck, pulled him closer and opened her mouth, prepared to yield all she had to give.

He ended the kiss and sighed. In the next instant, he threw off the bedcovers and got out of bed, naked. "It's early yet," he said, without any hint of embarrassment. "You don't have to get up, but I've some errands to run. Make yourself at home, sweet. I'll be back soon."

After a quick wash, he threw on fresh clothes and put on his boots. "You'll be all right on your own, won't you? You won't be afraid?"

"I'll be fine, Captain Spencer."

"Nicholas. I'm Nicholas." He smiled. "You might like to look the house over—make changes, if you like. I'll see you later, sweet." He gave her a hard kiss and left.

It took several minutes for her cheeks to cool. She'd turned into someone she couldn't recognise. Refusing to dwell on her strange response to the captain, she got out of bed. She threw open his wardrobe. Army uniforms took up half the space. The silky feel of the good quality fabric reminded her of the clothes the Rustands wore, nothing that Jeremy owned.

Dressed, she went downstairs to the kitchen. Having seen his clothes, she decided he was a man of means and, knowing he held the rank of captain, expected his household to be overrun with servants, but there was no one in the kitchen. She peeked into the large cooking pot held by a chain hung on a hook in the cold fireplace. Did the captain expect her to cook, or merely to supervise the cooking?

She waited a while for a servant to show, but the silence that surrounded her suggested there was no one else in the house with her. She found bread and cheese in the larder, broke her fast and continued exploring. The backyard was shaded by several tall eucalyptus trees. She squinted into the distance, in every direction, and saw scrub and more scrub and a scattering of tall trees. There was no sign of another dwelling to indicate the presence of a neighbour.

She stepped back into the house and, after a thorough examination, decided the captain cared for two rooms only—his bedroom and his library. Recalling his parting words, she wondered if he expected her to make changes to his home.

In the library, she made a list of things lacking in the house. The ideas came easily—curtains and wallpaper, carpets and rugs. She recalled the kitchen in the Rustands' household and began to note down every piece of equipment she remembered there. The list grew until she could think of nothing else to add.

She left the desk and examined the rows of books on the bookshelves. The important sounding titles made her take out a volume and turn the pages. She recognised many of the words, but not enough for the sentences to make sense.

She tensed at the sound of wheels crunching on gravel. She looked out the window and heaved a sigh of relief. It was the captain, not visitors, and he had returned with two women, convicts to judge by their clothes. She returned the book to the shelf and tucked her list into her pocket and went to open the front door for her new master.

He stood talking to the two women at the back of the wagon, glanced her way, then tossed a few more words at the women before he left them. With a smile on his face, he strode up to her and swept her off her feet. Then he kissed her.

"Missed me?"

Kate mumbled something, incensed that he could be so indiscreet. Didn't he know the two approaching women could see and hear him?

He chuckled and though he set her down, kept one arm around her waist. "My dear, this is Betty Wilson and Jane Blake, our cook and housekeeper. Ladies, this is Kate O'Neal. You're to take your orders from Mistress O'Neal. Is that clear?"

Kate started. "Don't you already have a cook and housekeeper?"

"I thought you'd be more comfortable in the company of women."

"But I don't mind—"

He put a finger on her lips. "I do. Show the ladies to their rooms, my sweet."

"The ones next to the kitchen?"

He nodded. "Tell them what you want done, then we'll go shopping. You need some new clothes."

Kate's gaze lingered on the two woollen dresses, before moving on to the heavy velvet gown in green and black. The captain had picked these for her himself, and lots more. There were the underclothes, a pile of them, as well as gloves, kerchiefs and a shawl. He had also had her fitted for footwear—a pair of comfortable slippers and soft leather boots. She pinched herself to be sure she wasn't dreaming.

"Do you want anything else?" he asked.

Kate hesitated, afraid he'd think her greedy, but finally decided she needed to be practical. "May I have two more gowns?"

He arched a brow, and Kate hung her head. He tilted her chin up with one finger and smiled. "Of course, my dear. Which ones would you like?"

Sure, she loved those beautiful clothes he'd picked for her, but she couldn't possibly wear them every day. She needed sturdy garments that would weather countless washing. She went through a stack of rugged-looking gowns, picked out two and passed them to Nicholas.

He stared at the gowns and frowned. "Are you sure you want these?"

"Oh yes."

He nodded. "Anything else?"

Kate bit her lip.

"What is it?"

She blushed. The captain had been generous. Should she suggest he dig deeper into his pockets? She straightened her shoulders and handed him the list she'd written earlier.

He looked over the list, then he frowned once more.

"Is it my writing?" she asked. "Can you not read it?"

"The writing's fine." He gave her a sharp look. "I didn't know you could write."

"Just a little."

He reached out and ran a finger gently down her cheek. "These are things for the house, sweet. Is there nothing else you want for yourself?"

She unclenched her fists and shook her head.

He smiled. "You're certainly full of surprises, my dear."

Kate decided she must be the most ungrateful woman in the world. How could she be so dissatisfied with the life of luxury that Nicholas had provided her? She stared out the library window and recalled a pair of lovebirds that Lady Rustand kept as pets. She'd thought them lucky. Now she wondered if they felt no gratitude either, not for the splendour of their cage, or the emptiness of their pampered lives.

She approached the bookshelf, returned a book that made no sense to her and paced the floor again. It'd be several hours before Nicholas came home. Time certainly dragged when there was nothing to do.

She heard faint laughter coming from the kitchen. If she had her druthers, she'd get rid of both Betty and Jane and do all the cooking and cleaning herself.

"I'll be cook," Betty had said that first morning, out of Nicholas' hearing. "Jane here can be maid."

Kate hesitated, then slowly nodded. "Do you want me to show you—"

Betty snorted. "I got eyes. I'll find things on me own. You better toddle along to the master before he comes panting after you."

Kate shrank at her tone and walked away. There would be plenty of other opportunities to make friends with the two women, when they were in a better mood.

Used to getting up early, Kate thought to give the two women a helping hand that second morning. She found them still asleep. Later she watched Betty prepare breakfast. "You're making dumplings?" she said.

"What's wrong with dumplings?"

Kate disregarded the icy tone. "Nothing. Maybe two boiled eggs—"

"I like dumplings," Betty insisted.

Later, Kate complimented Betty on the breakfast and thought to share a cooking secret with her. "You'd get a better dumpling if you—"

"Better? Are you trying to learn me me job?" Betty glared at her. "Who do think you are?"

Kate fled the kitchen. Later, in the backyard, by the kitchen window, she overheard Betty talking to Jane. "Bloody bitch! I been cooking all of me life, you know, and no one's ever complained about me food. And now here she comes, telling me how to do me job! She can keep her bloody ideas to herself! Bitch!"

"She ain't so bad," Jane said. "She helped me with the fireplace—"

"Don't you be fooled, now. She was snide about me dumplings. Thinks she can do better. I tell you, that girl's just too full of herself! Who's she? Naught but another bloody convict. Sure, she's spreading her legs for the cap'n. How does that make her a better cook than me?"

So long as Betty did her job and Nicholas didn't complain about the meals, Kate told herself to ignore Betty and keep out of her way.

She turned her attention to Jane, an easy-going woman. With a bit of help, Jane would make an excellent housemaid.

"Jane, have you forgotten? Clean the fireplace before you dust the room—"

"Betty says you're just pushing me around to feel important. We do our jobs all right. Why don't you do yours? Go pleasure the cap'n and leave us be."

Kate recoiled in shock, then walked stiffly away, vowing she'd get Nicholas to send the two women back to the government, back to the Parramatta Women's Factory where they could rot for all she cared. Or she could have them flogged. That would teach them to mind their sharp tongues.

When her temper cooled, she realised she was behaving like a child. She couldn't send the women away out of spite. Besides, she didn't want Nicholas to think she couldn't handle the household.

Bored with nothing to do, Kate left the library and wandered around the yard. The barren landscape compared poorly to the well-kept gardens she knew at Rustand Park. She recalled the flowers: their wonderful variety of scent and colours. Indeed, if she planted daffodils and tulips now, they'd be blooming come spring.

She went to the garden shed and dug out a shovel. Marking out a patch of ground not far from the front door, she began to dig. The hours passed. The sun beat down on her, and her clothes began to stick to her skin while the rocks and stones she'd removed from the dirt piled high behind her.

"Kate?"

She twisted around and looked up. "Nicholas! How nice. You're home early."

"Not earlier than usual. What are you doing?"

"Gardening," she said and smiled. "I'm going to—"

He helped her to her feet. "Kate, you're not to toil like this. It's not necessary, my sweet."

"But—"

"If you want a garden, tell me. I'll send a couple of men over, to take care of it. I won't have you spoiling your hands with calluses or tiring yourself for no good reason."

She wiped a trickle of sweat on her face with the end of her sleeve. "I'm only trying to keep busy, Nicholas."

He brushed away the spots of dirt speckling her face. He kissed her warmly and gave a rueful laugh. "I've a better idea how to keep you busy," he said in a suddenly husky voice. "Come with me."

Unable to stay in the bedchamber all day, and dissuaded from working on the garden, Kate spent her time in the library, away from Betty and Jane.

She closed her eyes and leaned back into her chair. The thick book she held open on her lap made her head ache. How could she be this discontented with her life of leisure? She must be daft. Never mind. Nicholas would be home soon.

The library door opened. She looked up, startled, wondering if her thoughts had conjured Nicholas up in reality.

Spencer walked into the room, stooped low and kissed her. "You look vexed, sweet. Is anything wrong?"

Kate closed her book and held it up. "I can't make any sense out of this. I swear, Nicholas, I'm about to toss your fancy book out the window—"

He chuckled, relieved Kate of the book and glanced at its title. "Hmmm. Maybe I should get you a few of Mrs. Radcliffe's romances." He settled in a comfortable chair next to her. "Who taught you how to read and write, Kate?"

"Mistress Smith, the governess." She reached out and plucked the book back from Spencer.

"Governess! You had a governess?"

She giggled. "Don't be silly!" In a few short sentences, she explained her special lessons with Mistress Smith, governess to the Rustands' two young daughters.

Nicholas held her hand. "Would you like to continue with your schooling?"

"What? I mean—"

He kissed the knuckles of her hand. "I could get you a teacher. Would you like that?"

"Oh yes!"

Kate thought Nicholas had forgotten all about her school lessons when, in the middle of the week, he brought home a tall woman with a pointed chin and a sharp nose. He introduced her as Mrs. Johnson, her teacher, and left her in the stranger's care.

"It's Captain Spencer's wish," Mrs. Johnson said, "that you receive an education, Mistress O'Neal. I've assured him you'll get one from me. I'm a woman of my word. Do you understand me?"

"Yes, ma'am."

Four hours every day, for five days a week, rain or shine, Mrs. Johnson called at Dunover. She drilled Kate in the rudiments of reading, writing and arithmetic. Suddenly, Kate's days became full, and she was happy.

Unlike Governess Smith, Mrs. Johnson treated her like a grown woman, but she never allowed Kate to forget their differences. She was the teacher and a free-woman, and Kate merely a convict girl, the captain's whim for the moment. Kate ignored her attitude, told herself to learn all she could from the woman. Soon she found her teacher had less and less to teach her. She'd always been quick with numbers, and often she'd have the answers ready before Mrs. Johnson even finished presenting her problems. "History" made her life miserable, for she couldn't understand why she had to learn stupid things that made no difference in her life. How would knowing why King John signed the Magna Carta benefit her?

The knock on the front door startled her. Nobody but Mrs. Johnson ever called at Dunover, and Kate didn't expect to see that lady again till the next day. She waited for Jane to answer the knock, but when the rapping sounded again, she went to answer it. The two men at the doorstep introduced themselves as Sergeants Cross and Latham.

"Is Captain Spencer home?" Cross, the stout one, asked.

An approaching rider made her answer unnecessary.

"It's all right, Kate," Spencer called out as he dismounted. "I'll handle this. Go on inside."

At the end of September, Kate was in the garden waiting for Nicholas to come home, when the two sergeants came calling again.

"Captain Spencer's not home yet. Would you like to wait, or shall I take a message?"

"Oh, no, ma'am!" Sergeant Latham smiled. "The captain told us he'd be late. We're to hand you the payment. Would you like to check the amount?"

"Maybe I'd better do so." She invited the men into the library and offered them brandy. More than the need to count the money, she wanted to know what was going on. Nicholas would tell her nothing.

"Dreadful weather we're having . . ." she rambled on as she sorted the coins, piling them into stacks of ten each—as if that was the only way she knew how to count. She kept talking and refilling their glasses. As she'd hoped, the fine liquor soon loosened their tongues.

"Do you like soldiering?" she asked.

"Can't complain. Me officers always treat me decent," Cross said. "But Captain Spencer's the best officer I've had yet."

"Hear, hear!" said Latham. "'Twas our lucky day when Captain Spencer became our commanding officer."

"Why do you say that?" she asked.

"Made us rich men, now, didn't he, George?" Cross said.

"I'll say he did."

She smiled. "Tell me more."

Latham chuckled. "Ah lass. Can't hear enough good things about the captain, eh?"

She looked down at her hands. "I'm sorry."

Cross cut in, "It's like this, see? It'd be our wages and nothing more for us if the captain didn't come along with his offer. He says, 'Sergeant, here's the deal—I provide you with merchandise. You sell them goods and pay me the sum I ask. Your profits be your business. What do you say?' I say, thank you very much, Captain."

Kate recalled how Jeremy used to rant about the fortunes to be made in trade. This must be the kind of deal he'd been dying to get, but never did.

She refilled their glasses. "Profits? Is that a lot?"

The two men roared with laughter.

"Ain't it just!" Cross said. " 'Tis because of the profits that everyone wants to get into trade. 'Tis where fortunes be made, but the Trading Officers Fraternity controls supply, see? They don't allow nobody to buy them goods off the ships, so everybody has to buy from the Fraternity."

Latham added, "The trading officers decide who shall trade, and they can name their price for the goods. The captain got us into trade, and we're right grateful."

"The Fraternity makes a lot of profit then?" Kate asked.

Cross grinned. "What do you think? We hear the Fraternity pay eight shillings a gallon for rum off the ship. Don't know what Captain Spencer pay for it, but he sell it to us at two pounds a gallon. We add water and sell the grog at four pounds a gallon. See? Everybody makes a profit."

Kate spent the next several days in furious thought. When Mrs. Johnson remarked on her lack of attention, she pulled herself together. She waited four weeks before she approached Spencer with her plan.

"No," he said. "You just don't realise how much hard work is involved, my sweet. You'd be run ragged, and I don't want you to exhaust yourself."

He caressed her bottom. "Am I not enough to keep you occupied?"

She blushed. "But Nicholas, I've nothing to do during the day. It'd be fun for me to run a store. Think of the extra profits you'd make if you didn't use the services of your sergeants—"

He arched an eyebrow. "Been talking to my sergeants, have you?"

"Well. A little."

"How's your lessons with Mrs. Johnson?"

Kate shrugged. "I don't think she's teaching me anything new anymore. Perhaps it's time to let her go."

Spencer smiled.

"Look, I know how to read and write now. Learning about English kings and of things English is all very interesting, but I don't see the point. How would knowing all that help me here in Parramatta? And stop distracting me, Nicholas." She brushed away his roving hands.

"I can do my adding and subtracting and all the rest. I write a good hand; I can spell, even the hard words. What more do I need to learn? Nicholas, I'd be happier being a shop girl. I'd be able to deal with things I can see and touch, and I promise, I'll make you money too!"

Spencer chuckled. "Let me see what you've learned from Mrs. Johnson."

Kate handed him a thick pile of papers. She watched him study the exercises she'd done for Mrs. Johnson. Why couldn't he see that working at the store would fill her lonely hours? It could be a start to building their future together. Marriage would come next and then children. Well, why not? Officers of the Corps had been known to wed their convict mistresses. She'd overheard Jane tell Betty that.

Spencer beckoned. When she approached, he settled her on his lap and began nuzzling her neck and kissing her shoulders.

"Nothing more to learn eh?" he whispered. "Let's see if I can change your mind—"

Kate sighed. The wretched man was in no mood for a serious talk now.

Three days later, Spencer told Kate he'd paid Mrs. Johnson off. He'd be teaching her from then on. "We'll see how much you do know."

Spencer proved a tough teacher. He taught her the principles of bookkeeping, made her keep fictitious accounts for all sorts of merchants, and Kate enjoyed the challenge he presented.

One day, she asked, "Have you given any thought to the store, Nicholas?"

"Store?"

She handed him a sheet of paper. "It's a plan of my store, just a small building where we can display the goods. It wouldn't cost very much to—"

He smiled. "Very pretty."

She gritted her teeth and flounced out of the library.

"Kate. Come back!" His laughter followed her down the hallway.

In the following weeks, Nicholas did everything to please her. He paid particular attention to her plans, listened to her ideas and offered suggestions for improvements. Kate's hopes soared till she felt a vague sense of unease.

Eejit! Blooming eejit! How had she missed it? Nicholas was being indulgent, treating her as he would a child. He hadn't taken her ideas seriously, and rightly so. Her plans for the store had grown into such monstrous proportions, no sensible man would risk his hard-earned money on it. *Damn.* She'd have to do some hard pruning.

Oh yes. She'd get her store yet.

CHAPTER 19

The fly, Spencer's own nemesis, made a figure of eight, then swung away towards the window before heading back to Spencer's desk. It perched on his stack of reports, rubbed its hands, as if in glee, then flew into his face, seeking to rest on his nose. Spencer brushed it away, knowing the nuisance would be back yet again.

There was no escaping the flies. They came in through the doors and the windows, and keeping these shut tight was not an option. No one working in the building moaned about the flies anymore. Better the flies than suffocating in the summer's sweltering heat.

Spencer stared at the stack of documents which called for his attention. He slipped his hand into his jacket pocket and pulled out a sheet of paper. It was Kate's latest sketch of her store, and he studied it once more. A smile trembled on his lips, and he shook his head. She was his little honey pot, to attend to his personal needs, not someone to be taken seriously. Still, he had to admit her ideas made excellent sense. Had they come from a man, he'd have invested in the store at once and have it open for business in short order. He folded the paper and tucked it back into his pocket and walked out of his office. He needed some fresh air to clear his head.

The corporals and sergeants, busy at their tasks, looked up when he passed them. He averted his gaze from a fat lieutenant chatting with another officer at the end of the corridor. He liked neither man and doubted they were discussing work. These two boasted of hiring out their convict mistresses as whores to advance themselves, and Spencer avoided their company when he could.

He stepped outside the building, took a brisk walk down the road and back. It was refreshing to have a mistress who wanted to improve his circumstances; his past mistresses only waited to bleed him for all they could get. But to use Kate to better his fortune? Wouldn't that make him no better than those officers who used their mistresses to whore for them? But what was the alternative? Kate would be bored with nothing to fill her hours till he came home from work. He didn't think a bored Kate would get into mischief. She was not that kind of woman. No, she would give him no peace till he gave in to her wishes. He took a deep breath and made his decision, the only one he could make. He would indulge Kate and profit by it.

In the following weeks, he acquired an acre of land near the town centre and hired a builder to construct the store and warehouse as Kate had drafted. Later, he let it be known he sought the services of two shopkeepers.

He had no shortage of applicants. He liked the MacGregors best and sent for them again.

They came trooping into his office, the two teenage boys following behind their father. They were big men, about Spencer's own height, and they looked capable enough to protect one small woman. And though Robert MacGregor kept fiddling with his cap, he met Spencer's gaze without flinching. Spencer liked that.

"I would have all three of you work for me," he said, "but there are conditions. I give you fair warning. I'll not tolerate the slightest breach. If one of you makes a mistake, I'll dismiss all three of you. Is this clear?"

"Aye, sir," MacGregor said. "There wilna be any breaches. I'll see to that."

"Good. Mistress O'Neal is very dear to me. She's taken a fancy to become a shopkeeper, and I'm inclined to indulge her. She'll be in charge of this store, and you'll take your instructions from her."

The three men nodded.

"Now, I don't want her to do any hard lifting. More importantly, I'll not have her bothered by any man. Should you think a situation is likely to turn dangerous, you shall send word to me at once, but only after you've made sure Mistress O'Neal is safe."

"Aye, sir."

"The wages I've proposed—are they satisfactory?"

"You're more than generous, sir."

Spencer nodded. "You'll have to meet Mistress O'Neal. If she approves, then you'll start work on Monday week."

That evening, he smiled as Kate snuggled up close in his arms. He liked it that she'd lost her shyness. "Now, what's this?"

"My sketch of a desk for myself in this store we're going to build."

"No, this desk is too big for you."

"But Nicholas, I need the space to keep all those books you say I must have." She counted on her fingers. "My order book, my purchase book, my creditors' book, my cookbook, my stock book—"

Spencer laughed. "Your cookbook? What—"

A knock on the door interrupted him.

"Come in."

Jane hovered in the doorway. "Sir, there be three MacGregors to see you."

"Show them in here."

"Visitors?" Kate scrambled off his knee. "Should I leave?"

He shook his head. "Stay."

An hour later, the MacGregors departed.

"What do you think of them?" Spencer asked.

"They're nice. So respectful, too. Didn't you like them?"

He pretended to consider the question, then smiled broadly. "If I didn't, would I hire them for your store?"

"My store? Nicholas, we don't have a store yet."

"Ah. That's where you're mistaken."

"Nicholas!" Her eyes glowed, her smile dazzling.

Spencer laughed and hugged her. "What will you name it?"

"I get to name it, too?" She paused for a moment. "How about D-Store?"

"I beg your pardon?"

She laughed. "D-Store? It's easy to remember. D for Dunover."

"You lucky dog, Spencer!" an officer said. "I hear your store is doing very well, thanks to your Kate!"

"Wasn't she Kendrick's woman?" another officer said. "Never mind. Name your price, Spencer, and I'll take her off your hands. What do you say?"

"Sure, when I'm done with her. I'll let you know when that happens. Just don't hold your breath." He smiled and walked away. He wasn't happy that Kate had attracted so much attention, but it couldn't be helped. Anyway, she was the least of his problems at the moment. Hunter, the new governor, was giving him the headache.

For three years, Major Grose, their Corps commander had been Acting-Governor of the colony following the resignation of Governor Arthur Phillip in 1792. Grose allowed his officers a free hand to run the colony for him. They did a good job all right and, in the process, used their official authority to enrich themselves, oftentimes at the expense of the colonial government.

London took its time to appoint a new governor, and Hunter arrived to take up his appointment in 1796. Hunter made it known he didn't like what he had inherited from Major Grose and would be correcting the iniquities.

Spencer shook his head. The officers who'd benefitted most under Grose's administration would resist any attempt to reduce their power and privileges. And, as much as he'd like to side with his fellow officers in a show of solidarity, he could not, in good conscience, join them. Right was not on their side.

Back in his office, Spencer worked through a stack of reports on his desk when, suddenly, the door crashed open and a red-faced officer came charging in. "I tell you, Spencer, the governor's run mad!"

Spencer couldn't understand why, with so many officers he could pick on, Lieutenant Hathaway had chosen to bend his ear with endless complaints. It was a pity that Hathaway saw him as his friend, while he considered the officer no more than a colleague. Likely the lieutenant thought he'd done him an extraordinary favour on the infamous night, when he gamed with Kendrick.

Spencer looked calmly into Hathaway's face and quelled a surge of annoyance. "How tiresome of him. What is it this time?"

"He thinks to please London by cutting down government expenses. That fool of a meddler wants to expand public agriculture!"

Spencer looked at Hathaway, wondering what his visitor expected him to say?

When Governor Phillip left the colony in 1792, public agriculture had taken up 1,014 acres of land. When Major Grose sailed for England three years later, the figure had dropped to 340 acres, while the officers' private farms expanded. The Commissariat was forced to buy from the officers in order to meet its obligation to feed the settlers. The new governor could hardly be expected to allow this practice to continue. Surely Hathaway must have expected Hunter to start expanding public agriculture to reduce public spending, except, maybe not so soon.

"How can you be so calm?" Hathaway demanded.

Spencer shrugged.

"There's more! He wants the convicts to be paid extra for their services—"

"For time beyond the prescribed hours? A trifling."

Hathaway's chest swelled, his face turned purple. "That's fine for you to say. You only have a score of convicts. I have more. But that's not all. That madman is going to stop government entitlements to assigned convicts! We are to feed and clothe them, if we want their services! They are convicts, for heaven's sakes. They are the government's responsibility. Why must we bear the burden of feeding and clothing them? It makes no sense to me."

"Hathaway, breathe deep before you explode."

"Are you listening?" Hathaway demanded. "He'll bankrupt us, I tell you."

"Sit down, Hathaway."

"What? Now look here, Spencer, don't you see the danger? First, he expands public agriculture, then he makes it expensive for us to raise our crops. Next, he's going to stop buying our harvest. If we don't sell to the Commissariat, where are we going to sell them? Think! Without hard currency from the treasury, how are we to finance our trade? Damned old meddler. His mother should have drowned him when he was a babe."

Spencer suppressed his laugh and coughed instead.

"Why couldn't Major Grose have stayed on as governor? He wouldn't have to lift a finger to do anything—we would run this colony for him." Hathaway lowered himself to a chair and sighed.

Spencer leaned back and waited for more complaints.

"Damn fool thinks to bribe us, you know?"

"The Governor? How?"

Hathaway scowled. "By allowing us two convicts each at government expense. Two! That's nothing! My farms take forty. Damn."

"Perhaps Hunter won't be governor for long. After all, the man's old. He must be all of sixty, wouldn't you say?"

"I don't know, but he'll live to be a hundred just to plague us! Why is he taking the part of the convicts? Doesn't he know they don't count for anything?"

"Why should you worry? If you think upon it, Macarthur or some other will find a way to outwit Hunter."

"Dammit. Why couldn't he be like the major? Leave us to run the colony?"

"Cheer up, Hathaway. Hunter can issue all the edicts he wants, but who's going to see them carried out?"

For a long moment Hathaway was speechless. His lips then curved into a smile. "Glad we had this little chat, Spencer. Well, goodbye. I'm off to spread some good cheer now."

Kate came home from D-Store one evening to find Spencer dressed in his best uniform, complete with braids and medals.

"Where are you going?"

"I'm attending a little party given in the governor's honour. I'll be home late, sweet. Don't wait up for me."

Kate wanted to ask why wasn't she going too? After all his consequence was large enough to allow him to bring along his convict mistress. Other officers had done it. Kate restrained herself. She feared the answer.

That evening, she paced the floor. Was he ashamed of her?

No. Nicholas loved her. Had he not done everything to spare her? Spared nothing to please her? She never had to do the housework, the cooking or the gardening. He gave her a teacher. He bowed to her wishes: built her a store and let her run it. He loved her. He did! And he'd marry her one day. Of course, he would, when he felt the time was right.

Spencer said nothing to reassure her in the days that followed. Anxiety ate into her soul. "Why didn't you take me to the party, Nicholas?"

"You wouldn't like it, sweet. 'Twas all very boring."

"Weren't there any women?"

"They're more tiresome than the men." After a small hesitation, he ran a finger gently down her cheek. "They can be very cruel, my dear, and I don't want you hurt."

Kate wanted to meet his friends, but Spencer seemed oblivious to the hints she dropped. She hated it when he went out in the evenings for she feared staying home alone and forced to deal with her imagination running wild.

She told herself nothing had changed. Nicholas behaved no differently towards her: he was just as tender, just as caring and most importantly, just as passionate. But like maggots feeding on a carcass, doubt nibbled into her core of contentment.

Her friends at Red Roo had become family to her. Now that she felt so lost, she needed to be with them to renew her self-confidence.

"Nicholas, can we visit Red Roo? It's been a year since I saw any one of my friends. Can we go this weekend? Please?"

"I'm sorry, sweet. Mrs. Barnes' party is this weekend."

"How about next weekend?"

"Kate. You know I don't like planning that far ahead."

"Why can't I go to Red Roo on my own? I could do it—"

"No." He pulled her close. "I'd miss you, sweet. Would you really leave me on my own? Hmmm?" He nuzzled her neck.

"It'll only be for a few days. Please? Ian or Hamish could drive me—"

"No. You're not going anywhere without me."

"Nicholas—"

He released her. "Cease this foolishness at once, Kate."

She watched him march out of the house. *Selfish bastard! Why do I love him? I must be an eejit.*

Spencer tossed the report down and shook his head. Another incident in a string of senseless atrocities. This time the Hawkesbury settlers had set out to attack the aborigines—they'd killed and mutilated seven, two of them women. Where would it all end? Did both sides have to be shocked by their countless dead to learn violence served no man, neither black nor white?

The settlers didn't always have right on their side, but neither did the natives. Before the settlers came, the natives hunted for their meat, but now they'd taken to killing the occasional sheep. The settlers complained about the theft and often took the law into their own hands. They claimed the natives were no different from the dingoes and had to be taught to keep away from other people's property.

Then there was the issue of native concubinage. He understood why some settlers had acquired native women for female company and household help—there were just too few white women in the colony to meet the needs of the settlers. He'd heard how some of these men used these aborigine women brutally: how they offered them to their friends as entertainment, hired them out to strangers as whores and would kill them on a whim. He found it abhorrent that some of these men had not been brought to justice. As such, how could he blame the natives for taking revenge for the dishonour done to their kin? Obviously, the natives had the advantage in their overwhelming numbers, but their wooden spears and clubs were no

216

match against the settlers' muskets. The attacks and counter-attacks only left many dead, both black and white.

The governor had tried to be fair to the natives, but he had a greater duty to defend the colonists. No one seemed to know how to end the hostilities.

Indeed, Spencer considered himself lucky that Red Roo had so far been free of such violence. And dear foolish Kate—she wanted to travel to Red Roo, into the heart of these hostilities—to visit her friends? He would not permit it.

He sighed. How could she be so sensible one minute and so silly the next? She'd been crying lately too. He could tell from her red eyes, but he wasn't about to become embroiled in her female upsets.

Ah, well. Kate would see reason soon enough and come out of her sullens.

The crowd in D-Store thinned around noon. Kate returned to her desk at the back of the store and reached for her stock book. A loud voice jerked her out of her world of numbers. She listened to Robert's conversation with a regular customer for several minutes, then decided to join them. "I'm happy for you, Mr. Jenkins. What wonderful news for Mrs. Jenkins."

Jenkins beamed. "Why, thank you, Mistress O'Neal. Wonderful indeed. I wasn't happy that me Bessy got seven years' transportation for pick-pocketing—such a harsh sentence for a childish trick, don't you agree? Now, with the Governor's Pardon, the offence is forgiven, and me Bessy has a clean start. We're right pleased the pardon came before our babe is born."

Kate's knees trembled. Had Nicholas obtained her a Governor's Pardon without telling her? Was it possible? She couldn't settle to work the rest of the day and hurried home after closing D-Store early.

The moment Spencer arrived home, she confronted him.

"The Governor's Pardon. Did you get one for me, Nicholas?"

"Do we have to discuss this in the hallway?" He removed his cloak and hung it in the closet.

"The library then?" She led the way.

He closed the door behind them. "Would you like a drink?"

She shook her head, leery of the way he'd avoided answering her question. "Nicholas?"

He poured a drink and drained it in two swallows. "No. You don't qualify for a pardon yet, my sweet."

"Will I qualify?"

He looked at her for some moments. "Not for another two, three years."

"Will you apply one for me then?"

"Maybe. I haven't thought about it."

"Think about it? If the pardon can turn me into a free woman, do away with the taint of being a convict, why would you even hesitate?"

He shrugged, then stretched his neck. He poured himself another brandy and sat down. "I'm tired."

He looked weary, and Kate's heart softened. She'd been thoughtless, pestering him when he must have had a hard day at work. She could have picked a better time to ask her questions. She stroked his face. "You need a shave."

"Yes." He pulled her onto his lap, lifted her hand and kissed it.

"Have you thought of marrying me, Nicholas?" Kate clapped both hands over her mouth in shock and stared at Spencer. She didn't know how those words had slipped from her mouth. The silence became oppressive.

He lifted her from his lap and stood. "Well! You do have a lot of questions for me tonight, haven't you, my sweet?" He went to refill his glass.

She closed her eyes. "You have no plans to marry me."

"I have no plans to marry anyone. I confess I find my present circumstances very pleasant. Do *you* have a complaint?"

Kate couldn't speak.

"Would you have preferred I left you at Red Roo?"

She shook her head, turned and slowly walked towards the door.

"Kate?"

"Yes?" She kept her gaze on the doorknob, her back to him. She didn't want him to see the tears.

"I'm sorry."

With her head held high, she walked out of the library.

No plans to marry anyone. Was that supposed to reassure her? *Bastard!* But no. Nicholas loved her. Of course, he did. So why wouldn't he marry her? How could she change his mind? Would a baby do it?

She couldn't understand why she wasn't pregnant yet. It'd been a year. Jeremy had planted his seed quickly enough, considering he was almost always laid low by seasickness or alcohol. Nicholas had no such problems. Had her use of the sponge and vinegar soured her womb, closed it to new life? No, it couldn't be. Could it?

One afternoon, a raging headache forced Kate to ask Ian to drive her home from the store. She took a long nap. When she awoke, she felt better and longed for a cup of hot tea. She made her way into the kitchen.

Betty ignored her. Kate didn't care. She was moving a bunch of carrots and a chunk of meat aside to make room for her teapot and a cup, when a bowl of mushrooms caught her eye. She'd learned a lot about mushrooms from Nellie. Leaning over, she plucked out a plump brown-spotted one.

Betty whisked the bowl away. "You leave me mushrooms alone!"

"Check your mushrooms, Betty." She held out the one in her hand. "This one is poisonous, and there could be a few more in that bowl."

"Nothing's wrong with me mushrooms! You always think you know better. Let me tell you, you don't!"

Hateful woman! Kate flicked the mushroom onto the table. "Please yourself, Betty. You will, anyway." She should get rid of her, and Jane too, but how could she do it when she couldn't be sure she'd be better off with their replacements?

She made her cup of tea. On her way out of the kitchen, she said, "I don't want supper tonight, and you can have my share of the mushrooms."

She woke to Nicholas' kiss. "Are you not well?" he asked.

"Just a headache. Have you had supper?"

"Not yet."

"Don't wait for me. I'm not hungry."

He gave her hand a gentle squeeze. "I hope you feel better soon."

Should she warn him about the mushrooms? No, let him take his risk. A little suffering might teach him to be more considerate of her needs.

Time seemed to drag. Did Betty serve the mushrooms? Or did good sense prevail? Kate's eyes grew heavier. She woke when Spencer joined her in bed. Within minutes, his light snores filled the room. Kate's disappointment was so painful, her eyes burned.

She woke to Spencer's groan. Her heart pounded. She watched him get out of bed and used the chamber pot. It was one thing to wish Nicholas ill, quite another to see him suffer. "Nicholas? Are you all right?"

"My stomach's churning—" He retched and vomited.

She went to his side and rubbed his back as he alternated between sitting on the chamber pot and emptying his guts into it. She made endless trips to the kitchen to fetch hot water for him to use. She heard Betty and Jane moaning each time she passed their rooms and smiled.

The next day, Kate found Betty looking doughy and moving sluggishly about the kitchen. "Captain Spencer was sick last night, Betty, from your poisonous mushrooms."

"Fat lot you know! 'Twas the bloody meat! 'Twas tainted!"

Kate shook her head. "The mushrooms. If you can't tell poisonous mushrooms from edible ones, you should keep away from them altogether. Don't serve the captain any more mushrooms."

Betty sneered, "You always think you know everything. You don't! 'Twas the meat, not the mushrooms!"

"Please yourself, Betty. Just don't serve the captain any more mushrooms," she said and walked out of the kitchen.

"Stupid bitch!"

Kate ignored the remark and kept walking. She'd speak to Nicholas about getting rid of Betty and Jane. Not today. Maybe tomorrow . . .

Two days later, she was in the library when Spencer came home. He kissed her gently and then smiled at her. "How would you like to go to Red Roo this weekend?"

"What?"

"You deserve a reward for taking such good care of me."

CHAPTER 20

Just five days for her to prepare for the trip—if only she was given more time. Still, she made sure that nothing of her dissatisfaction showed. She would make a success of the visit, make sure Nicholas would have no cause to regret his decision. And if she could, she would put him in such a pleasant mood, he'd be ready to consider more visits in the future.

Providing him with a warm bed—consisting of a comfortable pallet, soft pillows and warm blankets—would be a start. She'd make sure that at Red Roo, he'd still have all the comforts of home. Indeed, she planned to bring along food supplies to cook up a banquet to impress him. It would also serve as a peace-offering for her friends—for not visiting them sooner.

She wanted to shower her friends with gifts. The only problem was the wagon couldn't carry all she wanted to take to Red Roo.

The night before their trip, Nicholas told her that Ian and Hamish would be joining them for company. She couldn't understand why he wanted them to come along and was glad she'd not gone overboard with her gifts, or there'd be no room left for Ian and Hamish's belongings.

Upon getting up early the next morning, she looked out the window and smiled at the sight of a clear blue sky. It would be a lovely spring day. She ignored Betty's snide remarks as she gulped down a light breakfast, then hurried back to her room to put on her new dress.

"Good morning, Ian, Hamish," she called out as she stepped out of the house. They gaped at her, which made her smile. She turned around to show them the fashionable bustle at the back. Perhaps her new dress wasn't entirely appropriate for the journey, but she'd endure the discomfort, if only to dazzle her Red Roo friends with her splendour.

Spencer gave her a long look. She pretended not to notice when she moved forward to join him. If he was displeased with her dress, she didn't want to know about it. Her gaze fell upon three Brown Besses on the driving seat. *Firearms*. She shuddered. Nicholas was being unnecessarily vigilant, alarmed no doubt by the fanciful tales that had been making their rounds in the settlement.

How foolish of him to believe the black fellas were dangerous and hostile. The black fellas were such gentle and friendly people, if you really got to know them—well, maybe not if they fancied white-settler meat for their dinner. She chuckled, remembering the time she believed the natives were cannibals.

"Three muskets, Nicholas? Are we going to war?"

Spencer helped her board the wagon. "Nothing to worry you, my sweet. 'Tis merely a precaution."

"Aye, don't you worry, Kate," Ian said. "Hamish and I are good shots now. We've been practising, like the captain told us."

Spencer rode his big roan and led the way. Ian followed in the wagon with Kate and Hamish sitting beside him. Not long after they left Parramatta, Kate tried to entertain the boys with tales of her time at the farm. Somehow their attention kept straying to the trees and bushes. How curious. They never struck her as nature lovers.

Hours later, they turned into Red Roo. The changes she saw left her speechless. The scrub land she remembered had become endless fields of wheat.

"It's Kate! Yo! Fellas, Kate's here!" Roger's voice came roaring out of the trees. Three of her friends came running into the open. The others followed, not far behind.

"Stop here, Ian!" she said. "I'm getting off."

The wheels had barely rolled to a halt when Kate jumped off the wagon. Sam reached out in time to steady her. She hugged him, then she moved from one pair of arms into another. About to launch into a string of questions, she caught sight of Nicholas watching her. She waved to him, as did her friends. Nicholas dipped his head, then he spurred his horse to catch up with Ian and Hamish who had continued down the track to the cook-house.

Kate turned to her friends. "Look at you, baked golden by the sun. I'll have to call you 'brown fellas' now!"

Amidst the laughter, Sam said, "And you're all grown up—at seventeen!"

"She's grown posh too," Tom said with a wink at Kate. "You must like it living with the captain."

Kate gave him a push. "Stop being snide, Tom. I've not seen you all in over a year, so be nice!"

"Good Lord, she's also turned into a bold piece!"

She laughed. "Come on then, let's get that wagon unloaded. I've come bearing gifts!"

"Oh! What did you get me?" Tom asked. He didn't wait for his answer, just quickened his steps. Kate and the rest followed.

Someone tugged on Kate's sleeve. "You look so pretty, Kate."

"Why, thank you, Artie." She smiled, then looked into the other bearded faces. "We're going to have a feast tonight, and I'll be needing some help. Where's Nellie?"

"She'll be back soon," Ben said.

"Kate," Artie said. "I'm an emancipist now. I finished serving me time three months ago. Did you know that?"

She stumbled to a stop. *An emancipist!* "That's wonderful, Artie! Will you be leaving us then?"

Artie's eyes rounded in confusion. "Leave Red Roo? But this is me home. The cap'n said I could stay, when I asked him. That's all right, ain't it?"

"Of course, it's all right. I'm so glad you're staying. Red Roo wouldn't be the same without you." She gave Artie a one-arm hug as she looked for Nicholas. He was moving away from the cookhouse, leading the two boys down the path to the river. She wondered why he never told her about Artie.

She looked at Ben and Rory. "What about the rest of you? Will you leave when you've finished serving your sentence?" *Holy Mother of God, no. They're family. What would I do without them?*

Peter shrugged. "We have a ways to go yet."

"Whether we stay or go depends on the cap'n, surely," Sam said. "If he say we can, perhaps we will. If not—"

"Of course he'll want you all to stay. Who could farm this land better than you?"

"How's it been with you, Kate?" Ben asked. "Has the cap'n been kind?"

"He's all right." Kate tried to curb her impatience. "What will—"

Roger gave her a wink. "The man guards you like a mangy dog guards his precious bit of bone, Kate. He's a right jealous man, the cap'n."

"What?"

Tom called out to the men. "Here! Help me unload." Then with his gaze on Kate, he said, "Aye! The cap'n don't trust no man with you. He don't trust us neither! Why do you think we've been forbidden to call on you?"

"Forbidden?" Kate closed her eyes for a moment and took a deep breath. If Nicholas cared that much, why wouldn't he marry her?

Artie pushed a cup into her hand. She disliked hard liquor,

but she took a small swallow to please Artie and immediately spluttered and coughed. The fellas laughed. Peter gave her one big thump on her back and was about to deliver another when she twisted out of his way.

"Stop it, Peter! You don't know your own strength! And Artie! You could've warned me!" She gave him a mock punch on his shoulder. "This almost took my head off!"

Roger grinned at Artie. "Did you forget to add water, mate? Remember now, a woman can't drink like a man."

Artie nodded. "Do you like it, Kate?"

"It's good, Artie, but I'm like Nellie, you know. We like our tea." She peered into the cup. "I didn't know we've been selling such strong stuff."

"Kate, do you know what you're drinking?" Ben asked.

Kate raised her chin and looked down her nose at him. "I brought this. I should know."

"Did you now?" Ben smiled.

The others snickered.

She scowled. "What's going on?"

"This be our very own brew, Kate," Harry said. "I made it."

"Not without our help, you didn't," Roger said.

An idea set her heart racing. She looked around. "Nicholas must try this."

"What are you up to, now?" Rory asked.

"Patience," she said. "Somebody fetch me a bottle of this brew and two more cups."

Armed with a bottle and the cups, she went in search of Spencer. She found him with the boys by the river, chatting as they looked up at a koala sleeping on a high branch of a eucalyptus tree.

"Nicholas," she said. "Here's something to quench your thirst."

He gave her a level look. Ignoring a niggling of unease, she filled the cups and handed them out.

She waited for Spencer's reaction. "Do you like it?"

He shrugged. "I've tasted better."

She could have cried out of disappointment. "It's no good?"

He took another swallow and smiled. "It's not bad."

"Would you buy it?"

"Not for myself."

"How about your friends?"

He laughed. "My friends, as you call them, would buy anything they can pass for liquor. And *your* friends have been doing a spot of brewing."

Kate blushed. She turned to the boys. "Do you like it?"

They nodded.

"Don't like it too much, all right?" Nicholas grinned, then looked down at his hand as Kate linked her fingers to his.

"We'll see you later," she told the boys and led Nicholas away. They had walked some twenty yards when she said, "Nicholas, we have our very own liquor supplier. Isn't it wonderful?"

He said nothing.

She shook his arm. "Nicholas, are you listening?"

"No."

"What?" She giggled uneasily. "You're not listening?"

" 'No' to what you're suggesting, my sweet. You have your visit with your friends. We'll go home tomorrow, and I don't want to hear anything more about this place for at least another year."

"Why? Why won't you even consider it? Do you have something against becoming richer?"

"Damn it, Kate! I won't have you arguing with me. What you're suggesting takes a lot of work. It's just too damned complicated! These men here won't be able to organise a large enterprise on their own."

"Complicated? Of course it isn't, Nicholas! I've got it all figured out—"

He laughed. "Now, how did I know you were going to say that? But no." He put his arms around her and pulled her close. "Isn't D-Store sufficient to keep you busy? Am I not enough to make you happy?"

"That's not the point. How can you even think of turning down an opportunity like this? Sure, the fellas here might not be able to handle a big job by themselves. I could stay back a couple of weeks to help them get started. We'll pick a safe area—"

"No."

"Why not? Why are you so unreasonable?"

"I'm unreasonable?" He laughed.

Furious with his attitude, she quickened her steps. He reached out and stopped her, then turned her to face him.

"Kate, you know I don't like to explain myself, but just this once—Listen. This entire Hawkesbury region isn't safe at the moment. Haven't you heard? The aborigines have been attacking the settlers—"

"Nicholas! Those are foolish tales."

"They're not foolish tales, Kate, and I don't wish to see you hurt. If you must know, I was wrong to bring you here today, but I thought to please you. Never mind. I'm certainly not leaving you in this place for a few weeks!"

"With nine men to watch over me, why shouldn't I be safe? And you're making too much of the foolish rumours. The black fellas have always been kind and friendly. Why would they attack the settlers, or the settlers attack them? They're lies, Nicholas, told to frighten children."

"Lies? Kate, I can tell you exactly what—"

"You've been lied to, Nicholas. Trust me. I know the black

fellas. They're good people. Most of them here are Nellie's friends."

He stared at her. "Never mind. We're going home tomorrow, and we'll not speak of this anymore."

Kate couldn't let the matter go. The fellas' future was at stake. She had to make sure Nicholas depended on them so he'd want to keep them at Red Roo. This way, she'd have her family together and close at hand.

After supper, she joined Nicholas on the pallet and snuggled up close. "One week, Nicholas. Just one week. It's not such a big risk. Think of the money we can make."

After a moment of silence, he said, "Money's not everything. Certainly not worth risking your life."

"Well, it's my life! If I want to risk it, why should you care?"

Spencer seized her by her shoulders. "Would you like to repeat that?"

She buried her face in his chest and whispered, "I'm sorry, Nicholas. I didn't mean that." She planted remorseful kisses across his broad chest. She felt him relax, then respond. Without giving herself another moment to wonder, she whispered soft words of praise into his ears. She took erotic nips, then laved the spots warmly with her tongue. She caressed him in intimate places that made him moan in pleasure, then begged him to reconsider, to let her stay. She employed every trick she'd learned from the Petals and prayed he'd change his mind.

Doubts pricked her during the night and continued to do so into the early hours of the morning. Would Nicholas remember his promises given in passion?

"Stop fretting," he said, as if he could read her mind. "A week, Kate. If you haven't finished with all the arrangements by then, you'll return to Dunover and never raise this subject again. Is it a bargain?"

"Yes."

"I'll leave Ian here with you. You're not to leave his sight, is that clear?"

Outside his office, Spencer tightened the cinch, then patted his horse's flank. He had two situations to check out and decided he'd first investigate the destruction to a settler's home by a drunken convict. He grimaced at the irony. With Kate's help, he'd be contributing to this growing unruliness.

He shrugged. It wasn't his fault if settlers, both convict and free, had an enormous thirst. If he didn't supply them the liquor, someone else would.

"Captain Spencer!"

Lieutenant Hathaway waddled up, panting heavily and beading sweat. Spencer's lips thinned. He had taken a strong dislike for the lieutenant's company. He couldn't understand why Governor Hunter, who could pick any one of the officers to be his aide, had settled for Hathaway. Could the lieutenant be presenting a different face to the governor and gained his confidence?

"You won't believe this, Spencer. I swear Governor Hunter has rats in his attic. He's raving on about how liquor is giving the settlement a bad reputation of lawlessness."

"What's he planning to do about it?"

Hathaway scowled. "Damned fool won't be satisfied till he's made a pauper out of me! 'Twas bad enough that we're not allowed to brew alcohol for sale. Now the fusspot wants to place a quota on liquor imports. You know we can't import enough liquor to meet the demand for it, and he wants to cut down on what we can get? Madness. Why are we cursed with this man?"

Spencer controlled his impatience. Hathaway was a nuisance, but not a bad sort really, just a man easily driven to panic. No, the lieutenant didn't deserve the cutting remarks ready to roll off his tongue.

Hathaway frowned, then looked at Spencer hopefully. "Perhaps he needs London's permission to do this?"

Spencer shook his head.

"Damn. He's done nothing but given me a headache ever since he took office! What are we going to do? Our largest profits come from the liquor trade. This new ruling is going to ruin us. Don't laugh! It's not just the trade. You forget—without rum, we can't get any work done. My farm workers, damned rascals, won't work for anything but their portion of liquor!"

"Oh. I shouldn't worry, Hathaway."

"Not worry! Haven't you heard a thing I've said?"

"Putting a quota on liquor imports isn't going to change the demand for liquor, not as I see it. What it will do is drive the trade underground."

"Underground?"

"If Governor Hunter imposes a quota, the price of liquor will soar because merchants would blame the shortage. Some enterprising people will engage in smuggling to take advantage of the higher prices. Why, Hathaway, I believe Governor Hunter is going to help you make a bigger fortune."

Hathaway blinked, then drew a deep breath. "Always a pleasure to talk to you, Captain."

Kate was pleased to be with her friends. They consulted her over their problems, and they made her feel important, clever and in charge again. She had Harry explain to her the brewing process in detail and committed to memory all the materials he needed for his alcohol stills. Some materials like barley, wheat and sugar were readily available. Other materials, like the copper pots and tubings, were less easy to obtain, but through Nicholas' influence, she hoped to get them all. She discussed possible substitutes and alternatives in anticipation of difficulties. She almost left it too late to find a safe place to locate the

231

alcohol stills—tracking through the bush over wide distances took a lot of time.

"This is silly," Harry said. "We have the cap'n to protect us. Why do we have to hide our stills?"

"Because it's illegal to brew alcohol for sale, and it's our responsibility to keep ourselves out of trouble, not just depend on anyone else, and especially not the captain, to do it for us. Look, you don't all have to come with me looking for a proper site, not if you don't want to."

"Good. We've got better things to do. Just remember to pick a spot by the river."

A different fella accompanied Kate each day on her little trips around the property. Only Ian stuck close to her, until Ben objected. "Go make yourself useful somewhere else. I can protect Kate all by meself."

"But Ben, the cap'n—"

"What he don't know won't hurt him."

After a slight hesitation, Ian said, "All right. But take me Brown Bess."

Kate discussed her findings with the men in the evenings. She didn't want to make a mistake with a hasty decision, but time ran out. Nicholas would be back the following day.

"There are three likely places," she said, "but I'd like to look them over one last time . . ."

Rory accompanied her on this last inspection tour. She had more or less made up her mind after seeing the area nearest to the camp, but there was still enough daylight left for her to inspect the other two sites, and she decided not to waste the opportunity. Rory didn't have much to say, and Kate's thoughts began to wander. She was delighted to have secured for her friends a safe future at Red Roo. If only she could find as easy an answer to her own future with Nicholas.

She needed to give Nicholas a push in the right direction, but how? Sensing Rory's gaze upon her, she turned towards him. The tender expression in his eyes made her look away. Some moments later, she stole a look at Rory, and a wild idea took hold.

No, she couldn't. It wouldn't be right.

But what has right got to do with anything? If Nicholas had done the right thing by her, she wouldn't be in this position.

No, she couldn't lead Rory down a path that would lead nowhere. She couldn't.

But if she didn't, she might regret it the rest of her life.

Perhaps she could just give it one chance? Just one chance . . .

She took a deep breath, then deliberately stepped on a loose rock. She staggered, as she knew she would, and fell awkwardly.

"Are you all right?" Rory's pale face reflected his concern. Kate felt the sting of tears for what she was about to do. She cried, clinging hard to Rory who held her close. She wriggled to get closer to him and felt his response. She encouraged him. In the hour that followed, neither she nor Rory brought up their errand for the day.

It was getting dark when they started for home. Rory wanted to talk, but Kate shook her head. " 'Twas a mistake."

"No, Kate. How can you say that?"

"Because it is. We must never speak of this, ever. I want your word."

"Kate—"

"Your word."

Rory's eyes reflected pain, but he finally nodded.

Nicholas came with Hamish to fetch Kate and Ian home. In the weeks that followed, Kate was pleased that Nicholas found her most of the materials Harry needed for his stills. She had Ian and Hamish deliver them to the farm. Harry never seemed content with all she sent him. He kept asking for his metal pots and tubing until she ran out of patience. Did he think she'd forgotten? How, when he'd never stopped reminding her? Or did he think she'd kept them from him for the fun of it?

Minor things began to annoy her. She waited for the *curse* to show, but the weeks passed with no sign of it. Then her breasts grew tender, and her waist thickened. She was forced to admit that the baby she'd wanted so badly was now a reality, except she was no longer sure if having a baby was such a good idea. Would Nicholas do right by her or would he allow his child to be named a bastard?

If not for a blunder she'd committed seven weeks ago, she wouldn't be burdened by spiraling fear and savaged by her wild imagination. Flushed with her success in getting Nicholas to change his mind about Harry's liquor production, she'd decided to use the same ploy to push Nicholas for marriage, expecting an easy victory.

He'd turned cold on her, cursed and pulled away. "Kate, I'll not have you act the whore to get your way! It's a mistake to think you can rule me through my lust."

She shrank from the biting words and the icy contempt on his face. All that night she'd wept silent tears, while Nicholas stayed unforgiving, on his side of the bed.

Would the baby change his mind about marriage? Or would he show her the door once her belly swelled, and she became less than nimble?

Jeremy's baby had given her no trouble. This one made her sick every morning. Uncertain of Nicholas' reaction, she'd steal away from his side when dawn broke. She'd hurry into the backyard and empty her belly. Then with a handy wet rag, she'd remove all traces of her ailment.

She was on her knees, heaving into some bushes one morning, when she heard familiar footsteps approaching from behind.

She held her breath as Spencer hunkered beside her.

He gave her back a gentle rub. "Are you all right? Is it the baby?"

CHAPTER 21

A raucous bird-call ripped through the treetops, then another. Kate wiped her mouth with the wet rag and took a deep breath. Nothing, it seemed, had escaped Nicholas' notice. And she thought she was protecting a secret. "Yes, the baby's making me sick."

She might as well know the worst. "Will you marry me now, Nicholas?"

He rose to his feet. "I thought we had this matter settled."

She clung to fading hope. "You'll let your baby be a bastard?"

He shrugged. "Bastards have been known to do very well for themselves, my sweet. Some move in the best circles of Society in London, a few even have Royal blood in their veins. There's no shame to be born a bastard."

"Please?"

"I'm sorry." He walked away.

She glared at his back. Her eyes blurred. Oh Lord, she should have believed the rotten swine and stuck to her sponge and vinegar.

In the days that followed, she waited for him to tell her of his plans for her and the baby, but he said not a word.

"Nicholas, would you get me a Governor's Pardon? This baby won't be tainted with a convict for a mother then."

"Stop fretting, my sweet. I'll take good care of you and your baby."

"*My* baby?" She took a deep breath. "Don't you feel it's your baby too?"

"Of course. I fear you read too much into my words."

I hate him.

A voice inside her head sneered, "Liar!"

The days of summer proved inhospitable, hot and humid. Kate longed for the cooler days of autumn, but like an obnoxious guest, summer lingered through March. Kate felt ugly, with her belly sticking three yards in front of her. She thought herself unwanted, for Nicholas had taken to spending more evenings away from home. Images of other women keeping Nicholas company—every one of them beautiful and slim—tormented her. She told herself to stop thinking of things she could do nothing about and to live one day at a time. It didn't help.

Two hours after she'd gone to bed in mid-April 1797, she woke up to a terrible pain. She lit the oil lamp and glanced at Nicholas' side of the bed. Empty. Pain assaulted her in waves, and Kate knew her baby was ready to face the world. She wished the baby had better timing. Presently, there was only Betty or Jane to help her. She'd cut off her right arm before she appealed to those two witches for help. The pain had grown stronger when heavy footsteps sounded on the stairs.

In the throes of pain, she stared into Nicholas' face, glad he was home, yet furious because he looked so calm.

He smoothed the wet strands from her face. "Is it time?"

She panted. "Yes."

"I'll fetch the midwife."

The pain seemed never ending in the hours that followed. She couldn't remember suffering this long with her first child, but she forgot the agony she'd endured as soon as the midwife placed her beautiful son in her arms. Despite the midwife's protests, she undid the swaddling and counted ten little fingers.

Her throat closed up when she saw that his left foot had six little toes.

"Nothing for you to fret about," Nicholas said. "It's a family trait. My grandfather and father had six toes too, on their right foot."

Kate looked up, open-mouthed. She'd not heard him enter the room.

Clucking her disapproval, the midwife came forward and re-wrapped the baby before picking him up. "Ain't he a bonnie lad?" she cooed. "What's his name?"

Spencer looked at Kate. "Richard? After my father."

"I believe Christopher will suit him better. Don't you think it has a nice ring to it—Christopher *O'Neal?*"

He shrugged. "As you please."

"I'm tired." She pulled up the blanket and turned to face the wall. She heard Nicholas leave, then the soft click of the door closing.

Some hours later, when she felt stronger, she moved her things into the baby's room. Nicholas had not touched her in over two months. Better she removed herself than have him toss her out of his bed for disturbing his sleep. There was no deny-ing the fact that Christopher would cry during the night for her attention.

Nicholas made no comment about the change, and Kate's heart shrivelled. Would he find another to replace her in his bed? She wished she could gather up her fears and set a match to them. Instead, she battened them down and made her baby her new world.

A few times she caught Jane hovering over the cradle, or in the doorway. Kate offered her no encouragement to touch the baby. When she returned to D-Store to work, a month later, she took the baby with her. Christopher charmed the MacGregors. They'd pick him up when he cried, play with him when they had a free minute.

It took little more than a week for Kate to catch up with the paperwork. The MacGregors had done a good job in her four-week absence. Her only complaint was Robert had severely reduced the number of farmers buying on credit.

"What happened?" she asked.

Robert frowned. "There's this rumour saying the harvest might be poor this season. I dinna think it wise to let the farmers run up large debts. What if they canna pay?"

"You shouldn't worry if the farmers have a poor season or two, Robert. The good times will return and the farmers would pay all they owe. They'll surely remember that we gave them credit when they needed it most. If we stand by them in their times of need, they'll be there for us when we need them."

"Why would we need them?"

Kate smiled. "You can never tell. But should a time come when we can't buy enough wheat or barley, they'll be there to sell it to us, even if they can get the same or better prices from another buyer. Don't forget, Harry will need plenty of barley, wheat, corn—"

Robert nodded. "I'm learning lass, just not fast enough."

Nicholas showed scant interest in Christopher, and Kate tried not to care. The weeks passed. Kate came home from D-Store one day to find Nicholas, with Jane at his side, waiting for her. At his nod, Jane stepped forward to take Christopher.

"Let Jane have the baby, Kate. I want to talk to you."

Kate hugged Christopher close and shook her head. Despite a fast-beating heart, she lifted her chin. "We can talk, but I'll hold Christopher."

He stared at her, then waved Jane away. "Come into the library."

He waited for her to come through, then closed the door behind her. He indicated a chair. "Do you want a drink?"

When she shook her head, he poured himself one. "I've been very patient with you, Kate. The baby is two months old and I want things back to how it was before Christopher came along."

Kate blushed and lowered her gaze to hide her relief. She had thought he meant to send her away.

"Leave Christopher with Jane. I want you in my bed, where you belong."

"No!"

"What?" Spencer's tone turned harsh.

"I m—mean I don't want Jane to take care of Christopher."

"Oh." He nodded.

"And I don't want Betty to do it either."

"Hire another woman, if that pleases you."

So Kate hired Julie Bates, an emancipist woman who'd lost her baby only two weeks ago, whose milk was still flowing. During the day, Kate kept Christopher with her, letting Julie have him only when Nicholas came home.

Kate finished adding a long column of figures, glanced at the basket at her feet and smiled. Christopher looked very comfortable in his sleep.

". . . frightful?" a voice said. "Not two weeks ago, me neighbour's son died. Now 'tis the daughter. And I wonder if me children will be next."

Kate moved to stand at the door of her office. She could see Robert in conversation with two of their customers.

"I have me fears too," the other man said. "Me wife's been feeling right poorly—"

Kate walked up to them. "I'm sorry your wife's feeling poorly, Mr. Taylor."

Taylor nodded. " 'Tis a worry, ain't it, Mistress O'Neal? People . . . especially children, dying after several hours of fever? And nobody knows why."

"Children are dying . . . ?"

Kate heard a similar account later that day and her fear for Christopher's safety burgeoned. She left him at home with Julie the next day, but the talk of deaths continued, and Kate's heart jumped at each new mention. That night she asked Nicholas to take her and the baby to Red Roo.

"Why?"

"Haven't you heard? Children are dying because of this dreadful fever. I'm afraid for Christopher. If anything should happen to him—"

"Nothing's going to happen to him. Calm yourself, Kate."

"Please, Nicholas? I can't work. I can't even think. All I do is worry . . . Please, you've got to take us to Red Roo."

"Kate, Red Roo isn't some magical place where Christopher can be safe from all ill. With doctors close at hand, he'll be safer here."

Kate could only think of safety at Red Roo. Why was Nicholas being so stubborn? That night and the next, she wept into her pillow.

Spencer sighed. "All right, Kate. I'll take you and the baby to Red Roo. Now stop your crying."

They started out early the next morning, just she and the baby, with Nicholas driving the wagon. They arrived at the farm shortly after noon, to the fellas' welcoming cries, but it was baby Christopher who commanded their attention. They enticed him away from his mother's arms and quarrelled with each other for the chance to hold him.

She turned to Nicholas who stood by her side. His expression revealed nothing of his feelings as he watched the fellas being silly with the baby. Nor did he make any comment. Kate lay a hand on his arm. "Nicholas, you're sure you don't want to stay the night?"

"You know this trip was not planned, Kate. I've work in my

office that needs my attention." He kissed her. "I'll be back for you and the baby in two weeks, by which time I expect the crisis would be over. I'll see you then. Goodbye, sweet."

Kate was sorry to see him leave, but she also knew the fellas wouldn't feel free to be themselves in his company. No. She would not think about Nicholas anymore. For the next two weeks, she would concentrate on having a good time with her friends.

It warmed her heart to watch the fellas having fun with her five-month-old baby. They marveled at how well Christopher looked, even without any teeth. They commented on his eyes, as green as her own and tried every trick to make him laugh: swinging him around, tossing him into the air and making funny faces at him.

"He be the spitting image of you, Kate!" Ben said.

She smiled. "You haven't asked why we're here."

Ben obliged. "Why are you here, Kate?"

She told them about the fever that had swept across Parramatta leaving a trail of deaths.

"You're right to flee that wicked place," Sam said. "You and Christopher will be safe here with us. We'll look after you."

Tears smarted her eyes. No wonder that Red Roo felt like home. Dunover never did, not with Betty and Jane there to remind her she was no better than they.

"When you have a free moment, bring my things to the cookhouse, will you? I've supper to cook."

Once she had the roast in the ground oven, she joined the fellas and Nellie who had come back from her walk-about. They were still engrossed with Christopher. She tapped Harry on his shoulder. "Will you show me how you make your liquor?"

Tom groaned. "Oh, no, Kate! Don't you encourage Harry!"

"God! He'll not stop talking now!" cried Roger. "Go away, Harry! Do!"

Harry glared at the two men, then smiled at Kate. "Ignore them, they're just jealous." He led her away.

She couldn't help marvelling at the change in Harry. Where before he'd been surly and rude, he now tripped lightly over his words. He explained how he'd put together the materials she'd sent to build his alcohol stills. "I could produce better liquor, you know, but Roger and Sam wouldn't let me make no changes." He scowled. "Old women, that's what they've become. The others ain't no better—"

"Never mind about them. Tell me how you turn barley into liquor. Do you do all the work yourself?"

He shook his head. He led her through an opening in a wall of leaves. " 'Tis too much work for one man. Usually 'tis Sam and Tom's job to crush the grain, boil the mixture then cool it in a barrel. I decide when to add the yeast and some sugar, then let the mixture ferment for a few days."

She looked around the clearing. It had changed from the last time she saw it. The fellas had cleverly built enough cover to hide it from curious eyes. Steam wafted this way and that with the breeze as she studied the neat arrangement of pots and metal tubing.

"Then I have Ben and Roger boil the fermented mixture in these here kettles," he continued, tapping one of the three boiling pots with a stick then ran it along the metal pipes. "The liquor travel through these tubes to these here containers. There you have it, Kate, how to make liquor from barley."

"You make it sound so easy, Harry." She smiled.

He beamed. He filled a cup. "Have a taste."

She took a sip and immediately spat out the foul-tasting liquid. She rubbed her nose to rid it of the sharp smell. "Can the liquor be spoiling?"

"Spoiling?" Harry reclaimed the cup, took one swallow, then closed his eyes. He drained the contents, licked his lips and sighed. "Pure nectar."

"Couldn't we add some herbs to make it smell better?"

He glared at her. "Nobody's putting no herbs in me brew!"

"No, of course not." She shouldn't have upset Harry. After all, D-Store couldn't sell enough of his liquor.

On his fifth morning at Red Roo, Christopher started fretting. Kate felt his forehead and immediately called out to Peter, "Can you get me fresh water. Christopher is burning up."

The men stayed close, ready to carry out any task she demanded of them. They also kept Nellie out of her way.

The hours passed. Then Ben and Rory came up to her, suggesting they leave for Parramatta at once.

"Christopher's going to be fine. The fever's almost gone," she said, knowing it to be more hope than truth.

Then Christopher started vomiting.

"Kate, don't you be foolish now," Ben said. "Rory, you ride on ahead. Explain to the cap'n so he can have the doctor fetched. Peter, you drive. You're used to the road. Tom, you ride in the back with Kate. Right. Let's go."

Kate cradled the baby close, to cushion him against the wagon's jolts and lurches. She rocked him, sang softly in his ear, but Christopher wouldn't stop crying. The wind turned colder, and Kate immediately tucked the blanket around Christopher to make sure he was well covered, then hunched protectively over him. "Hold on, my sweet. You'll feel better soon. Mama's going to get you to a doctor."

Then Christopher stopped fussing, and she became alarmed. She leaned towards Tom, "Tell Peter to go faster!"

Rory cursed his horse. He'd been a fool to gallop all the way, and now the beast was blown. It would take him a whole hour's walk at least to reach Parramatta. He decided to let the horse go. He couldn't afford to have the beast slow him down. He walked at a fast pace. The gathering darkness preyed on his mind. The cap'n could have gone out for the evening, but he hoped not. He ran the last fifty yards to the front door and began hammering it with his fists.

A woman answered. He brushed her aside and burst into the house, shouting, "Cap'n Spencer! Cap'n Spencer!"

"Hey, you can't come in here like this," the woman yelled at him.

Spencer emerged from a room. "It's all right, Jane."

Rory ran up to him. "Cap'n, Christopher's real sick!"

"Calm down." Spencer glanced at the woman, then looked at Rory. "Come into the library."

Rory followed him into the room. "Cap'n—"

Spencer raised a hand to stop him. He walked back to close the door. "All right. What happened?"

The words came pouring from his mouth.

"How far are they behind you?"

"I don't know. I only thought to get here, but—"

"Never mind. Wait here. I'll fetch the doctor."

For a moment, Rory stared at the door Spencer had closed behind him, then strode to the window. The brightly coloured sky had turned grey. Where were Kate and the others? He left the window to pour himself a drink, then settled in a chair. A short while later, a noise made him jump and run to the window. Nothing. What was keeping everybody?

The room was covered in shadows when he woke. He got out of the deep-seated chair to light the oil lamp. For a long moment he stared at the rows and rows of shelves on the wall full of books. He was drawn to take a closer look. Carefully, he eased out a volume and sniffed at the book-cover. Leather? How very odd. He took out another volume, then froze at the sound of hoof beats. He pushed both books back into the shelf and rushed to the window.

Two riders. He could make out the cap'n and another man, likely the doctor he'd gone to fetch. Rory hurried to meet them at the front door. "They ain't here yet, Cap'n. Shall we go look for them?"

"No. We'll wait for them here."

"Do you think they ran into some bushrangers, Cap'n? Had an accident, maybe?"

The doctor squeezed Rory's shoulder. "My dear fellow, spare Captain Spencer your fears. He has enough of his own."

They waited. Spencer and the doctor held a low-tone conversation, while Rory simply stared at the shadows on the wall, his ears tuned to the noise outside. How could the cap'n remain so calm? Didn't he care?

By the time the clock struck midnight, Rory had lost all hope that the party from Red Roo would arrive. At dawn, they rode out for the Hawkesbury—Spencer, the doctor and Rory on a new horse. The moment they neared the farm, Rory urged his horse to a gallop. He saw Ben and Peter and swung his horse in their direction. "Peter! Ben! What happened to you all?"

Peter shook his head, then looked over Rory's shoulder. "I'm sorry, Cap'n, but Christopher passed last night."

Spencer dismounted. "Tell me."

"We be just halfway to Dunover when Kate called me to stop, said there ain't no point rushing to Parramatta no more."

"Where's Kate?"

Peter indicated the cookhouse. "Inside. With the baby."

Rory clenched his teeth to stop himself from howling. He wanted to rush into the cookhouse, hold Kate and comfort her, but he couldn't. That right belonged to the cap'n.

Kate held Christopher against her breast. Her arms ached, but she couldn't bear to lay her baby down. It was her fault. If only she'd listened to Nicholas and stayed home at Parramatta, Christopher might still be alive.

The silence was broken by approaching footsteps. Kate knew it could only be Nicholas; the fellas wouldn't intrude on her grief. She closed her eyes, prepared for Nicholas' harshest words. She deserved the worst he could hurl at her.

He came into the room. She didn't resist when he took Christopher from her and laid him down. She closed her eyes instead. Hot tears streaked down her face when he drew her into his embrace.

"It's all right, Kate," he whispered.

The kindness in his voice cut her raw. She sobbed. "Nicholas, I killed him. I killed our baby. I'm sorry, so sorry—"

"Shhh."

The simple funeral was over. The doctor moved away first. The Red Roo fellas and Nellie followed. Kate stared at Christopher's new grave beside two older ones and couldn't stop the tears from overflowing. She had lost two babies, and she was to be blamed in both instances. Somehow, she felt the pain of losing Christopher was a lot harder to bear than that of her firstborn.

Spencer placed his hand on her shoulder. "Kate, it's time to go. It does you no good to linger here."

She resisted. "Please? Just a few minutes more?"

He brushed back a windblown curl from her face. "Don't be long."

Alone at last, she heaped more dirt on top of the new grave and patted it down. She touched the wooden cross with the words, *Christopher O'Neal* in Nicholas' hand, scratched across it. A whisper of a sound made her look over her shoulder. Rory stood some six paces away. He coughed and looked apologetic.

"Go away, Rory. Leave me alone."

"I'm sorry," he said.

Kate watched him leave, then turned her attention back to the grave, annoyed she'd been interrupted when time was so short.

"Was Christopher me son, Kate?"

Shocked, she whirled around. Rory stood a pace behind her, his lips compressed and his hands clenched as fists. She gritted her teeth and tried to remain calm. "No, he's not your son."

His face flushed. "You're lying."

She shook her head. "I have no need to lie."

"Didn't we lie together that day—"

She laughed without humour. "Once."

"You've been with the cap'n over a year, but you didn't have no baby all that time, did you? Then you lay with me, and you had Christopher."

She looked away. "Let's not quarrel over Christopher, Rory. He's gone . . . Well, believe what you will. I can't stop you."

CHAPTER 22

As the weeks passed, the pain of losing Christopher became blurred. Kate forced herself to accept the two undeniable facts: that her beloved son was gone and that Nicholas would never take her for his wife. She suppressed a rising feeling of bitterness and reminded herself she still had her "family", the fellas at Red Roo and the MacGregors at D-Store. Indeed she got to see the fellas regularly now, for they called at D-Store several times a month to deliver barrels of Harry's liquor and to collect their supplies of grain, sugar and other goods.

Then her sense of contentment shattered. Ben, Roger and Sam informed her they'd be leaving Red Roo when they finished serving their sentence. It had never occurred to her that the fellas might want to leave for their own reasons. Every day she prayed they'd change their minds, but they didn't. She'd tried to be happy for them, offering them good wishes, while she battled tears and the urge to beg them not to go.

Now it was Rory and Tom who would be leaving. They'd be calling on her some time today, to say goodbye.

She was losing her *family*. Telling herself that real families broke up too, when the children were grown, did not ease her pain. Reduced to half their number, the others might be persuaded to leave too, and they'd take Nellie with them. Kate winced, as if from a physical blow. She'd have no one but the MacGregors left.

Nicholas didn't appear bothered by the prospect of losing his

Red Roo workers, which could lead to shutting down their liquor production. He was a fair man, Kate had to grant him that. He had applied for Ben, Roger and Sam land grants of thirty acres each, their entitlement as free men. He'd done the same for Rory and Tom.

Kate knew the fellas would do well enough on their own. With their share of the profits, over five years, from the Red Roo harvests and Harry's liquor, they would have a good start in their new lives. She would miss them. Terribly. Well, whatever it cost her, she would show Tom and Rory a happy face too, when they said goodbye.

She'd been on the watch out for the fellas all morning and caught sight of them late that afternoon. She held herself back and allowed Robert and his sons to greet them and say their goodbyes first. Then it was her turn.

Tom kissed her lightly on the cheek. "Don't be sad, me dear. You'll be seeing me soon enough." He turned and gave Rory's shoulder a squeeze, then swung up on his horse. "Goodbye, all!"

She waved. Robert and his boys did too, then they moved back into the store.

"Kate . . ." Rory said.

Her heart thudded. She'd avoided Rory ever since Christopher's funeral, and when she couldn't, wouldn't give him the opportunity for a private talk. There could be no escape this time. She turned to face him.

"There's no other way to say this. Will you marry me, Kate? Will you?"

The question came as a shock. Tears welled. "I can't. I'm sorry."

"Why not? I love you, Kate, and I know you care for me."

"I do care for you, Rory, but I love Nicholas."

"You can't love the cap'n. You couldn't love him and lie with me."

"I do love him."

"Kate, the cap'n's not married you these many years. Think you, he'll change? To be sure I ain't got as much to offer you, but what I have, 'tis all yours, Kate. You'll have all of me love, and I'd never hurt you—"

"Stop! Please stop, Rory." She covered her trembling lips with her hand. "Oh, God. I wish I could! But the very thought of not being with him, of not seeing him . . . Rory, I know it's stupid, but it's true! I need him. It's no good talking about it. He'll not let me go, anyway."

"He'll have no say in the matter when you become an emancipist. I can wait. Just say you'll marry me."

"I can't." She wept. "Please, let's not talk about it anymore." After a while, she wiped her tears.

He gave her a sad smile. "So, it's goodbye then."

"I hate to have you leave, Rory. Why can't you stay, like Artie? It's not such a bad life. You make good money with the liquor."

"I'm hoping to build meself a future, Kate. I can't be working for someone else all of me life. And I ain't daft. I don't wish to be tormenting myself each time we meet. Well, you be good to yourself, then."

A month later, Kate was busy cleaning up a corner of the warehouse to stock new bales of fabric, when Hamish's voice floated in through the open door. "Kate! Look who's here!"

She couldn't begin to imagine, but she dusted her hands and walked out into the morning sunshine. She blinked, then screamed, "Ben! Sam!" She ran forward to hug one, then the other. "It's been four months! Couldn't you have visited sooner? I missed you."

Ben smiled. "We're coming back to Red Roo, Kate."

She tensed. "You're not teasing me?"

Sam shook his head. "We've just come from the cap'n. He said we can stay at Red Roo under the old terms."

"How wonderful! The fellas will be so happy too. They've been struggling with the farming and the liquor-making. Indeed, a week after Tom and Rory left, I suggested we hire some men, but Harry nearly bit my head off. He'll not have spies on the farm, he said."

Sam laughed. "Harry! That old scoundrel."

Ben smiled. "I've missed them all. Especially Nellie."

"Have you heard from Roger? Tom? What about Rory? Will they be coming back—"

Sam shook his head. "Rory says he's moving farther west, Kate and Ben here told me Tom and Roger sold their land and sailed for England."

"Never mind. I'm just so pleased to have you both back."

Kate suspected she was pregnant again in June 1798 and knew to expect nothing from Nicholas anymore. Her concern was only for the new baby. Poor mite, to have a father who didn't care, and a mother who didn't have the wits to know better. She could have used her sponge and vinegar, true, but she'd felt such an emptiness ever since Christopher died, she was hoping another baby might change that. And this time, she vowed to do a better job of taking care of this baby.

A month later, David and Sam told Kate they suspected Nellie was pregnant. They asked her to help them. Kate liked the idea of a visit to Red Roo, but feared Nicholas would object.

He surprised her. "How long do you plan to be away?"

"Two nights?"

He nodded agreeably.

Kate wasn't about to question her luck, though it struck her Nicholas appeared more distracted than usual that week.

David and Sam escorted her to Red Roo. Six new huts stood

a short distance from the ten humpies Kate knew so well. "David! Sam! You didn't tell me you've built yourselves new homes!"

David shrugged. "Thought the others might have done that already."

"It only made sense, Kate," Sam said. "If we mean to stay here forevermore, with the captain's permission of course, we should have better homes than them small humpies. What do you think?"

"I like your huts. They must be more comfortable than the humpies."

Sam pointed to the old cookhouse "We still do our cooking there, but you don't have to sleep there no more, Kate. You can have me hut, and I'll move in with David here."

Kate shook her head. "The old cookhouse will suit me fine. It's only for two nights." She stared at the cluster of old humpies. "You're not using those humpies anymore. So why don't you tear them down."

David's eyes rounded in horror. "We can't do that. We want to remember them old days. Anyways, they ain't hurting nobody by just standing there."

Kate waved at the four other fellas waiting outside the cookhouse for her. After the warm greetings were over, she planted her hands on her hips and smiled at them. "So, you're to become fathers come Easter?"

They beamed at her.

"Where's Nellie? Out bushwalking?"

Ben laughed. "That's our Nellie."

"And you're keeping a sharp eye on her?"

Ben nodded. "It's been so dry these days. We don't think she's going to slip over mud and lose the baby like last time. But we're looking out for her."

"All right then. Now, what are you fellas waiting for? Start unloading the wagon, and I'm going to take a closer look at your new home."

"We'll come with you," Peter said. They all followed her as she made her way to one of the new huts. The roof of shingles looked sturdy, as did the walls of cut timber. "Build it all yourselves, eh?"

"Of course," Harry said. "We ain't paying good money for things we can do ourselves. It ain't so hard to build these."

"I wouldn't mind paying a real builder," Peter said.

Harry snorted. "He'd only rob us blind."

"Whose hut is this?" Kate asked.

"Mine," Harry said. "Why do you ask?"

"Do you mind if I go through your clothes?"

"What for?"

"Just curious." She rummaged through his chest of clothes.

Harry tried to pull her away. "Stop it! Me clothes be clean, I tell you!"

"Oh, I wasn't checking for dirty clothes, Harry. There, I'm done."

At the next hut, Sam blocked the portal. She ducked under his arm.

"Don't you mess with me clothes, Kate. Hey, give me that. You know you're here to talk about Nellie, nothing else." Sam tried to recover his shirt from Kate's hold.

"Sam, don't tug. You'll tear the shirt." She examined the garment and handed it back to him. She looked at the other men. "I don't suppose your clothes are in any better shape? What on earth do you spend your money on, I'd like to know? Your clothes are a disgrace. Never mind. I'll get you some new ones. Shoes too. And these huts want a good clean."

"Oh, you don't have to clean—"

Kate laughed. "I'm not doing any cleaning. You all are!"

"Lord, you're a bloody tyrant," Peter said.

"You can start cleaning now, while I take care of supper. Do we have meat?"

"Aye," Peter said. "About Nellie—"

She headed back to the cookhouse. The fellas stayed close to her side.

"Kate," Sam said, "do you think we should hire a woman to look after Nellie?"

Kate stopped and studied her friends. "Is that what you all want?"

"Huh! If we did, would we bother you?" Harry asked. "We don't need no strange woman poking her nose into our business, I tell you. Nellie don't need no woman to take care of her. She got us."

Sam glared at him. "And you can deliver babies and all?"

"We have Kate," Harry said. "She can take care of that."

"Indeed, I will. Nellie can come stay with me in Parramatta." She turned to Ben. "What do you think?"

"I think one of us should marry Nellie. To give the baby a name."

The words punched the breath out of Kate. Why couldn't Nicholas feel as protective of her as the fellas did for Nellie?

"She should marry me," Sam said. "I thought of it first!"

David gave him a push. "No. She likes me better."

"Says who?" Peter demanded.

Kate watched them argue. Any one of them could be the father, but all of them wanted to be the husband. And Nicholas cared to be neither. Tears stung her eyes.

Ben touched her shoulder. "What's wrong, Kate?"

The others stopped quarrelling and stared at her.

"Nothing. We'll see what Nellie has to say about this."

Nellie wanted to marry all six men and rejected Kate's invitation to stay with her at Parramatta. She refused to leave Red Roo.

"Kate," Ben said, "don't you worry none. We'll get Nellie to you. Somehow."

"All right. Make it as soon as you can." She sighed. "I don't want you men fighting to marry Nellie. Perhaps we should let the baby take Nellie's name?"

The men looked at each other, then away.

Peter sighed. "Perhaps that's best."

Ben and David escorted Kate home. She went straight to bed and woke to a soft kiss.

"A tiring trip, my dear?" Spencer asked.

"Oh, no! I was just feeling lazy." She sat up. "Nicholas, can we have Nellie visit us for a while?"

"Why?"

"She'll be company for me."

"A half-wit for company?" He laughed. "Of course, if that's what you want. Just keep her out of my way."

"Thank you." She got out of bed. "Nellie says the Hawkesbury's going to flood. What do you think?"

"When?"

"Very soon." She ignored his raised eyebrows. "Nellie heard it from her black fella friends. Now, if the river's going to flood—"

"Kate, tell me you don't believe this rubbish."

"Nicholas, this is black fella land. If they say it's going to flood—"

He chuckled and shook his head. "I can't imagine what possessed me to think you're a woman of good sense!"

She smiled thinly. "Is that an insult?"

"Well, my pet, I never thought you could be so gullible."

She lifted her chin. "I am not."

"We've had no rain in months, almost a year. The ground is cracking up, the riverbed is showing. And the aborigines say it's going to flood? How on—"

"The black fellas must know what they're saying."

Spencer gave a heavy sigh. "Kate, for the river to flood, you need a lot of water. There's got to be rain, right? Plenty of rain? Well, have you seen a rain cloud in the sky lately? We'd be lucky to get a little rain, if only enough to break the bloody drought, never mind the flood."

She opened her mouth. He pressed a finger to her lips. "The aborigines are ignorant and simpleminded, Kate. Savages, really. They're like children. They want rain, and so it shall rain. Add a little imagination, and—"

He broke off, chuckling. Kate glared at him. That he had to struggle to control his hilarity made her angrier.

"Listen," he finally gasped. "These aborigines have been fighting a losing battle with the army and the settlers some years now. Why would they warn us, their hated enemies? They have good reasons to rejoice if the flood washed us all away."

"They're Nellie's friends. Why would they hoax her?"

"Enough! Forget about the flood. It won't happen."

Kate was not convinced. Harry had certainly taken the flood warning seriously. He'd demanded the others help him move his precious stills to higher ground. He wouldn't listen to any excuse, insisted it wouldn't take them long to do it. Peter's suggestion that it might only be a little flood moved him not at all. They finally yielded. Sam said they couldn't bear to be pestered by Harry forevermore.

Kate bit her lip. She couldn't tell Nicholas about Harry and his stills. He'd only make some cutting remark about her friend, and she couldn't bear that.

In February, Nellie came for the proposed visit. Kate stayed home the first day. She realized she couldn't leave Nellie at Dunover with Betty and Jane. Not only wouldn't they look after Nellie, chances were they'd bully her.

She took Nellie to work with her, and the MacGregors had

to go searching for her six times in two hours.

"Robert, would Janet look after Nellie for me?"

"Aye. I was about to suggest it meself. We really canna have Nellie here, Kate. We'll get no work done. Besides, you've got to look after yourself too."

She nodded, resting a hand on her big belly. "I'll pay Janet of course."

"You don't have to do that, lass. We'd be happy to help."

"Of course, I'll pay. We'll hear no more about it."

In March 1799, the rains came, putting an end to almost a year's drought. Ben's message told Kate the Hawkesbury river had started to flow again. It rained for four straight days, then the sky cleared.

Kate thought Nicholas was right after all. There'd never be enough water for a flood. Later that day, the Red Roo fellas showed up at D-Store.

"It's Harry's fault," Peter said. "We can't take no more of his foolishness."

Harry stuck out his chin. "Well, the river's still rising. How can I be sure it'd stop before it reached me still? You buggers don't care for nothing."

"Aye. You're the only one who cares," David said.

Kate couldn't control her sputter of laughter.

"Enough!" Ben said. "We agreed 'twas time to visit our Nellie, didn't we? Taking them stills with us for safety only made sense." He turned to Robert. "Can we camp in your backyard, to be near Nellie? We'll try not to be a bother."

"Sure, and you'll be right welcome."

The next day, Kate heard nothing but talk of the Hawkesbury river and its rising waters. Nicholas remained stubbornly quiet for two more days, then burst out, "God only knows how those aborigines knew about this flood."

"But where did all the water come from? It didn't rain that long or hard."

"From rain in the upper reaches, all draining into the Hawkesbury. It's a disaster, Kate. Already, 10,000 acres are under water. And they're saying the river will rise to 50 feet. It's a good thing your friends are here."

"Is it true five people are dead?"

"No. There's been one death. We had to use boats and managed to rescue the rest from their rooftops. That river is powerful, Kate. It carried the Government Store downstream like it was a tinder box!"

The flood finally subsided. Two days later, the Red Roo fellas made tracks home despite Kate's protests. They had work to do, they said.

The flood left many Hawkesbury farmers homeless and destitute. To add to their problems, prices of goods soared. Always ready to turn a quick profit, Kate, the businesswoman, shrank from taking advantage of this situation.

Nicholas, who had never interfered in her management of D-Store, suddenly took charge. "Kate, you're to trade strictly for money. No credit is to be given, do you understand?"

"No, I don't."

Spencer's glance fell on her belly, then shifted away. "Just do it."

She couldn't tell what that look meant. "Nicholas, these people can't pay for anything. They need credit now. If you like, we can charge them extra—"

"No. Accept only coins. Don't argue, my sweet."

"Nicholas, these people are going to remember we refused them credit in their time of need. This is no way to do business. Look at Andrew Thompson. He's offering very generous credit terms—"

"Let them all go to Thompson then. You're not to extend any

credit. I want your word, Kate."

Numbly, she nodded.

A week later, Janet sent news that Nellie was in labour. Kate sent for the midwife and then rushed to Nellie's side. Five hours later, Nellie gave birth to a baby girl. Within the hour, Ian rode off to Red Roo to deliver the good news.

Kate waited for her friends at the MacGregors'. They arrived that evening and looked like they hadn't wasted a minute to change their clothes. Judging from their dark expressions, she knew they'd been quarrelling again.

"Kate, don't you agree *Margaret*'s a pretty name?" Peter demanded.

"No, *Amber* sounds better," David said. "Kate—"

"I'm sure you've all picked a lovely name for the baby, but Nellie's waiting for you." She led them into a room.

Nellie, who had the baby cradled in her arms, beamed at them. "Come and meet Polly. Ain't she sweet?"

Silence fell on the men.

"P—Polly?" David coughed. "What a pretty name."

"Lovely," Ben said. The others chorused agreement. They crowded around Nellie and stared at the baby. Harry reached out and stroked the baby's cheek. Ben touched her almost hairless head, and Peter counted her small fingers and toes. Polly gave a loud wail and opened her eyes. The men retreated in confusion except for Artie, who leaned close.

"Why, she looks just like me," he said.

"What?" the others shouted. The baby started screaming.

Peter held Artie's shoulder. "What do you mean, Artie?"

"Look. She's got me eyes."

All five men moved closer and stared into Polly's eyes, then looked away.

"You're right, Artie," Ben said.

The others nodded vigorously. Kate bit her lip to stop from

laughing. The baby had blue eyes, and they'd remain blue for a while yet, and Artie had brown ones. No doubt each of them believed himself to be Polly's real father.

Two weeks after Nellie returned to Red Roo, Kate ignored a backache and went to work, as usual. The twinges of discomfort turned into pain. She promised herself she'd go home in another hour, but home with Betty and Jane held no appeal for her. A strong spasm had her gasping.

"Is it the baby, Kate?" Robert asked.

She nodded.

He raised his voice. "Lads, we're closing the shop now. Ian, go fetch the midwife, and Hamish, tell the cap'n."

"Robert—"

"Dinna argue, lass."

Four hours later, Kate gave birth to Lisa who had her father's brown hair and hooded eyes. This time she didn't wait for Nicholas to tell her to get the baby a nurse. She hired Mary Collins, a fifteen-year-old, to help her. When she returned to work, three weeks later, she brought Mary and the baby with her.

Robert protested. "Dinna you trust us MacGregors to run the store for you, Kate? We did—"

"No, Robert. I couldn't breathe at Dunover. You know I don't care for Betty and Jane. I needed to get away. Where better than here with you?"

Lisa was three months old when Kate left her at Dunover with Mary. She came home early one day, to retrieve several bills she'd inadvertently left in the library. She thought to check on Lisa. Upstairs, she caught sight of Nicholas in the nursery. He was cradling Lisa in his arms. Nicholas, who'd shown no interest in Christopher? What could it mean? Her immediate impulse was to join them. Second thought made her leave immediately. She wouldn't risk driving Nicholas away simply by making her presence known.

She took Mary aside later that night. "How long has the captain been visiting Lisa?"

"Three weeks now. It started that day when she cried and wouldn't stop. The cap'n came by to ask what's wrong. Lisa stopped crying right away, smiled and waved her arms at the cap'n. He stayed for a while to play with her. He's been stopping by every day now."

Kate tidied her desk, glad another work day had ended, when she heard two sets of footsteps heading her way.

"Ah, there you are, Kate. I thought to drive you home."

She stared at Nicholas, unable to believe her eyes. Not once, since D-Store opened for business, had he crossed its threshold. Sure, he'd helped her to obtain supplies for the store, but he'd conducted his business with the suppliers, away in Sydney Town. What was he doing here now?

He stepped aside and ushered a man forward. "My dear, I'd like you to meet my good friend, Lieutenant William Hudson. Bill, this is the lady who runs my life, Kate O'Neal."

She held out her hand. "How do you do, Lieutenant?"

Hudson clasped it with both of his. "How do you do. I'm Bill. May I call you Kate?"

She nodded, hoping her excitement didn't show. In all of their five years together, Nicholas had never introduced her to any one of his friends or fellow officers. Something had changed. Would she be meeting more of his friends now? Would he be offering her marriage next? *Holy Mary, Mother of God, please let it be so.*

CHAPTER 23

"I see you're almost ready to leave," Nicholas said as he slipped his arm around Kate's waist and dropped a kiss on her head. "Well, give me a minute to let Ian know I'll be driving you home tonight. In the meantime, why don't you show Bill around the store? You'd like that, wouldn't you Bill?"

"Indeed. If you wouldn't mind, Kate?"

Kate nodded, then lowered her gaze and swallowed hard. She was excited and nervous all at once. For the past several years, she had imagined being in the company of Nicholas' faceless friends. She saw herself chatting with them with the greatest ease, but now, when faced with the reality, she found her throat had closed up and her mind, a total blank. She looked up to appeal to Nicholas not to leave her alone.

Nicholas gave her hand a gentle squeeze and then he was gone before she could utter a word.

Bill Hudson was speaking, and Kate forced herself to pay attention to his words.

"I've always pictured your store much bigger than this for the amount of goods you sell," Hudson said. "How do you manage on such a small floor space? Didn't you think to expand, like having a bigger building and using this for another warehouse?"

Kate was surprised to find how easy it was to talk business with Lieutenant Hudson. He kept the conversation going, and in a short while Kate found her nervousness had vanished. Then Nicholas was back, urging them out of the store. He drove

Kate in the wagon, while Lieutenant Hudson rode his bay. For the first time in all their years together, Kate saw Nicholas with someone he considered a friend. He was open with Hudson, as he had never been with her. They chatted along the way, and Nicholas, whom she thought to be a man of very few words, seemed to have plenty to say for himself. She was content to listen to the two men. They spoke of the governor, of other officers and of their early days in Sydney Town. Lieutenant Hudson was very kind. He often included her in their conversation, if only to get her agreement on an opinion.

All too soon they arrived at Dunover. In the library, Nicholas busied himself with their drinks.

"I'm delighted we've met at last, Kate," Hudson said. "But it's not entirely my fault, mind, that I haven't met you earlier. I hate to say this, but my dear wife, bless her heart, keeps me on a short leash, you see? It's work and home, and no excuses."

He looked somewhat mortified by his confession, and Kate felt a little sorry for him.

Spencer looked from Kate to his friend and chuckled. "I wonder if your dear wife knows how you slander her, Bill. And what would you call your three children for clinging to your shirt tails? Leeches?"

Hudson squirmed in his seat, turned a bright shade of pink and burst out laughing. "Must you spoil it all for me, you devil?"

Kate smiled. "A fond papa?"

Hudson beamed. "Indeed."

"Supper is served, sir," Jane announced from the doorway.

During supper Kate and Hudson exchanged tales of the mischief children could get themselves into. Spencer watched them through half-closed eyes, joined in their laughter now and again, but didn't contribute to the conversation. Kate didn't care. She was too happy trading stories with Hudson, eager to show Nicholas she could hold her own with his friend or any other friend he'd care to invite home.

Then Jane interrupted them once more. "A soldier here to see you, Cap'n."

Spencer excused himself from the table. He came back a few minutes later. "Bill, the governor has asked for me—"

"At this late hour? He's getting somewhat demanding, don't you think?" Hudson dabbed his mouth with a napkin. "Let's go then. Kate, if you'll excuse us—"

Spencer held him down by his shoulders. "There's no need for you to come with me. You know how the governor is. It's probably nothing but a storm in a teacup. Finish your meal, and if you're not here when I get back, I'll see you in Sydney Town."

With a nod, he was gone.

Hudson gave a loud sigh, then picked up his fork and knife. "I can never win an argument with that man. So, tell me, Kate. Is your family in trade? Is that why you do so well with D-Store?"

"Oh, no. My father's a farmer. So was his father."

"I don't suppose Nicholas would have told you this, but do you know that many of my fellow officers are not too pleased with you?"

She frowned. "Why? What did I do to offend them?"

Hudson laughed. "You made them look incompetent."

Kate blinked, then waited for Hudson to give a more complete explanation.

"They're all somewhat embarrassed to fail in their business when you, a mere girl, seem to have done so well with D-Store. Oh, you needn't feel sorry for them. It's their own fault, and they don't blame you for their failure. Not really. They blame the governor, perhaps rightly so. Did he not keep trimming our authority, we might all be in business still."

"The Trading Officers' Fraternity knows of me?"

Hudson grinned. "How could we not? Nicholas is the envy of

many for having you in charge of his store, but the Fraternity is no more, Kate. It's ironic really. Nicholas, who never wanted to be in trade, has remained in it far longer than many of us. He's done very well too, with your help."

They chatted on till supper was done, then they retired to the library. The summer sky was still light, but Kate knew that Hudson would be leaving soon. He had his family waiting for him at home and over an hour's ride to reach Sydney Town.

"Can I pour you a brandy, Bill? Rum?"

"I'd rather have a cup of tea. You see, my dear wife doesn't approve of excessive drinking. Says it's bad for her health."

Kate thought she'd misheard. "How is it bad for *her* health?"

"I must admit I was puzzled too till she explained it all to me. Our fate became one the day we married, she said. Since her good health depended on mine, it was my duty to keep healthy so she'd be in the pink. If anything bad happened to me, worse would happen to her. I must forevermore be considerate. It's a husband's obligation, you see?"

Kate laughed and shook her head. "Well, tea it is then. I'll fetch it."

"Fetch it? No, no. That's too much trouble. Brandy will be fine."

"It's no trouble at all. You're not to get into strife with Mrs. Hudson on my account!" Kate smiled. "I won't be long."

Betty confronted her when she stepped into the kitchen. "What do you want now?"

Kate ignored her, sidestepped and reached for the teapot. She warmed the pot, scooped in three teaspoons of leaves from the tea caddy, then poured in hot water for two cups. She set up a tray of cups and saucers with spoons, a bowl of sugar and a small jug of milk.

"Well, don't give yourself airs, doxy. It don't make you no

better than me just 'cause you supped with the captain and his friend."

Jane said, "Betty, maybe you'd better—"

Betty glared at her friend. "Don't you take that trollop's part, Jane. I won't have it—"

"What goes on here?" a voice interrupted.

Jane gasped, and Betty's face paled. Kate turned and stared in horror at Hudson who stood in the kitchen doorway. *Damn.* She should have given him the brandy and spared herself this terrible humiliation.

Hudson walked up to Betty. "I'm sorry. Captain Spencer neglected to introduce us. How very careless of him. You sound like an important person in his household. Allow me to introduce myself. I'm Lieutenant William Hudson, and you are?"

"B—Betty Wilson. I'm the c—cook, sir."

"The cook?" He sounded amazed. "A free settler then? Of course. How else could you be so bold with Mistress O'Neal?"

Betty said nothing, only looked down at her feet.

"No? Hmmm. A convict cook then, and insolent too. Well!" He turned to Kate. "My dear, how kind of you to prepare my tea yourself. Allow me to carry that tray for you."

Back in the library, Hudson put down the tray. He waited for Kate to be seated, then occupied the chair next to her. "I must apologise for meddling, my dear. But, you shouldn't let a woman like Betty Wilson bully you. If you give a bully the merest inch, she'd take a mile and wrap it around your neck to choke you."

Kate couldn't look Hudson in the eye. "She does her job well enough, and I try not to get in her way . . ."

The silence stretched.

"Would you like me to speak to Nicholas for you?"

Kate looked at him in alarm. "Oh, no! Please don't! I try not to trouble him with my problems."

He gave her a long look, then dipped his head. He poured himself a cup of tea and another for Kate. "Nicholas is very fortunate. My evenings must be very different from his. My dear wife thinks it her duty to fill my ears with the happenings in the household when I get home. Methinks, she doesn't trust me. Sometimes she'd repeat herself, to see if I noticed. And if I don't, she'd make sure I never get to hear the end of it. Woe is me. I married a harridan."

He gave a long-suffering sigh, but Kate caught the twinkle in his eye that belied his words. She laughed and took a sip of her plain tea. "I think Nicholas is right. You do like to slander your dear wife, don't you?"

In the days that followed, Kate waited anxiously for Nicholas to announce his new plans for their future. He intended to marry her. She was sure of it. Why else would he have her meet Bill Hudson? But he said nothing. Then it was end of June, and Kate realised only a month remained of her seven-year sentence. Maybe that was the answer—Nicholas meant to surprise her, marry her as a free woman!

Kate wished July gone. Sure, she could've pressed Nicholas for some answers, but she'd learned it would yield her nothing. Nicholas only told her what he wanted her to know. She must be patient, she told herself.

A few days later, she came home early to be with Lisa because her little girl wasn't feeling well. She was halfway up the stairs with Lisa's cup of milk when the front door swung open. A blast of winter cold rushed in, followed by a grim-faced Nicholas. He usually came home after five, and it was just three in the afternoon.

Kate's heart began to pound. Something was wrong.

Nicholas shrugged off his cloak, as he looked up at her. "Kate, can you come to the library, please? I need to talk to you."

Her sense of unease increased. Nicholas had never been this brusque with her before. She came down the stairs and followed him into the library. He indicated a chair.

She shook her head. "I'll stand."

"Sit down, Kate." He poured a drink, removed her cup of milk and handed her the glass of brandy.

Kate's hands trembled. If Nicholas thought she needed fortification, it had to be bad news. She swallowed a mouthful of liquor and coughed.

He seated himself facing her. "Don't interrupt, Kate. Just hear me out. I'm sorry to have to say this, but—Well, all good things must come to an end, and that's how it must be with us."

"What?" She couldn't understand his words, and yet she knew she must try to do so, that it was important that she did.

He held up a hand. "Let me finish, please. I'm sorry, I've left it so late, but—I'm leaving you, Kate."

The glass of brandy slipped from her fingers. It fell with a dull thud, and the contents seeped into the dark carpet to form a widening wet patch. "Leaving me? Whatever can you mean?"

"I'm going home, my dear."

"Home? But this is home."

"No. Home to England."

"And leaving me and Lisa here? You're jesting! It's a cruel joke, Nicholas."

Spencer picked up her glass. "I've acquired new obligations in England, and I must return home to do my duty."

"What's there to stop you from taking Lisa and me with you?" She scrambled off her chair, knelt at his feet and grabbed his hand. "Please take us with you, Nicholas. We won't be any bother. None at all, I promise."

"Shhh." He stroked her hair and murmured soothing sounds.

After a while, he said, "I'm sorry, sweet. That's not possible."

"Please?"

Spencer got to his feet. Kate followed, slowly.

"I've bought passage to sail on Thursday on the *Lady Carolyn.*"

Kate frowned. Something was amiss. "In two days? How is this possible? You can't just drop everything and sail away."

He raised his voice. "I've made provisions for you and Lisa. You'll have the two farms, Random and Red Roo, this house, D-Store and the warehouse."

Kate stiffened. In that moment she finally understood it all. He wouldn't allow her to sell goods on credit after the flood. She should have realised something was wrong then. Why else would he interfere with her running of the store when he never had before?

Then he'd stopped re-stocking the warehouse. *Why wasn't I alarmed then?* Because she thought he was biding his time for the price of goods to fall even more before he started buying again. *Eejit! He was already planning to leave.*

"You bastard!" Stepping up close, she slammed her palms heavily against his chest. "Oh, you heartless bastard!" She hit him again, and again.

He grabbed her wrists. She struggled, her breathing turned ragged and her tears streamed. She slumped against him and sobbed. After a while, he loosened his hold and settled her into a chair. He offered her a new glass of brandy. She brushed it aside.

He set down the glass. "I'll leave you some money, Kate, so you'll be able to carry on trading, if you choose to do so."

"Damn your money! Can't you understand? All I ever wanted was you. Nicholas, please take us with you. Please?"

"Don't carry on like a fishwife. That's not you. Come on, Kate, where's this sensible woman I know?"

"Sensible? You expect me to be sensible? I thought you cared for me. What about Lisa? How can you—"

He cursed. "Why can't you be civil about this? I find all this emotional excess . . . distasteful."

"I'm supposed to laugh and be merry? I'm flesh and blood, Nicholas. When you cut me, I bleed."

"I can't talk to you if you're going to be this emotional. It's better for me to leave now." He walked out of the library. She wanted to chase after him, say anything, even promise him the moon so long as he changed his mind.

A voice inside her head whispered, "Where's your pride, girl? If he doesn't want you, let him go."

"I can't," she cried. *What has pride to do with anything? What is life without him?*

"He doesn't want you, girl," the voice repeated.

Kate had regained a measure of composure by the time Nicholas came down the stairs carrying two valises. She stared at him, battling her pride. He stopped before her. She opened her mouth, but her throat had closed up. The words she would use to grovel refused to take shape.

He dropped the valises on the floor. "I'm really sorry it has come to this, Kate, but I know you'll be all right."

She found her voice. "Do you really care?"

"Of course I do." He bent to kiss her. She jerked her head aside at the last moment, and the kiss went awry. For five years she'd lived with him, yet she knew him not at all. How could she have loved such a cold bastard?

His gaze swept over her face, as if he was memorising her features, then he picked up his valises. "I'm sorry. Goodbye, my dear."

CHAPTER 24

A distant cockcrow shattered the early morning silence. Before the cry could die, another followed, then another. Kate wiped away a tear trickling its way down the side of her face and struggled for another breath. Sleep had eluded her all night long. Now, she dragged herself out of bed and lit the oil lamp.

The mirror showed a pale face with swollen red eyes and nose. She didn't think a pound of powder and rouge would hide the ravages of the past hours, yet she must try. She needed to put on a bold front to face the world and give no hint her life had turned into a wasteland.

She pinched her cheeks, then glared into her mirror. *You're done with self-pity! Get on with your life.*

She put on a warm robe and walked out of her room, determined to treat this day as any other. Nicholas was right. She hadn't been sensible last night. Now she'd have to pay for it with uncertainty. Sure, she'd be a free woman, an emancipist, in four weeks, but with Nicholas gone, would she now be required to return to the government to complete her term? Nicholas had said he'd take care of her and Lisa. She'd never known him to lie, but what if he had this time? She shuddered and pushed the ugly thought away. She must keep faith. The alternative was too terrible to contemplate.

In the kitchen, she lit the fire, then put on some water to boil. Although she was not hungry, she knew she needed the energy to get her through the day. So she forced herself to swallow a slice of buttered bread and a cup of tea. Afraid to bump into Betty or Jane, she left the cup and plate unwashed and hurried back upstairs.

A noise from the nursery made her pause. She decided to check on Lisa. The little girl was sound asleep. Kate stroked her soft cheeks, whispering, "Lisa, sweetie, your papa has abandoned us." An image of Nicholas cradling Lisa in his arms flashed through her mind, and a swelling of emotions overpowered her. She choked back a sob and ran back to her room.

She dressed, then painted her face with a heavy hand. The garish image that stared back from the mirror urged her to wipe off some of the powder and rouge. She resisted. She would not look tired and pale and have her customers concerned about her health. She could not afford to listen to words of sympathy. Not today. Today must be like any other working day.

She sat on her bed, watching the sky lighten. She waited till she heard Hamish drive up in the wagon. It was time to go. She straightened her shoulders and made her way down the stairs, along the hallway and through the front door, but not before she passed Mary and Jane and noted their puzzled looks.

Hamish, who usually had a few things to say when he drove her to work, left her alone with her thoughts. At the store, a heavy traffic of customers kept her busy: measuring out four pounds of flour here, three lengths of calico there. She concentrated on each task, as if a slight mishap would cause a bolt of lightning to strike her dead. She smiled till she felt her face stiffening into a mask.

The MacGregors kept their distance, going about their tasks quietly, without once approaching her to have a question answered, and she was grateful. Then a lull in trade occurred around noon. She beckoned for Robert and his sons to join her. Apart from the Red Roo fellas, they were her only friends, and they deserved the truth.

"I've some bad news, Robert. Captain Spencer has left me."

Robert frowned. "Och. Nay, lass. Listen, all couples have their ups and downs. I've me bad days with Janet too—"

"No, you don't understand. Captain Spencer has left me. He's returning to England—" Unable to continue, she turned her face away.

Robert put an arm around her shoulder. "Och, lass, I'm right sorry. How can we help?"

She dug out a handkerchief, wiped her tears and gave a weak giggle. "You'd do better to think on your future, Robert, not worry about mine, but thank you." She attempted a smile. "Perhaps it's not too bad . . ."

She related what Nicholas had told her about leaving her well-provided. ". . . Oh Robert, and haven't I been fooling myself all these years?"

"I dinna ken what to say. I've always believed the captain thought the world of you, Kate, and I've never known him to lie—"

"But haven't I lived out his lie these many months?" She couldn't stop a bitter laugh. "Why do you think he refused to re-stock the warehouse after the flood? Or allow credit to our customers?" She blew her nose. "Because he was squeezing out as much as he could from the business, to take with him when he left."

Robert looked at her. His Adam's apple bobbed.

"Damn! I've become a watering-pot." Kate dried her eyes and put away her handkerchief. "I don't know what will happen to me or the store, but I'll be grateful if we could carry on as usual in the meantime."

All three MacGregors nodded.

"Our low supplies are a worry. We need to re-stock, but I've only ever handed Nicholas lists of what goods I wanted, and he had handled the rest. I'm not sure how I'm to go about this."

"Dinna you fash, lass. You'll find a way. You always do."

"And you'll all stay with me, Robert? You and your boys?"

"Aye. You canna get rid of us MacGregors so easily!"

Kate reached out for Robert's arm and squeezed it gently. "Thank you. I won't forget this." She led him away from his two sons. "I've another problem."

"Another? What is it?"

"I finish my sentence end of July. I'm wondering—"

"Good Lord! Nay. The captain would've seen to this before he left." He stared at Kate. "Dinna you say he hasna left yet? Well, I'll go look for him, sort this out. It canna harm just to be checking. Just to be sure."

"No. I don't want you seeking out the captain. He wants nothing more to do with me. It shall be as he wishes. I'll survive, Robert. Somehow."

He shook his head. "Lass, this is no time to be standing on your pride. 'Tis not too late—"

"No, Robert."

"As you wish. Our friends at Red Roo. You'll want to tell them about—"

"Yes. But later. I can't leave Parramatta until I know for sure what Nicholas has arranged for me."

"Kate, Ian could drive up tomorrow with the supplies and tell them—"

"All right. Send Ian."

"Perhaps Hamish should move in to stay with you, at least for now. You're a household of women, and 'tis not safe—"

Fresh tears rolled down her cheeks. She hugged him. "Yes, of course. I'm not thinking too well. Thank you, Robert, for looking out for me."

Three days had passed since Nicholas left. Hamish was driving Kate home, as usual, after a hard day at the store, when they rounded a bend and Dunover came into view. Kate's heart skipped a beat when she saw Mary, with Lisa astride her hip, come rushing out of the house. Then she raced down the driveway towards her, like the devil was at her heels.

Hamish immediately pulled up the horses and barely managed to avoid running over the foolish girl and little Lisa.

Mary didn't seem to realise she'd almost caused an accident. "They've both run mad," she cried. "Betty's taken over me room, and Jane, Lisa's. They threw out our clothes and everything!"

Rage blazed through Kate. She should have booted the two witches out long ago, but like a coward, she'd tolerated them rather than raised a fuss. No more. She'd sort them out, and right this minute. "Where are they?"

"The nursery."

She climbed down the wagon, picked up her skirts and stormed into the house. She pounded up the stairs and headed for the nursery. Betty and Jane, busy rearranging the furniture, appeared unaware of her approach.

"Get out of here!" Kate cried.

Both women whirled to face her. Jane gasped, then quickly ducked behind Betty, who showed her teeth in a feral smile.

Kate pointed to the door. "Move! Your rooms are downstairs. Stay there!"

Betty cackled. "If it ain't the bloody Queen of England herself come to throw us out, Jane."

"I don't want to argue with you, Betty. Get your things—"

"Ooh! She's right angry, Jane! See? I'm trembling, afeared!" Betty shook her hands and snickered.

Jane hunched her shoulders and sidled to the door. Betty grabbed her arm. "Stay!" She glared at Kate. "We ain't moving, bitch! So what you gonna do?"

Kate wanted to strangle the troublemaker. She took a step closer.

Betty raised a threatening arm. "One more step, and I'll brain you! You're nothing but the captain's doxy, and I know the captain's gone and left you. You're no one special now, you bitch, and we ain't taking your orders no more, see? We're just as good as you. If you sleep upstairs, we will too. So there!"

The words chilled Kate. Without Nicholas' authority, she had no power to impose her will on anyone. She closed her eyes and swallowed her humiliation. Clinging tightly to the remnants of her dignity, she turned and walked out of the room.

"And you can jolly well cook your own meals, your bloody highness!" Betty shouted. "And wash your own bloody clothes and do your brat's too."

Mary grumbled when Kate told her to move into Jane's old room and to keep Lisa with her. "It'll only be for a few days, till I sort out the confusion." In truth, she didn't know what to do.

Two days later, the longest two days Kate had experienced, a sergeant and two soldiers called on her at D-Store.

"Ma'am, I'm Sergeant Sharpe. I've these here orders to collect from you two convict women—Betty Wilson and Jane Blake. I'm to take them to the Parramatta Women's Factory. If you'll hand them over, ma'am, I'll be right grateful."

No other words could sound sweeter to Kate. "I'm happy to let you have them, Sergeant. They're at my house. If you'll follow me?"

Mary, with the baby riding on her hips, met them at the door.

"Where are they?" Kate asked.

Mary looked up the stairs. "In me old room."

"Mary, please take Lisa into the library now, and stay there with her till I call for you." She waited till Mary and Lisa were safe inside the library before she turned to the sergeant. "The women you want are up those stairs, Sergeant, behind the second door on your left. Please be careful."

"Careful?" The sergeant frowned. "Right, men, on your way. Don't take no nonsense from yon ladies!"

The two soldiers stomped up the stairs. The knocks on the door were quickly followed by Betty's shriek. Next came a noisy scuffle and an exchange of hot words between the soldiers and Betty. Then a man howled.

Sergeant Sharpe cursed. He pounded up the stairs. "Order," he thundered.

A short eerie silence was followed by a flurry of footsteps leading to the landing. The soldiers started down the stairs, dragging Betty along. Betty fought to free herself, spat foul words at them when she couldn't.

Jane appeared to shrink from Betty this time, pressing herself into Sergeant Sharpe's side. They made their way down the stairs in two groups. Then Betty's gaze fell on Kate, and all at once she began to buck and twist wildly. The two soldiers struggled to hold on to her. They cursed.

"What about her, you bastards?" Betty shrieked. "Why ain't you taking her too? Don't let her fine clothes and fancy ways fool you. She's a bloody convict too!"

"Don't you learn me me job!" the sergeant shouted. "Don't you give me no more trouble, you foul-mouthed bitch!"

In one violent move, Betty kneed one of the soldiers between his legs and sent him tripping down a step then tumbling down the stairs. The sergeant ordered the other soldier to hold Betty still. But Betty continued to twist and buck. The soldier couldn't hold her. She bit his hand then sent him crashing against the wall. A loud thud was immediately followed by a howl of pain.

The sergeant bounded down three steps, grabbed Betty by her hair, then punched her in her face. She would have collapsed on the stairs had the sergeant not held her up. The soldier on the stairs struggled to his feet, his face screwed up in pain. Then he was helping his sergeant carry Betty like a big sack of potatoes down the stairs.

"I can manage by meself now, Sergeant," the soldier said. Sergeant Sharpe nodded and watched as his man dragged Betty by one arm out of the door.

The other soldier got off the floor and stood very still with his knees bent and his hands hovering over his groin. He looked at the sergeant. "I would've let the bitch fall and break her neck for what she done."

"Enough. Go help Bill chain and iron her." He beckoned for Jane to approach. "Take her with you. Chain her too."

He turned to Kate. "Thank you, ma'am. We got what we came for, so we'll be going now."

Kate couldn't stop smiling. Free! Free of Betty and Jane, at last! That the sergeant had not included her with the two other women told her she was a free woman. Another worry lifted from her shoulders. *Thank God.*

The next day, Mary handed in her notice. Her mother needed her at home, she said. Kate didn't believe her. "That's all right, Mary. Have you packed? No? Well, give Lisa to me, and you can start packing now. I'll have your wages ready when you leave."

She was not sorry to see Mary go. She needed loyal friends, and Mary couldn't be counted as one.

The following morning, Kate took Lisa to work with her. She didn't even have to ask. Robert told her Janet would look after Lisa till she found a replacement for Mary. That evening, Robert came knocking on her door. He'd brought his daughter, Fiona, to look after Lisa. Janet thought this would be a better idea so Lisa wouldn't be frightened by a new place and new faces too.

The next day, Kate noted an unusual number of men visiting her store. They came to buy trifles, several stayed only to browse. They all looked her over, most of them furtively. She felt like a goose they were considering to serve for their Christmas dinner.

It was way past noon, when a man, dressed in his Sunday best, approached her to ask for her hand in marriage. Kate was astonished by his boldness. When two more men came to her with a similar proposal, she wondered no more. With so few white women in the settlement, many men were not particular about whom they got for a wife. Since she was young, strong and known for running a successful store, Kate knew she would be seen as prime material for some man's wife. Nor did she doubt the supposed fortune Nicholas must have left her had added to her appeal.

The marriage offers kept coming. She turned them all down, firmly but politely. After her experience with Jeremy and Nicholas, she knew her future and her happiness would be safer in her own hands.

After two weeks, the number of offers slowed to a trickle. She was glad that her decision not to seek a protector had finally spread far and wide. No stranger called on her on Sunday and Monday. Then late on Tuesday morning, a man in his fifties presented himself at Dunover.

"Mistress O'Neal? I'm Aaron Bernstein. Your man at the store told me I'd find you at home."

She stared at her visitor in surprise. Robert should've known better than to direct her unwanted suitor to Dunover.

She looked at Bernstein's grey hair, at his well-worn clothes that hung loosely on his tall and thin frame. Obviously, he was a man who dressed for comfort, not to impress.

Well, she had no time to waste on him. She had two big stacks of documents, mostly bills, to go through. Now that Nicholas was gone, she had to learn how to handle the details that would keep D-Store supplied.

"Mr. Bernstein, I'm sorry, but it's a wasted journey for you,

I'm afraid. You see, I won't be thinking of marriage for another year at least—"

The man chuckled. "Mistress O'Neal, I must apologise for not making my purpose more clear. I'm Aaron Bernstein, the solicitor hired by Captain Spencer to handle his business affairs here in the colony. I've some legal matters to settle with you."

"A solicitor? Oh dear!" Kate covered her hot cheeks with her hands. "I'm sorry. Please, do come in, Mr. Bernstein. You must think I'm raving mad, shameless too, to think every man in the world wants to marry me! The fact is since it became common knowledge that I no longer have a protector, strangers have approached me to propose marriage. I'm so sorry I mistook you for one of these men."

"No, no! Don't apologise, Mistress O'Neal. I understand. I've heard quite a bit about your suitors, but I didn't think you'd mistake an old man like me—"

"Sir, you're too modest."

Once they'd settled in the library, Bernstein explained to Kate the legal state of affairs that concerned her. There were no surprises. Nicholas' farming properties of Red Roo and Random, and the house, Dunover, had been registered in her name. Title to D-Store and the warehouse would be transferred to her only if she agreed to settle all of Nicholas' outstanding debts in the colony.

"These are relatively modest debts." Bernstein handed her a list. She gave it a quick glance. Nicholas continued to be the astute businessman while acting the gentleman. Kate passed the list back to Bernstein.

He shook his head. "You may keep that. I've another copy. If you reject responsibility for these debts, I've been instructed to sell the store and the warehouse to settle them. Any monies left over are to be given to you. I will, of course, provide a proper accounting—"

"That won't be necessary. Captain Spencer's debts will be mine." She had no choice, really. She couldn't allow Bernstein to sell D-Store and the warehouse. She needed them to trade, to earn a living. And Nicholas knew it.

"Good! That simplifies matters. The captain had anticipated your decision. He's made arrangements with his debtors to allow you three months' grace to settle the debts."

He handed her a document. The words made no sense to her.

"It's a legal document, Mistress O'Neal. You only have to make your mark at the bottom of the page," Bernstein said kindly. "It merely states that you accept responsibility for Captain Spencer's debts in the colony."

She reached out for a pen, signed her name and handed him the document.

"When you've settled the captain's debts, I shall proceed to have title to the store and the warehouse transferred to your name." He handed her another document. "And this is your Governor's Pardon."

Kate glanced at the date on the document and was not at all surprised to note she'd been a free woman three months before Nicholas left her. He was indeed very good at keeping secrets. She signed a receipt for it.

Bernstein next slung a heavy bag of coins onto the table. "Captain Spencer has left you six hundred pounds. Would you care to count it?"

Kate shook her head.

"All right. If you'll sign this receipt? Good. Thank you. And now, Mistress O'Neal, this is the captain's letter for you."

She accepted it with a trembling hand. Unable to stop herself, she tore open the envelope, fished out a piece of paper and scanned it.

"Well, that concludes my business for today," Bernstein said.

Kate looked up. The solicitor had gathered his papers together. "Mr. Bernstein? Will you be writing to Captain Spencer?"

"Indeed. Would you like me to give him a message?"

"Can I have his address? He seems to have overlooked it in his letter."

"I'm sorry. Captain Spencer left strict instructions. I'll be happy to pass on a message—"

Kate's face burned. "No. There's no message. Thank you, Mr. Bernstein. I'll see you to the door." When she returned to the library, she re-read her letter.

My dearest Kate,

We could have had a sweeter parting. I apologise for mishandling the situation. I trust Mr. Bernstein has made a better job in his explanation. You'll have discovered by this time that I've left both you and Lisa sufficient funds for your present needs. I know you too well and wouldn't be surprised if you turned this into a great fortune of your own. However, it's my fondest hope that you'll seek a different future, a future with a husband to care for you and Lisa.

Bill Hudson has agreed to extend his help, should you ever need it. If you require legal advice, you'll find no better man than Mr. Bernstein. He has served me well over the years. The man is honest.

I have every confidence that dear Lisa will be safe in your care. I shall miss you, and Lisa too. You may be sure you'll both be in my thoughts, always.

Nicholas

Kate crushed the letter and hurled it at the wall. When her temper cooled, she collected it, smoothed out the creases and locked it away in the desk drawer, to read it again whenever she needed reminding what a fool she'd been, living on dreams. She had only ever been Nicholas' convict mistress, nothing more.

She opened the bag Bernstein had given her and slowly fingered the coins. They wouldn't be enough to put D-Store on the footing it had enjoyed before the flood. However, if she was careful, she'd be able to keep the store open. With Harry's liquor, she should keep the customers coming while she built up the business for herself. It would be hard work, but the store would be hers, all hers.

The next day, Kate explained her financial circumstances to Robert and his boys.

"You can have me savings, lass. I'd be honored—"

Kate laughed. "Dear Robert, keep your savings. I'm only grateful you and your boys have decided to stick by me. I'd be in terrible straits if you left."

"Och, we'd never do that, lass! We're like family."

Kate met her various suppliers for the first time the following days. The first one called and introduced himself. He was very sorry, he said, but he needed to raise the price of his goods. The others too had the same message to deliver. A fortnight later, the first supplier returned with more bad news. He was sorry, he said, but he would sell his goods for cash only.

Kate's heart sank. No doubt the others would tell her the same thing. "Why are you doing this? We've always paid on time—"

"Ah, that was when Captain Spencer was here. How can I be sure you'll be able to pay for me goods two, three months from now? I must protect meself."

"You're making it impossible for me to carry on trading—"

"Now, now. Don't you fret, me dear. When you're married, your husband can take care of you and your store." He chortled. "There ain't no shortage of men waiting to marry you, I hear.

Why don't you pick one, and I'll be right glad to do business with him."

Kate wanted to slap the old fool, but she kept on smiling. "Couldn't you supply me with your goods as usual? Then when I get married—which can happen any time now because you know there are many men who want to marry me, and I need only decide on which man—then you can deal with my husband, and everything will be fine."

"Hmmm. You're clever with them words, ain't you?" The man wagged his finger at her. "But them tricks ain't gonna work with me. Oh, no. First you get married, young lady. Then me and your husband will talk business. You will look after your home, have your babies and raise them. Just as it should be. Just as God intended."

CHAPTER 25

Six weeks had passed since Nicholas walked out on Kate, and the problems his absence had raised continued to plague her. All these years, she'd not given much thought to the details of how the merchandise had been obtained. She'd only to hand Nicholas the list of goods she needed, and these goods would simply appear in due time. Nicholas had kept D-Store well-supplied, and he did it so unobtrusively, and without ever stepping into the store, that Kate had been deceived into thinking she ran the store alone. Now she knew differently. In her business, the acquisition of merchandise was just as important as their sale.

Kate took a sip of water and massaged her temples. The dull ache persisted. The figures she'd been studying for two long days remained grim.

Now her suppliers were acting as one, trying to squeeze her out of business by making it impossible for her to sell their goods at a profit. If only she had plenty of money to splash around. Wouldn't the merchants come running then, eager to grab their share of her money? They might even lick her boots to do it.

She sighed. A wonderful daydream, nothing more. She didn't have a fortune, only the six hundred pounds Nicholas had left her. And she had to be careful how she spent it for she had Lisa's future to protect.

Only Harry's liquor kept the customers coming, providing

her with an income. Would D-Store be reduced to a grog shop, serving only the thirsty in Parramatta? She couldn't bear the thought. She considered raising her prices to maintain a slim profit, but that could drive away her customers to stores that would charge them less. She cursed. The three months' grace Nicholas had obtained for her would soon melt away, and then she'd have to contend with the repayment of his debts too.

No matter how hard she searched for answers, she returned again and again to the same conclusion: if she could get no credit from her old suppliers, she had to find new ones. Discounts would only come with bigger purchases, and to be competitive, she might have to buy in substantial amounts. This meant she needed more funds than she owned. She would have to sell some of her assets.

She couldn't sell D-Store or Dunover. One spelt "business" and the other "home". Nor could she sell Red Roo which was home for her friends. That left Random. She didn't think the Parramatta farm would fetch very much, but it was all she had to sell. *Damn.* She needed fresh air to clear her head.

The blast of winter wind chilled her face as she stepped outside the store. She gathered her shawl close, breathed deeply as she gazed upon two eucalyptus trees a hundred feet away. She stared at their huge trunks, tracing their heights from the ground to the profusion of leaves above. They had triumphed over hard times of drought and heavy rain to emerge stronger than before. By God, so would she!

First, she must settle the question of Lisa's care. She couldn't impose on Fiona much longer. She must find an older woman to care for Lisa and to attend to household matters. She had to accomplish this quickly, so she'd be free to concentrate on her business problems, or she might not have a business left to worry over.

She called the MacGregors together. "Robert, you must know

there's not enough work here for the four of us now."

"Do you want some of us to leave, lass?" Robert asked.

"Good heavens, no! How could you think this?" She bit her lip. "Perhaps you're thinking of leaving?"

"Nay, lass. We'll stay as long as you need us."

"That'll be forever!" She sighed, then turned to the boys. "Hamish is staying with me, so that leaves you, Ian. How would you like to work on a farm?"

"Farming? Ian?" Robert shook his head and chuckled.

"Or you could go to the farm, Hamish, and Ian could stay with me. Oh. You don't fancy working on the farm either, huh? How about taking turns then? Harry could do with more help with his liquor. And when things here improve—"

"It's all right. I'll go to the farm," Hamish said. "Ian can stay with you."

Ian held up a hand. "No. We'll take turns."

Within the first five minutes of their arrival at Red Roo, Kate found herself struggling to contain her laughter. The fellas had trouble looking her in the eye. They kept clearing their throats and stumbling over their words.

She pretended to be offended. "What? Am I a leper, missing a nose?"

"No!" Artie said in shocked tones. "Are you a leper, Kate? Is that why we're not to bother you for now?"

"I'm not sure, Artie. Is it, David?"

"Don't you start your nonsense." David scowled. "We would've visited you sooner except for the wagon wheels. Two of them broke and Harry's still repairing them. Stubborn old fool!"

"Just 'cause he's in charge of the liquor, he thinks he can fix wagon wheels too," Sam said.

"I can too!" Harry cried. "You just have no faith and no

patience neither. But that ain't the reason, so don't you start blaming me." He turned to Kate. "They had this talk about you and decided—"

"Harry!" Ben roared. "You shut your mouth!"

Kate laughed. "And what didn't you want Harry to tell me, Ben?"

"Never mind that. How are you, Kate?"

"I'm fine." She patted his arm. "Honest."

He gave her a hug. "Good. We were worried some after Ian spoke to us. You know how we liked the cap'n after dealing with that horrible Kendrick. Thought the cap'n was quite the gentleman."

Sam added, "Aye, he treated us well. Fooled us all, didn't he? Should've known better than to trust them officers."

"No, Sam, I fooled myself. In truth, Nicholas never made me a promise he didn't keep."

"Look at me!" Peter cried, smiling broadly. He held Lisa and Polly on each arm. "I caught meself two angels." He bounced them. Polly laughed, but Lisa looked startled, then started crying. She leaned out, reaching for Kate.

"You silly bugger, Peter," Sam said. "You've frightened the child!"

"I didn't mean to frighten her. Sorry Kate!" He passed Lisa to her.

"It's all right. Lisa's just not used to you fellas yet." Kate looked at the other little girl on Peter's arm. "Hasn't Polly grown! Well, I must say Nellie's done a great job with her."

The men laughed. A few even stamped their feet.

"What's so funny?" she asked.

Peter choked. "You—for thinking our Nellie's looking after Polly."

"She's not?"

Sam shook his head. "*We* take care of our Polly. Did you

think our Nellie's changed? Not that we'd want her any different, mind. She comes and goes like before, Kate. She stops to play with Polly when the mood takes her and leaves when the urge moves her. One of us stays with Polly, makes sure she's safe."

"Aye," David said, "But Peter cheats all the time. It's always his turn to look after Polly."

Ben smiled. "Aye. Some of us have behaved quite shamelessly."

Harry frowned. "I remember that time when Sam—"

"Don't you talk!" Sam said. "What about the time you pretended you'd hurt yourself so you could stay back with—"

"Pretended!" Harry shouted. "I did no such thing. I stayed back to protect Polly from the likes of you!"

"Me! What did I do?"

"Piling on the clothes, that's what! 'Tis a miracle our Polly didn't smother!"

"Just 'cause you don't feel the cold, you think Polly don't neither!"

"Stop your shouting!" Kate said. "You'll frighten the children."

Ben grinned. "We need only worry about your Lisa. Polly won't care. 'Tis like this every day. We'd rather be with Polly than do any work."

"Yes, work. I had better start cooking too. There are so many of us to feed. What do you have, fish or meat?"

After supper, Kate got down to business. "Can you fellas use Hamish on the farm?"

Harry grinned. "Sure, I can always use an extra pair of hands at the stills."

Sam gave her a thoughtful look. "I don't understand. Won't you need him at D-Store?"

"We're not very busy at the store now. With the cap'n gone, I don't have as many things to sell."

"Why?" Artie said. "Did the cap'n take them goods away with him?"

Kate laughed. "I couldn't have said it better, Artie." She looked back at Harry. "Can you increase your liquor production?"

"Of course!" Peter and David joined Harry in a chorus.

"How come you need more liquor, Kate?" Artie said.

"It's like this, Artie: until I have more of the other things to sell, I'll sell your liquor. It'll keep D-Store open and the customers calling."

"Are things so very bad for you?" Ben asked.

"Yes, Ben. My suppliers think to squeeze me out of the business. They've put up the prices and won't supply me unless I pay cash."

"Bastards!" Harry said.

"It's all right, Harry. I'll manage, somehow."

" 'Course, you will!" David said. The others nodded.

"Who's looking after Polly tomorrow?" Kate asked.

Artie smiled. "Sam gets to look after Polly in the morning, and it's me turn after. Why do you ask, Kate?"

"Can you both look after Lisa as well?"

"No worries," Sam said. "We'll have us a great time."

"Good. Now, would any of you know of a reliable woman looking for work, but who wouldn't be asking a lot in payment? I need someone to take care of Dunover and Lisa while I tend to business at the store."

The men looked at each other, then shook their heads.

"Then I'll have to ask around. Ben, can you help me look?"

They started out early the next morning, calling on every farm west of Red Roo. Many of the farm houses along the Hawkesbury looked like ruins, their broken fences had gaps showing. Obviously, the farmers were too busy rebuilding their farms to worry about appearances.

As they drove along the quiet road, Ben pointed to a section of the Hawkesbury River. "During the drought, we cross the river just there, without getting wet. You should have seen how the water swelled during the flood, Kate. Nature can be right fearsome sometimes."

"Do you think it'll flood that badly again? Maybe this is the greatest flood for the next hundred years."

He smiled. "Don't matter. We'll be better prepared next time."

The day ended without Kate finding one woman interested in working for her. The next day, David drove her to cover those areas east of Red Roo. She couldn't understand it. Although many settlers were in terrible straits, no one seemed to be looking for paid work. Perhaps those who did had already found it—weeks, or months ago.

The wind rose, carrying with it a faint odour of mud and rotting carcass. Kate looked at the evening glow in the sky. "Let's take in one more farmhouse, David, then head for home. That should give me enough time to cook supper."

"That's all right, Kate. Peter can take care of supper if we're late."

They turned down a track, their wagon wheels crunching on the driveway's gravel as they rolled towards another dilapidated farmhouse. Within moments, a man and a woman stood outside their door, watching them approach. They were joined by five skinny children in patched clothing. The picture they made reminded Kate of her days on her father's farm.

She walked up to the farmer and his wife and introduced herself, then explained her purpose for calling. The couple exchanged glances, then the man gave a small nod.

"I think you should call on Sara Conway," the woman said. "Her farm's just down the road here. John, her husband, took sick after the floods. He died. She's been having a right hard time lately, taking care of her two children. We help where we can, but it's been hard for us, too. I think your offer should interest Sara. As I said, she's just down the road."

Kate thanked the couple. David followed their directions and stopped the wagon a short distance from the front door of an even more broken-down farmhouse.

The flood had left its mark: a dark ring along the walls of the farmhouse, just a foot under the roofline. Little was left of the fence: a few timber pieces leaned at precarious angles, and others lay broken and scattered on the ground, partly buried in dirt.

Kate walked up to the door. No one answered her soft rap. She knocked harder. No response. She pushed open the door, calling out to announce herself.

The bareness of the room spoke of abject poverty. The walls and the timber floor scrubbed clean of all evidence of the flood told Kate Sara Conway was house-proud.

A sniffle startled her. A little girl of five or six summers peeked out of the only bedroom in the house. Afraid of alarming the child, Kate stood very still, then she smiled. "Hello there. Is your mama here?"

The girl shook her head. Her rounded eyes didn't blink.

"Are you by yourself?"

Again the girl shook her head. She displayed no alarm, only curiosity. Kate took a step forward. The girl retreated a step, then disappeared into the room. Kate followed. The girl stood beside a younger child, who was playing with some rags on the floor. Kate smiled. "What's your name, dear?"

"Brenda."

"Can you fetch your mama for me, Brenda?"

She stared at Kate, then looked down at the child.

"That's all right, Brenda. Your little brother will be safe with me."

She gave Kate another long look, then slipped past her and out of the room. The front door slammed.

The rags seemed to command all of the little boy's attention. Kate looked around the room. There didn't seem to be anything around that could hurt him. She decided to leave him on his own.

A widow with two children couldn't possibly rebuild the farm. A lump suddenly appeared in her throat. She'd resented Nicholas for abandoning her and Lisa. She'd cursed him for making it almost impossible for her to carry on trading. Now, after seeing Sara Conway's circumstances, she realised she had a lot to be thankful for.

The sound of running footsteps grew louder. A tall, thin woman, with Brenda running at her side, came into view. They drew to a stop a few feet away. The bun at the back of the woman's head wobbled; her hair looked about to tumble free. Sara Conway wiped her dirt-stained hands against her gown. She straightened her shoulders. "My little girl says you're looking for me."

"I'm Kate O'Neal. I'm sorry if my presence alarmed you—"

The woman raised a hand and shook her head. "That's all right. I'm Sara Conway. How can I help you?"

Kate explained her quest. Sara's eyes slowly filled. She blinked. The twin streams of tears unsettled Kate. She let her last words trail away when the woman buried her face in her hands and began to sob. Brenda, looking frightened, clutched her mother's skirts.

"Are you all right, Mrs. Conway?"

"Sara, I'm Sara, and now everything's going to be all right. Thank God!" She brushed away her tears, wiped her hands on her skirts again. With a smile trembling on her lips, she clasped Kate's hand in both her own. "You'll take the children too? I've got two children—"

"Yes, the children too," Kate said. "There's room enough in my house for all of you."

"Oh thank you, thank you, mistress."

"If you're accepting my offer, Sara, we'll have to discuss your wages. I'm sorry, I can't offer very much."

"I don't care about the money! We've been starving for months and living on charity. I'll be glad to work for room and board—"

"That won't be necessary. I can afford a small wage, and as long as I can afford it, you'll get paid."

"You're the miracle I've been praying for, Mistress O'Neal!" Sara cried. "God in His Mercy has sent you to help me and me children."

"Sara, please. It's only a job, and I'm not even paying you much. So it's settled? Can you be ready to leave by noon tomorrow? Good."

After supper that night, Kate told her friends about Sara. "Maybe you can get a woman like Sara to help with Polly—"

Sam looked appalled. "And what are we going to do with ourselves without Polly to look after?"

"Stop your meddling, Kate. We don't need it, you hear?" Harry said. "I ain't having no strange woman poking her nose into me stills."

"And if she's a Christian woman, she'll give us more grief with Nellie than we need. No!" Ben said. He pulled Nellie close and kissed her.

"All right, all right," Kate said. " 'Twas just an idea."

Artie tugged at her sleeve. "Kate, we've got something for you. A surprise."

"What is it?"

Artie looked at the others, as if asking for permission to proceed. Ben nodded. Artie laughed and rushed away. Sam went with him. They came back moments later, each carrying a bunch of bulging coin bags. They dropped these on the dining table in front of her.

The clink of metal was loud, and several coins spilled onto the table. Kate counted a dozen bags.

"What's this?" she croaked.

They grinned broadly at her. "We thought you could use them," Ben said.

"But—"

"What's the fuss?" Harry said. "We ain't using them coins anyways."

Kate started to weep. Was it any wonder that she took these men for her family? Indeed, she doubted her father would be half as generous, supposing he had the money.

"Why are you crying, Kate?" Artie asked. "We thought this would make you happy."

"Oh I am, Artie. I'm so happy!" She kissed Artie on the cheek. "Thank you." She moved to give each of her other friends a kiss too, then returned to her seat. She picked up a bag and weighed it in her hand. "How much is it?"

David laughed. "We didn't count. What for? 'Tis yours now."

"You have to know how much you're lending me."

Ben shook his head. "No. It's yours, Kate. It ain't doing us no good, buried in the ground. We just like owning it, but if it can help you, we're glad for it."

Sam shrugged. "We never had no reason to use them coins to buy anything. You sent us everything we needed—in fact, we get stuff we never even wanted."

Kate stared at the coins. Never in her wildest dreams did she suspect her friends had so much money. There had to be at least three thousand pounds sitting on the table. Well, her friends might see this as a gift to her, but she would pay them back one day, every penny of it.

She faced the men. "My suppliers had better watch out, now. If they're not careful, I shall buy from other suppliers. I'll make them regret they ever thought to treat me badly, just because I'm a woman."

CHAPTER 26

After the excitement subsided, Kate wondered if it was safe to keep her little fortune at Dunover. What if someone should break into the house and rob her? *Eejit!* She was being foolish. No one knew she had the money. They'd all seen her poorly stocked store. If she had money would her store not have more merchandise to sell? No, they wouldn't think to rob her. But what if they did . . .

She gnawed her bottom lip, started when she felt a hand on her shoulder.

"What's wrong, Kate?" Ben asked.

She laughed sheepishly. "I was worried when I didn't have enough money. Now that I do, I worry someone is going to rob me of it. I guess I must be a born worrier."

Ben smiled. "You didn't think we'd send you home on your own, did you now? Peter and I will ride to Parramatta with you. We'll help you bury the money in your backyard, see that everything is safe before we leave. Now stop worrying."

Ian coughed. "Kate, don't forget your new housekeeper. We have to be careful with her. We shouldn't let her know where we bury the money. We don't know how honest she is yet."

Peter nodded. "Well, let it be your job then to keep her busy with something while we bury the money."

A surge of affection choked Kate, and with tears stinging her eyes, she smiled at her friends. "I'm so lucky."

★　★　★　★　★

Sara made no secret of the fact that she thought herself very lucky to have found safe haven for herself and her children under Kate's roof, but Kate knew she had the better of the deal. Not only had she found an efficient housekeeper, cook and baby-minder in Sara, she had also found a friend. Better yet, in Sara's children, she had provided Lisa with playmates. Not since Sara and her children came into their lives, had she seen her little girl greet each morning so eagerly.

Knowing that she could leave Dunover and Lisa in Sara's safe hands, Kate felt free to concentrate her efforts in keeping D-Store in business. Flushed with funds, she began working on her lists of goods she would buy. Ever conscious that the money was not really hers, she reminded herself to be careful how she spent it. Should she make a mistake and lose the fellas' savings, she would not get another chance to make a recovery.

With time to reconsider, Kate discarded all thoughts of taking revenge on her suppliers. It would be to her advantage to stick to them for she knew them all, and they had proved themselves over the years. Taking on new suppliers could be a risk she couldn't afford. They might prove to be less than honest and unreliable to boot.

She thought of different ways to approach her old suppliers, to persuade them to reconsider their position and wasn't quite ready to deal with them, when one came calling. He never gave her a chance to say one word beyond her greetings. He told her he wouldn't be supplying goods to D-Store anymore. "I'm sorry, but I cannot do business with a female. Find yourself a husband, Mistress O'Neal, then he and I can work something out. In the meanwhile, I'd be obliged if you'll settle Captain Spencer's account now. I've honoured me promise to him to allow you three months' grace. I pride meself in being a man of me word."

Kate knew it was useless to argue. She paid him and silently vowed never to do business with him ever again.

Her next supplier delivered the same bad news, then took her breath away when he said, "I'll do you a favour, Mistress O'Neal. I'll buy your store from you, while it's still worth something, provided we can come to a reasonable price. What do you say?"

A favour? Were all her suppliers so arrogant they thought she had no choice but to give in to their demands? She was to get herself a new husband, then let him take over D-Store, or lose the store altogether for lack of merchandise to sell? Well, she'd surprise them. She'd show them Kate O'Neal would not go away just because they wished it. But first, she needed to find out what the eejit was offering.

She preserved a pleasant expression on her face. "Business has indeed been slow, but I hadn't thought to sell D-Store. How much do you think I would get for it?"

"Not much, I don't think. Your shelves are almost empty. You cannot have many customers left." He looked around. "This is not a good location for a shop, but as I said, I've a mind to do you a favour. I'll give you one hundred pounds. You'll not get a better price anywhere else, I promise you."

"Without stock?"

"With what liquor stock you have now. My offer would be a lot less without stock. I'm sure you understand."

A surge of anger almost overcame her good sense. "Indeed, I do."

"All right. I'll wait for word from you then."

Her other suppliers had the same message for her. She was forced to accept their decision and calmly paid off all those who held Nicholas' vouchers. She had no choice now, but to reach out to other suppliers. And no matter how nervous she was to approach these strangers, she would have to do it, or her old suppliers would have their victory.

She kept her mounting worries to herself. She didn't wish to alarm Robert and his boys. D-Store was finished if all the other traders in the settlement refused to deal with her. But she would not think of failure, not till it stared her in the face.

No! There had to be at least one merchant in this whole settlement who would be brave enough to supply her store! But how long would it take her to find this man?

In desperation, she thought of contacting Lieutenant William Hudson. Nicholas had said he'd help, if she approached him. Although the army officers were no longer as powerful as before, they were still a force to be reckoned with. Her suppliers wouldn't dare risk offending an officer. And if she had Lieutenant Hudson's protection . . .

No. She couldn't do it. The lieutenant had struck her as a kind man, but what would it cost her to have his protection? Besides, she'd be damned if she'd be beholden to Nicholas again, if only for his friend's help. If D-Store was to be nothing more than a grog shop, so be it.

In the meantime, she would knock on every supplier's door to find that one merchant who would supply her, and she would find him even if it took her a year or more to do it. The sooner she started, the sooner she would solve her problem. And the more she knew about the goods she wanted to buy, the better prepared she'd be to deal with the suppliers.

At the store, she kept a bold face. Back at Dunover, she spent most of her time in the library, drawing up lists of goods she wanted to buy, the range of quality she would consider acceptable and the prices she'd pay for them.

She had just finished writing out her latest list, when she decided it was time for her cup of tea. She put down her pen and stretched herself to ease the stiffness in her shoulders. She tucked her stack of lists into the drawer, then made her way to the kitchen.

At the kitchen doorway, she paused for a moment to watch Sara on her knees, scrubbing the floor. Betty and Jane had turned the kitchen and the house into a pigsty in a couple of days. It would take two weeks or more to clean up the mess and repair the damage, but Sara seemed determined to do it in shorter time.

Kate walked into the kitchen and took down the tea caddy. "I'm making a cup of tea, Sara. Would you like one?"

Sara mumbled. Kate gave her a sharp look. "What's wrong?"

Sara sniffed. "Nothing. I'm fine."

"If you're fine, then why are you crying?"

Sara got to her feet. She wiped her cheeks and her nose with her sleeve. "I was just thinking of me narrow escape. Thank God, you came along when you did. I was about to give in to those men who came calling with their fancy offers. It fair tore me up to listen to me children crying themselves to sleep on empty bellies—"

Kate walked up and placed both hands on Sara's shoulders. "You're safe now, Sara, unless I let you work yourself to death."

"Honest work never killed nobody, and I'm right grateful to you, Kate. You saved me children from having a whore for a mother. I dread—"

"Sara, enough! 'Tis best you leave the past behind you." Kate smiled to soften the harsh words. "How about a cup of tea?"

"A cup of tea will do me fine."

Kate reached for Sara's hand and gently squeezed it. "Good. We may still have hard times ahead of us, Sara, but together, we'll make our tomorrows better than yesterday."

Kate moved this way and that and watched herself in the mirror. She adjusted her long sleeves that covered her hands to the knuckles, then gave her skirts a twitch. The narrow flounce at the bottom fell gently into place. Her plum-coloured gown of sprig muslin had always looked good on her.

She glanced at Sara. "I hope the merchants will be suitably impressed." She picked up a shawl that matched her dress and wrapped it around her shoulders. "Do I look nervous?"

"You look charming, and Robert's been waiting a while, downstairs."

Robert, who was pacing the floor, stopped and smiled at her as she came down the stairs. He gave her a theatrical bow and showed his leg clad in corduroy breeches. "Your carriage awaits, ma'am."

Thirty minutes into their journey, Kate said, for the tenth time, "Now, there's no need for you to be nervous, Robert. I know what to do and say. Trust me, it'll be fine."

"Aye, Kate."

She fiddled with her reticule, heard the crackling of sheets of paper inside and resisted the urge to open her purse again. Lord, the journey seemed endless, but she must not hurry Robert. He seemed extraordinarily quiet. Scared stiff, probably. Poor man.

Eventually they reached the outskirts of Sydney Town. The traffic moved briskly along the streets. Robert negotiated his way to a huge wooden building that housed one of the settlement's largest importers/wholesalers.

"Good luck, lass," Robert said as he helped her down from the carriage.

She nodded, straightened her shoulders and walked towards the building. Maybe it was just her wild imagination, but she fancied everybody was looking at her. Did they expect her to fail too? She wouldn't fail. She mustn't.

A short man met her as she stepped through the door. She gave him her name and asked to see the owner. He left her, then returned to say Mr. Pritchard was busy. She told him she'd wait for Mr. Pritchard to be free. He shrugged and pointed her to a chair.

An hour passed. The heat got to her. She feared her sweat would soon show through her garment. How long before she started to smell? Dear Lord, please let Mr. Pritchard see her soon.

Another hour and a half passed before the short man approached her again. "Mr. Pritchard will see you now."

The merchant listened to her reasons for calling. He interrupted her saying he already had more customers than he needed. He couldn't possibly take on a new one.

She didn't believe him. Goods were not in tight supply in the colony so it was more than likely that all honest merchants would welcome new customers. Pritchard was a bastard too—making her wait in the heat for so many hours when he never meant to oblige her.

The next two merchants she met were bold.

The first one, an elderly merchant, shook a finger at her. "Unnatural creature! Stop meddling in men's affairs. Get yourself married, missy, and let your husband take care of you and your business. You should know, trading be man's work."

The other leered, "Precious, don't you worry none about your business. Be me love, and I'll be taking good care of you. I'll even make you very happy." He fondled himself and cackled.

Kate ignored his insult, simply walked away. She knew if she responded, he'd be encouraged to say more. Berating these eejits, or taking a stick and cracking their thick skulls open, might give her great satisfaction, but she'd still not get the supplies she wanted for her store.

She gained nothing but frustration from all the waiting, and sore feet from trudging from one building to another. Still, she wouldn't give up, and, thankfully, Robert asked no question, made no comment.

Nightmares haunted Kate's sleep. Earlier, she'd worried D-Store might be reduced to a grog shop. Now, all too conscious of the trading community's hostility towards her, she feared she could lose the store altogether. Philip Gidley King, the new governor, shared Governor Hunter's abhorrence for liquor. He blamed drunkenness for every ill that befell the colony and would, if he could, issue edicts to outlaw liquor altogether. With a little encouragement from those who would see her fail, Governor King could be persuaded to close down D-Store.

"Oh Kate. I wish I could help you," Sara said.

"You are helping, Sara, by just being here, listening to me ranting and offering me a shoulder to cry on."

"I guess the merchants want you to be like me, Kate, tending to home and family. I'm right glad you're more than what they expect you to be! And you'll beat them at their game. I know you will!"

Kate laughed and gave her a hug. "Your faith humbles me, dear Sara. The truth is I cannot afford to fail. Damn! If only I could deal directly with the ships' captains, bid for their cargo. Except I don't know any ships' captains to approach. And even if I did, he'd probably refuse to deal with a woman too."

Much as she hated the idea of hiding behind a man to conduct business, Kate thought she no longer had the luxury of a choice. She was not above practising a little deceit, but she didn't have a man who could act for her.

None of the Red Roo fellas would serve. As simple farmers, they'd be fodder for the crafty merchants who would swallow them whole. The MacGregors offered no better advantage. Ian and Hamish were too young to command respect, and Robert was too gentle. But, gentle or not, Kate knew it had to be Robert, or no one else.

Robert looked at her in horror. "You canna be thinking right.

I couldna work me own farm and lost it in two years. How can you expect me to handle the merchants?"

Kate patted his arm. "You can do it, Robert. I'll work with you."

"You're fooling yourself, lass."

"I'll take the risk."

Two weeks later, Robert threw up his hands. "Kate, I canna do this! If I could read and write, things might be different. Damn! I get muddled too easily when I'm nervous. It's different in the shop—I know all the prices, and you're there to correct me mistakes."

Kate forced a smile. "It's all right, Robert. I'm sorry I put you through this, but I had to give it a try."

Once again she had Robert drive her all over the colony, trying out the smaller or more remote merchants. Surely she'd find a man who would help her. Just one, who would see beyond her skirts and treat her as an equal. But the repeated rejections assaulted her confidence, and the frequent humiliation tore into her pride. Pure stubbornness, however, would not allow her to accept defeat. Where was this one merchant who would help her?

CHAPTER 27

Bert Rowley ignored the knock on his door and continued to add a column of figures. He intended to finish balancing his books, a task he'd avoided for over two months. Sometimes, he wished Captain Pollard, his employer, would be a little more demanding, force him to do the books on time. But did he want the captain always looking over his shoulder? He'd hate that, and likely the captain knew this too, for he never interfered with Bert's management of the store. The captain trusted him, a trust he'd earned through four years of hard work.

The knock came again. "Yes! What is it?"

The door opened. "Bert, the lady's here."

He looked up and frowned. "What lady?"

The short, bald man in the doorway winked. "Kate O'Neal."

"Who?"

His worker snickered. "You know—the one who's been callin' here every day, three days now, tryin' to catch the owner?"

"I don't have time for anybody. Send her away."

"That ain't gonna work, Bert. You best see her, or she'll be back tomorrow. She's right persistent."

"Damn!" Bert threw down his pen. He didn't like people wasting his time, and he tried not to be guilty of the same offence. "All right. Send her in. I'll get rid of her quick enough."

The woman who stepped into his office barely reached his shoulders. From the bits and pieces he'd heard about this troublesome female, he'd pictured her as an unappealing piece of baggage, some sort of shrew. But Kate O'Neal looked like a young girl who'd dressed in her mother's clothes, a child who needed leading by her hand.

"Mistress O'Neal, I'm Bert Rowley." He offered her a chair, then moved to sit behind the desk. "I understand you wish to see me?" Now, at closer range, he realised he was facing a woman full grown, and she didn't appear to be nervous at all.

"I thought to meet Mr. Pollard. He's the owner, isn't he?" She had a surprisingly sweet voice.

"Indeed. Captain Pollard owns this store, but I run it for him. How may I help you?"

"I find myself in a difficult bind, Mr. Rowley. Perhaps you've heard of my difficulties?"

A slight lifting of the corner of her lips in a smile charmed him. He dipped his head and waited for her to continue.

"I was hoping you might be able to help me, supply goods to my store."

"Ah."

"Indeed, I don't wish to waste your time any more than I have to, Mr. Rowley, but what am I to do? My store no longer keeps me busy. I'm now obliged to fill my time visiting merchants like yourself, to see if someone, anyone, who might want to help improve the situation for me."

"My man must not have made himself plain then. He thought turning you away the past few days was enough to indicate Pollard and Company is unable to help you with your problems."

She smoothed back a tendril of dark hair from her face and smiled. "I'm afraid the fault is mine, Mr. Rowley. I prefer the owner to look me in the eye when he turns me down."

Bert laughed. "I see. It needs but a word from me to send you away?"

She laughed. "You wouldn't be so unkind, would you? I'll pay cash if you don't wish to give me credit."

"Correct me if I'm wrong, Mistress O'Neal. Rumour has it that you can live very well on what Captain Spencer has left you, without your having to remain in trade?"

"Indeed, for several years at least. Then what happens to my child and me, Mr. Rowley, when the money is all gone?"

"Then your husband will provide for you. I doubt you'll remain unmarried for long, Mistress O'Neal. You're a very attractive woman."

"Certainly, while I'm still in possession of my small fortune. I hope you'll understand if I say I'd rather not trust my future to fate."

"A woman with spunk. I like that."

"Enough to sell me your goods?"

Bert chuckled, then got to his feet. "Perhaps."

Digging deep into his memories, Bert swiftly pieced together a fuller picture of Kate O'Neal. This tiny woman had become the bane of the trading community. She might have pleased Captain Spencer with her success with D-Store, but she had gained the enmity of many merchants for that success. These men found insupportable the fact that a mere woman could do as well as the best of them. Worse, it was not to be tolerated that she had thrived when some amongst them had gone into bankruptcy.

So they had acted together to force her to abandon her business and assume the role of wife and mother. Likely they would succeed too because Captain Spencer was no longer around to stop them.

But where other women might have yielded to the merchants' bullying, Kate O'Neal seemed to be made of sterner stuff. She was putting up a good fight. He liked her spirit. Indeed she had his admiration. Not many years ago, he too had suffered from prejudice directed at him by a great number of merchants. He had hated that.

He looked down at her for a long while, struck by indecision. He wanted to help her, but feared his reasons might be less than pure. Quickly, he quelled the disturbing thought. Did he wish to invite the animosity of his fellow traders? Captain Pollard would not be pleased. He preferred a peaceful life. Bert reminded himself that he had enough on his hands: a backlog of work. Could he afford to champion anybody's cause, no matter how righteous?

However, now that he'd met Kate O'Neal, he thought it a great shame that a large group of men had conspired to drive one small woman out of business. Dammit! Yes, he would help her. If she was prepared to pay his price.

He strolled to the door and reached for the key. He turned and half-faced her, made sure their gazes engaged, before he locked it. She held very still, but said nothing. She stared at him, as if trying to read his mind.

He waited for more reaction, and when none was forthcoming, gave her an approving nod. "You realise, of course, if one of my workers should try this door and find it locked, your reputation would be ruined?"

"I cannot imagine why you would do me this disservice."

He could detect no tremour in her voice. "I wanted to see how far you'd go to get goods for your store."

"Not as far as some people would like me to go, I assure you."

Bert threw his head back and roared with laughter. "Very good."

He moved away from the door. "Like you, Mistress O'Neal, I'm an emancipist. I've had my share of difficulties serving my time as a convict in this new colony. Had some kind people not given me a helping hand, I would not be where I am today. Now, when I can, I try to help others less fortunate. Sadly, I'm not a gallant sort of fellow. I've got a great respect for self-interest."

"But I'm willing to pay cash for your goods, and you'll make your profits."

Bert smiled. "I expect more than profits."

"I'm listening." Her gaze followed him as he moved to support himself at the edge of his desk.

"I hate to say this, but many of the traders I deal with can be very unreasonable, men who should have lived a hundred years ago. I've had to endure their insults, and I've tried to ignore their arrogance. After all, one must earn one's living, and business is business."

"Yes."

"I like to play them for a fool. I've been known to throw a rub in their way now and again, to have my bit of fun. I think I see another major opportunity to strike at them in helping you."

"You'll help me?"

Her eyes gleamed with unshed tears. He looked away. "I'm rarely this impulsive, Mistress O'Neal, but yes, against my better judgment, I will help you and enjoy myself in the process."

"Better judgment? Why do you say that?"

"They may be hypocrites, and some of them are even dishonourable, but I share their opinion. You'd do better to get married and have your husband take care of your business. On the other hand, you have done very well on your own and would continue to do so, if some self-important bigots didn't decide to interfere in your business."

She bit her lip, then burst out, "But—would helping me get you into trouble with Captain Pollard?"

Her concern pleased him. He liked it that she could still consider his position when hers was so shaky. "Captain Pollard is a man with a keen eye on his profits. I doubt he will interfere with my decision. However, has it dawned on you yet that what

I'm proposing does no honour to a gentleman?" He tilted his head towards the door. "Your good reputation would be sacrificed. But it's not too late for me to unlock the door."

"First, explain why I must sacrifice my reputation."

"Consider this: powerful merchants are determined to close down your store, or, if you're willing, buy it from you. And no trader in his right mind would challenge the decision of his brethren to help you survive in your business. But who can blame a besotted man for wanting to please his mistress? They might curse me for a fool, but they'd envy me my good fortune."

"Your m—mistress?"

Bert smiled and winked. "A charade, Mistress O'Neal, nothing more."

She hesitated. "Charade?"

"We will pretend to be lovers to deceive the world."

"And 'besotted'? You'd become a figure of contempt."

"My dear lady, don't you own a looking glass?"

Kate's face turned a becoming shade of pink. She held out her hand. "You have a deal, Mr. Rowley, and thank you."

"Bert, please. We're to be lovers, remember?" He grinned and rubbed his hands. "Allow me to muss up your hair, my dear, so you'll present a vision to satisfy every gossip in town. Yes, indeed. This little charade will be fun."

In the space of a week, eight wagons, one after another, arrived at D-Store to deliver goods Kate had ordered through Bert. The MacGregors grinned as they unloaded the first wagon. Kate couldn't hide her delight either. Until the merchandise arrived, she'd been uncertain about Bert, afraid he might forget all about their bargain.

He called on her at D-Store, ten days later. Kate stared at him, unable to believe her eyes. He presented a splendid figure in a frock coat of green silk over fashionable pantaloons of ivory. His widening smile made her realise she was gawking. She looked away, wishing she'd worn something more present-able than her faded cotton gown.

He removed his hat and held out a hand. "Kate, my dear, you look ravishing. Simply ravishing."

Well-aware the MacGregors were watching and listening, Kate blushed, embarrassed by his familiarity, yet flattered by the compliment. She was also at a loss, uncertain how to play the role she'd accepted, or deal with the situation he presented. They were, after all, strangers.

She gave him her hand. He kissed it, straightened and even as he smiled, flashed her a wink. "I've come to take you for a drive into town, maybe do a little bit of shopping. You'll like that, wouldn't you, my sweet?"

She leaned forward and whispered, "I'm not dressed to go anywhere."

"Of course, my dear. Allow me to drive you home and help you select a more appropriate garment for our outing."

Kate started, blushed again, then stole a look at the Mac-Gregors. All three looked at her with mouths agape. She couldn't blame them. They knew nothing of her bargain with Bert, but how could she tell them about a bargain when she didn't know the rules?

Bert drove her home to Dunover. She was too bemused to carry on a conversation, but he appeared very comfortable with their silence. They had almost reached Dunover, when he said, "I gather you didn't take your workers into your confidence?"

"Not because I didn't trust them. I was too embarrassed to do it. But I shall have to explain it all to them soon."

"Would that be wise?"

"I don't have many friends, but those who are, are all to be trusted."

"I hope your trust is not misplaced."

"I would put my life in their hands."

Much to her relief, he didn't accompany her to her room. He stayed downstairs with the children. She heard laughter as she changed into a pink muslin gown she'd not worn since her days with Nicholas. A sense of uneasiness swept over her. Lisa and Sara's children were usually wary of strangers and yet Bert had won them over easily. She feared for her heart. Bert Rowley must be nothing more than a business connection.

Not ten minutes into the journey to Sydney Town, Bert covered her hand with one of his. "Kate, you don't have to worry about my intentions. They're entirely honorable, I promise you."

She took a deep breath. "Am I so obvious?"

"Yes. I don't blame you. You'd be a fool not to worry, and I have no time for fools."

She smiled, not entirely reassured.

"Fact is, I'm a married man, Kate."

She started. "I didn't know that."

He smiled. "I've told no one else about it, not even Captain Pollard. I plan to return to England, to my wife, one day soon."

He'd met and fallen in love with Olivia, he said, when he was still a lad and wild in his ways. Her father was the local squire, and Bert's father was a country parson. Bert had refused to go into the ministry. He left home instead and worked for a successful timber merchant. He dreamed of owning a business one day. At twenty-three, he'd listened to his heart when Olivia, who was seventeen then, wrote to him, begging him to save her. Her father, she said, planned to marry her off to his friend, an old man. She insisted they elope to Gretna Green at once. They did that and spent a fortnight together, before her father caught up with them.

Squire Stanton snatched Olivia away and had Bert charged with stealing a pair of horses. On the day Bert was sentenced to seven years' transportation, Squire Stanton told him that his marriage to Olivia had been annulled. Bert didn't believe it.

"Olivia is my wife, Kate, and will always be until she tells me different. Her father is my biggest problem, but soon, I'll have sufficient wealth to impress him. I'll claim back my bride and happiness then."

"Olivia is a very lucky woman."

"Do you know, you remind me very much of her? It's your fighting spirit, and your determination to get your way."

"Then I'm grateful to Olivia."

"Enough said about me." He smiled at her. "So, did the goods I sent meet with your approval?"

"You must know they did. Will you tell me something? Why did you use eight wagons to deliver my goods over the course of a week when three would have done the job in one day?"

Bert chuckled. "You may trust your workers. I don't trust any of mine. I had to convince them of my devotion to you. You should see how I fussed to get the merchandise for you. I made sure to exclaim frequently, within their hearing of course, 'I'm sure Kate would like to have some of that!' I'd change my mind, and change it again. Then have some goods, only those you've ordered, dispatched to you immediately. I'm the besotted swain intent on pleasing his new love, you see?"

Kate pressed her hands to the sides of her hot face. She'd never met a man like Bert, so direct with his speech. Jeremy had only been interested in his needs and desires, and Nicholas did not believe in long conversations with her. Now, here was Bert who could speak of intimate things so casually.

"That's not all. I also make sure I remind myself—aloud of course—to pay for the goods. I didn't want them thinking I'd be cheating Captain Pollard in any way. So now, my workers are whispering, they hope I wake up from my foolishness before I'm left without a sixpence to scratch with! But I've also hinted at several romantic rendezvous I've had with you, and they're all green with envy."

Kate laughed and fished out a bag of coins from her reticule. "To pay for what you wish to buy on this shopping trip. If you'll give me a bill for what you've supplied me—"

"Keep your money for now. You can settle your account later, when I take you home."

"And what would you have me do—when we're shopping—as part of our charade?"

"Well, you could call me *Bertie*—the fellows know how much I hate to be called that—and I could pretend to go into transports over it."

"You're enjoying this, aren't you?"

"Indeed. It'll be my greatest pleasure to hoax those pompous jackasses in their stores, play them for the fools they are. Not only am I supplying goods to you, I'll have them selling you their merchandise too! And today's the day!"

CHAPTER 28

Kate's life had become easier since she met Bert. In the beginning, she resisted from handing him a big shopping list, afraid that might scare him away. She knew her fears made no sense. Why should Bert be scared away? She never quibbled at the prices he charged, and he never had to ask her twice for payment for the goods.

As the weeks passed, she gained confidence. She began to order larger quantities of merchandise. Then Bert began to give her hard looks and the occasional frown.

"Kate," he said, "don't let your recent experience scare you. Really, you have no need to keep large stocks of anything. I'm here. I'll see to it that D-Store is kept supplied. You can count on me to do that."

She smiled. "I do trust you, Bert. It's just that I have a big warehouse, and I hate to see it empty. It'll be good to have it as it was during the time when it was always full."

But Bert was right. She knew she was stocking up for a 'rainy day.' It took another two months before she shed her fears. Even so, she was cautious not to allow her stock to fall below a level she had set for the store.

One day, she was serving Mrs. Ashby, a woman in her thirties, when she noticed her fine garment. She complimented Mrs. Ashby on her dress.

"Where did you buy it?"

"I didn't buy it." Mrs. Ashby laughed self-consciously. "I

made it from a piece of material given me by me mother before I left home."

"You make all your dresses? How wonderful."

"I've always been good with the needle. So is me daughter. We like to sew."

Kate decided to try her luck. "Mrs. Ashby, I wonder if you would sew me a gown like yours? I'll pay you, of course."

Mrs. Ashby looked uncertainly at her equally well-dressed husband.

He smiled. "Go ahead, if you'd like to do this."

From persuading her customer to sew her one dress, Kate managed to get her to produce a couple of gowns each month which she proceeded to sell in her store. The gowns sold very quickly. And why not? Lizzy's gowns were well-sewn. More importantly, they were made of lighter material which proved more suitable for the colony's warmer winters and hot, hot summers.

Lizzy and Kate quickly settled into a business relationship, where they split their profits down the middle. Kate would supply the materials, Lizzy Ashby would sew up the dresses, and Kate would sell them. Soon, Lizzy recruited more helpers to increase production, and Kate began thinking of expanding her clothing business.

"We have to offer our customers more choices, Lizzy. If you can, produce gowns with new designs every few months so those who have already bought our gowns would happily buy the new ones."

Lizzy's face lit up. "Yes! Perhaps we can sell these gowns at higher prices in Sydney Town too."

Kate gave Lizzy a hug. "Yes. I think I may be able to get the town merchants to carry our gowns in their stores! The promise of large profits would persuade them, I'm sure."

Lizzy looked uncertain, so Kate smiled at her. "They will, trust me."

Kate decided they'd have to provide these merchants with samples. They had to produce gowns whose quality could not be doubted. This meant Lizzy would have to use better quality material and accessories. Kate realised she couldn't just order such goods through Bert. She couldn't expect him to know exactly what was wanted. No, she would have to go shopping herself, with Bert by her side, of course. Thus far, he had never allowed her to go shopping in Sydney Town by herself.

The thought of being in Bert's company again gave Kate a jolt of pleasure. She loved being with him, especially in the company of merchants and strangers, when he acted the besotted lover. He would be particularly attentive then, acting as if nothing was too good for her.

"Bert is married!" a little voice inside her head said sternly.

As usual her heart jumped to defend her. What would be the harm? Surely, she could enjoy Bert's friendship and company if she wished. They were friends.

"No harm?" the voice sneered. "He will leave you weeping when he sails for England to claim his wife! You are an eejit. Who, but an eejit would choose to be willfully blind to reality?"

Enough! Kate shook her head, willing the troublesome voice to be silent.

The voice would have the last word. "You depend on him too much. You will live to regret this!"

After a sleepless night, Kate decided to go shopping on her own. She had Ian drive her into Sydney Town, to the largest store there.

Mr. Bagley, the store owner, approached to greet her with a broad smile. What a difference Bert had made in her life. It seemed she no longer had to wait to see the proprietor of any store anymore.

Mr. Bagley showed her his stock of materials. She made her purchases and boldly announced that Bert would settle the account for her. Mr. Bagley didn't even blink; he merely nodded and smiled. Kate had Ian drive her from one store to another, and soon bales of materials piled up at the back of her wagon. She decided she would visit one last store, and then they would head for home.

As luck would have it, she was just going through a collection of ribbons and lace when she heard a commotion outside the store. Within moments Bert was at her side, his hand cupping her elbow. With a smile on his lips, a smile that didn't reach his eyes, and a nod to the proprietor of the shop, he began urging her aside for a private word.

"I wouldn't have known you were here if one of my workers had not caught sight of you and reported the matter to me."

Kate could not understand why Bert was so upset. She sought to placate him. "Bert, I'm sorry I didn't tell you I was coming into town."

"Kate, that's not the problem. You don't seem to understand that any of these men here could turn cruel and insulting. You're supposed to be my mistress, not my wife. Didn't it occur to you that you'd be fair game to them?"

"No, surely not!" She was about to say more, argue even, when she overheard a snigger.

"Trouble in paradise, you reckon?" The remark was spoken loudly, the speaker obviously intended to be heard.

Bert's lips tightened, and Kate decided she'd best get them out of this awkward situation, and quickly. She stepped away from Bert and calmly finished purchasing the ribbons and lace she had chosen. With a bright smile she let Bert lead her out of the store.

Ian looked from her to Bert and back again. Without a word,

he yielded the driving seat to Bert and hopped into the back of the wagon.

They had turned a corner before Kate realised that Bert intended to drive her home. She said nothing because she could sense that he was still upset. A half hour passed before she touched his arm. "I'm sorry Bert."

He sighed. "Kate, I don't mean to be a scold. Please, do me a favour. Don't think to go shopping on your own again. Just let me know, and I'll make time to go with you."

In the next week, Kate's mood turned somewhat brittle. She had always felt safe as Nicholas' mistress. The men kept their distance from her. It now seemed she was not as safe being Bert's mistress. What would happen when Bert sailed for England to be reunited with his wife? What would happen to her then? To D-Store?

I'd be back to the time when Nicholas left me.

"Kate, you're frowning again," Sara said. "What troubles you?"

Kate turned, but couldn't summon any warmth in her smile. She rubbed her arms to warm them. "Nothing."

" 'Tis not Bert, is it?"

Sara knew her too well. Kate nodded.

"But why would he worry you? He's ever so nice, ever the perfect gentleman. The children likes him—you can never fool the children, I say. He's got a good heart, Bert has."

"I depend too much on him, Sara. I remember how it was with Nicholas, and I don't wish to be so dependent on a man again. There's always the danger he'd leave me floundering when he goes away."

"Bert's not going away, is he?"

"Not yet, but he will one day."

"And maybe not. Maybe 'tis just your fear that makes you

think he'll go away." Sara smiled. "You care for him, don't you?"

Kate turned her face away. "Yes. I must be daft. It all began as good fun. He makes me laugh. He makes me feel important, even beautiful. He's tender, he's caring. Damn. I even deceive myself into thinking he means all the wonderful words he says to me in company."

Sara nodded. "He's a rascal I grant you, but ever so charming."

"But I know those words were not meant for me. They were meant to fool an audience."

"I'm sure he cares for you, Kate. It cannot be all pretend."

Kate closed her eyes. "But he's married, Sara."

"What?"

" 'Tis true. He told me about his marriage right from the start . . ."

A frown gathered on Sara's forehead as Kate explained.

"Seventeen! Olivia was but a child when they married. Think you she's waiting these eight years for her husband to come home to her? Likely, she's married another and has little ones clinging to her skirts. Kate. Don't you let this ghost of a woman get in the way of your happiness."

"Don't you think I've considered that? I love Bert, but I can't rob him of his dream of claiming his bride. Anyway, I don't want a man who would forever be looking back to what might have been if he'd followed his heart."

"Bert wouldn't do that—"

"I've been thinking of cutting him out of my life, Sara, but what would happen to D-Store then?"

"Cutting him out of your life?" Sara looked alarmed.

Kate placed her hand on Sara's arm. "It's all right, Sara. I'm too much of a coward to do it. At least, not yet, but I'll have to do it soon, before he beats me to it when he sails for England."

"Fight for him, Kate. He's a fine man—there ain't too many

like him around."

Sure, she loved Bert, but did he love her? How could she tell? When he behaved outrageously as the besotted lover, he was merely performing for an audience of strangers. He had never overstepped the bounds of propriety when they were alone. Never. And even if he loved her, what difference would that make? Olivia was still his wife.

A week later, she had Ian drive her into Sydney Town to call on Aaron Bernstein, the solicitor who had handled legal matters for Nicholas.

"Mistress O'Neal, what a pleasant surprise!" the old man greeted her. After pleasantries were exchanged, he asked, "What can I do for you?"

Kate wondered if she should forget her idea. Bert would be hurt should he find out about this. No! She had to take some measures to protect herself and those she loved, who depended on her.

Kate made her assessment of Bernstein's office at a glance. Business couldn't be good: the room appeared too spare, the furniture and furnishings needed replacing. Dust and dirt lay thick in the corners, which suggested the old solicitor did his own cleaning. Maybe he wouldn't be difficult to enlist to her cause at all.

"Mr. Bernstein, could I interest you in a job?"

He smiled. "I'm always interested in a job."

She took a deep breath. "I need an agent, a purchasing agent—"

"You mean you want me to find you a purchasing agent."

"No. I want *you* to be my purchasing agent."

He stared at her. "I'm a solicitor, Mistress O'Neal. I deal with legal matters, draft legal documents . . . dull things like that. I'm not a business agent."

"True, but I could teach you to become one. It shouldn't

take long for a man of your experience and schooling to learn all you need to know about my business. Will you represent me, Mr. Bernstein?"

"This is an astonishing request."

"But not an impossible one, I'm sure. I'll gladly pay you for—"

"Oh dear. This is really not my field of work, and I can't, in good conscience, collect an agent's fee when I've no expert service to offer."

Kate sensed his weakening. "So charge me a fee of an 'apprentice-agent.' I shall be glad for the discount."

He raised his hand. "You mustn't tempt an old man like this."

"Be a devil, Mr. Bernstein. Who knows? You might like being an agent, and I could surely use your help."

He coughed. "I'll tell you what I'll do, Mistress O'Neal. Let me ask around for a suitable agent for you, and you can pay me a finder's fee."

"No. I don't want it to become common knowledge that I'm seeking the services of a purchasing agent."

"I can be very discreet in how I go about this matter."

"No. I would like to have you as my agent, no one else."

His eyes widened. "Why are you so insistent on this?"

"Because I know you for an honest man and fair-minded. You also come highly recommended. I do not doubt you'll make me the perfect agent."

"Oh." Bernstein gave her a sharp look before he stared into space, lost in his thoughts.

Kate waited patiently for his answer.

"All right," he finally said. "I'll be your agent, Mistress O'Neal, your apprentice-agent, for three months. I only hope you don't regret this decision."

"Thank you, Mr. Bernstein. I'm Kate." She extended her hand.

He shook it. "My name is Aaron."

Kate tightened her hold on Bernstein's hand. "It's been a month Aaron. I promise you, you're ready."

"I don't feel as though I'm ready."

"I've taught you everything you need to know about my business. It's time for you to go shopping."

"Slow is best, Kate. There'll be less mistakes made this way." He looked around the store. "Anyway, you still have plenty of goods to sell. There's no hurry, surely?"

Kate laughed without much humour. "Obviously, you've not seen D-Store at her glorious best. The fact is, Aaron, I'm dying to know how well you will perform. Surely you realise your performance would be a reflection of my teaching? Your success will be my success. And you need practice to improve."

She sighed. "You're right. I shouldn't push you in this. You need to feel comfortable when you deal with the suppliers."

Two weeks later, Bernstein handed Kate a sheaf of papers.

"What's this?"

"My account of the goods I've purchased for you."

"What!" She studied the lists and laughed. "When can we take delivery?"

"The goods are right outside. The MacGregors are—"

Kate hurried out of the office. The MacGregors were already examining the goods. They looked up at her and grinned broadly.

"Aaron's done a wonderful job," Robert said.

She turned to Aaron and gave him a big hug. "Thank you!"

Ever since the day Aaron purchased that first load of merchandise for her, Kate had waited anxiously to hear from Bert. She could not be sure of his reaction, but she suspected he would not be pleased. Likely he'd think she didn't trust him, that she'd used Aaron to get better prices for her elsewhere. Or maybe, he'd heard of Aaron's purchases and didn't care. If he was already planning to leave for England, surely he wouldn't care if his store lost the profits to be made from her purchases. It'd be Captain Pollard's loss, not Bert's.

Damn! She didn't know what to think anymore.

A few days later, Kate was working in her office when she heard Bert's familiar footsteps. She put down her pen and smiled when he appeared in the doorway. His grim expression started her heart racing.

"Is it true?" he asked, without his usual friendly greeting.

"Is what true?"

"Is Aaron Bernstein buying goods for you?"

"Yes." She waited a heartbeat before she asked, "Are you angry with me?"

"Why would you think that? You're free to get your goods from anywhere you please. It's too much to expect perhaps, but you could have told me about Aaron Bernstein before I heard of it from the others."

"Please, don't be angry. I wasn't sure a solicitor would make a good purchasing agent, and I haven't seen you in two weeks to tell you about it."

"So? Do you mean to terminate our arrangement now?"

"Oh, no. Aaron will just be my other buyer."

"Aaron?"

The underlying tone of jealousy thrilled Kate. *He cares!*

She calmed herself. Didn't Nicholas care too? Just not enough. "Bert, I'd like to depend on you, and you alone, but it wouldn't be wise, would it? One of these days, you'll sail for England to claim your Olivia. Where would that leave me?"

CHAPTER 29

Bert couldn't stop thinking of Kate. He couldn't fault her for wanting to protect her future, a future that couldn't include him. Reaching for a half-full bottle of rum, he knocked down two empty ones. One rolled off the table and crashed to the floor. He kicked aside the shards that landed around his feet, then stared at the bottle in his hand. Tomorrow he would have a devil of a headache. So what? Tonight, he needed some peace. He tilted the bottle and drank some more.

Damn! How had he got himself into this muddle? Could a man possibly love two women at the same time? Well, it wouldn't do. He was married, and a man must cleave unto his wife. He had no business to be jealous of Aaron Bernstein.

But like a splinter festering under his thumbnail, his father-in-law's words needled him. His marriage had been annulled. Olivia wasn't his wife anymore. He was free to love where he pleased. Indeed, he could marry Kate, if he had a mind to do so.

But he didn't feel free. Not at all. Why couldn't he accept Squire Stanton's word and get on with his life? He sighed. He knew exactly why. Olivia had stood by him through these eight years. She'd stayed steadfast in his mind, kept him strong, helped him get through his darkest hours and stopped him getting lost in the bottom of a bottle. Would he be a man of good standing today, if not for her?

He must forget Kate. He should buy passage to return to

England tomorrow. Yes, that was what he should do. Flee while he still could, before temptation made him forget his obligations. The voyage home would be long. He would have months to sort out his confusion. He knew where his loyalty lay. And when he arrived in England, he'd confront Olivia's bastard of a father and reclaim Olivia for his wife.

Forget Olivia? Abandon his wife after all she'd been to him? That would be beyond being dishonourable. No, he couldn't do it. He mustn't.

He had no right to be angry with Kate. She'd done the sensible thing. Right. Only trying to protect her interests. Why, he should be glad that she'd found Aaron Bernstein to help her. He wouldn't have to feel guilty about abandoning her when he sailed for England. Yes, he should be glad.

But he wasn't glad, not one little bit.

Her conversation with Bert yesterday continued to haunt Kate. She couldn't forget the expression of hurt and bewilderment on his face. She wondered if she had made a mistake in engaging Aaron as her purchasing agent so precipitously. Perhaps she should have consulted Bert. The last thing she meant to do was to hurt Bert, who had been so kind to her.

"Kate, aren't you feeling well?" Robert asked.

"I have a bit of a headache," she lied.

"Why don't you let Ian take you home? It ain't so busy now that Hamish and I can't manage the store on our own."

"Thank you, Robert. I think I'll do just that. It'll be nice to get home early, to spend some time with Lisa. If I'm not careful she might mistake Sara for her mother!"

Ian left her to her thoughts on the journey home. He drove up to the front door, waited for her to get off, before driving on to the stables. She entered the house and headed for the kitchen.

"You're home early," Sara greeted her with a smile.

A ball of energy came storming through the back door. "Mama, I'm playing tag with Brenda and Daniel!" Lisa cried as she rushed up to Kate and hugged her leg.

"Are you having fun?"

Lisa nodded her head vigorously. "I'm thirsty, Mama!"

Kate handed her a half cup of water then watched her drink the water down.

"Lisa!" Daniel called out from the backyard. "C'mon we're waiting for you!"

Lisa started coughing, spewing water to the floor. Kate wiped her mouth, then gently rubbed her back. "It's all right, Lisa. Take your time. Daniel will wait for you."

Lisa thrust the empty cup into her mother's hand and ran for the back door, skipped down the steps, hopping from the last two to the ground. Kate held her breath when the little girl wobbled on her feet, trying to stay upright. In a moment, she regained her balance and ran off into the backyard to join Brenda and Daniel. The children screamed in greater excitement when Ian joined them in their game.

"She's a strong little girl, Kate," Sara said.

"I know, but she's so little." Kate moved away from the door to the kitchen table. She put away the cup and began shelling the peas into a bowl.

Sara had her hands deep in flour, kneading bread dough. "I know the feeling. I remember how it was with me Brenda. . . ."

They chatted on for a while, when several loud knocks on the front door interrupted them.

"I'll see who it is," Kate said, wiping her hand on a wet rag.

The knocks came again, before she even moved out of the kitchen. She wondered if it was Bert, but it wasn't like him to be so impatient. Who else could it be when it was almost supper time? She opened the door and squinted into the blinding setting sun. She shielded her eyes with her hand and, despite the glare, could make out the shape of a large man who stood some ten feet away. He appeared to be looking at the side of the house, or maybe at the rose bushes growing there. He was not someone she recognised.

She stepped out of the door and down the steps. "Hello? Can I help you?"

The man swung around unsteadily on his feet. He approached Kate, his arms open wide to embrace her. Instinctively, she stepped aside.

"Kate, I came as soon as I heard!" he boomed.

She gasped. *Jeremy Kendrick!* She could not mistake the voice, but the Jeremy she knew was now buried in almost three hundred pounds of blubber.

Jeremy kept talking, his words, somewhat disjointed. Kate, long used to his drunken stutter, only heard sounds as she stared at the layers of flesh under Jeremy's chin that quivered with every word he spoke. She took in his red and teary eyes and shrank from the blasts of his liquor-laden breath. The hell he'd put her through, eight years ago, came flooding back.

She started when he took a step closer and touched her arm. Her skin broke out in goose flesh, then the buzz in her ears turned into words.

"As soon as you knew?" she repeated.

"Yes! And here I am, Kate, as I promised!"

"Promised?" She could have kicked herself for sounding like a halfwit, when she should be firm and send the bastard on his way.

"Don't you remember? I told you I'd come for you as soon as I could. That bastard Spencer. I'll wager my last penny he arranged for my transfer to Norfolk Island. Been there all these years. Can you believe it? He stuck me in hell, I tell you! God rot his soul."

Kate took a deep breath. "What do you want, Jeremy?"

"You, of course. That bloody bastard parted us, but now he's gone. Good riddance! Everything's all right, love. Your Jeremy's back!" He grinned at Kate, then nodded approvingly at Dunover. "Good, strong building. This is just the kind of house I would've built for us if those bastards had worked the farm as they were supposed to. Or if the Trading Officers' Fraternity had let me into trade. Looks like your five years with Spencer has gained us some welcome benefits."

The pleasure in his voice had Kate clenching her teeth. The bastard had not changed. He was as lazy and greedy as ever. Now, he seemed intent upon claiming her fortune for his own. Well, that was not going to happen. She would be damned before she allowed him back into her life again.

"Jeremy! You're not listening. I don't want you here. Go away!"

"You're just angry I didn't come for you sooner." He patted her cheek then turned to examine Dunover once more. "Well! Who would've thought I'd get my grand house through you? Let's go inside, love, and you can show me around."

Kate stared at him in disbelief. Was the man mad that he didn't realise he was not welcome? She started when he headed for the front door.

"Oh, no, you don't!" She grabbed his arm and held him back with all of her strength. He proved extraordinarily strong, dragging her along with him for several steps. Stopping him was definitely beyond her, so she let go of his arm and ran for the door.

"We shall have parties here. We'll invite everybody who is anybody in this here backwater. Ah, Kate, you'll be the envy of every woman in this colony. I'll see to it."

Kate stood blocking the doorway. "You're not getting inside. Have you not heard a word I've said? I don't want you here, Jeremy."

Jeremy's mouth dropped open. He snapped it shut, and his face turned an ugly shade of red. "Why, you trollop! Don't you dare take that tone with me!"

He thrust his pudgy hand forward to grab Kate's arm. She slapped it away, then slipped into the house and slammed the door shut. The door bounced off Jeremy's boot. She snatched the door back and pushed hard on it. He gave a shove. The door swung open, flinging her away. She yelped, then struggled to stay on her feet, but by the time she did, Jeremy was inside the house.

His gaze was fixed on her, and Kate recognised the expression on his face. The years slipped away, and the instinct to stay away from his fists took over. She retreated. Jeremy advanced, loosening the belt from his trousers as he did so. "I'll teach you to respect your betters, you slut!"

Kate stared at his hand fumbling on his belt, and suddenly she went back further into time. Lord Oliver sprang into life before her. She froze.

Just today, Bert had stayed back at Pollard & Company after the store closed. He thought to work on the accounts. He even hoped for something unexpected to occur that required his attention. Anything so long as he could put off his visit to Kate. After dallying in the empty store for a half hour, he set out for Dunover on his horse. He knew he had to offer Kate his apologies, put things right between them quickly, or he'd have no peace. And by God, he'd do it too, then get the hell away from her, as fast as he could, before he lost his resolve.

Dunover came into view. His heart thudded when he spotted Kate in the distance. She was talking to a man, a big man, but not someone he recognised. He'd only heard of Aaron Bernstein recently—had no idea what the man looked like. Could that fat man be Bernstein? Bert looked away, as he tried to calm himself. Damn! If he couldn't control his jealousy, he'd best stay away from Kate altogether.

He took a deep breath and looked again. His belly became a cavern, cold and empty. Kate and the man seemed locked in an embrace. She broke away and hurried into the house, the man followed, close at her heels.

Bert turned his horse around. Perhaps it'd be better for him to call on her another day. He hadn't gone ten yards when he pulled on the reins and turned his horse around. Dammit. He needed to meet the bastard, to check out this new man in Kate's life.

Was he Bernstein? How on earth could Kate find such a fat man appealing? What did this fat man have that he didn't? Well, he surely had something that the fat man didn't: a wife. *Damn!* Why had his life become so complicated?

He rode up close to the door of Kate's house. Leaving his horse tied to the hitching post, he strode towards the front door which stood slightly ajar. At the sound of heavy breathing, he stumbled to a halt. No! Kate could not be this indiscreet. There were children in the house.

"Ian, help! Help! Ian! Ian!" Sara's voice, urgent and shrill knocked him out of his anguish. He catapulted up the steps and into the house. He froze for a moment, astounded by the sight of the fat man pinning his small, helpless Kate to the wall with his hand. Then as if in a dream, he watched the man take a step back, then hit Kate with his belt. She screamed.

With a roar, Bert leapt at the man. He snatched the belt and threw it away. With his hands wrapped around the man's neck, he squeezed. The man choked, releasing Kate. He turned on Bert, punching him in his belly.

Bert gasped, let go of the man's neck and immediately slammed his fist into the man's fat face. It landed on his left ear. He yowled. The next blow connected with the man's right jaw. He grunted and retaliated with a fist into Bert's ribs. Bert cursed. Furiously, he let loose another punch. It snapped the man's face to the right and sent him staggering past Ian and Sara. He bounced off the wall and slumped to the floor, moaning. Bert grabbed the fallen man's arm to pull him up. Damn. The tub of lard wouldn't shift. Frustrated, and though out of breath, Bert kicked him, again and again.

"Stop, Bert," Kate yelled. "You'll kill him!"

"I want to kill him!"

Kate stepped forward and wrapped her arms around Bert. "No, don't. He's harmless now."

"He's harmless when he's dead!"

"No, Bert, don't." She reached out for his hand. "He didn't hurt me. I'm all right. Really."

He hesitated, shook his head to clear it. "You're sure?"

"Yes, yes. I'm all right, Bert."

He looked down at the mountain of fat. "Who's he?"

"Jeremy Kendrick."

"Filth! We had better throw him out. Ian, can you give me a hand?" He reached for the man's arm. Ian set down the Brown Bess he held and grabbed hold of Kendrick's other arm; together they dragged him past Sara, who held the door open for them. They dropped him outside, on his back.

Kendrick scrambled to his feet and would have fled had Bert not quickly given chase, then stopping him by pulling on his jacket. He gave Kendrick a hard shove, sending him tumbling into the dirt. Bert forced him to rollover. Kendrick immediately raised his arms to shield his face.

Bert placed a boot on the man's expansive belly instead, to hold him down. Then bending over, he growled down into Kendrick's face, "If you ever lay a finger on Kate again, I'll kill you! Do you understand?"

Kendrick nodded. Bert applied more pressure on Kendrick's

belly. "Do you?"

"Yes, yes! I do."

"All right. Get up. Be gone, before I change my mind."

Kendrick staggered to his feet, then ran to his horse. He scrambled into the saddle and galloped away. Satisfied the man was gone, Bert gestured for Ian to precede him into the house. Kate closed the door behind them.

Bert looked at Kate. "You're sure he didn't hurt you?"

"I'm fine, Bert, honest. How about you?" She looked him over for signs of injury, then gasped at the sight of his bruised knuckles.

He tingled all over at her show of concern. He forced a smile. "I'm fine."

"I'm sorry I wasn't much help, Kate," Ian said, picking up the Brown Bess.

Bert chuckled. "You did fine, Ian. Let's hope you don't ever have to use that musket. Better put it away now." He looked down, noted Kate's pale face and pulled her into his arms. Her hair smelled of flowers. Oh yes, he certainly liked the feel of this bundle of softness. Just then he remembered his resolve. He loosened his hold around Kate and took a step back.

Sara came out of the library bearing two glasses of amber liquid. She handed one to him and the other to Kate. "I was never so scared, Bert. Thank God you were here to take care of that bloody swine." She turned to Ian. "Would you like a glass of brandy too?"

"No thanks. Now that it's all over, I can't believe it happened." Ian cleared his throat. "I guess I had better go check on the children. Thank goodness they stayed put in the backyard and missed the violence!"

Sara hooked her arm in Ian's. "Yes, and I'd better finish making me bread. Will you be eating with us tonight, Bert?"

"I don't think so, but thank you for asking." He watched Ian and Sara head for the kitchen, then turned to look at Kate. She was trying to drink her brandy, but each time she did, a sharp tinkling noise rang out. Her teeth were knocking on the glass. She giggled.

Gently, Bert removed the glass from her trembling hand, then put both glasses away. He gathered her close.

"I don't know what's wrong with me," Kate stammered tearfully. "This is stupid! It's not as if I'm hurt. And Jeremy's gone. Why am I shaking like this?"

"Shhh. It's all right." He kissed the top of her head. "Hush!"

When Kate's shakes subsided, he released her. "Come. We'll be more comfortable in the library." He led her into the room and closed the door. Once seated, he placed Kate across his lap. She slumped into him. He bit back a smile. He wasn't sure what he'd expected, certainly not for her to be this docile.

"Who is Jeremy Kendrick?" he asked.

Kate sighed. "An officer of the New South Wales Corps. He . . ."

As Bert listened, his fury blazed anew. He wished he'd gelded the bastard when he had the chance.

". . . now he thinks to come back into my life, take control of me and what I own . . ."

"Don't worry. He's gone now and he won't be back, not if he's smart."

"You don't know Jeremy. He was never smart."

"I don't wish to know him, and though I may not have Spencer's power, I do have my ways, Kate. Kendrick won't be back to trouble you again, I promise."

She snuggled closer and sighed.

He closed his eyes. Kate was chipping away at his resolve, and still he couldn't push her away. "Kate? About yesterday? I'm sorry I took my temper out on you. You were right; you had to look after your interests. It wasn't Aaron Bernstein I objected to, you know? I would've objected to any man because I want to be the only one to look after you."

She remained very still as if asleep. He drew a deep breath. "Kate?"

She stirred. "What about Olivia?"

"I don't know. No other woman had appealed to me before, so it was easy enough to keep faith with my marriage vows. Kate, I love you. I don't wish to lose you because of a dream I hold dear for so long."

"What will you have me say?"

"Do you love me?"

"I don't wish to steal you from Olivia."

"Listen. Will you give me a month to put my past behind me?"

"What do you mean?"

"I've been sending Olivia a letter every few months. I've never heard back from her. If she doesn't get in touch by the end of January, I shall take it her father had not lied—that our marriage is no more. Likely, she's married to another and has a family of her own. Whatever it may be, my conscience would be clear. We can get married then, if you'll have me."

Kate hesitated. Bert's heart rocked. He wanted to say, "To hell with the waiting! Let's get married now."

"What about Aaron Bernstein? I can't—"

"No, no. Keep Bernstein as your purchasing agent. I shan't interfere with that." He kissed her hands. "You'll have me, then?"

"Oh yes!"

Kate wondered if there were other women as confused as she in the world. How could she be this contrary? She'd wanted to marry Bert so badly she ached. And now that he'd proposed, her doubts kept growing. Did Bert intend to take over the running of D-Store and have her stay at home—to run the household, to take care of the babies, when they came along, and to stay out of *men's business* altogether?

Would she still marry him if he demanded such a sacrifice from her?

Unable to bear the suspense of uncertainty, she took her courage into her hands when he called on her a few days later. "Bert, have you thought of running D-Store after we're married?"

He frowned. "Why? Do you want me to?"

"I just wondered what would happen after the wedding?"

"We'd be married, of course," he grinned, leaned over and kissed her.

Kate gave him a playful slap on his arm. "Be serious!"

"I haven't planned on any changes."

"Where would we live? At your house, or here, in mine?"

"If you wish to live in my house, which is in Sydney Town—we can do that. It would mean uprooting the children. It'd be easier for me to move into Dunover. What do you think?"

Kate smiled. "That would be lovely, except you'd have to do so much travelling. Do you mind?"

"Perhaps we could live a little closer to Sydney Town, but it's something we might want think about later."

Kate decided to push. "We could both work at D-Store, you know, then you wouldn't have to do so much travelling."

"What are you saying? That you prefer me to work with you at D-Store? Why? You've managed very nicely on your own all this time—you don't need me to hold your hand. Besides, I'm quite happy working for Captain Pollard. I like the benefits that come from working for him—like access to cheaper merchandise and to the power the captain wields as an officer of the Corps. Do you really want me to run D-Store and give up these benefits?"

"No, you're right. Stay with Pollard & Company." Kate

reached for his hand. "Will you stay for supper?"

He shook his head. "I have a busy day tomorrow, and it's a long ride home."

She tightened her hold on his hand. "You could stay overnight sometimes."

"Kate, don't tempt me."

She blushed. "I'm not. I do have a spare room."

He shook his head, urging Kate towards the door. "You'd still be too close. I will not have you become the subject of a scandal."

They stepped out of the library. "Bert, don't be silly. More scandal? How? The whole settlement believes I'm your mistress already."

He smiled. "But we know the truth. I didn't anticipate my marriage vows with Olivia. I will not do so with you. A month is not that long to wait."

Kate sighed. "It might not be long enough for me to prepare for the wedding. Will you be inviting many guests?"

"No. Just Captain Pollard. But don't let that stop you inviting as many guests as you wish." He kissed her. "Oh I almost forgot. I've good news for you. Kendrick should be back in Norfolk Island next week, courtesy of Captain Pollard. That swine can consider himself lucky if he gets to see Sydney Town in another ten years."

"Norfolk Island?" Kate laughed. "Oh, you are wicked!"

"If Kendrick hates it so much, then he deserves to be stuck there forever. There! Can you see how useful Captain Pollard can be?"

A murmur of voices halted further conversation.

Kate flashed him an uncertain look. "It's Aaron." She'd not expected him to call and wondered how Bert would react to his visit.

The front door opened wider and Ian followed Aaron into

the hallway. Bert surprised her by greeting Aaron with a grin and an outstretched hand. "Mr. Bernstein? I'm Bert Rowley."

Aaron shook his hand. "How do you do." He looked at Kate. "I'm sorry to call so late, Kate, but can you spare me a few minutes?"

"Of course. Come with me to the library."

Behind Aaron's back, Bert cocked an eyebrow at her. She widened her eyes and shook her head. He smiled, blew her a goodbye kiss and left.

Aaron refused her offer of a drink. He waited for her to be seated before he settled into the chair next to her. "Kate, do you still think of Nicholas Spencer?"

A sense of dread caused her mouth to become very dry. "Not lately. Why do you ask?"

He hesitated.

Her heartbeats quickened. "He's not back, is he?"

He shook his head.

She released a sigh of relief. "Well! Why talk about him at all?"

"Captain Hudson directed a Lord Hopkins to see me this afternoon, Kate. His lordship claims Nicholas Spencer has sent him with a personal message for you. He's rejected my offer to arrange for a day when you might be 'at home' to him. He plans to call on you tomorrow. I thought I should warn you."

CHAPTER 30

The night was unseasonably warm for August. Kate plumped up her pillow yet again before she lay her head on it. Minutes passed, but Kate remained as wide awake as ever. Nicholas, whom she thought well and truly buried in the past, had returned to haunt her. Why? What did he want? Damn! She didn't need Nicholas to complicate her life just now, not when she was about to be married to Bert.

Sure, she thought she'd loved Nicholas, but she was only young then. And after her horrible time with Jeremy, anybody kind would have looked very good. And Nicholas had been exceptionally kind and generous. And of course, he'd been passionate too, and she'd mistaken their lust for love, a mistake she was not likely to repeat.

Kate tossed around the bed, seeking a cooler spot.

If Nicholas had a message, why had he not just sent it through Aaron, his solicitor? What was so important about the message to warrant a viscount to deliver it? Had Nicholas changed his mind? Except why had he? For five years he had resisted marriage to her. Why would he change his mind now? Ridiculous. That couldn't be it.

But what if it was indeed a proposal of marriage?

Well, he was two years too late. Let him learn the world didn't wait upon his pleasure. But could she reject Nicholas' proposal out of hand? Yes! She would marry Bert, and that would be that. But . . . Could she deny Lisa the opportunity of growing up under her father's protection?

Kate frowned. An offer of marriage? Well, what else could it be? To resume their old relationship? A letter to Aaron saying he wanted Kate and Lisa to join him in England would have sufficed surely? So why would he send a viscount to do the job? It had to be a marriage proposal. What, if it wasn't?

Her thoughts went round and round in her head, exhausting her. She finally slept and woke up with a headache. She told Ian to go to D-Store without her, said she'd be in later—or maybe not.

She couldn't settle into doing anything after Ian left. She dawdled over her breakfast.

"What's wrong?" Sara asked. "I've not seen you this troubled in a long while. 'Tis not Bert or the wedding, is it?"

Kate started. "No. I'm to have a visitor today—a viscount."

"A viscount?" Sara's eyes widened in surprise. "Imagine that!"

Kate laughed. "He's just a man, with a pair of eyes and a pair of ears, a nose and a mouth—just like you and me, Sara." She sighed. "I suppose I had better dress for the visit. Will you help me choose the right gown? I don't wish to be taken for a rustic, a wild colonial."

Within half an hour, several garments lay helter-skelter on Kate's bed. She picked up a gown of pink muslin with an embroidered hem and gave it a shake. Pressing it against her front, she turned to Sara. "What do you think?"

"Very nice."

She pointed to the gown of green lawn on the bed. "But I like the long sleeves of that one better."

Sara shook her head. "Ain't you a bundle of nerves?"

Kate blinked. She hadn't realised she'd allowed Lord Hopkins' visit to rattle her.

"Do you want to impress him so badly?" Sara asked.

"No. I just didn't want him to think poorly of me, that's all."

Sara rolled her eyes as she picked up a silk garment. "Never mind. How about this one?"

"The neckline cuts too deep. I don't mean to seduce his lordship."

Sara laughed. "This one? Kate, stop dreaming!"

"You're right, Sara. What does it matter what his lordship thinks of me?"

"Wh—what?"

"Why should I pretend to be better than what I am? He means to surprise me with this visit. Well then, he should find me dressed as I am everyday. I'll wear this old thing. Why not? Nicholas has seen me in this before."

Sara glared at her. "You will not!"

"I will too."

"Oh that Bert! He's to be blamed for this."

"What do you mean?"

"Full of mischief he is, and getting you to play his games." She inhaled sharply. "And you think to treat this viscount as a game."

Kate fell on the bed, laughing. "Poor Bert. He's more proper than you know, Sara! And you're mistaken. I'm not playing any games with the viscount. I wouldn't dare!"

Glad to remain in her comfortable old dress, Kate worked on her accounts in the library. She paused now and again, listening for the viscount's arrival. A loud rap on the front door was the first indication that her visitor had arrived. She cleared the desk in haste, then hurried out of the library. She almost bumped into Sara in the hall. With a smile, she waved her away. "I'll let his lordship in."

She opened the door and stared at her caller. All at once she was back in time, in England, and working with the Rustands again. *How uncanny.* Lord Hopkins could have been one of the many noblemen who called on Lord Rustand—portly in figure, dressed in the latest London fashion.

Kate took a little more time to examine his lordship's elegant attire: the blue jacket, white pantaloons and a beautifully arranged neck cloth. A flush warmed her face. *Damn.* She should have listened to Sara. Now she felt drab and at a disadvantage.

A loud clearing of the throat brought her attention back to her visitor. She attempted a smile. "Good—"

"I'm Lord Hopkins, James Hopkins." He handed her a calling card. "Please tell your mistress Viscount Hopkins is here to see her."

Kate bit down on her lip. She dared not laugh, but the urge to do so washed away her nervousness. She decided to correct his mistake. "My lord—"

He glared at her. "Well? Do you mean to keep me standing on your doorstep forever?"

"I'm sorry." She opened the door wider. "Please, come in, my lord." *What a horrible man.* She was glad she hadn't put herself out for his visit.

He brushed past her, stopped in the hall and looked around.

"This way, my lord." Kate led the way to the library, stopped when she realised her visitor was in no hurry to follow her. She didn't think the viscount would examine the hallway so boldly, or reveal his feeling of distaste in the curl of his lips or the twitch of his nose, not if he knew he was in the presence of his hostess.

She had not changed a thing at Dunover since her early days with Nicholas. Now, she tried to see her home through her visitor's eyes. The carpet looked a bit worn and stained in spots. The furniture bore battle scars from their encounters with the children, and the curtains looked somewhat shabby.

Kate started when Lord Hopkins lurched sideways to avoid treading on a wooden horse and a box of paint on the floor.

Lisa and Daniel. Somehow those two had always managed to

keep a few steps ahead of the grown-ups, discarding their playthings on the floor faster than anyone could pick them up. Perhaps they'd left a stray marble around? She choked on the image of his lordship felled by one small marble.

Inside the library, Kate indicated a chair. "Can I offer you a drink, my lord? A brandy, perhaps?"

Lord Hopkins nodded. He lifted his coat tails and sat down. His gaze moved about the room, marking the furniture and the wall hangings, even the carpet. He stopped examining the room when Kate handed him his drink.

"Where is Mistress O'Neal? Isn't she home?"

"I'm Kate O'Neal, my lord."

He shot out of his chair and stumbled. Brandy splashed on his hand. His face reddened. "I beg your pardon."

She took a seat facing her visitor and watched him squirm. After a moment, she said, "Please, do be seated, my lord. I'm sure the chair is comfortable. It used to be Nicholas' favourite seat."

The colour on Lord Hopkins' face receded. "Forgive me, Mistress O'Neal. I'm sorry if I was rude . . . Uh . . ."

"There's no need to apologise, my lord."

He dipped his head, then he smiled. "It's a great pleasure for me to meet you at last, Mistress O'Neal. I've heard so much about you from Nicholas—"

"How kind of you to say so, my lord. I'm rather amazed Nicholas mentioned me at all. How is dear Nicholas?"

Kate blinked, amazed at the ease with which she'd adopted the affected speech and aristocratic manner of Lady Rustand, who had socialised with British royalty.

Lord Hopkins shifted in his seat. "He's very well, thank you. And be assured he often talks about you."

"Ah. I trust he has only good things to say."

"Of course. In fact, Nicholas wished to make this visit

himself—he booked passage to sail no less than three times last year, but he was forced to cancel. . . .”

His lordship looked at her expectantly. What? Did he expect her to be impressed? Flattered? “Oh. Three times?” she said obligingly.

He gave her an approving smile. “Indeed, but you know how it is with business emergencies and unexpected social responsibilities.”

Kate didn't think he expected her to know any such thing. When she said nothing, he continued, “They do have an unpleasant way of disrupting one's plans. Wouldn't you say?”

Oh, no. She couldn't be expected to spend the whole afternoon with this man, aristocrat or not. Already his condescending manner pushed her to the edge of saying something rude to shock him.

She reined in her impatience. The man had in his possession a message from Nicholas, and she'd like to know what that message was. “Of course. Nicholas keeps very busy, then.”

“Oh yes. Nothing is too private between us. We're the best of friends, you see?” He gave Kate a long look, as if to make his point.

She smiled. “How nice.”

“Knowing his difficulties, I felt obliged to offer my services. It's rather fortunate my personal engagements are few and far in between. They allow me greater freedom to attend to many things, like giving friends a helping hand.”

“How very fortunate for Nicholas.”

“No, no. It's my privilege to help him. Glad to do it. There've been too many changes in London in his long absence, and he couldn't be expected to know what was what. He needed guidance, and I gave it freely. Not a day passed without my popping in to offer Nicholas a word of advice. I didn't want him to commit a social blunder, you see? The ton can be quite merciless.”

She nodded agreeably though she was not interested in the whims of London's ton. Somehow Lord Hopkins' revelations had given Kate a possible reason for Nicholas' action. The viscount had been plaguing the life out of Nicholas and making it impossible for him to take a step without the viscount snapping at his heels. Likely, he had sent the viscount halfway across the world to get rid of him. The image of Nicholas trying hard to avoid Lord Hopkins tickled her funny bone. She quickly lowered her gaze and bit her trembling lips to stop bursting into giggles.

His lordship coughed. "Nicholas wishes me to tell you that he thinks of you and your daughter . . . Lisa? . . . very often. He misses you both very much."

Kate's amusement died. She wondered how Nicholas could have endured this tiresome viscount. "I'm obliged to you for this information, my lord. It pleases me to know that Nicholas still thinks of Lisa and myself in his so very busy life. One does like to be remembered. So Nicholas depends on you to attend to things that he's too busy to handle himself? How very gratifying for him."

His lordship's eyes narrowed. She gave him a vacant smile. After a long moment, he gave a nod and dug out a snuffbox from his pocket. "Nicholas trusts me to deal with very confidential matters, and this time, you might say I'm on a delicate mission."

Kate took a shuddering breath. She couldn't bear to have Lord Hopkins under her roof a minute more. "So, what can I do for Nicholas?"

His lordship froze, his hand with a pinch of snuff hung in the air several inches from his nostrils.

"I don't mean to rush you, my lord, but like Nicholas, I've become a busy person, and I do have another appointment I must keep. You have a message for me?"

Sudden anger blazed in his eyes. "You lack manners, young lady! It does not bode well for your future!"

She clenched her fists. *Lack manners?* What? Was she to be scolded like a ten-year-old child? She took a deep breath. "I'm sorry, my lord. I see you need more time to deliver Nicholas' message. Please, take all the time you need to gather your thoughts. I've noticed that as one grows older, one's thoughts tend to wander. Never say I can't wait for my answers."

Lord Hopkins glared at her, his face turning scarlet; his breathing became laboured. "Nicholas has asked me to remind you of your wish to share his life, Mistress O'Neal. I'm here to find out if you're of the same mind. If so, he wants you and your daughter to join him in England. I'm to provide you escort and smooth the way for you."

Her disappointment battled with her outrage. Nicholas had not offered marriage. *Damn you, Nicholas. Why are you unearthing a past best forgotten? Why have you sent this arrogant buffoon to plague me?*

"Forgive me, my lord, if I appear less than excited by this offer. How long does Nicholas expect us to be together? The last time lasted five years. Is this invitation good for another five years, do you know?"

He glared at her. "I tell you now, Mistress O'Neal, I will not tolerate rag-manners!"

"Oh dear. Nicholas should have warned you. I'm that dreadful creature: a female merchant. It's my wretched custom to wrangle for the best terms I can get. It's a deplorable flaw—"

"Well, it is to be hoped—"

She raised her voice. "When Nicholas left me, he did so abruptly, with hardly a word of explanation. Now he wants me back in his life again. Is this to be for another five years? I don't mean to quibble. I need to know. Nicholas might want a younger woman in five years' time, and I'd be five years older. You looked shocked. I'm sorry, my lord, but such is the reality of life. I've a need to be cautious, you see?"

"No, I don't see, Madam. Nicholas has done you an honour, a signal honour! You cannot know this, of course, but Nicholas has London at his feet. He has his pick of the beauties there, all diamonds of the first water, but he's decided no one would suit him as well as you would. He's put himself to the expense of sending me all this way to put his offer to you. I've just undertaken a long and hellish voyage—"

She raised a hand. "I'm properly chastised, my lord. So, what is Nicholas' offer?"

"You get a townhouse at St James Square," he snapped. "I've already left instructions with my staff to get it ready to receive you. I will, of course, attend to the necessary once we arrive—introduce you to your household staff and help you settle in. Rest assured, I'll see that you're attired in the latest prevailing fashion. Of course, Nicholas will bear the responsibility for all of your expenses, including a generous quarterly allowance."

"And where will dear Nicholas be all this time?"

"No doubt he'll visit as soon as you arrive, Mistress O'Neal. He's waited a long time to be reunited with you."

Kate cringed at Lord Hopkins' smirk. Her lips tightened. "Visiting me? He'll not be staying with me then?"

"Oh I'm sure he'll be staying with you, and frequently, too, Mistress O'Neal. After all the trouble he's taken, and the expense, he's not likely to neglect you."

Arrogant bastard! "Where does Nicholas live then, if he's not expected to live with me? I presume he has another home?"

"Nicholas owns several homes." His lordship made a show of brushing a speck of dirt from his sleeve. "The townhouse at Grosvenor Square is his official residence."

"I don't quite understand. Why is it necessary for my daughter and me to live separately from Nicholas? Why can we not make our home with him?"

For the length of several heartbeats, Lord Hopkins stared at her, his mouth unbecomingly agape. He snapped it shut. "Confound it! You must be insane! You cannot be so insensible to the proprieties! A man doesn't simply install a mistress in his own home! It'd be a gross insult to his wife! Nicholas wouldn't do that to Lady Gwendolyn. Society wouldn't stand for it, either! It'd be the season's scandal!"

Wife? Kate heard that piece of information and became almost deaf to the rest of his lordship's words. The bastard was married? After telling her marriage was never part of his plans, he got married? How dared he! Married, and he wanted her for a side dish!

Breathing became difficult. She resisted the urge to clutch her belly, to bend over and empty its contents. Instead she clung to her outrage. *Damn him! Damn him!* Why couldn't he stay out of her life?

She forced a smile. "I wasn't aware Nicholas was married. When did he marry? Does he have children?"

"Nicholas has been married over a year, and as far as I know, he has no legitimate children."

She winced and resisted the urge to ask if he knew how many bastards Nicholas had sired. "I see. Did it occur to Nicholas that I might be married now?"

"Of course, the possibility crossed his mind. In fact, he told me he'd urged you to get married before he left this settlement. But you're not married, are you? I don't see an obstacle. Do you?"

"I'm obliged for Nicholas' offer. Now, let's see if I've got the situation right. Lisa and I are to travel with you to England, where you will install us in a townhouse in London. A luxurious townhouse, I presume? With all the trimmings? A houseful of servants, clothes and jewels and—What else? Ah, yes, carriages to take me wherever I want to go? Good. No doubt, I'll be squired around town by Nicholas, attend parties he chooses to attend with me, but not those where Lady Gwendolyn will be attending?"

Lord Hopkins dipped his head in agreement.

"Ah! I've got everything right so far? Good! So, I'm to be offered all these marvelous things, these wonderful opportunities, for the pleasure of being the captain's doxy?"

Lord Hopkins jumped in his seat, his face flushed. "Allow me to inform you, Mistress O'Neal, Nicholas Spencer is the fifth Earl of Brompton, after his brother, the fourth earl. His family is an old and distinguished one. Captain's doxy indeed! You do have a nice turn of phrase, Mistress O'Neal, that is, if you're bent on being vulgar!"

"I'm sorry." She remained silent for a moment longer, marshalling her strength for one last push. "So what are your plans, my lord, if I accept Nicholas' offer?"

"If you accept?" His lordship choked, his eyes rounded.

"Yes, if I accept."

"Why, you may leave everything to me, Mistress O'Neal. You need only pack your personal belongings and attend to your child."

"I expect you'll be selling—" She stared at the viscount. "Who gets to keep the proceeds from the sale?"

His lordship froze for a moment, then waved his handkerchief under his nose, as if he'd detected some foul smell. "You need not be alarmed on that score, Mistress O'Neal. Money isn't at issue here. Nicholas has no need for your money. He has plenty of his own."

She wanted to scream at him, kick a chair maybe, something, anything, but she told herself to bear up for a little longer. She would be civil to her visitor, pretend to be unaffected by his visit. She would make sure the toad didn't know how badly his news had hurt and angered her. She forced a smile. "How reassuring! So I get to keep the money? Hmmm."

"Do you have any other questions?"

She ignored the icy tone. "One more. When do you expect to sail for England?"

His lordship leaned into his chair. "As soon as I've disposed of everything you don't wish to keep for yourself. Within a month, not much later than that."

"Indeed, much sooner than that, Lord Hopkins. I'll see to it."

"What do you mean?"

"If the disposal of my property is the only thing that's holding you back, why then, my lord, you may sail tomorrow if you wish!"

"I don't understand."

"You won't have the problem of disposing off my property, my lord, for I've no intention of selling. Nor do I wish to become bloody Lord Nicholas' doxy!"

Lord Hopkins' eyes bulged. "Is this a jest?"

"I never jest about business, my lord. That could prove dangerous. Let me explain. I can't accept Nicholas' offer because it's just too paltry."

"Paltry? Why, you silly chit!" Lord Hopkins hissed.

"Yes, paltry."

"Good God! He's more than generous, you madwoman! You don't know what you're turning down!"

"Paltry," she repeated firmly. She stood, praying her knees wouldn't buckle. They didn't. *Thank God.* She took two steps forward. "Well, my lord, I don't wish to delay you any longer. Let me show you out, and when you see Nicholas, tell him I wish him well."

She led the way to the front door and opened it.

Bert stood in the doorway, his arm raised, reaching for the knocker. All at once, the exhausted expression in his eyes changed into a glow of pleasure and his teeth flashed in a broad smile. "What a lovely—"

Kate blinked at him in disbelief. She couldn't have conjured up a more welcome sight. Her heart filled with thankfulness and her vision blurred.

The look of delight on his face faded, replaced by a look of concern. He reached out for her. She shook her head and blinked away her tears.

"You've got company," he said, looking over her shoulder.

She turned to her visitor. "Lord Hopkins, may I present my betrothed, Bert Rowley. Bert, this is Viscount Hopkins. His lordship has come from England to offer us his good wishes on our upcoming wedding. Isn't it just too kind of him?"

The viscount ignored Bert's outstretched hand and glared at Kate. "Madam, you don't want to know what I really wish for you! It's certainly not good wishes. And you. Rowley, is it? Well, I pity you, sir. Good day!"

He marched off without a backward glance.

"Now, what have you done to upset that nice nobleman, Kate?" He looked her over and shook his head in mock despair. "Has no one told you that you cannot receive a member of the British aristocracy dressed like that?"

"Is that why he mistook me for the maid, do you think?"

He laughed. "Did he?"

Kate nodded.

He laughed even louder, then wrapped his arms tightly around her and kissed her. "You're such a delight, my dear!"

As she stepped back from his kiss, she smiled. Bert's presence had swept away the air of foulness Lord Hopkins had left behind. Still she was glad for his visit. Now she was assured Nicholas and the rest of her past would trouble her no more.

She urged Bert to come into the house. In the library, she began her tale with Aaron's visit last night. To her surprise,

Bert's face darkened when she told him of Nicholas' offer.

"What's wrong?"

"Kate, you must know I cannot offer you all the things Spencer can—"

She put her fingers on his lips to silence him. "Someone once told me that money isn't everything, and he's right. I love you, Bert, very much."

Bert smiled and kissed her forehead.

Kate placed her hand gently against his cheek. "Now, why would I want anything Nicholas has to offer? He can't give me what I want. Not laughter and certainly not love. Would he go into transports when I call him *Bertie?* Now, would he?"

Bert laughed, as she meant him to do. She snuggled into his arms, feeling very much beloved. *I must be the luckiest woman in the world.*

ABOUT THE AUTHOR

Born in Malaysia, **Sanchona** is a graduate of the University of Malaya (1968) who now makes her home in Sydney, Australia. After obtaining her Masters of Commerce (MIS) degree from the University of New South Wales (1991), she went into partnership with a friend to buy and operate a busy Asian supermarket.

She has always been a voracious reader and, in absolute ignorance, thought she could write as well as any published writer. She decided to write a novel about the Chinese in Australia during the gold rush of the 1850s but, as a history graduate, got lost in the research, going backwards in time to the 1780s and extending from today's United Kingdom to Europe, Australia, China and the United States of America. Her little project became so unwieldy that she has since divided them up into sequels.

She is hopeful her first novel, which covers the period 1793–1802, will be well-received so she will get to tell her story of the Chinese in Australia in the 1850s.

Read more about Sanchona at http://www.sanchona.com.